IT WAS UNSPEAKABLE PUNISHMENT . . . FOR A WOMAN WHO HAD DONE NO WRONG. BUT ONE MAN WOULD NOT GIVE UP HIS SEARCH UNTIL HE'D SAVED HER FROM THE DAMNED . . .

Rolf came to a halt, breathing hard, and moved toward her cautiously, as one would approach a wild animal. He spoke slowly, softly. "Annette, it's me. Rolf. I won't hurt you. You're safe now."

Annette stood up, facing Rolf's advancing figure. She snatched a loose board from the garbage-littered ground and waved it threateningly. "Go away!" she cried. "Leave me alone! I'll kill you!"

She was the image of avenging fury, all wild hair and staring eyes. Rolf stopped short. She was so brave, so beautiful in her wild state. His heart went out to her. Cold hatred filled him. What had O'Neill done to turn a gently bred society girl into this creature?

"It's Rolf, Annette," he repeated.

"Rolf?" She looked through the darkness, confused, scared.

What had her captors done to her? Slowly, ever so slowly, she lowered the board. Rolf waited, hardly daring to breathe. He held out his hand. "Take my hand, Annette. I want to help you, to take you home."

Falteringly, she held her hand up to her throat, searching his face as if she didn't trust her own eyes. "Rolf?"

"Yes, Annette. I'm here to take you home."

A WOMAN OF SAN FRANCISCO

SAN FRANCISCO
A WOMAN OF

LYNN ERICKSON

A Dell/Banbury Book

Published by
Banbury Books, Inc.
37 West Avenue
Wayne, Pennsylvania 19087

ISBN: 0-440-09845-9

Printed in the United States of America

First printing—December 1982

This book is dedicated with gratitude to Al Zuckerman and Merrilee Heifetz.

San Francisco in 1890 has been described as the most lighthearted, most romantic, most pleasure-loving city of America. It was also truly the hotbed of corruption pictured in this story and "Blind Chris" Buckley did hold court in the Snug Café. His thug, Tansy O'Neill, is an imaginary character, but "Little Pete," the Tong chieftan, was a real person. The Barbary Coast was the hellhole of San Francisco, depraved as described herein, the "cribs" full of Chinese slave-prostitutes existed, and so did the fabulous opulence on Nob Hill.

William Keith, the landscape painter, lived and worked in San Francisco in 1890 and, strangely enough, was fundamentally influenced by the Impressionists after 1891. Fernand Cormon, as described, was the teacher of such famous painters as Van Gogh and Toulouse-Lautrec.

The Montgomery Block building, or Monkey Block, was indeed the dwelling place of struggling young artists, and Coppa's restaurant provided them with a gathering place, hot food and unlimited credit. The more elegant restaurants named did exist at the time and catered to such nabobs as the Stanfords, the Crockers, the Huntingtons and the Hearsts.

Chapter 1

Annette Tofler deftly tied the satin ribbon on the neckline of her black lace camisole giving it a final, purposeful tweak, then ran her hands down her tiny, whalebone-stiffened waist.

Her maid of long standing, Vivian, shook her red head and from pursed lips began to chastise gently in her soft Irish lilt. "Miss Annette, sure'n you'll be a scandal! Black lace underwear indeed! Why, if your mama knew, she'd—"

"Well, Mother is no longer here to see and certainly no one else will see it either, so what's the harm? If I don't wear my new Paris things, they'll rot in my bureau." Impulsively, Annette twirled across the rose Aubusson carpet and, stopping in midstep, gave the maid an imploring look. "Please Vivian, don't scold. It's our secret." Her large hazel eyes begged Vivian's forgiveness, but in their tawny depths lurked a hint of mischief and unquenchable deviltry.

Once again, Vivian was the loser, a role to which she was quite accustomed and to which she had learned to submit with dour grace. No one had ever been able to control Miss Annette's shenanigans and likely no one ever would. Far be it from Vivian to try too hard.

"Now for the dress," announced Annette. "Are you sure it's properly ironed?"

"I did it meself, miss," replied Vivian sourly. "It's ironed all right . . . what there is of it."

"Oh hush, Viv. It's a beautiful dress, a glorious dress!" Annette spun around to face the wood-framed upright mirror in the corner of her spacious, rose damask bedroom. "It's perfect for today." Her carefully styled auburn ringlets bounced and swung with her graceful movements, and her eyes gleamed with anticipation. "It's my first social event since I got home. I want to make a splash, a big splash! I want all of San Francisco to know I'm home."

Vivian pursed her thin, bloodless lips again and went to the mahogany wardrobe to fetch the costly dress. She helped Annette into it and fastened the tiny pearl buttons up the back. After fluffing the ruffles on the bustle, she stepped back to examine the effect.

The dress was stunning, a glistening shot silk in copper tones that varied according to the light. It was sleek, fitting tightly over Annette's tiny waist and rounded hips and flaring slightly at the hem. In the back it was pulled into a graceful bustle. But it was mostly the neckline that Vivian studied, hands on hips, shaking her head morosely. "Are you bein' quite sure you want to wear it, Miss Annette? It's not decent. Why, it's still afternoon . . ."

"Of course I'm going to wear it! In Paris, all the most fashionable ladies wear dresses exactly like this. I'll show these provincial blue bloods what's what."

The neckline that Vivian disapproved of was trimmed with black ostrich feathers and plunged outrageously low, revealing the swell of Annette's creamy breasts that were pushed up by her corset. Delicate, transparent black lace covered the white skin from the feathers to her graceful neck and formed long sleeves that ended in a deep ruffle.

"Please stop scowling and fetch my cape. Jensen will be furious if I'm late. He says he's not used to waiting for ladies anymore, at least not at home." She rolled her big eyes. "I'll bet Jensen knows more about waiting for ladies than he's letting on!"

Annette pulled on black kid gloves and snatched her cape from Vivian with an apologetic smile. She removed her parasol from its stand on her way out of the room, then hurried down the wide, curving oak staircase. In the spacious entrance hall, her dashingly handsome older brother was waiting, impatiently tapping his pointed, black patent leather shoe.

"Oh Jensen, really, I'm hardly a second late," she gave him a charming pout. "Here, help me on with my cape."

"You do look beautiful, Annette." Jensen smiled affectionately down at her as he draped her black velvet wrap over her shoulders. "It's good to have you back."

Returning his smile with pleasure, she thought how immensely glad she was that Jensen hadn't scolded her about the daring dress. Oh, he had lifted one eyebrow, that she had noted, but he wouldn't mention a thing. Not Jensen. Four years her senior, at twenty-three he was the so-called catch of the city. He had more on his mind than her choice of dress.

Jensen offered her his arm and she took it. Looking gay and carefree, they swept out of the magnificent mansion that their father had built for their mother twenty years before. Outside the ornate brass gate, on Mason Street, the carriage awaited them.

"We're going to the Golden Gate Gallery on Kearny Street near Market, Tom. Do you know it?"

"Sure, Mr. Tofler. It's that big fancy one next to Stein's Jewelers."

As her brother was helping her into the carriage, Annette swung around. "Oh! I forgot!" she cried and dashed back through the gate and into the mansion before he could stop her. In a few moments, she was rushing down the marble steps, two large carrots in hand.

"What the devil?"

"They're for the horses, Jensen. Be a sport. I won't be a minute."

Jensen watched somewhat impatiently as his radiant sister fed the horses just as she had always done. That was Annette. One moment she could be curtsying before a queen, dressed in the most elegant of gowns, and next moment she'd be picking up some mangy mutt with no care whatsoever for what people might think. Animals of all sorts fascinated Annette.

"You'll soil your gloves, Annette. Come on, now. We're late, and not fashionably. You should buy yourself a zoo!"

"And maybe I just will." Giving the horses one last affectionate pat on their velvety noses, she came back around to the side of the carriage and allowed Jensen to help her up.

The matched pair of blacks finally clip-clopped swiftly down from Nob Hill, that bastion of wealth that viewed San Francisco from the Olympian heights of boundless wealth, and headed toward the city's chic shopping district. It was a cool but brightly sunlit day, unusual for autumn in the notoriously foggy city. In the bay, cobalt-blue waves danced under the sun. The air was fresh and sharp and carried the tang of the sea.

"Oh, it is so good to be home," breathed Annette. "Paris is beautiful, but the air is too musty there. There's nothing like San Francisco, I must admit."

"Of course not. That's why we live here," Jensen laughed.

"Oh, I'm so excited! It's my first time out into society. I can't wait to see everybody. And the paintings, of course. It will be interesting to see how they compare."

"We have quite a growing colony of artists here, Annette. They won't disappoint you. The two men whose works you'll see today are quite well-known, quite established. They have more commissions than they can handle."

"Interesting," she mused. "Now, tell me who they are again, please." She settled back into the comfortable seat, promising herself not to forget a thing Jensen said.

"Well, there's William Keith. He does the most marvelous landscapes, all tranquil and soft colored. And then there's Rolf Karman. He's quite a phenomenon, really. Perhaps a scandal. Rumor has it that he was an orphan and grew up someplace in the South in dreadful poverty. Then he became a professional gambler on a Mississippi riverboat. He must have been a good one, because he won a bundle of money and was able to retire from that profession and move out here to paint."

"How very unusual." She looked pensive. "I wonder if he cheated. You say he won a bundle?"

Jensen laughed. "I doubt that he was a cheater—they don't live too long. It is an interesting question, though. And they say Karman is quite a ladies' man, too. I suppose it goes along with the image."

"Oh, Jensen, really! But how good is he as a painter?"

"You'll have to judge that for yourself. We're nearly there."

The gallery was on the second floor of a new

building made of brick and stone. Several carriages were disgorging gaily dressed people at the inconspicuously elegant entrance. Annette and Jensen joined the throng of people who streamed into the building and up the marble stairs to the sweeping, well-lit room. A placard on a stand announced: "First showing of new works by William Keith and Rolf Karman. October 15, 1890."

The moment Annette had shed her cape, a Chinese manservant appeared with a tray and offered them glasses of champagne. Jensen handed her a glass and they began to stroll slowly through the huge room, studying the dozens of paintings mounted on the white walls.

Much as she might have wanted to, it was difficult for Annette to concentrate on the canvases. She had been away in Paris attending school and old friends and acquaintances whom she hadn't seen for two years kept saying hello, welcoming her back, asking after her health. And there was another reason. Recently she had been kept awake at night by fantasies of an afternoon such as this where she was dressed daringly and floating through a sea of attractive men, their eyes turned always in her direction, admiringly. And yes, she blushed at the thought, the men in her visions had looked at her with open desire, too. Now her afternoon was taking on the quality of a dream come true. It was thrilling. She was sure her beautiful dress had helped to create the reality. The men's eyes followed her with approval. The women, however, looked at her critically, some even with shock.

Good, she thought, swishing the rich fabric of her skirt. Now they know I'm home and they won't forget me.

Jensen leaned down and whispered in her ear. "You've made quite a hit, little sister. The artists should be jealous of you today. You've stolen the spotlight from their work."

"If their work can't stand up to my dress, then they'll just have to improve, won't they?" she whispered back wickedly, tilting her delicate chin upward.

"Ah, but you have an advantage. They can hardly compare with your—shall we say—natural talent?" Jensen's hazel eyes sparkled with laughter.

At her brother's remark, Annette dropped her gaze demurely. Perhaps she was carrying her fantasy too far. Nevertheless, inside she was swelling with pleasure. Jensen had impeccable taste. If he approved of her, then she was satisfied. She wasn't doing anything wrong, was she?

Finally, Annette had an opportunity to study a number of the paintings. There were some excellent black and white sketches of the city, especially the ones of Chinatown, which evoked the exotic atmosphere of that area. She admired them for a while, losing herself in the art, forgetting the stir caused over her dress. Then she moved on to the oils and watercolors of William Keith. He had a good sense of nature's beauty, but his colors looked dim and boring to Annette, who had just returned from the brilliant artistic turmoil of Paris where the new Impressionists used startlingly bright colors that shocked the eye into comprehension and approval. She clucked her tongue and unconsciously shook her dark red curls, thinking how this artist could benefit from the fascinating work being done in Paris these days.

She strolled on, consumed by her inner thoughts, losing Jensen along the way somehow. She stopped in front of an arresting watercolor of a rocky coast somewhere near San Francisco, she guessed. It was all sea spray and grey-green rushing water and heavy, solid rocks. Something powerful stirred within her as she stood, head cocked to one side, studying the painting. She felt a vague professional jealousy. Could she herself have captured so well those forceful waves, those enduring rocks, the glowering grey sky? It was a question she could not answer.

She peered at the brass name plate on the frame: Rolf Karman. Ah, the orphan, the gambler. So he really could paint. *Devil's Cove* it was called. A supremely dynamic work, bold and intense. He had used the strong brush strokes and incongruous color combinations of the Impressionists. Had he studied in Paris, too? Or was his style instinctive? Who was this Rolf Karman anyway?

"Good, isn't it?" drawled a lazy, masculine voice.

She turned, startled out of her reverie, expecting an old friend, perhaps one of her father's acquaintances. But the soft, compelling voice belonged to a stranger who was standing beside her, eyeing the seascape. He was tall and extremely well dressed in a dark cutaway jacket, striped pants, and a beautifully pleated white shirt. His clothes were the height of elegance, but his face somehow didn't quite belong with his outfit. He had rough, curly, sandy hair that was streaked with blond, a strong jawline, hollow cheeks below high cheekbones and deep-set brown eyes that seemed to hide his thoughts. A thin mustache lined his upper lip. Below it, his wide mouth was curved into an insolent smile. His face had an untamed quality that gave the impression of the outdoors, whereas his clothes were the very essence of civilization. His aura overwhelmed her. Perhaps it was the hint of well-suppressed violence in those dark, unreadable eyes, the leonine carriage of his blond head, the way he looked at her as if she were a small animal that he was stalking.

How ridiculous! she told herself, bristling at her own intimidation. "Good?" she echoed, finally responding to his question. "Well, it does have a measure of feeling to it. But look at those awkward lines there," she pointed with a slim, gloved finger, "and that heavy mass of color here. It's a bit amateurish, I'd say. Rushed." She turned her full gaze eloquently on the stranger and saw him smile more broadly—perhaps mockingly, it occurred to her.

"And where did your critical eye get such a marvelous education?" he asked, his low voice full of laughter.

Annette grew uncomfortable as his gaze dropped deliberately to her décolletage. It made her want to look down to see if she was decently covered. Instead, she straightened her back and put on her haughtiest look. In a voice a little louder than she'd expected it to be, she said, "I'm a painter myself and have just returned from studying under Fernand Cormon for two years. I know a little—"

"Yes, you do know a little, perhaps," replied the tall man, still smiling infuriatingly down at her, his eyes burning through the black lace.

"I'd venture to say everyone here could benefit from some study in Paris," she said, trying to control her anger. The man was really too insulting!

"I'm sure they could, ma'am," he offered, closing the subject by his light treatment of it. "And what do you think of this one, then?" he asked her, pointing to a quick charcoal sketch of a mare and a foal running in a field.

"Passable," replied Annette. "Ordinary. And the foal's legs are too long."

"Ah, of course. The legs *are* a bit too long. But perhaps the artist exaggerated on purpose, to make a point." The soft voice washed over her, mocking her with its easy, dispassionate tone.

"Perhaps," Annette replied coldly.

"But you could be right, ma'am," he continued. "Perhaps the legs are just a mistake. Or perhaps horses' legs are shorter in Paris."

Her gold-flecked eyes flashed him a curt, angry glance. The very nerve of the man! He was insulting her. Openly. He certainly was no gentleman, despite his clothes. A man his age, at least thirty and probably older, should know better. There was no imaginable excuse! Her eyes narrowed in mounting outrage. He wasn't looking at her now and she saw only his profile as he pretended to study the sketch. He had a strong, high forehead, a generous nose that hooked unashamedly and long sideburns that ventured onto the tanned skin of his flat cheeks. Her temper simmered near the boiling point. If she weren't a lady, she'd tell him what she thought of his behavior!

"Excuse me, but I believe my brother is looking for me," Annette said coolly, controlling her wrath. She turned away, swishing her silk skirt and refusing to acknowledge his mockingly polite bow. Her head held high, she strode across the crowded gallery.

"Oh, Annette," she heard her brother call above the din. "There you are. I was wondering what happened to you."

Jensen obviously had been talking to the girl standing next to him, but Annette couldn't see her face yet. Leave it to Jensen, she thought, to attract the ladies.

"Annette!" cried the girl in a vaguely familiar voice, turning toward her. "It's been ages!"

"Why, Arabella Sims! How are you?"

"I guess I don't have to introduce you two."

"Of course not," replied Arabella. "We went to school together. How could you forget, Jensen?" The plump, blonde Arabella fluttered her eyelashes at Jensen so rapidly that Annette thought the girl would surely make herself dizzy.

As Arabella turned to greet another friend, Annette took the opportunity to lean close to Jensen for a moment. "Who on earth is that rude man over there?" she whispered, turning and nodding to where the tall stranger had stood only seconds before. He was gone.

"Who?"

"Oh, never mind. He's disappeared." Suddenly she felt foolish.

"Did he bother you?" asked Jensen. "Just point him out."

"Oh, no, nothing like that," mumbled Annette, embarrassed now at the fuss she had started. How on earth could she explain to her brother what had gone on between her and the tall stranger? She hardly understood it herself. "Really, Jensen, it was nothing." Quickly, she tried to change the subject. "And what have you been doing with yourself, Arabella? And how's Frederick?"

"Oh, Freddy's fine. He's awfully busy these days, working for the *Examiner*. But he still finds time to check on my beaus. Older brothers, you know!" Arabella rolled her big, round blue eyes drolly. "Now, you must tell me all about Paris. Is it true that bustles are on their way out?"

And so went the next hour as Annette had to answer a hundred questions from nearly as many people. Almost everyone wanted to know about Paris fashion trends. It piqued her that she couldn't study the paintings as closely as she wished, but socially, the afternoon was a complete success. She received several invitations to tea and five requests for her appearance at parties and dances. It was a nice feeling to be welcomed home by so many, a secure feeling, even if she did feel slightly different from everyone else, after having lived in Paris for so long. Her goals, too, had diverged from theirs.

If the truth were to be known, Annette realized, most of the rich and influential people at the afternoon exhibit were not really interested in art of any kind. They made their appearances in order to be seen and admired and remarked upon. They wanted to show that they really did have some culture. That they were patrons of the arts and no longer single-mindedly interested in amassing their fortunes. The knowledge made Annette feel uncomfortably superior. Although she too had come to make an appearance, she truly was interested in art for its own sake. She was no dilettante who painted pretty flowers to amuse herself. She honestly felt the call of the artist. There were images in her head that she felt compelled to put on paper. Ever since she was a child, she had sketched and painted and searched only for the skill and technique through which to express herself. She considered herself a step above the ladies whose hobby it was to reproduce their flower garden or their pet Pekingese. She wanted one day to be famous, to see her paintings hanging on walls like these, even in museums like the ones she had toured in Europe.

Her study in Paris had helped enormously, but she knew she still lacked something. Old Cormon, sparrow-faced and scrawny, Van Gogh's teacher, had put it into words. "Mademoiselle, you have not suffered enough. You are too young and carefree. There is no depth to your work. Your technique is fine, but *il y a quelque chose qui manque*. Something is lacking." Someday, she knew, she would succeed. But first she had to live fully, to fall in love, to fulfill herself as a woman.

Sometimes the notion frightened her, made her shiver with a delicious tremor of anticipation. But she felt an irrepressible urge to feel everything, do everything, experience everything that life offered. She felt strong and adventurous, ready for anything that would allow her to grasp, to comprehend, to penetrate the mystery of life itself. She needed a bit more age, more seasoning. Then she would really be able to paint, and the world would stand and take notice.

Jensen was beckoning her. "Annette, come and meet Francis Turner, the owner of the gallery. Mr. Turner, my sister, Annette, just recently returned from Paris. She's an artist, too."

"Miss Tofler." Turner kissed her hand. He was a short, heavy, grey-haired man and very prosperous looking. For a long moment his eyes did not leave her décolletage. It was almost embarrassing.

"Mr. Turner, how nice to meet you," babbled Annette, hoping nobody had noticed the man's audacity. "My brother exaggerates. I'm not an artist. Not yet. But someday I hope to be one." Perhaps Vivian had been correct. Perhaps it was a mistake to have worn a dress with such a low bodice.

"Miss Tofler," Turner still held her hand in his, "with your beauty, you should be a model, not a painter. You would inspire an artist to heights of skill."

"Oh, but I have modeled," she corrected quickly, pulling her hand from his. "In Paris. I sat for several artists there. But I still wish to do my own work." She knew from the way the man wetted his lips pensively that he was envisioning her as an artist's model. She cringed within her black camisole at his perusal. She certainly was glad she had never sat for a man like this.

"Of course. And when you complete a few, perhaps you will bring them to me and we might arrange a showing?"

The man's oily manner was beginning to irritate

her. He was obviously more interested in her feminine charms than in her canvases. "Perhaps," she replied coolly, her cheeks flaming.

Jensen got the hint. "Excuse us, Francis, I must introduce my sister to another friend." They walked away, mingling with the crowd.

"What other friend?"

"No one. I thought you needed rescuing. Old Francis is a known womanizer." Jensen's eyes danced with merriment.

It was clear to everyone that they were brother and sister. It was also clear that they belonged to the upper crust of San Francisco society, the nabobs, the railroad magnates, the forty-niners who had made good, the silver barons. It was not old money, but by now it was good, solid, established money. No one in San Francisco questioned how it had been accumulated, certainly not Jensen or Annette Tofler. They enjoyed its benefits far too much.

Later, as she sipped another glass of champagne and gazed at one of William Keith's lovely landscapes, Annette felt the distinct, unsettling sensation that someone was staring at her. She tried to ignore it. After all, she had come here not only to view the art but to be stared at, hadn't she? But she could not ignore for long the impression of someone's eyes boring a hole into her lace-covered back. Finally, she was forced to turn and search for its source.

The instant she turned, she knew she shouldn't have. The tall, rough-faced stranger was leaning negligently against a fluted column across the room, watching her, one elegantly shod foot crossed over the other. Even in nonchalant repose, his body appeared ready to move, to leap, to react. A taunting smile still played on his lips and his dark eyes rested precisely on the spot where Annette's dress left uncovered a substantial part of her translucent white skin.

She glanced around almost desperately searching for Jensen, but he had drifted away and she couldn't find his curly brown head in the crowd. Her natural pride made her ignore the man's rudeness, but his mocking gaze continued to disturb her. It was as if he saw right through her. The tiny hairs on the back of her neck prickled.

Quickly she turned away, knowing that the stranger's eyes still were fastened on her, knowing also that he was quite aware that she had noticed. She looked at the picture for endless minutes, not really seeing anything, unable to concentrate. Finally, she felt able to move casually into the crowd without seeming to be running away. She'd never give him that satisfaction!

At last she found her brother, surrounded by three lovely young ladies. "Can we go now?" she asked him. "I'm afraid we might be late to meet Daddy."

Jensen pulled his gold watch out of his waistcoat pocket. "Yes, perhaps we'd better be on our way. Good-bye, ladies. I trust I'll see you soon?" He grinned charmingly, bowed to the disappointed trio and took Annette's arm. "Thank God! This time you rescued me. I think those girls are after my scalp."

"Hardly that!" trilled Annette. "What would they do with your scalp?"

As they waited for the carriage to be brought around, Jensen eyed her warily. "What did you do, really, in Paris? I don't think I like the way you're talking, Annette. You've changed somehow."

She laughed, showing her small, white teeth. "Oh, silly, it's only talk. All I did in Paris was get sophisticated. Aunt Mercy was too strict for anything else."

"Good for her," muttered Jensen, still eyeing her speculatively.

They climbed into the carriage and set off down Kearny Street in the direction of the harbor where their father, Edward Tofler, had his offices. The familiar brick building, slightly seedy on the outside, was labeled "Tofler Transport Company." It was the hub of Edward's far-flung business ventures, and he spent more time there than he did at home. His children often joked that he felt more comfortable in its unpretentious, vaguely run-down disorder than he did in his meticulous, Greco-Roman-Italianate mansion. Their observation was more accurate than they realized.

"I'm lucky I got the afternoon off," remarked Jensen. "And I only did because you're home. He works me like a slave!"

"You love it," said Annette lightly. "Go on, admit it."

"I guess I do," he replied sheepishly. "It's a fascinating business, controlling all the things the city needs, the staples of our civilization. We've made the world a hundred times smaller than it ever was before."

When they arrived at the front door of Tofler Transport, Jensen asked Tom to wait for them as they wouldn't be long. Edward Tofler was taking his children to dinner at the Marchand restaurant and they were only picking him up.

Upon entering the musty reception room, Annette was greeted by many of the company's employees, people who had known her before she'd gone to Paris. Some of them remembered her as a child romping around the office, occasionally getting underfoot. Annette and Jensen climbed the stairs to their father's second-floor office and were met by his private secretary, Ned Plunket, who had been with Edward for fifteen years.

"Go right on in. He's expecting you. And welcome home, Miss Annette."

"Thank you, Ned. It's good to be back." She smiled at the thin, balding man, then leaned conspiratorially over his desk. "What kind of mood is he in today? Good or bad?"

"Oh, good, I'd say," answered Ned, grinning at Annette. "Nothing serious has gone wrong. In fact, he's just about tied up a big army contract." He looked at Jensen. "You know, the one you've been working on. I'd say he's feeling good."

"Wonderful! Then dinner will be fun," said Annette, knowing that her father, in one of his black moods, could ruin everyone's time.

Without bothering to knock, she swept into her father's office followed by Jensen. "Daddy! The opening was lovely!" she cried, settling herself into the deep leather chair in front of his enormous desk. "Thank you for letting Jensen off work to take me."

Edward Tofler raised his eyes from the proposal he was studying and looked at his youngest daughter. "Humph!" he growled. "Wasting time, as usual."

"Now Daddy, that's not true. Don't we have a social position to uphold? Goodness, you'd have Jensen a monk in this dusty old office! And you should have seen the ladies coo over him today!" She laughed prettily, throwing off her velvet cape.

"Annette!" pleaded Jensen, slightly uncomfortable, as usual, in his father's presence.

"It's true," she giggled.

"Good God," her father rasped. "Did you wear that dress to the opening? In the afternoon?" He was eyeing the neckline relentlessly.

Unconsciously, she put her hand to her breast as

if to reassure herself. She had never seen her father look at her in quite that way. He certainly was angry. She gave a small, nervous laugh. "Of course, Daddy."

"That dress is . . . disgusting," he said harshly.

A sudden, uncomfortable silence filled the room. Annette felt her cheeks begin to burn. Even her skin under the black lace was beginning to grow warm and prickly.

"Dad, it's not quite that bad," intervened Jensen, trying to lighten the tense atmosphere.

Abruptly, and with surprising agility for a bulky man of sixty, Edward spun around his chair to face Jensen. His eyes bored into Jensen's. "No one asked you! And I won't have my Annette displaying herself like a . . . a fallen woman!"

"Oh, Daddy," sighed Annette uneasily. "Everyone wears dresses like this now. It's not the dark ages anymore." Still, for all her brave words, she felt tears just under the surface and sensed that their evening was well on the way to being ruined. She glanced at Jensen surreptitiously from under her dark lashes. His face was pale and drawn and he had the look of a man who had been hit in the stomach. As if he were willing his consciousness elsewhere, his eyes were focused far away, beyond the wall of his father's office. Hard, white lines radiated outward from his mouth.

Oh dear, Annette thought, they're going to have an awful quarrel again. And it's all my fault.

Chapter 2

Sunday dawned grey. A heavy blanket of fog rolled up from the sleeping waterfront, crept into the alleys off Pacific Street and enshrouded the dozing forms of sailors passed out from Saturday night's shore leave on the Barbary Coast.

The air was damp and miserable. The sailors didn't care. A night in San Francisco's exotic area of debauchery was worth ten leaves elsewhere. Some had had their money stolen by dishonest gamblers, several had contracted syphilis, others who were more fortunate had simply drunk themselves into a deep stupor. But when they set sail with their captains on the evening tide or steamed out of the harbor with the sun at their backs, a San Francisco memory would go with them and they would tell tales of the Barbary Coast in ports around the world.

A weak autumn sun touched the elevated hills above the murky fog on the infamous coast. Those who knew San Francisco and had amassed the necessary funds built their homes on one of those hills, which the fog did not have the audacity to climb. Telegraph Hill attracted many. Nob Hill, however, was reserved for the ultrarich, those to whom money was so plentiful that it had lost all value. Edward Tofler was one of these moguls of wealth. Although he kept a close eye on his transport business, he belonged up on the Hill, away from the stream of lesser humanity he had struggled so hard to avoid all his adult life. His circle of friends was comprised of the unapproachables of the West, families such as the Hearsts, the Stanfords and the Crockers. They socialized among themselves, their conversations revolving around the shipping lines, the great railroads, their vast real estate holdings. What went on below them in the throb of the growing city was of little value or interest. They were above it, above the banks of fog and petty theft, ensconced in their own world of corruption and power.

Jensen Tofler understood and lived by the nabob rules. He was content with his position. Annette Tofler was not. To her the money, the glamour and the huge mansion in which she had been born meant little. She knew there were other valuable things in life. Although she wasn't quite sure yet what they were, Annette was determined to find out. And that had been the subject of her argument with her father at dinner several nights before.

Now, as they returned from church, it seemed to Annette that her father was determined to do battle once more. Today's argument had started when she had asked Jensen to drive out south of the city with her so that she might sketch a bit in the countryside.

"But Daddy," she drew off her long gloves and tossed them onto a polished drawing room table, "it's Sunday. Jensen doesn't have to work and all I want to do is to take a harmless ride. Maybe we'll have a picnic. What's so wrong in that?" The bustled skirt on her green velvet dress spread out around her as she sank into a chair, annoyed.

Edward Tofler's light brown eyes narrowed beneath his bushy, grey brows and his normally ruddy complexion deepened in color. "Not a damn thing if that's all you wanted to do! But I know you, my dear. You're determined to pursue this notion of painting. Women, Annette, do not pursue careers. Especially Tofler women!"

"You're a snob, Daddy." She pursed her lips defiantly and watched him as he paced the long room in agitation. "Lots of women paint. Why, even Mrs. Hearst dabbles in the arts. Think of all the money she's donated to struggling artists."

"Mrs. Hearst paints the roses in her garden and perhaps her cat. Besides, you have no idea who donates money where. It's all anonymous. And stop trying to talk your way around the subject." Angrily, he strode across the room and towered over her. "You shall not pursue this career."

"Oh, yes I shall!" Annette's hazel eyes sparked fury into her father's face. "And if you don't let me, well then, I'll just leave."

"Without funds?" he scoffed, his hands trembling in tight fists at his sides.

"Of course, Daddy." Annette rose and walked across the room to the long, velvet-draped window. Her back to her father, she winked at Jensen who stood in the doorway, watching his rebellious sister carefully. Then she spun around, facing Edward. "I'm not unattractive, Daddy. I'm sure I'll find a sponsor!"

"A what!" he exploded.

"A sponsor. Someone who will set me up in lodgings and finance my work." Her eyes sparkled with devilment. "And I'm sure it won't be a woman," she added coolly.

"By God, daughter, I'll see you locked away first!"

Jensen laughed and stepped into the room. "Lock

Annette up? Why, she'd tear the house down brick by brick."

"Keep out of this, Jensen," Edward sputtered, to which his son bowed mockingly.

The huge room filled with a pregnant silence as Edward looked from his son's face to Annette's. He realized there was nothing he could do.

"All right," he muttered finally, "go for your damn Sunday drive. Paint your fields and flowers. But you be back here for dinner, and that's final." He left the room, grumbling beneath his breath.

"I don't see why he let me go to Paris," Annette said to Jensen. "And he didn't even object when Aunt Mercy wrote to him about my studies with Fernand Cormon. So why is he suddenly so angry?"

"He's angry, Annette, because he thought your interest in art was a passing fancy, something you'd drop once you got back to San Francisco and rejoined society here."

"You mean he thinks I'll spend all my time going to teas and balls and batting my lashes until I snag some wealthy, boring bachelor? Ha!"

Jensen shook his head. He looked both amused and troubled. "It's not such a terrible idea, little sister."

"Oh, not you, too!"

"All right. Let's drop it. Now go change your dress and I'll see to a picnic basket."

She walked over and hugged him. "Jensen, you're wonderful."

They stopped some eight miles south of the city on a rolling hill overlooking a clean farmhouse and a horse pasture surrounded by a white fence and dark eucalyptus trees. Annette jumped out of the buggy before Jensen could assist her and twirled gaily, exhilarated by the crisp autumn air.

"It's so wonderful here, Jensen! What a marvelous place." She fetched her sketch pad and her charcoal from the buggy and strolled over to a comfortable spot beneath a giant oak.

In a few minutes, she had sketched the farmhouse, meadow and fence with artful strokes. "Dull," she commented under her breath, tearing off the page. She began anew, this time concentrating on a young foal.

"Have you ever painted in oils?" asked Jensen, who was stretched out beside her on the blanket. "I mean, have you really done a canvas?"

"Several," she replied without pausing in her work. "They were awful though and Monsieur Cormon said I should concentrate on my form before tackling another canvas. I suppose he's right, but it's so frustrating. I left all my efforts with Aunt Mercy. She thought they were wonderful." She made a winsome little face.

"Then you really are serious about becoming an artist?"

"Absolutely." She ripped off the page and crumpled it. "I've dreamed about becoming famous ever since I can remember. It's become almost an obsession."

Jensen sat up and took off his grey jacket, leaving on the vest. "It's getting warm," he observed. He placed a hand on Annette's arm. "Can we talk?"

Annette put down her sketch pad. The gold in her eyes, which matched her crisp cotton, floral print dress, turned a darker, wondering shade. "You're going to lecture me, like Daddy," she stated flatly.

"No. And please, for God's sake don't compare me to him."

"All right."

"Our dear father," he uttered the word with

venom, "would close you up in a nunnery if he could. He'd keep you all for himself."

"I don't understand."

Jensen looked away, focusing his eyes somewhere on the lea below. "I simply mean that he guards your innocence jealously, like he did Cecile's. He wants to keep his children under his thumb, that's all, and I think you'd better watch your step."

"Well, Cecile left, didn't she? Jensen, I've often thought our older sister disappeared because Daddy was too strict."

"She was only fourteen, for pity's sake. I don't recall her as being anything other than the perfect child. I've thought a lot about it, and I can't find any reason for her sudden disappearance. And Dad won't discuss it."

"I barely remember it," she reflected. "I was far too young, I guess. It's strange that we've never heard from her."

"Yes. Strange. At any rate, I would try to settle down some if I were you. This talk about a sponsor and all only infuriates him. And I'm sure you can't possibly mean a word of it."

"Oh, but I do." Annette tossed her copper ringlets defiantly. "Why shouldn't I have a lover?"

"Annette!"

"Oh, don't look so worried, Jensen. I haven't taken one . . . yet."

"And you won't! My God, this may be 1890 and all, but a woman's virtue still counts with a decent man."

"Decent men are boring, I've found," she revealed. "In Paris, women are shrugging off the so-called Victorian ideals and living their own lives. It's exciting, Jensen. I want to be a part of the new era. Why, you take lovers all the time! Nice women, too!"

"I don't marry them, though, do I?"

"You're such a prude. As though marriage were all a girl wants out of life!"

"That's no answer."

"Well, then, you're archaic. There are lots of men who would, well . . . bed me and then marry me, too. If I wanted them, that is. It is done, you know."

"Occasionally." He studied her for a moment. "You are beautiful, little sister. I just suggest you give these things more thought, that's all."

She laughed. "I think about them all the time." If only Jensen knew how much I do think about having an affair, she thought to herself. How many nights had she lain awake in her spacious four-poster, dreaming, fantasizing. She always envisioned a wonderful painting and people admiring her great skill, oohing and ahing over the canvas. There was always one man, a handsome, virile man, who was stunned by her artistry and her beauty. He pursued her, devoured her with his eyes, protested undying love. And then they were alone somehow. She would approach him, let him know that she found him attractive. The edges of the dream would blur as they became locked in an ardent embrace. . . .

Smiling to herself, Annette rose and strolled away from the tree. She stooped to pick an autumn wildflower and examined it. Jensen watched her every movement, the soft provocative sway of her hips, the casual way in which her curls tumbled down her back, the proud line of her delicate nose. Annette was a beauty, all right. Already, many men had asked after her, even Jensen's own friends. Did she know the stir her return from Paris had created among the menfolk? How long could Annette keep winding their father around her little finger? Edward, for all his faults, was not stupid. Annette should be more careful about angering Edward. The man could be ruthless, even cruel.

The truth was Jensen hated their father. Perhaps it was because of their older sister, Cecile. Jensen was sure Edward had driven her away somehow. He certainly had alienated their mother, Elizabeth. Oh, she hadn't gone away as Cecile had, but Jensen could still remember the bitter arguments which frequently had raged long into the night, echoing through the dark halls of the mansion. It was then that he had begun to hate his father. And then his mother had died so suddenly. . . . And now Annette was taunting Edward. Jensen didn't know how long he could protect her.

She returned from her stroll, having fetched the lunch from the buggy. "Are you mad at me? You seem so quiet."

"No," he sighed. "I just worry some."

"Please don't." She smiled warmly at him. "I'm sorry if I worry you, truly I am, but I can take care of myself. I just feel terrible when you take my side against Daddy. You shouldn't have to. I can see how he hurts you and I hate that."

Jensen leaned over and kissed her cheek. "That's sweet, Annette. Thank you. But I can handle our father. Besides, the fights aren't really over you. We always argue. I guess we always will."

They ate lunch. There was cold chicken, potato salad and a small bottle of red wine which Jensen had thought to bring along. They talked more about Edward and then about Jensen's growing role in the transport business and the fact that he was being groomed to take over someday.

Annette understood little about the technicalities of the transport business. As far as she was concerned, it was simply too dull. The money had always been there, she reasoned, so why should she worry her head over business? Still, she had to admit that her brother made it sound almost exciting, but then Jensen would. He was a wonderful conversationalist. At times, perhaps, he was a little too sarcastic, but he did have a gift for words. The ladies of San Francisco loved his deep, smooth tones, his knowledge of the inner political circles, his dashing good looks.

Jensen was filling her in on recent local news and gossip that she'd missed. She found herself alternately torn between laughter and horror. ". . . and the wonderful leader of San Francisco, the man behind the political machine, Blind Chris Buckley—"

"Blind? You mean because he turns his back on corruption?"

"Yes, that too, but he really is blind. All day, every day, he sits locked up in the back room of the Snug Café, running the city."

"Does Daddy deal with a man like that?"

"I don't think so. I hope to hell not. If he does, he keeps it well hidden from me." Jensen shrugged and returned to his subject. "Anyway, last week one of the Barbary Coast saloon proprietors needed to renew his liquor license, so he came to Chris' office with a huge tale of woe. It seems there'd been some kind of flood in the saloon. The man's stock had been ruined, the carpeting in several of the rooms upstairs had been destroyed, and to top it all off, he was robbed several days later."

"He probably deserved it," she commented.

"Perhaps so. Still, he didn't have the money to renew the license, so he went to Chris to beg off. Chris said no. The man grew irate and threatened him. Well, Chris' bodyguard and general thug, Tansy O'Neill, kicked him out of the office, and the next day the health and fire inspectors showed up at his saloon and closed the place down. The man rushed over to Chris' office again, supposedly half-crying in apology. Do you know what Chris did?"

Annette giggled. "No."

"He told the poor chap that the license price had just doubled. I guess the man called him a thief and then," Jensen chuckled, shaking his head, "Chris raised the price again, doubling the former one."

"What did the poor man do? Did he pay it?"

"Of course. If he hadn't, Chris would have seen to it that the man never reopened."

"But if he didn't have any money, then how—"

"Oh, no doubt Tansy will show up every Saturday night to collect a portion of the dues."

"That's terrible."

"It is. But that's the way it's done here, and Chris never bluffs."

Annette's back stiffened as a thought occurred to her. "What if he makes Daddy . . . well, pay him money for something?"

"He won't. The nabobs are above all that, silly. They're just too powerful."

"I hope you're right."

"I am. Now," he began packing up their picnic items, "what about you, my sister? What are your plans for the immediate future?"

"Painting. Nothing's going to stop me. In fact," she confided hesitantly, "I'm thinking of renting a studio in the Montgomery Block building."

"The Monkey Block?" Jensen was almost shouting.

Annette ignored his shock. "Why yes. Lots of artists keep rooms there."

"My God," he exclaimed, still horrified, "you can't be serious!"

"Oh, but I am. And you won't tell Daddy, either."

"The hell I—"

"Oh, no you don't, Jensen. It wouldn't be fair. I told you this in complete confidence."

"Jesus . . ." He rubbed his clean-shaven chin thoughtfully. "Look. Why not the Astor House or something? At least the artists there are reputable. Anywhere but the Monkey Block."

"The Astor House is too highbrow. If I'm going to experience things, to live, it will have to be somewhere more seedy."

"It's seedy all right."

"Promise you won't tell?"

"He'll find out."

"Promise!"

"Oh God. I . . . promise."

On Monday morning, Edward and Jensen left for the company offices bright and early. Annette lazed in bed until late morning, toying with the idea of renting the studio that very day. Then she thought of another plan, one which would broaden her horizons even further. It was far racier than anything she had done or thought of doing since her return. If her father found out, well, that would be the end of her freedom forever. Finally she rose and called for Vivian to help her dress. While drinking a glass of chilled orange juice, Annette pondered what to wear. Finally, she selected a green tweed skirt and a matching jacket with fitted sleeves. Under it she wore a crisp white blouse which encircled her throat with lace. To complete the ensemble, she chose a simple hat with a few feathers. She looked very businesslike and that was exactly what she wanted.

"Where are we going today?" inquired Vivian.

"*We* are going nowhere. *I* am going downtown." She pinned a gold brooch at the throat of her blouse.

"Alone?"

"Quite."

"But—"

"Now don't fret, Viv. I'll be back shortly."

"What if your father should come home?"

"He won't." Annette opened her bedroom door and started down the curved staircase.

Vivian called after her, "Should I send for the carriage?"

Annette shook her head. "I'm taking the cable car. It'll be fun."

As she left the mansion alone, she imagined Vivian racing to the kitchen where the servants would gossip for the rest of the morning about the young mistress's brazen behavior. Let them. Just as long as Edward never found out.

She rode the green painted cable car, the one the Nob Hill residents had built for themselves, down California Street to the central business district. She then strolled over to Montgomery Street and into the ground floor of the so-called Monkey Block building. There was a restaurant there, next to the small lobby, called Coppa's. It was brimming over with artists. Some were drinking coffee, some whiskey, and their voices were loud and animated. For the most part, they were dressed badly. As were the Bohemians in Paris, they were trying to live up to their role of struggling young artists.

It was exciting. Annette wondered where she could shop for such clothes. And wouldn't they look too terribly new?

She walked into the lobby and found a slim, poorly dressed man behind the desk. He eyed her warily at first, as if to say, "Go back where you belong." However, as soon as she produced enough cash to hire a studio apartment for six months in advance, his manner changed abruptly.

"Certainly, miss. I have just the one."

When Annette was shown into the tiny room, she gasped in delight. It was just what she had dreamed of. The walls were white and the small bed, chair and table were spattered wonderfully with old paint. It was the window facing northeast, however, that captured most of her attention. It was large and caught the late morning light. It was perfect.

"I'll take it," she told the clerk instantly, handing him the cash.

He produced the key and disappeared down the dimly lit hall. Annette closed the door, locked it and walked over to the window. Not much of a view, but plenty of light. She turned around and went to the paint-encrusted table, touching it almost reverently, wondering if the drops had fallen from the brushes of some now famous artists. She realized then that she would need to add her own touches. She would bring a vase, perhaps buy a new carpet. And she wanted a colorful quilt for the narrow cot, although it was unlikely that she ever would sleep there. She glanced at the bare walls. Those would be easy to fill. To tell the truth, this tiny room thrilled and excited Annette far more than her opulent rose-colored boudoir at home. This was hers, all hers, and no one could take it away from her.

The first thing she wanted to do was to meet the local artists, study their works and gain experience. Would they accept into their circle a rich woman from Nob Hill? Most likely not. But then, who was to tell them?

Experience. Yes, Annette thought, she must make an all out effort to study the work of at least several local artists. It certainly wouldn't hurt. And therein was her most daring plan. Her stomach fluttered at the prospect. Did she dare? She had done it in Paris, but somehow that was different. There no one really had known her and the artists were old hands at their trade. Still, what was so different about it here? Nothing. Artists were artists the world over.

She left the room, locking the door behind her. Tomorrow she would bring a few things to the studio. But first, today, she had to hurry over to the *Examiner*. The streets were crowded with shoppers, businessmen on their lunch hours and beggars. A peddler stood on the corner selling medicinal potions that he claimed would cure anything from a headache to an unwanted pregnancy. On the opposite corner was a saloon offering a free lunch with the purchase of a drink. There were hundreds of such saloons in the city, all competing for customers. It was a buyer's market.

Crossing the street through the heavy carriage and horse traffic, Annette saw a woman on the corner who was eyeing her suspiciously. It took a moment for Annette to realize that the woman was a harlot, for her dress was more ornate than most. Of course, she realized, this wasn't Chinatown or the waterfront. The woman was of a higher class of prostitute. As the whore's dark, limpid eyes followed Annette, she wondered what it would be like to stand on a street corner and sell oneself. If the man were attractive, she guessd it might be an adventure and not unpleasant. But suppose he was old and balding and fat?

She shuddered inwardly as she passed by the woman and headed toward the newspaper office, the one owned by William Randolph Hearst, her father's friend. Good Lord, she thought, what if she ran into Mr. Hearst while she was there? But no, he most likely would never be in that department.

As she approached the *Examiner* building, she

considered the wording of the advertisement. It would have to read something like this: "Young attractive woman seeking employment as model. Qualified. Paris experience. Inquire for Annette, the Montgomery Block building."

Chapter 3

It had been a frustrating, dull week since Annette had placed the advertisement. She had expected to spend a good deal of her time at the new studio, but every time she turned around there was another tea to attend, or another supper party. She had to accept the invitations. That had become obvious the first time she'd tried to refuse one.

"What do you mean you're not going?" Edward Tofler had exploded over breakfast. "What better things do you have to do with your time? My Lord, Annette, you don't sew, you don't take Vivian shopping with you. How, may I inquire, do you spend the days?"

Annette had hesitated, catching Jensen's amused gaze from across the wide, mahogany table. "I've been, well, I've attended several teas and then, oh yes, I've been reading lots."

"Reading?" Edward arched a bushy eyebrow.

"Well, yes. Why just yesterday I finished *Les Miserables*," she fibbed wretchedly. In truth, she had read *Les Miserables* three years before, at school.

"I see," Edward commented thoughtfully, dabbing at his mouth with the napkin. "I suggest you attend this tea, Annette. You won't find a husband if you keep sulking about the house with a French book."

"A husband? Why, Daddy! Do you want me to

marry and leave you and Jensen all alone?" She folded her hands in her lap demurely. "I thought you were glad I came home."

"Stop playing the little girl with me," he'd chided sternly, but Annette had sensed he wasn't all that angry. "And don't look at me with those puppy dog eyes of yours, either. You're going to the tea. That's final."

"Yes, Daddy."

"Humph!" he'd muttered, leaving the table.

And so Annette had been to the Montgomery Block only once, and that was several days ago, to check her studio and the mail. Now, having slipped away from Vivian while she was busy, Annette entered the building again.

She had dressed fashionably for shopping, just in case she ran into anyone who knew her. She'd chosen a sapphire blue wool dress with a high, lacy collar and long leg-of-mutton sleeves. Her hair was arranged in a loose pompadour. A stylish, matching blue felt hat with brilliant peacock feathers streaming behind sat perched neatly on top of her head. The color of her dress set off her eyes, making them appear more green than golden brown. She looked young, self-assured and very beautiful as she walked through the lobby.

"Would there be a letter for me?" she asked the clerk behind the desk, her eyes wide with anticipation.

"Why, yes, I believe so," he said, recognizing her. Her heart leapt wildly. "Funny, though, there's no last name on the envelope. But being as how you're our only Annette, miss, I suppose it's for you."

She took the small white envelope as nonchalantly as possible, smiled and walked up the two flights of stairs to her studio. Her hand trembled as she placed the key in the lock. It had to be a reply to her ad. It had to be.

Once the door was securely closed behind her, she

sat down in the chair, let her breath out, and ripped the seal open.

October 23

Dear Annette:

I have read your advertisement in the *Examiner* this day and am most interested in your experience in Paris. At present I seek a young female for a sculpture I hope to complete by Christmas. I should like very much to interview you. If it is convenient, would the afternoon of October 25 be suitable? If so, I shall see you at my lodgings at 178 Powell Street on that date. If you have made other arrangements, would you be so kind as to inform me?

Sincerely, Bernard Maduro.

Bernard Maduro. A sculptor. Hadn't she heard his name somewhere? She clutched the note to her breast. Bernard Maduro wanted to interview her! It was too wonderful! Quickly, she reread the note. But wasn't the date . . . today?

"Oh God!" she cried, leaping to her feet. It must already be one or two in the afternoon. And she hadn't anything to wear! There had been no time to shop for the right clothes. Oh, what could she do? Surely, she thought, if she went dressed up so finely, he would think her too highbrow for the work. But there was no time to remedy that, no time at all. What were her choices? Either she could show up in her expensive dress or not go at all today and risk losing the job. When put in that light, she had no choice. She had to go and quickly.

In front of the Montgomery Block, breathless from running down two flights of stairs, she hailed a carriage and gave the driver the address on Powell Street. As the horses clip-clopped along, she thought of a thousand excuses she could give this Bernard Maduro about her elegant attire. In the end, however, she decided that anything she might say would only draw more attention to her clothing.

She tried to envision the sculptor. But that, too, was futile. She would know in a few minutes, anyway. Still, she couldn't help wondering if he was attractive. If he turned out to be old and ugly, she decided, she would be his model and nothing more. A business deal, that was all. But if he were handsome, or even just intense and sensitive, an insecure artist type, then anything might happen.

Her familiar fantasy unfolded before her eyes, routine and pleasant and just wicked enough to be tinged with the excitement of the unknown. She was posing and the handsome young artist approached her, dazzled by her beauty. He could not help himself. But she was kind and gracious and womanly and made everything easy for him . . . and then the fantasy blurred. Exactly what she and the young, vulnerable artist did together was indistinct and vague. But whatever it was, she was sure she would love it. After all, in the romances she read, the women just pined for it.

When the carriage stopped in front of 178 Powell Street, Annette paid the driver and walked briskly to the door of the brick apartment house. On the outside, she appeared calm and even businesslike, but inwardly she was as nervous as a cat. Would he hire her, or would he brush her aside, thinking she was a society lady seeking an afternoon's thrill?

She found his apartment at last. It was on the top floor, so she was certain he must have a large window or skylight, perhaps even a door onto the rooftop. She closed her eyes, took a deep breath and knocked.

The door swung open. "Yes?" A dark-haired man, thirtyish, stood before her.

"I'm Annette."

"Annette?" He stared hard at her, momentarily puzzled. Her heart pounded furiously. "Oh," he said finally, "Annette . . . the model. Why yes, come in, please." He stuck out his hand for her to shake. "I'm Bernard Maduro."

And then she was inside, the door closed behind her. The studio was spacious, a sculptor's dream, with lots of light pouring in from a glass roof on the front of the building. Several large, unfinished figures were placed at random around the room. There was an odor of dried clay and a grey, powdery dust covered everything from the floor to his single cot to the tiny kitchen counter near the rear of the room.

Even Bernard Maduro himself was chalky. She'd felt the roughness of his cracked hand and there was a smudge of plaster on his ample nose. He was a handsome man, very southern European looking, with dark hair and pale olive skin. He wasn't much taller than she and he had a slight, well-proportioned build. His large, light brown eyes were serious looking and surrounded by extremely long, dark lashes. His lips beneath the bent, full nose were fine and stern.

He showed her to a dusty chair, paused, then brushed at it with his hand. "I'm afraid you'll get your beautiful dress all—"

"That's all right," she said quickly, embarrassed, making herself comfortable in its dusty depths.

"You've modeled in Paris, your advertisement said." He stood over her, arms folded, his eyes studying her closely as if he could not believe her beauty, or her presence, was quite real.

"Yes, many times," she fibbed. The truth was she had sat only for her master, a sheet covering most of her young body at all times. But she would have posed naked in front of him, or any man, for that matter. Annette knew her body was perfectly shaped for a model. She was proud of the full breasts and hips, the long legs and slender waist. And as an artist, she knew there was only beauty in the human form, no shame, nothing to hide.

"Whom, may I ask, have you sat for?"

He was doubting her. But she was well rehearsed. She rattled off several names easily, knowing full well he could never check. They were all in Paris.

Still, Bernard seemed skeptical. An idea came to her. Abruptly, she stood up. "Would you like to start now?" she asked quickly, confidently, and began to look around for a screen. "Is there somewhere I might change?" Now she knew he must make his decision. She had shown her willingness and the ball was in his court. She stood waiting, her chin held high, her hazel eyes meeting his dark ones levelly.

After endless moments, he broke the strained silence. "The screen's behind you," he nodded. "I suppose, if you like, we could start now. I'll be doing several sketches at first and then I'll begin sculpting. Perhaps," he added to her disappearing form, "we'll do a simple sketch today so that I might have time to study it."

Annette was glad that the screen hid her face from him. Her insides were twisting so madly that she had to take several quiet, deep breaths before she could begin undressing. Behind her there were hooks and a single, white sheet which she assumed was to be draped around her when she reappeared. Good. That way she wouldn't feel quite so naked when she walked back out.

Do I dare go through with this? she thought for an instant. But of course she would. Annette Tofler would not go back on a bargain struck. Never. It took her several minutes to unclothe as she was dreadfully overdressed and the buttons on her dress and the strings on her corset were terribly awkward to unfasten by herself. Next time she would dress accordingly.

"Do you have a last name, Annette?" came his solemn voice.

"Why, yes. Tofler," she replied uneasily, immediately regretting it. "I don't use it often, though," she added. She should have given a false name.

"I hope you realize I can't pay much—"

"Whatever you can afford will be adequate."

At last she was ready, the sheet wrapped around her soft curves. Her cheeks were hot and probably a flaming red, but there was nothing she could do about that now. Mustering all her courage, she stepped out from behind the screen before she could dwell too long on what was to come. She would not back out. He was an artist, she told herself. He had no interest in her body except as a work of art. And besides, she was secretly dying to know what modeling would be like.

"Over here, please," he instructed in an impersonal tone, showing her to a bay window seat under the glass roof. There was a long, narrow, grubby cushion on the seat. Annette sat down gingerly.

"How would you like me?" she asked, matching his professional tone.

She wondered then, as he fussed with her position, a thin finger to his lip, if she should undrape herself now or wait. The situation grew tense. He seemed to be having a great deal of trouble deciding on how she should stretch out, so she took a chance and let the sheet slip down. At first only her breasts were bare, but then she let go of the sheet completely.

Bernard spoke almost at once. "Yes, that's better," he said. She was amazed that he never once faltered in speech or let his hands slip or his eyes linger on her.

How easy this is! she thought in relief. Bernard continued to have her twist this way and that, suggesting positions, until he was satisfied. All the while, Annette felt as if she were a piece of modeling clay instead of flesh and blood. It came to her that, in a way, she was almost disappointed. This was, after all, the first time a man had ever seen her naked. Surely, she wondered, she must have more modesty than this? But it seemed she didn't, and she had to admit, it took a little of the secret excitement away.

At last, Bernard turned away and picked up his sketch pad. "I hope the position isn't too uncomfortable," he offered, turning to face her and taking a seat on a hard, wooden stool. "If it is, we can take a break. Just say so."

"I will."

Bernard had chosen a position for her which suggested a portrait of a woman stretched out on a velvet settee. It made her think of a painting that might hang over a bar in a saloon. One hand was resting on her hip and the other was draped over her head, elbow bent. She felt exotic. She liked the feeling of a man's eyes on her naked flesh. Her head was facing toward him, but slightly to the left. Still, from the corner of her eye, she could watch him as he sketched.

He worked for a while, ripping off several pages. "Could you move your right leg a little?" he said finally. "And bend the knee a touch more. There." He went back to his drawing.

It had all happened so fast that Annette really had not had the time to think. First they had been talking, then he had positioned her and now there was only silence.

She could feel the afternoon sun beating on her

hip and legs, its strength magnified by the glass. Beads of perspiration began to form on her skin. Soon they were trickling down between her breasts. His eyes were fastened on her bosom, on the two full mounds that swelled toward him, the rosy peaks standing pert under his absorbed scrutiny. An alien sensation tingled in her lower abdomen.

"I suppose you've been told this often, Annette," he said, "but you have an exquisite shape for modeling. How old are you?"

"Twenty-one," she lied.

"Young, yes. Your skin is still fresh. And your bosom," he laughed unselfconsciously, "is absolutely marvelous. I couldn't have asked for better."

Annette was so taken aback by his bold, blatant words that she forgot he was only viewing her as a professional and blushed crimson.

He seemed not to notice at first, but then, as his hand sketched in the lines of her face, he stopped. "I've embarrassed you," he said stiffly. "I'm so sorry, Annette. Sometimes when I see a work of art before me I forget that the person might have sensibilities. Please, forgive me." He rose then, tossing aside the pad. As he came toward her, Annette almost drew back in confusion. What was he going to do?

"Here," he said, picking up the sheet and offering it to her. "That's enough for today."

Annette came to a sitting position. Her eyes averted, she allowed him to cover her nakedness. As he helped her, his fingers inadvertently brushed an erect nipple.

She recoiled automatically.

"Sorry," he said, looking at her thoughtfully. And then, "Listen, I want to recreate you, Annette, no matter what. But I have a feeling you haven't really modeled this way before. Have you?"

"Of course I have," she replied quickly, afraid to be caught in the lie. And then she got up and headed for the screen.

"We'll talk about it next session," he said easily, without humor. She prayed he wouldn't go back on his promise to sculpt her.

She dressed quickly, in silence. When she was done, she came bravely out from behind the screen.

"Might I offer you a cup of tea?" He turned from his place in the tiny kitchen to face her.

"No, thank you. I must be going. When shall I come again?" she asked with as much confidence as she could manage.

"How is tomorrow? Say about one?"

"Fine." She smiled then and went to the door. "At one."

That night, having bribed and begged Vivian into silence, Annette found sleep long in coming. First there was Vivian; it wasn't really fair to sneak out on her. And then there was her father; that was the worst deception. She had arrived home late, after Edward and Jensen, and had been forced to lie miserably to avert an argument. She told Edward that she had gone out for a short walk and been detained by neighbors. God help her if he ever checked on her story!

Still, while it nearly made her sick to lie like that, it wasn't really fair that a woman was allowed so little freedom. Society forced her to be devious. And even then, it would be so much simpler if her father would consider her career as a genuine possibility. But he wouldn't. And Jensen wasn't too much better. He was overly protective. Somehow she would have to keep fighting for her dream. She would use every weapon at her disposal, tooth and nail if need be, whatever it took to reach her goal.

On the following morning, Annette went shopping

with Vivian on Kearny Street, where she purchased a peasant style skirt, a loose blouse with long sleeves and a drawstring neck, and a warm, simple cape to cover it all.

Vivian was amazed. She asked a hundred questions. And when Annette shipped her off to lunch alone, she was aghast. "You're off again, are you, Miss Annette? Well, I'll not be hearin' of it. Not this time, I won't."

But for all her arguments, Vivian did indeed leave Annette alone in the end. The moment the maid was out of sight, Annette went to her studio in the Monkey Block. After she had changed, she headed straight for Bernard Maduro's.

During her wakeful night, she had spent a lot of time thinking about the handsome man who was going to sculpt her. All her thoughts had been pleasantly expectant. Not only was he attractive, but his calm air of maturity was appealing. She liked that in a man. Still, she sensed a vulnerability in him which he kept under tight rein. The right woman, she thought, could tap that innocence and use it to her advantage.

She imagined that Bernard, as she'd come to think of him, most likely would be a gentle, caring lover who would treat her body with reverence and delight in it, as if it were a work of art. Hadn't he told her she was exquisite? He must, then, be somewhat attracted to her.

But no, she didn't dare flirt with him. Why, she hardly knew him at all. He might turn out to be a molester of women. Or worse. Still, her curious mind kept fantasizing a union between them. She tried to shake off the sensual vision, reminding herself that she was a model, not a seductress. It was simply that for years she had wondered what it would be like to sleep with a man, naked, his hands possessing her, his body joining with hers. There was nothing wrong with physical union, and marriage was not, she insisted to herself, a prerequisite for lovemaking.

She stood at Bernard's door for the second time, realizing that the carriage trip over to Powell Street had been a blur in the face of her musings. She giggled mischievously, sobered, then knocked.

Bernard's manner was much the same as on the previous day. He was unerringly polite, the perfect gentleman. He even carefully avoided her while she found the proper pose once more. If she was a little off in her position, he said nothing.

Absent-mindedly, he made small talk while sketching. "Tofler wouldn't be French, would it?"

"Why yes," she answered. "My family's originally from Lyon."

"And now they live in San Francisco?"

"Yes. My father and brother."

"Your mother?"

"She died when I was a child."

"Umm." He looked up from the pad. "Would you like to take a break?"

Annette was thoroughly exhausted from holding the same position. She had never realized how tired keeping perfectly still could make you. "Why yes, if you wouldn't mind too awfully." She sat up stiffly and glanced at Bernard, who had gone to make tea. She started to reach down for the sheet, then hesitated.

Why should she hide her nakedness from him at this point? She crossed her legs, remained seated, and waited.

When he returned with the steaming brew, Bernard did not seem surprised that she had not bothered to cover herself. He handed her the cup as if she were clothed and sitting in an elegant café. Then he turned his back on her and walked across the wide room.

Annette grew piqued. How could he ignore her? She glanced down at her body. It was nice, but was it desirable? How could she know?

On an impulse, Annette rose to her feet and began moving toward him. It did cross her mind that she might be asking for something she was not yet ready to handle. But the thought died on the air like a forgotten breeze.

She was standing behind him. She swallowed. "Bernard?"

He turned around abruptly, nearly bumping into her. His eyes met hers. One dark brow lifted questioningly for a moment, then settled. He remained silent.

This wasn't easy. She felt her breasts rise and fall. Her hands at her sides were sweating. She tried her voice. "Are you sure I'm the right model? I mean, perhaps my, my bosom is too small or something?" My God, she realized suddenly, I'm being wanton! What had she started?

Bernard smiled, a lazy, slow parting of his thin lips. "I doubt I have ever, or will ever, see such perfect breasts, Annette. Is that what you wanted to hear?"

Yes, of course it was, but why did he have to put it that way? For a fleeting moment, she thought she would turn and run.

But he spoke again before she could. "Would you like me to touch you there, Annette?"

Slowly, her eyes lowered self-consciously and she nodded. A slim finger reached out and lightly touched her nipple.

She sighed, feeling the peak harden and grow. He continued to touch her in the same way until she was sagging with weakness. "Kiss me," she whispered finally. "Kiss me."

He bent his dark head, his mouth found her delicate lips and his arms drew her into an embrace. For a few moments, Bernard did nothing more than move his mouth gently over hers. Then, without warning, his careful manner altered. He opened her mouth with his lips and thrust his tongue into her, while one hand seized her tender breast and pinched the nipple.

Annette stiffened. He was hurting her!

Bernard ceased the assault almost as soon as he had begun it. He drew his head back and chuckled softly. "Is that what you wanted, little virgin?"

"Oh!" She tried to spin away.

"No. Oh, no you don't. You can't just go around flaunting that body of yours in my face and then run." His hands imprisoned her arms. "Come on now, little virgin, aren't you still curious?"

"Let go of me! How dare you!"

Again Bernard laughed. "How dare I? I could hardly refuse. Who, may I ask, is throwing herself at whom? Would you like me to rape you?"

"No! I . . ." Tears sprang to her eyes, hot and burning. She felt so humiliated. "Please, let go of my arms."

"So you aren't curious any longer." The humor left his face. "And I'd say it's because I took control. Isn't that it?" He released her.

Annette's eyes were flashing with hatred as she rushed over and snatched the sheet. "You . . . You're unspeakable!" she cried, flinging it around her, trying to cover herself from neck to ankle.

But Bernard was not put off. "It was all fine when you thought I was like a piece of clay in your hands, wasn't it? But that's not the way things are, Annette. When I want a woman, I take her, not vice versa. Frankly," he concluded, "all you virgins are alike."

Her tears of pain and frustration rolled freely then. She was speechless. A knot formed in her chest, threatening to choke off her breath.

What was he saying? How could he be so cruel?

Furious, she ran behind the screen and somehow managed to get the skirt and blouse back on. She thought she might kill him with her bare hands if he said one more mortifying word to her. He was so wrong. Yes, she had wanted to experiment, but she hadn't meant to be the aggressor. Not at all. It was just that he had treated her so casually. That in itself had made her curious about her own femininity.

"Can we talk?" she heard him say.

"No. I hardly think we have anything to say to each other."

"Come now, Annette, I just saved you from a fate I don't think you're ready for just yet."

Silence.

"All right then, I admit I want you. But it wouldn't be fair. At least give me credit for being a gentleman."

Finally, her eyes still flashing, she came out from behind the screen, regally.

"What about the modeling? Are you going to just walk out on me and return to Nob Hill?"

"To Nob Hill!" she gasped.

"That's correct. Nob Hill. Did you think I'm unfamiliar with the name Tofler or with the fact that your father is one of the wealthiest men in the West?"

"I . . ." She bit her lower lip in thought, her anger lessening. "I meant to fool no one, Bernard. I am an artist and genuinely pursuing a goal. My father's money means nothing to me."

"Ah," he mumbled, studying her closely. He looked intently at her hazel eyes still moist with tears, her heaving breasts, the defiant, proud tilt of her lovely chin.

"It's true," she was saying. "And frankly, the reason I lied to you about several things is because you are not better than the other men in this world. You think a woman belongs in the home, nursing babies—"

"That's unfair. And untrue. I have met several fine women artists, working in all media. I have nothing against a woman seeking her own destiny."

Annette watched him warily. "Then why am I any different? Is it my wealth?"

"No. Not that. I think it's your age, your innocence."

"But I can't help my age. And I'm not without experience. I *have* studied in Paris. I've seen the masters' works. I'm trying to learn."

Bernard was silent, digesting this knowledge. Perhaps he had misjudged her, overlooked her determination. There was a depth to this beautiful girl, but as yet it was still undefined. Of course, ten years ago, he himself had been floundering about helplessly in his art. It did take time, a lifetime, and often even that was not enough. Maybe he ought to give this child the benefit of the doubt.

"What medium do you work in, Annette?" he asked finally.

"Oils. Well, that is, I want to work in oils. But my teacher, Monsieur Cormon, suggested that I spend time sketching in charcoals first, defining my lines and angles."

She was a different person when she spoke of her work, a genuine, unaffected one. He liked her better this way. "I see. A wise man. So you actually have not painted yet?"

"Oh," she corrected hastily, relaxing, "that's not exactly true. Ever since I was a child, I've been painting everything in sight. Animals, especially. I've also been studying human form for years. It was just that Monsieur Cormon thought I should back up, begin anew, rethink my work."

"Sit down, Annette." With a slim hand, he indicated the single overstuffed chair. His voice became gentle. "Now tell me, is your family at all behind this desire of yours?"

"No. Well, my father certainly isn't, but Jensen, my older brother, is somewhat receptive."

"So you must prove yourself?"

She laughed. "Prove myself? Why, yes, to the whole world."

Bernard observed her, amused. "We all feel that way, at least in the beginning. May you have the luck to achieve your ambitions. Fortunately, you don't have to worry about starving to death while you prove your talent." There was a tinge of bitterness in his voice.

"Oh, but you don't understand. My father is adamantly against the idea of women having careers. He'll try to stop me. We fight about it all the time. It's awful. I've threatened to leave home once already."

"Somehow, I can't see him letting his daughter starve. Some of us aren't so lucky."

"I don't feel lucky," Annette said, trying to be truthful.

"Well, you are, nevertheless. Don't you realize how many people in the world are literally starving to death? They live in abject squalor and disease while you people on Nob Hill lord it up." Bernard's black brows drew together and two spots of red stained his cheeks. His voice had become louder.

"I . . . I'm sorry," murmured Annette, a little frightened by him.

Bernard appeared not to notice that he was intimidating her. He ranted on, swept up by a vision that Annette could not understand or imagine. "Someday there will be a revolution and everything will change. The rich will be destroyed and their fortunes will be shared by everyone. Then and only then will there be real equality. Then we all will be free!" He stopped, a little out of breath, his brown eyes sparking fire. "I'm sorry. Sometimes I get carried away."

"It's a very interesting idea," Annette said carefully, not quite sure of what she'd just heard.

"Interesting!" laughed Bernard. "Karl Marx would be so delighted to be called interesting by such a beautiful young lady."

"Who?"

"Never mind. He died seven years ago, anyway. Just a man who had some new ideas."

"Oh . . . I see."

"So, tell me more about your father's cruel and tyrannical opposition to your painting. Perhaps we can think of a way to foil him. I'll try not to get carried away on the subject of revolutions again." Bernard smiled kindly at her, his eyes a little sad.

As the afternoon shadows lengthened in the bright room, filling the corners and absorbing the tension, Annette felt more at ease with Bernard. They talked about her aspirations and about him, too, about his struggles and successes. Even for a man, she discovered, the path was rocky. But that was all right. She could take the vinegar with the honey.

They never mentioned her flirtation; it might not have happened. Annette sensed that he thought her too naive for an affair. She thought he was wrong, but she wouldn't tell him. And she was grateful to him for not hurting her any more than he had to, for respecting her as a person and as an artist. There would be other men, other times for her to discover herself as a woman.

It was quite late when she got home. She had prepared what she hoped was a convincing story for her father, but was immensely relieved to find that he and Jensen were still at the office.

When they finally appeared around nine, she met them at the door, dressed in an elegant burgundy dressing gown. Her hair was still damp from a bath and her eyes were glowing.

"A long day, Daddy?" she asked, taking his hat from him dutifully.

"Yes," he muttered, "too damn long." Then he smiled at her. "And how was your day, dear?"

"Oh," she cast her glance away demurely, "quite dull, I'm afraid."

Chapter 4

This time Annette was not sure she would make it home before her father and Jensen did. Inadvertently, Bernard had kept her late again. Her clothes were at the Montgomery Block building, so she had to race back to the studio, fling off her peasant blouse and loose skirt and change quickly into her Nob Hill attire.

She didn't mind. Usually Bernard was most considerate of her tight afternoon schedule. In fact, he was fast becoming a true friend. In spite of his occasional crazy ramblings about Marxism, which confused her, he was interesting to be with. She had posed for him several times, and she no longer blushed or felt even vaguely uncomfortable under his perusal. She was beginning to believe she might turn out to be an excellent model.

She grabbed her small hat, perched it on her head and locked the studio.

As she was hurrying through the lobby, the skinny clerk stopped her. "Miss Annette?" he called out, waving a white envelope. "A letter for you."

"Oh. Thank you," she smiled, taking the envelope and continuing on her way to catch the cable car.

She found a seat, caught her breath and prayed that her father would be late arriving home. Then she remembered the letter. It must be another reply to her advertisement of several weeks earlier. No one else would send her a letter addressed to her first name only and in care of the Montgomery Block building. Her heart squeezed with delight. But, really, she shouldn't open it here, not in public. Besides, she would be home in a few minutes. Perhaps she would have a moment to read it alone in her room before dinner.

She stepped lightly down from the cable car and hurried up Mason Street. She wished she were carrying a package, something, in case her father was already home. Naturally, he would demand to know where she had been and why Vivian had not accompanied her.

The sun had already plunged into the Pacific beyond the Golden Gate and a soft, pearly dusk was settling over the constantly changing skyline. Muted sounds of the city's evening bustle ventured into the closed world of Nob Hill.

She passed through the gate. Long shadows stretched in thin columns across the broad drive. It was quite late. Surely her father was home. She opened and closed the front door as quietly as possible, then crossed the grand entrance hall toward the steps.

A voice emerged from the drawing room. "Annette?" It was Jensen.

"Yes," she replied, her heart lifting momentarily. But then, if Jensen was home, surely her father was, too.

She turned and saw her brother, who now was standing in the doorway. His handsome face was grim. "And where, might I ask, have you been?" he demanded.

Annette frowned in confusion. Was he angry? "Why, I've been out . . . at the studio. What on earth is bothering you?"

"Come in here, Annette," he said curtly. "I want

to talk to you." Shrugging her slim shoulders, she followed Jensen into the drawing room. He walked to the sideboard and poured himself a stiff brandy. "Dad's not home . . . lucky for you." He nodded toward a chair. "Sit down."

"Really, Jensen . . ."

"Sit down!"

She murmured something in irritation but did as he asked. "Well?"

"I think, little sister, that Father has about had it with you," he began.

"Oh, no!" interrupted Annette. "Not another lecture!" She rose.

"No lecture, Annette. Just watch your step. He's not going to be working every night. One day he's going to make it home before you and then all hell will break loose."

"So what?" She walked back toward the door, pouting with annoyance. "I really don't care what Daddy thinks. I'm having fun and I'm learning lots. Jensen," she turned back to face him, softening her tone, "I'm going to be an artist someday. A good one. I really am."

"That's all fine and dandy. But I suspect," he approached her, his glance measuring, "that there is more going on in your life right now than painting."

"And what is that supposed to imply?" she asked in a haughty voice, trying to conceal her shock.

He studied her for a moment. Raking a hand through his thick, light brown hair, he said, "I suspect that you're involved with someone."

She looked at him uncomprehendingly for an instant, then laughed. "Why Jensen, you're so protective!" she replied, avoiding his accusation, teasing lightly.

"Laugh if you like, Annette. But if you're not

careful, you may arrive home some night with a swollen belly."

Her smile faded. "You really are concerned, aren't you? But Jensen, let me assure you that there's no need to worry. And besides," she lifted her chin proudly, "it's my choice, isn't it?"

Jensen threw back his head in exasperation. "Oh, how naive you are! Good Lord, Annette, don't you know the first thing about men?"

"Of course I do," she defended quickly, meeting his eyes with determination. "I can take care of myself."

Again, he shook his head. "Poor, young little Annette. You've so very much to learn. I just hope, my innocent little sister, that you don't get hurt."

"Well I won't. And besides, as I've been trying to tell you, it's my concern." She placed a warm hand on his arm, a consoling hand. "Please. Try to understand me just a little, Jensen. I do know what I'm doing. Honestly."

He sighed. "I hope to God you do, Annette. I couldn't bear to see you hurt."

Lovingly, she embraced him. "Thank you, Jensen. I appreciate your concern. Don't worry, though. Please?"

"Well . . ."

"Now, Jensen." She laughed lightly. "Say, have you eaten dinner, yet?"

"No. I've got an appointment with some friends. I'm afraid I won't be home for dinner tonight. I only waited here this long because I wanted to see you."

"Well, you needn't have." She walked out of the room and started toward the steps. "I suppose you and your friends are off to Chinatown or somewhere exotic?"

Jensen smiled at her retreating form. "Why not? It's the latest fad, you know."

"And," she said over her shoulder, "women, I take it, are not invited?"

"Most assuredly not."

Annette decided to have a light supper in her room. Her father might not be home for hours. Recently, she remembered, he had even spent whole nights away, telling his children he had slept at the office.

That was fine with Annette. Lately, every time she saw her father, he scolded her for one thing or another. At least when he was gone, she wasn't forced to endure his tedious lectures. Still, she did love her father and the thought of him working such long hours worried her. At sixty, he was not a young man. She thought he'd been looking a touch pale lately. His normally ruddy cheeks were lined and gaunt. Perhaps, Annette reflected, as she peeled off her gloves, she should speak with him about taking it easier. After all, she was the woman of the house now. It was her duty to care for the menfolk.

As she seated herself at her dresser and glanced in the mirror, she noticed the lines of concern creasing her brow. What if Edward really were ill?

There was a tap at her bedroom door. "Yes? Come in."

Vivian entered, still attired in her brown and white uniform. "So here you be, miss. I thought for sure your daddy would be getting home before you." She shook her frizzy head ruefully. "And where have you been all day?"

Annette sighed. "I suppose the kitchen help are dying to know," she replied tiredly.

"Well, now, I wouldn't be knowin' that, miss. I don't sit in the pantry gossiping all day, you understand." Vivian picked up Annette's boots and hat and stowed them neatly in the wardrobe. "It's just that having been with you since you was a baby, miss, I worry. It's unkind of you to snap at me."

"I'm sorry, Viv. You're right. I'm sure you don't gossip with the downstairs help. It's just that no one is on my side, lately. No one understands me."

"I understand you, miss. You'll be wantin' your freedom. It's not easy being a woman in such an exciting city."

Annette brushed her long, auburn hair absentmindedly. "Oh, Viv. Didn't you ever want to come and go as you pleased? To visit . . . well, a man in his lodgings if you chose to? Anything you wanted?"

Vivian came over and took the brush from Annette. "Here, you'll be ruinin' your hair. Let me fix it." She studied the young girl for a moment. "If I was to tell you a secret, could you be keepin' it?"

"Of course," replied Annette, her hazel eyes lifting in curiosity to meet Vivian's in the mirror.

"Well now, I wouldn't be telling you this except I think it might help you. Once, when you was a baby, I met this man. He was a bartender down on the docks, real handsome and so strong. He tells me he loves me. And then he pays me court and all."

"Oh Viv," said Annette, seeing a great sadness in her maid's eyes. "I didn't know you ever had someone—"

"Had him?" She laughed harshly. "It was me that was had! Why, he got me into his bed, he did. A real smooth talker. Then," she paused, "he gets me with child."

"Oh!" Annette's slim, dark eyebrows arched in surprise.

"That's right. And when I tells him that I'm going

to have a baby, he says outright to me that it's my problem."

"He wouldn't marry you?"

"Now that's the joke. The bloke was married already, he was, and his wife and babes were back in Ireland."

"Oh Viv, how terrible! But . . . what about the baby?"

"I lost it soon after. And it was a blessing I did, 'cause your Daddy would've fired me sure if he knew. As it was, he just thought I was sick with a fever."

"I'm glad you told me, Viv. I often wondered why you never found a man. But, Viv," she turned to face her, "that's not going to happen to me. I am curious about men. And I would like to have an affair, to be perfectly honest. But I'll be careful."

"Oh, Miss Annette! Please, don't let a man touch you. Wait till you're married! It's too risky, I tell you. Why your daddy'd put you in a home for wayward women, he would. Sure as I'm standing here."

Annette giggled and raised her delicate chin defiantly. "You're probably right, Viv. Either that or he'd kill me, and I mean literally!"

Vivian grimaced. "You watch yourself, Miss Annette."

"That's funny," she interrupted thoughtfully, "Jensen just told me the same thing."

"You have that look about you lately, miss. I think your daddy senses it, too."

"Then I'll just have to look more virginal, won't I?"

"Humph."

"Go on to bed now, Viv. I'll put my nightgown on by myself. I don't mind. Really."

"You sure, now?"

"Yes. Just tell the cook to send up a light supper, if you would."

"Well, all right. But you remember what I told you."

"I will."

But as soon as Vivian had left, Annette remembered only one thing: she had that look about her. What did it mean? She studied herself in the mirror. How could you tell? Perhaps it was in her eyes. Or maybe it was her mouth, the soft, expectant way the lips were parted.

She tried several poses, watching her reflection in the mirror. She decided Vivian must be quite mad. She didn't look a bit different. And besides, Bernard was not interested in her that way—

The letter! She jumped up and fetched it from her purse. With all the lectures, she'd forgotten. She ripped open the envelope.

> Dear Annette,
>
> I am most interested in your experience. Please forward more information about yourself and your modeling ventures. A few lines of description would also be helpful, as I seek a particular form. If you fit my needs, I'll be in touch immediately to set up an interview.
>
> Sincerely,
> Rolf Karman
> In care of the Astor House

Rolf Karman. The artist whose works she'd criticized to the stranger at the opening. Well, she thought, she hadn't meant it. His work was good. She remembered it now as dynamic, intense. And to think, the very same man wanted to interview her!

Not so fast, she reminded herself. First he wanted to know what experience she'd had and he also wanted a description of her. So the job was not for certain. He must be interviewing several models. She decided she should make an all-out effort to get this particular job. Rolf Karman was a well-known, established artist who reportedly had more commissions than he could handle, so obviously he was good and people liked his work. How should she reply? Should she exaggerate her experience and write a glowing description of herself? Or would that be too presumptuous?

As she picked at her supper, Annette pondered the matter. Should her reply be modest but firm or extravagant and insistent? Finally, she reached a decision. She must grab his attention, no matter how absurd her reply. She must make him curious enough to want to meet her. If she could see him in person, surely she could persuade him to hire her.

Annette sat down at her writing desk and began her reply. In her very best and boldest script, she wrote a grossly exaggerated account of her previous modeling experience. She mentioned sitting for Monsieur Cormon, Emile Bernard and even Henri de Toulouse-Lautrec, who was well-known in San Francisco. She threw in the names of several sculptors in Paris whom Rolf Karman probably had never heard of, feeling certain the long list would impress him. Any experience was better than none. She also mentioned her recent work with Bernard Maduro, who had told her once that he and Rolf Karman had met on several occasions. Verification from Bernard would lend credibility to the other references.

She put down her pen. So far, so good. Then she reread what she had written, checking the spelling and punctuation. It was fine. Naturally, most of it was a lie, but so what? She wanted this job.

She picked up the pen again and tapped the quill against her chin. Now for the description. This was the difficult part. What would he be looking for in a model? His work was dynamic, so certainly he would want a woman whose appearance was compatible with his bold brush strokes. Nothing too soft. And not angular, either; that would be too harsh. She must find features in herself that would meet almost any requirement. It occurred to her that he might be looking for something specific, a blonde or a brunette, for instance. Oh well, she thought, some things must be left to chance. Taking a deep breath, she began.

> I am twenty-two, of medium height, and I weigh approximately one hundred and six pounds. My hair is a deep auburn color and my complexion is pearly white. My eyes, which have been described by artists as unusually tilted, are hazel. My shape is rounded, full-figured, but my legs are quite long. Lautrec described my body as perfect for a model and said there was mystery in my eyes.

Annette blushed. How could she write such awful lies? This was outrageous! But in spite of herself, she giggled.

> In description of myself, I must confess to having a nice, full bosom and a small, nineteen-inch waist. I feel certain that I would meet your requirements, Mr. Karman, and I hope you will allow me an interview. Quite frankly, I am in desperate need of em-

ployment, as my mother has taken ill. I do hope to hear from you soon.

Sincerely, Annette Tofler

In care of the Montgomery Block building

There, she sighed, done. Again, she reread the letter, first for grammar, then for content. It was more than outrageous, it was ludicrous. But no doubt it would get his attention. And even if he didn't hire her, surely this womanizer, as Jensen had described him, would be dying to meet such a brazen woman. He wouldn't be able to resist.

Instead of posting the letter, Annette decided to hand deliver it to the desk at the Astor House. That would both save time and show her good, if not desperate, intent. Anything to catch his eye.

The next afternoon, on her way to Bernard's, Annette did indeed march herself into the elegant lobby of the Astor House and ask the desk manager to put her letter into Rolf Karman's box. If he replied that very day, she would know the results in two or three days.

But it was a week before Annette received her reply. One day, as she and Vivian were on their way home after a shopping trip, Annette instructed the driver to stop in front of the Montgomery Block building. Leaving Vivian in the carriage, she went inside to check for mail. By this time she had all but given up hope.

But there it was. The handwriting on the face of the envelope was the same as before. Clutching the letter to her breast, she rejoined Vivian.

"So this is where you go," the maid observed dryly.

"Yes. I have a studio here, Viv. But you and Jensen are the only ones who know."

In answer, Annette received Vivian's usual "humph," but mercifully, no more.

Once back in the mansion, alone in her room, Annette tore open the envelope, her stomach fluttering with anticipation.

Dear Annette:

Your experience and description have piqued my interest. Be at the Astor House on Monday morning, November 20, at ten.

Sincerely, Rolf Karman

With an excited cry, she tossed the letter on her bed and twirled gaily around the room, hugging herself. It had worked! Rolf Karman, *the* Rolf Karman, wanted to meet her! It was too wonderful to be true!

On Sunday night, Annette couldn't sleep. She already had decided to wear her peasant blouse and skirt, so that wasn't the problem. What plagued her were the lies she had told. What if he laughed in her face? What if he knew her experience was a pack of lies?

These questions tormented her for the better part of the night. The only thing she could think of was to fall back on the truth. If Rolf Karman exposed her, she simply would tell him how badly she wanted to work with him. She would flatter him, anything to make him understand her plight and why she had lied so terribly. But then, of course, there was the other side to the coin. Maybe he would hire her on the spot, no questions asked.

It occurred to Annette, as she changed clothes in her studio on Monday morning, that she was far more nervous about this interview than she had been when she had gone to Bernard Maduro's for the first time. It must be Karman's reputation, she decided, the fact that he was famous in the city. And then there was his dubious background, too—the things Jensen had said about him.

She was unnerved, yes, but excited, too. What would this orphan, this gambler, look like? Was he old? Young? Would he be rakish, a real riverboat gambler with dark, narrow eyes and a black, curling mustache? If only she had spotted him at the opening that day, but it had been so crowded and she and Jensen had left early.

At nine forty-five, Annette arrived at the Astor House. She walked to the desk. "What is the number of Mr. Rolf Karman's room?" she inquired.

"Mr. Karman's *suite*," the desk clerk emphasized the word, "is on the third floor, miss, number three ten." And then the elderly gentleman gave her a speculative look, as if to say, Another young morsel for the artist to enjoy.

Annette ignored his open rudeness. She had far more on her mind than what this stuffy desk clerk thought of her visit. She climbed the wide staircase to the third floor and found the door to three ten. It was not yet ten. She waited.

The hall was carpeted in a dull green floral pattern and the walls were papered in a similar dull green with a gold diamond pattern. It was quiet in the hallway, oppressive. She disliked hotels. They were so impersonal, so without character. She continued to wait.

It must be ten by now, she thought, but then waited a few moments longer. Finally, she approached the door. She raised her hand to knock and saw it trembling. Was he waiting for her, or had he forgotten she was to come this morning? Perhaps he did remember and was laughing already. The breath caught in her throat.

She steeled herself and knocked three times, more confidently than she felt. There were footsteps. Someone was coming to the door. What would he look like?

She heard the click of a latch. The door swung open. The bright light from inside the room splashed in her eyes for an instant, blinding her. A man stood in the portal, filling it. He was quite tall.

Her eyes adjusted to the sudden brightness. She looked up into his face, placed a smile on her lips. And then she recognized him. It was the man from the gallery opening! The rude stranger!

Chapter 5

"Jensen, your father would like to see you," said Ned quietly. "In his office."

Jensen looked up from his paper-strewn desk with an irritated frown. "What does he want now, Ned? I'm just in the middle of checking this consignment."

"I don't know." Edward Tofler's long-time secretary shrugged amiably. "But he wants to see you now, before lunch." Ned's attitude, Jensen could see, was apologetic, but when his employer's wishes were not met, Ned could become very firm. He'd taken care of Edward Tofler's business for so many years that Jensen often thought Ned could run Tofler Transport all by himself.

Jensen gave in. "Oh, all right." He pushed back his chair and stood up, stretching. He reached for his frock coat, which was hanging on a hook behind him, and put it on. Unconsciously, he smoothed down his light brown hair and tugged his waistcoat straight. "Let's go. We mustn't keep Mr. Tofler waiting, mustn't we, Ned?" He grinned.

Ned flashed Jensen a disapproving look.

"Now, now, you know I'm only fooling, Ned. Don't take everything so seriously. This place could use a little livening up."

The two men walked down the dusty hall to Edward's office. Ned pushed the door open, held it and stood aside for Jensen to enter. With a respectful nod to his employer, Ned closed the door and returned to his compulsively neat desk.

"Sit down, son, sit down." With a thick, age-speckled finger, Edward indicated the deep leather chair facing his desk.

Jensen sat and waited. There was no sense in asking what this was about. Edward would get around to it in his own time. So far as he could tell from his father's expression, it didn't seem to be anything serious.

"Good job you did on the proposal for the army contract. It's coming along just fine." Edward took out a fat Havana cigar and tapped a pile of papers on his desk with it. "Very lucrative to work for the government."

"Thank you, Father." Jensen felt an unbidden spurt of pride and happiness at his father's compliment. How could this reprehensible old man's approval still have the power to move him? he wondered. But it did.

Edward leaned back in his chair and searched in his waistcoat pocket for his key chain. When he finally found it, he used the tiny knife that hung from it to cut off the end of his cigar. Jensen waited patiently as Edward lit the cigar with a long wooden match, shook out the match flame, clamped his fleshy lips around the cigar and leaned forward across the desk. "What in hell's going on with Annette?" he asked suddenly, the words emerging from a puff of pungent, grey smoke.

Jensen was caught off guard. He'd thought his father wanted to discuss business. For a second, his mind whirled uselessly. "Annette?" he asked stupidly.

"Yes, your sister, Annette. Damned little vixen's gone God knows where half the time, usually comes home late." He stabbed the air with his cigar to punctuate his words, leaving trails of smoke. "I tell you, I don't like it. The other day, she said she was reading. Reading! I ask you! I may not understand the so-called feminine mind too well, but that was too much even for me. She thinks I'm blind." He took a gargantuan puff on his cigar, squinting a light brown eye to avoid the smoke. "Now I know you're very close to Annette, and I suspect that you know where she goes and what she does." He leaned forward and stabbed the cigar into the air in front of Jensen's face. "And I want to know. She *is* my daughter, after all," he finished sardonically.

Jensen kept his voice very low and pleasant. "Why don't you ask her, Father? I'm sure there's nothing to it—"

"Ha! Ask her! I have. And believe me, her answers are just as insipid as the one you just gave me. I'm not stupid. I want to know what's going on."

"Why, nothing, Father, nothing at all." Jensen felt a fine sheen of sweat form on the back of his neck. If Edward found out about the studio, Annette was in serious trouble. He had to think of something, and quickly.

Edward Tofler leaned across the table again, his narrow, deep-set eyes boring into Jensen's. "The little twit is painting again, isn't she?"

Jesus! thought Jensen. The old man's still pretty sharp. "Actually, Father, I really wasn't supposed to tell you this. Annette asked me not to." Pretending to hesitate, he looked down at his knees. "She's in love," he said in a conspiratorial tone. "She's spending a lot of time with a certain beau."

"Who is the son of a bitch?" Edward's face reddened dangerously.

"She won't tell me. Someone suitable, she says."

"Damned well better be. I won't have my only remaining daughter going off with some chimney sweep." Edward took another furious puff of his cigar. "Is she seeing him alone?"

"I believe Vivian accompanies her," lied Jensen primly.

"God damned tarts. That's what they all are. So it's a man. Well, at least that's better than painting. If he touches her, so help me God!" The cigar stabbed again, as if it were the weapon of Edward's vengeance. A grim smile touched the lips that were fleshy on the father but sensual on the son. "Then again, if this beau of hers gets her knocked up, she'll have more to worry about than paintings. In the long run, it might solve a lot of problems. Knowing Annette, though, I'd lay odds the fellow's a spineless fool that she can wrap around her pretty little finger. Women!"

Jensen cringed inwardly at his father's crudeness. If Annette knew what he'd said, she'd be insane with rage. She'd better not find out.

"Father, please don't let on you know. She's frantic to keep it quiet. After all her talk about a career in painting, she's afraid you'll laugh at her. She may even pretend she still wants to paint to keep you from being suspicious."

Edward leaned back, closed his eyes, and smiled grimly. "Of course I won't. Stupid little twit."

"Father," said Jensen, unable to control himself any longer, "Annette may be spoiled and headstrong, but she is not stupid!"

"I know my daughter." A smug look crossed his lips. "She's just as flighty and empty-headed as all women are. Believe me."

Jensen felt his control slipping. How dare Edward speak of his own daughter in such a way? He shifted uncomfortably in his chair, the squeak of his leather shoes conspicuous in the stillness that had descended over the room. His father's eyes probed his own and Jensen knew he was being baited. Edward was angry at Annette but taking it out on Jensen, as always. Well, if the old man was spoiling for an argument, he'd get one.

"You know nothing about women. You made Mother miserable and I have a very good idea that you chased Cecile away, although I doubt if you'll ever admit to it. And if you're not damned careful, you'll do the same to Annette." Jensen kept his voice low, but every word was as clear and sharp as a splinter of ice.

"I did not drive Cecile away. I . . . I loved her. She was my daughter, just as Annette is. How dare you talk to me like that? You don't know anything about it." Edward's voice faltered and he stood up, struggling to regain the upper hand.

"I dare because it's the only type of language you understand," replied Jensen coldly. "Now, if you'll excuse me, I have work to do." Stiffly, he rose and left his father's office. He felt the hellfire of rage boiling up within him. Why did it always end this way? Why was there this wretched competition between them, as if they were deadly enemies on a hideous battlefield? Who had set up the rules that kept them forever at each other's throats? Was it his fault or Edward's?

Jensen stalked past Ned, whose salt-and-pepper head was bent judiciously over his desk. Then he noticed the man sitting on the bench against the wall of the outer office. It was Tansy O'Neill. His rage ebbed and a chill question took its place. What was Tansy O'Neill doing here?

He paused imperceptibly as he passed the man and almost stopped before he thought better of it. He was in no condition to talk to O'Neill right now. Let his father deal with Blind Chris Buckley, his hired thugs and the whole stinking, corrupt machine that ran San Francisco. Most likely O'Neill was there only because of some mix-up in delivery of those cases of whiskey to Buckley's headquarters at the Snug Café. As Jensen brushed past the waiting man, he heard Ned say politely behind him, "Mr. Tofler will see you now, sir."

Tansy O'Neill unfolded his tall, skeletal frame from the bench, gave Ned a chilling smile and followed him down the hall to Edward Tofler's office. He moved smoothly, with long, heronlike strides, and his eyes were everywhere at once, checking, prying, gauging. His face was gaunt, every bone showing under the skin, and his pale eyes were sunken and surrounded by bruised, purple flesh. He had a bony nose and his mouth was incongruously small and pursed and pink. He looked so like a death's-head that small children sometimes cried when they saw Tansy striding the hills of San Francisco.

"Morning, Mr. Tofler," he said, entering the office and sinking into the chair across from Edward without an invitation. His voice had a high, thin twang.

"O'Neill." Tofler nodded his head, acknowledging his visitor. Neither man made any move to shake hands. "What can I do for you today?"

"Chris sent me with a message. He said to tell you the girls didn't make it. You owe him, he figures, about five thousand dollars. He'll forget the wasted time."

Tofler's face grew ashen. "What?"

Tansy took a knife out of his pocket and flicked open the long, wicked blade. Calmly, he trimmed his fingernails. After a long moment, his small, pale eyes met Edward's dispassionately. "Chris don't like to be double-crossed, Mr. Tofler."

"The girls didn't make it? Why, the arrangements

were the same as they've always been. How could they not have made it?"

"I don't know, Tofler. That's your part of the deal. All I know is what Chris told me. He said the girls got picked up by the port authorities before they reached their destinations. Now they're all being held in jail until they can ship 'em back to China. The organization's lost a lot of dough. Them girls was expected." Tansy flicked a tiny bit of fingernail onto Tofler's desk.

Edward shifted his eyes, pretending not to notice the man's rudeness. "But I don't understand. It was all fixed, just like always. They were to be moved from the harbor to the city at night. What happened?" Edward's heavy jowls quivered.

"That's your problem, Tofler. Chris wants his money."

Edward was silent for a time, thinking. Finally he looked up. "I think I can guess what happened. It's the only possibility. That new man at the port authority, what's his name? Fredrickson? He must have done it. He's not in your boss's pocket yet, O'Neill. It isn't my fault. I did everything that was expected of me. All the arrangements were made and checked. I refuse to accept any blame. Obviously, you've got an honest man working down there at the port. It's that simple."

"You said you had everything fixed." Tansy's eyes were cold, relentless.

"I did. That Fredrickson was a surprise. There's nothing I can do about it. Tell that to your boss." Tofler's voice began to regain some of its normal strength and the color came back to his face. "Some things are beyond even the powers of Blind Chris Buckley." He smiled, leaning back in his chair and reaching for his cigar.

"Not a hell of a lot." Tansy grinned his death's-head grin. He flicked another piece of fingernail onto the enormous mahogany desk. Then he turned the blade of the knife until the light from the one dirty window hit it and flashed into Tofler's eyes. Deliberately, irritatingly, he kept the tiny light dancing on the blade.

"What do you want from me?" asked Edward. "I've done every rotten job you've asked me to do. I've cooperated. Tell Chris that." He had to squint to keep the annoying light out of his eyes.

Suddenly, Tansy leaned forward and rested his bony elbows on the desk. He poked his long, skinny finger almost in Edward Tofler's face. "Just remember, Chris has his eye on you. He thinks you sold him out with this Fredrickson."

"Of course I didn't. Do you think I'm crazy?"

"I don't know about that. But Chris ain't sure about you anymore. You messed up."

"I tell you, it wasn't my fault."

"That's for you to prove, Tofler."

"How on earth am I supposed to do that?" asked Edward with heavy irony. "Ask Fredrickson?"

"Like I said, that's your problem."

"One of these days," growled Edward, relighting his cigar and deliberately blowing a cloud of smoke in Tansy's face, "someone is going to break your boss's hold on this city, and I hope I'm around to see it."

"Doubt that," said Tansy flatly. "I don't think you rich, uppity, muckamucks know quite how smart old Chris is. He may be blind, but he's got more eyes than the Pinkerton Agency. He knows everything." His narrow lips curved chillingly. "For instance, last night you left Matilda Grueter's house at ten." He paused for effect. "And right at this very minute, your daughter, Miss Annette, is sitting in her studio in the Montgomery Block building."

"She's what?" rasped Edward.

"Yep."

"You're insane! She wouldn't dare!"

"You'd be surprised what people dare," said Tansy insolently.

Edward Tofler fumbled with the letter opener on his desk. He stubbed out his cigar. His gaze met Tansy's as he strove for control. "Look O'Neill, forget my daughter. I'll take care of that. But listen, about Tilly—Matilda—you aren't planning on letting anyone know, are you? My children, you understand . . ."

Tansy smiled grimly. "We never let out any information like that, Tofler. Unless we need to. You keep your nose clean and follow orders and no one'll ever know what you been up to." There was barely hidden glee in his voice.

"Tell Chris I'm sorry about the shipment of girls. It wasn't my fault. We'll have to make some other arrangements for next time."

"You'll be hearing from him." Tansy rose and stalked across the room on his stiltlike legs. He paused at the open door and gave a ghostly leer. "By the way, that daughter of yours—she ain't bad, ain't bad at all."

Edward's heart gave a sick lurch and the familiar palpitations began. He put a hand to his chest as if to stop the terrible, irregular beating. The thought of Tansy watching his beautiful, innocent daughter made him physically ill. He'd never before paid much attention to Blind Chris and the Democratic machine that had a strangle hold on the city. He'd just accepted it as part of doing business. Now he realized just how personal Buckley could get.

A low groan escaped from Edward Tofler's lips. As his fingers automatically reached for a new cigar, his eyes stared unseeingly at the door that Tansy

O'Neill had closed behind himself on his way out. What had he done? Edward wondered. Had his business dealings with Chris Buckley put his only remaining daughter in danger?

Chapter 6

"Miss Tofler, I presume?" drawled the man, holding out a hand to her. His eyes met hers unflinchingly, their dark depths filled with droll mockery.

"Mr. Karman? Rolf Karman?" she managed to stammer, shocked to the core, barely able to think.

"Yes, of course." He paused, still gazing at her.

The moment stretched out, endlessly long. Her mind spun. Her first meeting came flooding back, humiliating and sickening her. The gallery opening. The painting—*Devil's Cove*—the foal with the long legs. Oh, how could she have said such critical things to him? She should have known, or at least guessed, that he was the artist. It was mortifying. No wonder he had teased her. Oh God, Annette thought, why did I come? She wished the earth would open up and swallow her.

She heard his familiar drawl. "Would you care to step inside?"

Wordlessly, she walked into his suite of rooms, gathering her shredded dignity. He barely moved aside as she entered, causing her to brush so close to his loose, white ruffled shirt as to be embarrassing. He exuded an alien, male odor, far different from the scent of Jensen's hair pomade or her father's cigars. The combination of paint, turpentine, expensive brandy and pure healthy maleness assailed her nostrils. It reminded her of something from a foreign land, exotic and terribly attractive.

Annette didn't know what to say. The stranger—she must begin to think of him as Rolf Karman—was frankly studying her. She started to bristle, but then she remembered why she was there. Of course, he had to study her.

"Well, Miss Tofler, ma'am, I do think you may have exaggerated your measurements a bit, but certainly not your charms," he was saying.

Her cheeks flushed pink. He was unspeakably rude, just as she'd remembered. In a flash of intuition, it struck her that this man had known who she was all along, ever since the showing. She wondered if he had lured her into this trap, knowing she was ignorant of his identity. It was humiliating. She had to regain her wits, her poise, and show him she didn't care, show him she could play his little games.

"Do I get the job or not?" she blurted out, feeling the need to say something, anything. She met his arrogant gaze with what she hoped was calm assurance.

"Yes, why not? The other girls couldn't compare with you." Gracefully, he stepped closer to her and ran a casual, knowing hand through her loose auburn hair. "And your coloring, ma'am, is so perfect."

"Good. Shall we begin now?"

"Why not?" he grinned, showing his strong, white teeth.

Why did she feel so unnerved around him, so immature? He had a way about him, a way of mocking her and perhaps himself, too, that grated on her nerves and made her strangely unsure of herself. She didn't know how to act. He was a man unlike any in her experience, neither smooth nor flirting, neither openly crude like her father nor gallant. He defied classification. It was unsettling.

He led her down a carpeted hallway, past a kitchen, a dining room, and a pleasantly untidy bedroom, and showed her into a large sunny room on the west side of the building. Obviously the living room of the suite had been made over into a studio. Stacks of canvases lay against the walls on the beautiful old wainscoting, and paint was splattered on the old table and chairs that had obviously replaced the original elegant furniture. Only a space in front of the costly marble fireplace was cleared. The wide mantel, however, was littered with tins of linseed oil, jars of brushes in turpentine and tubes of paint.

"There is where I paint, as I'm sure you can tell. But before we get started, perhaps you'd like some tea?"

"Yes, thank you," she said quickly, glad to postpone disrobing and letting this bold stranger view her body. His manner was not at all like Bernard Maduro's analytical, professional one. He was much more intense, much more personal.

He disappeared down the hallway, into the kitchen, Annette presumed. With a sigh, she let herself relax into one of the chairs at the table. Rolf Karman. Of all men for her to have insulted at the Golden Gate Gallery. If only she'd known! She cringed, remembering how she'd called his painting amateurish and rushed. And right to his face, too. It had been cruel of him not to introduce himself to her. Perhaps he thought everyone knew him. Then it occurred to her that he was the one who had started the whole, ill-starred conversation. Yes, he'd begun it all by asking her in his superior, insolent manner whether she thought the painting was good. Then he'd dragged out the conversation until he'd managed to insult her back. Here she was, scarcely able to face him and all because of her awful temper and his even worse one. He'd probably planned this whole fiasco and was gloating over it right now as he fixed the tea.

Well, there was only one thing to do about it. She'd hold her head up and model for him and never, never say another word about his work. She'd learned her lesson.

Idly, curiously, she began to look around at the paintings she could see. Some were lying on the floor or leaning against the wall or a chair leg, others were half covered by another unfinished canvas.

She had to admit they were good. The power that she'd noticed in the seascape was evident in all his work, even in the high society portraits. She could see why he was popular. There was a fresh, American strength to his work. The Impressionists had influenced him with their bold strokes and colors and configurations, but he'd taken their techniques and adapted them to his own style. She was envious of his talent.

He entered the room again, filling it with his commanding presence. As he poured them each a cup of tea, she was surprised to see how graceful he was for a big man. Pushing some brushes and paint-stained rags off a chair, he casually sat down across from her.

Annette sipped the scalding liquid, lowering her eyes to hide her confusion. She felt him studying her, measuring her, perhaps even taunting her. She steeled herself to meet his gaze, to say something, but he forestalled her intention.

Stretching his long, muscular legs out in front of him, he began, "So Miss Tofler, you are experienced, correct? You have sat for Toulouse-Lautrec and Emile Bernard in Paris?"

She felt that he was challenging her, piercing her flimsy facade of sophistication. He knew she had lied in her letter. Of course he knew. He was playing with her. She lifted her chin and met his insinuating eyes. "Yes, and also for Bernard Maduro here. Of course, I have just returned from Paris, so there hasn't been time for me to line up too many jobs yet."

"Ah yes, lovely city, Paris." His voice was non-committal. The slightly Southern drawl was noticeable only if you listened for it. "I work a lot in the early mornings," he continued. "Can you sit for me between, say, seven and nine?" His eyes regarded her lazily from under straight, sandy brows.

Annette's heart squeezed with apprehension. This was something she had not foreseen. She would never be able to get out of the house at that hour. "Well, I . . . I . . . couldn't come then." She felt her heart sink at his look of satisfaction. "It's another job, you see."

"So early?"

"Yes."

"Every morning?"

"Well, yes."

"I see." His mouth curved slightly upward, faint humor gathering at the corners. "I guess I'll have to work later in the day then. An experienced model such as yourself is too valuable to pass up."

Annette's lips pressed together tightly. She wanted to shout something rude at him, but instead, she smiled brightly and ignored his sarcasm.

"By the way, did you like the gallery showing last week?" he asked casually. "That is, of course, except for the amateurish seascape and the foal with the ridiculously long legs."

Her eyes flew to his.

So he remembered it all, every detail. She was mortified. She was trapped. There was only one way out. She would have to apologize. After all, she had been at fault. "I'm awfully sorry about that." The words were hard to get out. Humble pie was not Annette's favorite dish. "I had no idea who you were."

"Which doesn't change the fact that you disliked those works," he observed dryly.

"Oh, no. Really. I loved them, especially the seascape. It's just that"—her gold-flecked eyes met his with sudden, disarming candor, catching him off guard—"I guess I was jealous and it made me spiteful. I do so want to be able to paint like that, or at least that well, although I think I'd prefer to do animals."

For the first time, his expression softened. She really was quite charming when she was being herself and not trying to act the role of the society girl. Perhaps she really did have the soul of an artist, although Rolf rather doubted that she'd get far in her chosen career. She'd be married and pregnant before she turned around, what with those huge hazel eyes, the riot of auburn curls and the creamy skin that showed above the low neck of her glaringly new Bohemian peasant blouse.

"Perhaps you'd do a little something for me sometime. I'd like to see your work," he said, smiling at her. He really was curious.

"Oh, would you? I'd be so grateful."

"Certainly. Now, we'd better get started." He noticed that her open smile faded a bit. "You can change over there while I set up my easel," he said pointing to a corner of the big room.

Slowly, Annette stood up and looked at the curtained alcove. He had turned away and was busying himself with his materials. No doubt this was routine for him. Annette felt oddly reluctant to take off her clothes and allow this stranger to rake her body with his cynical scrutiny. Strange, she hadn't felt that way in front of Bernard Maduro. That had seemed like an innocent, exciting adventure, a pleasure cruise. This, however, was a voyage into dangerous, uncharted waters, a voyage with no promise of a return to home port.

Forcing back her reluctance, Annette strode purposefully to the alcove. She pulled the curtain shut and stood in the semidarkness with her eyes closed and her hands clenched into fists. To calm herself, she took several deep breaths. She took off her shawl, then untied the drawstring neck of her blouse and pulled it over her head. Next, she removed her dirndl skirt and her shoes and stockings. All that remained was a simple camisole top, one petticoat and her drawers. How much simpler this was than her usual complex outfits, with their corsets and various other elaborate underpinnings. Smirking to herself at her own cleverness, she stepped out of her petticoat and tried to untie the waist of her bloomers. But the strings were knotted and her fingers were clumsy. Vivian usually did this. She began to tug frantically.

"Is something wrong, ma'am?" she heard Rolf call.

"No, I'll be along directly," she replied breathlessly, fumbling with the stubborn ties.

"Maybe you need some help?" she heard him ask, and then the curtain was pulled aside and light bathed her in sudden brightness. She saw him silhouetted against the glare—tall, intimidating, powerfully graceful.

Inadvertently, she gasped and her hands flew to her breast. Then she felt more foolish than ever.

He smiled indulgently. "I've had a lot of experience helping ladies off with their things. Infernally complicated items, aren't they?"

"Yes," she whispered. "My ties are knotted."

"Nothing to it." She could feel his gentle breath on her shoulder, stirring the hairs on her neck, and his large, strong fingers were hot on the bare skin of her midriff. They seemed to sear her flesh, but when he took his hands away, his task completed, she felt strangely bereft. "There," he said matter-of-factly.

"Thank you." Her voice was barely audible.

Letting the curtain fall, he left her. She wanted to laugh hysterically at the fact that she'd thanked a man for helping to undress her. Quickly, she shed the rest of her underthings, wrapped the sheet around her naked body and stepped out into the studio. The floor felt cool to her bare feet and she shivered slightly as she walked across the large room toward the tall window where Rolf had set up his easel. He was busy arranging his materials and ignored her approach except to wave a hand toward a bare wooden bench that was placed under the window.

"Over there," he said offhandedly as he busied himself behind the easel.

She sat docilely on the bench, clutching the sheet to her breasts. She could feel the sun on her bare back. She wasn't sure whether she was glad that he was ignoring her or strangely disappointed.

Finally, he looked up at her as if he'd suddenly become aware of her presence. He stood still, studying her endlessly, a slight frown creasing his brow. "Ah, yes," he murmured eventually, "the light's good."

He stepped closer and her heart began a drum beat in her chest. "Like this," he said, arranging her arms and torso as he wanted them. She sat turned to one side, her head cocked slightly as if she were listening to something and her hands in her lap. The pressure of his fingers on her cool, bare flesh sent shivers down her spine. Every time he touched her, she felt as if she might jump or scream with tension. It took the utmost control not to grab that casual, strong hand that was as tanned as a woodsman's and fling it away.

At last he had her posed to his satisfaction. Standing back, he scrutinized her again. Oddly, he'd left the sheet in place. Perhaps he wasn't interested in nudes, Annette began to think, unaccountably relieved. When he moved up close to her again and extended his arm, she knew . . .

She closed her eyes, steeling herself. Suddenly, the cool air of the studio caressed her skin, raising goose flesh all over her. She could feel the pink tips of her breasts harden. She wanted to keep her eyes closed forever, pretend she wasn't there, pretend he wasn't there. But that would not do at all for an experienced model. She forced her eyes open.

Rolf stood utterly still in a kind of mute reverie. His eyes were half closed and his mouth was a thin, forbidding line. A muscle in the flat plane of his cheek twitched. There was an air of absolute concentration about him that was almost frightening. Incongruously, it reminded Annette of people she'd seen in church sometimes. It was the way they looked at the bleeding, suffering, glorious figure of Christ. It was the way they worshipped Him.

Then Rolf moved as if in a trance and picked up a piece of charcoal. Quickly, deftly, he began to sketch, his eyes almost never leaving her body. Once he paused for a moment. "Are you comfortable?" he inquired, but he hardly heard her murmured reply.

"Yes," she said, but the truth was that she was so tense that her muscles were quivering and aching with strain. She was afraid to move, afraid to ask for a rest. He was completely absorbed in his work.

Annette decided to study this man, to try to take her mind off her discomfort. Oblivious as he was to all but the artistic passion that consumed him, she could watch him easily. She studied each feature separately, analyzing it.

His mouth was wide and sensual and a well-groomed blond mustache outlined the curve of his upper lip. He had a strong, square jaw and chin. His nose was piratelike and almost cruel in its determined hook. She noted the flat muscle of the cheek, the high cheekbones, the deep-set, dark brown eyes that drank in her nudity as if it were water to a thirsty man, the curling, sandy hair that had been streaked by the sun. Yes, she thought, with his tanned skin, the crinkly lines around his eyes, and his broad, powerful shoulders, he looked like a man who spent a lot of time outdoors. He could have been a mountain man, she mused, feeling his air of danger and grace and constant readiness to pounce.

Annette remembered what Jensen had told her. Rolf Karman, he'd said, had been an orphan and had made his fortune as a gambler on a Mississippi riverboat. Ah yes, she could see him at a card table, studying his hand as he now was studying her, willing the cards to be good. She could imagine him raking in the money, flaunting his infernally mocking smile at the other players. She could even imagine him challenging someone for cheating, then fighting and winning again. Fantasies crowded her brain. What kind of man was he, really?

A very attractive one, to begin with, and dangerous and powerful. And, she suddenly remembered, a renowned artist. The varied roles didn't mesh. She couldn't resolve them in her mind, couldn't comprehend this man. He was beyond her experience.

He was also quite fascinating, she realized as she considered the strange hold he had on her thoughts. Idly, she began to wonder if he had a lady friend. She recalled her brother saying that Rolf Karman had a reputation for being a womanizer. She could believe it. He certainly had a way about him. Although she tried to picture the kind of woman he'd be attracted to, she couldn't. Did he see beyond her as a model and find her attractive? Or was she too young and inexperienced for him? If nothing else, he seemed experienced. She wondered if he liked older women, women closer to his own age. Perhaps, to him, she was just a silly child.

Annette again became aware of her cramped, protesting muscles. Surreptitiously, she tried to ease into a more comfortable position.

A moment later, she noticed a distracted frown on Rolf's face. He put down the charcoal and strode toward her. Anticipation clutched her heart. She was fearful and eager at the same time.

"No, like this." He arranged her arms. "You moved."

"I'm sorry," she murmured, raising her eyes. His eyes were dark, distant.

"Are you tired?"

"A bit," she admitted.

"Well, I'm almost done with the sketch. A few more minutes, all right?"

"Yes, certainly." She set her mind for a few more minutes of discomfort.

He leaned over her and turned her head a bit, his hand gentle. When he stepped back, the loose sleeve of his shirt brushed against her breast. Instantly, and quite unexpectedly, a surge of pure, naked pleasure shot through her, burning a trail of raw sensation that became a vortex of desire whirling in her abdomen.

But Rolf went back to his easel and turned his attention to the canvas, leaving her stunned and quivering.

Annette tried to analyze the sensation, but it was foreign to her experience. Was this, then, what they wrote about in the romantic novels? Was this passion or desire or love?

She forgot her discomfort and stared unblinkingly at Rolf as he worked, wondering why he, of all people, had awakened this feeling in her. Why not another man? Was he to be the instrument of her fulfillment, her guide to experience?

Her breath quickened. Her lips parted slightly in wonder. Well, he certainly was a man, but not at all what she would have chosen. He was too blunt, too ungallant, too strong. She felt he could best her and that was not at all what Annette wanted. If anyone had dared to ask her, she would have replied that she wanted to have an affair, yes, but one in which she was the pursuer, the seductress, the controller of destiny. Instinctively, she sensed that Rolf Karman would let no one, female or otherwise, control his destiny.

"There," he said finally, dropping the charcoal. "Done."

Grateful, Annette relaxed. She wondered whether she should cover her nakedness with the sheet or sit there nonchalantly. What did other models do? Would he think her disgraceful if she remained uncovered, or ridiculously modest if she wrapped the sheet around her? She sat there in a quandary, shivering a little. It was all so awkward, so uncomfortable. Rolf, however, seemed not to notice her. He was studying his sketch.

"Well," he said finally, glancing up over the easel at her, "you can get up and walk around, Miss Tofler. Then I'd like some more of your time, if you don't mind. Just for a little color."

Annette's decision was made. She certainly wasn't going to strut around in front of him nude. Somehow this whole thing was not following the path of her fantasies. She wrapped the sheet around her toga-fashion and stood up. Turning, she stepped closer to the tall, uncurtained window and began to study the view of the city. Past the new skyscrapers and the city bustle, she could see the treetops in Golden Gate Park to the west and beyond that, the hazy blue expanse of the Pacific. Suddenly she felt Rolf's presence at her shoulder.

"You must be tired, Miss Tofler, ma'am. Sometimes I forget my poor human model in my passion to get an image on canvas. I must apologize," he said in his soft voice.

She turned, finding him uncomfortably close to her. She backed up a little, hoping he didn't think her afraid of him. Breathlessly, she replied, "Oh, I understand. Really I do. I've felt the same way myself."

"Then you will forgive me," he said, imprisoning her gaze.

"Of course," she murmured, mesmerized by his dark, unfathomable eyes. She felt weak all over, giddy, and was tingling with a kind of eager fragility at his closeness. He made no attempt to move away from her. She was agonizingly aware that only a thin sheet covered her nakedness and that all he had to do was reach out a finger and pull it aside . . .

"It must be hard to sit still for so long. You did well, Miss Tofler."

"Please call me Annette," she said. It was ludicrous for this man who had seen her naked body to call her Miss Tofler.

"Annette." He turned the word in his mouth, rolling the sound around, drawing out the second syllable a little as a Southerner would. "Thank you," he said soberly.

She wondered whether he was being serious or making fun of her.

"Here, let me massage your shoulders. I do this often for my models. It releases the tension and helps them to relax after a long sitting." The gentleness in his voice surprised her.

"Well, really, I don't think . . ." she began, flustered. What were his motives?

"I assure you, I only wish to make you more comfortable, Annette. You seem a bit nervous." He took her hand and led her back to the bench in front of the window. "Sit down." Gently he drew her down onto the seat. "There, like that." He stood behind her and began to knead the muscles of her shoulders and neck expertly. His warm, strong hands sent exquisite ripples of pleasure through her body. There was some kind of magic in his touch. "Ah, I can feel your muscles relaxing," he said softly. "You see?"

As the kneading went on, Annette closed her eyes, swept away by the delicious feeling of his hands. When he stopped, her eyes flew open. Her body felt lost and lonely without the wonderful sensations that his touch could produce. She quivered for more and a sigh escaped her lips.

"Feels good, doesn't it?" He was still standing behind her so that she couldn't see him at all.

"Mmm."

Rolf put a hand on each of her arms and brought her to her feet, as if she weighed no more than a feather. Slowly, carefully, he turned her around to face him. Her amber eyes, fringed with long, black lashes, were wide and expectant. She stood silent, unmoving, waiting. His dark eyes devoured her face, her white skin, the swell of her breasts above the sheet, her lovely shoulders.

Finally, unable to bear his scrutiny for another instant, yet unable to break away, Annette closed her eyes. Time stood still. She could feel his hands on her arms, his breath fanning her face. His gaze, she knew, still possessed her.

"And does this feel good, too?" he asked in a low, resonant voice as he lowered his face to hers and brushed her lips with his. "And this?" He pressed his mouth to the spot where her neck met her shoulder, the sensitive hollow where her pulse jumped in sweet anticipation.

Annette moaned very softly. Her knees were like rubber, and as if she were a frightened bird, her heart began to flutter. She felt his arms encircle her and press her against his tall, strong body. Waves of ecstasy flooded her.

Was it to be now? Was this what she had planned for, dreamed about? Would it really happen to her now? Was she ready?

But Rolf did not ask if she was ready. He merely swung her up into his arms easily and strode across the studio and into the hallway, his eyes magnetizing hers. It was too late to wonder whether she really wanted this. There was no turning back.

Pushing open his bedroom door with his foot, Rolf carried her to his rumpled bed and placed her gently on it. He knelt beside her and kissed her full on the lips. When he pulled back, he was smiling a little. "Ah, now you are really relaxed, Annette. I like you much better this way." Hooking a finger under the sheet, he slid it off her, slowly and deliberately.

She lay there, mute, excited, her body all languorous and warm and waiting.

Expertly, he kissed her neck, her shoulders, her ears, sending shivers of sensation through her body. He lowered his head to her breasts and brushed the rosy tips with his rough, curly hair. Immediately, they stiffened and tingled. Teasingly, he touched them with his tongue, withdrew, touched them again until she moaned and pulled him to her.

"Wait, my anxious little beauty, we have time," he whispered. He stood and took off his white shirt. He started to unbutton his trousers, but paused and looked at her intently. "Are you sure you want this, Annette?"

She could not meet his gaze. "Yes," she whispered. She was too caught up in his spell to ponder seriously her own reservations. This is what she'd wanted, wasn't it, to be swept along with the tide?

He finished undressing and came to her. She caught a glimpse of his body before shame at her own curiosity made her look away. Oh, but he was beautiful. His body was tall and lean, the flat stomach widening into a strong chest, and his muscles were clearly defined and solidly square. His long, sinewy arms were covered with golden hairs. She dared not look further down. That would come later.

He lay next to her. With a gentle hand, he stroked her skin from her shoulder to the tips of her breasts and down her stomach and thighs. She quivered like a taut string. Then he bent his head and kissed her, his tongue darting into her mouth, seeking, caressing. Her breath began to come in gasps and her body groped for something she could not define, for some kind of release. Only he could satisfy her longing; that much she knew instinctively.

Gently, carefully, Rolf's hand traced circles on her belly, lower and lower, until he brushed the soft triangle between her legs. Inadvertently, she jumped. Then his hand searched and found the secret spot that she'd never even known was there, awakening in her an exquisite agony. Her hips began to move under his expert fondling. It was as if she'd known the rhythm all her life, or as if her hips moved of their own accord, without thought, without direction.

"Now," he whispered, "now you are ready, my Annette." And then she felt his weight on her and something hard and hot thrusting between her legs, into her. It was something that belonged there, something that she had always needed. It fulfilled her, made her whole.

She sighed. "Yes, yes," she whispered. Mindlessly, her hips moved in the ancient dance. There was a burning pressure, a moment of pain, and he filled her.

She had thought that was all there was to it. But soon her body began to beg again, to reach for something, she knew not what. She was in its grip, nonetheless, writhing, gasping. His body was above her, in her, helping, pushing her further and further.

"Ahhh," she heard herself cry, the sound so earthy, so unadorned and without any social graces, that she felt ashamed for a moment. But then her body began to spasm, taking her far, far beyond thought. Now she knew exactly what she'd been searching for all along. Before the explosions of sensation could die down, she felt his rhythm increase and he filled her harder and deeper than she'd thought possible. Then his rhythm broke and he gasped in her ear.

She lay exhausted and wondering, his long body melded to hers and both bathed in perspiration.

After a time, Rolf rolled over onto his side, rested his head on his hand and gazed at her. "You should have told me," he said, his voice somber.

"Told you what?" She was puzzled.

"That it was your first time."

"Oh." Annette tried to be nonchalant about it. Airily, she waved a hand. "Well, there has to be a first time, doesn't there?"

"You shouldn't give away what is precious to you."

"Precious? Goodness, no! A mere annoyance. In this day and age—" she began.

"In any day and age," Rolf interrupted, "a woman's virginity is one of her most valuable possessions."

"Not anymore."

"Do you regret all this?"

"No. Do you?"

His answer was a while in coming. "No, not if it's what you wanted."

"It was," she replied smugly.

"Than I am merely the instrument of your fulfillment?" he asked, a taunting grin on his face.

The question stunned her and she couldn't think how to answer. When put like that, the experience seemed utterly without grace, even cold and calculating. "Certainly not," she answered.

"Then you must be madly, truly in love with me." His grin widened.

"Lord, no!" she cried. "Of course not!"

"I think, Miss Annette Tofler," he said, leaning over her and tickling her breast with his mustache, "that you're kidding the hell out of yourself."

"What do you mean?" she asked, suddenly irritated by his smugness, his insolent, matter-of-fact attitude.

"I mean, my dear, that you have no idea what you've done. Your little adventure is merely the fantasy of a spoiled little rich girl. It means nothing, really, either to you or to me. You have a great deal to learn about life and love and even, to tell the truth, about modeling."

Annette sat up quickly and covered herself with the quilt. Her hair was in wild disarray, her eyes all iris, stormy and hard, and her cheeks were crimson with fury. "How dare you speak to me this way! After what I just let you do, you are no gentleman, sir! I should have known better. I thought you were an artist. I thought you were different." She rose from the bed, desperate to leave.

"Different from whom, my dear?" he asked, placing a restraining hand on her arm. "I am, after all, merely a man." His white teeth gleamed in the gloom of the bedroom, and his eyes were dark pools of shadow. "I'm not about to reject a woman who flaunts herself openly, who obviously wants me. That would be too cruel."

"Oh, you're disgusting!" she gasped.

Throwing his head back on the pillow, he laughed, while Annette stood in the middle of the room, fuming and quivering with hurt rage. How had she lost control of the situation? She thought everything had gone according to plan: seduction, passion, fulfillment. But now he was throwing it all in her face, insulting her. It made the whole act of her initiation into passion a farce, a tawdry, childish whim. She felt betrayed by Rolf and by herself. What should have been beautiful and gracious had become ugly. What had gone wrong?

He chuckled from the bed. "Does your daddy know how you spend your days, Miss Tofler, ma'am?" he drawled in an insinuating tone.

Annette snatched her clothes, whirled and ran from the dim bedroom. Tears of rage and frustration filled her eyes. Rolf Karman would pay for this!

Chapter 7

Annette questioned herself ruefully. Was she really lazing in a tub of steaming, fragrant water in the middle of the afternoon, home hours before her father? It seemed too easy. Especially on this occasion.

She had thought that everything in her life would change on the auspicious day when she lost her virginity, or at least that something would. Fireworks exploding overhead would be too much, of course, but this sense of languid lethargy came as a surprise. Even as she had ridden the cable car home, still furious and hurt to the quick by Rolf's cruel taunts, she still had found it hard to believe that she was no longer a virgin.

She hadn't planned it that way. She had been sure that the man she chose would fall at her feet, vowing undying love. She had imagined many things, anything other than Rolf's cold, unfeeling manner. As the cable car had climbed California Street, she kept expecting heads to turn, kept expecting to see men whispering behind their hands. "See that woman over there? She just lost her virginity. You can tell, you know. Look at the swollen lips and those glassy eyes. Even her hair is still mussed. It's so obvious." But nothing like that had happened. Even Vivian had noticed nothing unusual while preparing Annette's bath and helping her undress.

As the water cooled, Annette mentally explored her body for some sign of change and could feel only the dullest ache between her legs. Her stomach was a little queasy, she realized, but that she attributed to nerves and to the fact that Mr. Rolf Karman had turned out to be such a beast. How she detested him!

She should have known he wouldn't be putty in her hands, for men of his type were incapable of softness. Oh, how he must be laughing, how proud of himself he must be. It was mortifying. Worse still, she had only herself to blame. Her first affair had turned out to be nothing like her fantasies. But then, she mused, things in life seldom did.

Stepping out of the tub, Annette wrapped a soft linen towel around her body and unpinned her hair. She looked down at the swell of her breasts. It was hard to believe that only a short while ago Rolf's hands had explored her flesh, his mouth following the path of his touch. It seemed unreal. She wondered if she regretted it.

Of course, she would have selected a different lover had she known his true character, but there was nothing to be done about it now. In the future, she would choose more wisely. At least, she told herself, she was learning. She was gaining experience.

Quite honestly, she felt no guilt or shame. For all his rudeness and arrogance, Rolf had been a marvelous lover, if nothing else. Naturally, she had no one to compare him with, but she had enjoyed his caresses. That much she grudgingly admitted.

She seated herself at her dressing table and brushed her long hair until it shone richly. At some point, while she was lost in contemplation, she was vaguely aware of a carriage pulling up in front of the house. Most likely Jensen and her father were returning home from the office. She knew she should dress, greet them in the drawing room and sit with them while they had a before-dinner brandy. But it was so difficult to move, to think about dressing, to do anything at present. Vengeance kept plaguing her mind. She should find some way of paying Rolf Karman back for his insults. But that would be stooping to his level of behavior. It would be more mature to ignore him if and when they ever met again.

She rose finally, tugged on her underclothing and selected a rich green velvet dress to wear downstairs. She left her hair cascading down her back in loose ringlets. She was too relaxed after the bath to pin it up herself and Vivian was off now for the rest of the evening.

Would Jensen or, God forbid, her father notice a change in her? Perhaps she should tell Jensen what had happened, how badly Rolf had treated her. It really hadn't been her fault. Rolf had seduced her. She hadn't planned it that way. Maybe Jensen would avenge her. On the other hand, maybe Rolf would do something awful to Jensen. He did seem dangerous.

No, she mustn't let Jensen find out, even if he was as much her friend as her brother. This was her problem. She was just suffering from wounded pride right now and time surely would heal that. Soon Rolf Karman would be only a dull ache, a bad memory.

Annette greeted her father and Jensen in the drawing room. She might have been imagining it but Edward seemed oddly cool toward her. He hardly spoke. Jensen was uncharacteristically quiet, too. Could they know? Her heart clutched in sudden fear. Of course not.

"Shall we eat?" she finally offered, breaking the

long silence. What was the matter with the two of them?

Edward seated himself at the head of the long table. Annette and Jensen sat in the middle, across from one another. Years ago, her mother had decorated the large dining room, giving it an Oriental touch. The polished wood floors were covered by a huge Persian rug, which was patterned predominantly in tones of blue and green. The breakfront was also Oriental in design, with dragon legs and a Great Wall inlay framing it. The plates and goblets were Chinese porcelain, gleaming and priceless. Two tall Chinese urns sat near the door, filled with slender rushes and ostrich feathers. Near the large window overlooking the gardens stood a lush silk screen, partially open.

With its leaves inserted, the dining table could seat up to thirty, but dinner parties were rare at the Toflers'. When her mother was still alive, there had been gayer times and the house often had brimmed over with guests. Annette had been quite young then, but Vivian sometimes had let her watch from the balcony before bedtime. She still had pleasant memories of the noise and laughter.

Dinner was brought in by Henry, who had been serving dinner at the Tofler mansion for twenty years. All the servants had been with Edward for years. Their quarters on the third floor were comfortable and they were paid quite well. As Edward often said, "Better to pay a high wage than to have them steal you blind."

The fare tonight consisted of lamb with boiled potatoes, mint sauce and peas. And, as usual, following the French custom, Edward insisted on a cheese platter after the main course.

Although normally her appetite was healthy, Annette could only pick at her food. When her glance met her father's, she was confused by his measuring coolness. And Jensen? Strangely, he avoided her eyes altogether. Could they tell? If not, why were they treating her as if she were a leper?

Finally, unable to bear another moment of the awkward silence, Annette asked, "Did everything go well at the office today?"

Silence.

At last Jensen spoke. "Routine." As he dabbed at his mouth with a napkin, his eyes slid away from hers.

She looked from one to the other. What was wrong? "Daddy," she began again, "is there something the matter?"

Edward groaned and put down his fork. His hooded eyes met hers. "I was going to wait until after dinner to speak with you in private—"

"Father," interrupted Jensen, "don't you think it would be best to wait—"

"Stay out of this, Jensen!" he roared, suddenly furious.

Annette's heart skipped a beat. He did know! her mind screamed. Someone must have seen her going into Rolf's apartment. And Jensen knew, too. He was trying to defend her.

Edward's eyes shifted back to her, red-rimmed with anger. "I want you to tell me where you go during the day, Annette, and I demand an honest answer."

She swallowed hard. "I . . . I paint . . ."

"Dad," Jensen rose to his feet. "Please. Annette is doing nothing wrong—"

"Damn you, Jensen!" Edward pounded a heavy fist on the table. The glasses tinkled uneasily. "Stay out of this." He whirled back to Annette. "Do you keep a studio? Tell me. Now."

"Why . . . why, yes. I do." How did he know?

"Good God!" he blustered. "At that revolting hovel—the Montgomery Block?"

"Yes." She dropped her eyes uncomfortably. "And nothing you can say or do—"

"Enough!" His voice thundered, shaking the air. "Enough, I say! God almighty, am I not your father? Have you no respect for me whatsoever? Well? Damn it, girl, answer me!"

Tears sprang to her eyes. "Yes, Daddy, of course I respect you," she whispered hoarsely. "But you don't even try to understand me."

"Understand you? By God, I think I understand you only too well. You've no respect. None! When I found out about this studio, I was never so humiliated in all my life." He flew to his feet. "Up there all day, alone, where any man can walk in and . . . and . . . touch you. Hanging around that filthy place. Why, everyone knows what those artists do there. They're disgusting! And you're right in there with them, my own daughter!"

"I'm not doing anything like that!" Annette cried, shocked at her father's outpouring of venom. "I'm painting. That's all. I hardly see anyone there—"

"I want you home, where I can look after you. Not in some dirty hole—"

Worrying her lower lip, Annette forced herself to meet his outraged gaze. "I am going to keep the studio, Daddy."

"Never!"

"Yes I am. I'll move out if that's what you want. But I'm keeping my studio." She held her breath for a long, agonizing moment.

Edward was shaking now. He took a trembling step toward her, knocking over his chair. She was afraid for a moment that he would hit her, knock her down. Then she was afraid that he would collapse from the force of his rage. Her eyes locked with his. She tried to show him, by her look, that she loved and respected him, but that she also would remain firm in her ambition.

The tension between them mounted until the atmosphere in the room pulsed with it. Annette knew she could not back down, but she was aware, also, that her father was in the habit of being obeyed. It was an impasse.

She began to tremble. Everything in the room grew fuzzy around the edges, seemed to disappear. Only she and her father existed, staring endlessly at each other in a kind of vacuum. It was as if she were clinging to the side of a high, high cliff, afraid to climb down but unable to climb up. She hadn't even the strength to scream for help. Her fingers were growing numb, and she knew she couldn't hold on for much longer. The terror grew, swelled like a horrid beast, its shadow hovering over them.

Jensen rounded the table, blocking his father's path, coming between them. "Stop this," he begged, breaking the deadlock. "Father. Please. Do you really want Annette to leave? Do you want to drive her away like you did Cecile?"

Edward froze. His face contorted strangely. "Cecile?" he muttered, his hand going to his chest.

"Yes," Jensen replied, confident that his words were making an impression. "Like you drove Cecile away—"

"No," whispered Edward. "I never . . . I didn't mean to . . ." And then, to his children's utter disbelief, he turned away stiffly and stalked from the room, his face as pale as death.

"Jensen?" Annette whispered. "What . . . what happened?"

The young man's brows drew together pensively. He stood perfectly still, staring at the door through which their father had retreated only seconds before. At last he said, as if to himself, "I honestly don't know."

Edward Tofler's carriage rolled to a stop in front of a brightly painted, gingerbread-style house on Oak Street.

He climbed the steps to the second floor, placed a key in the lock of number three and pushed open the door wearily.

"Edward!" gasped a young woman clad in a black, filmy robe. "Why, you startled me. I wasn't expecting you." The girl's hips swayed seductively as she approached Edward, a smile on her wide mouth.

"I . . . I had to come, Tilly. Something awful has happened."

She laid her fair head against his wide chest. "Awful? Oh, poor Edward. Come." Matilda Grueter led him to an overstuffed couch. "Sit down and tell me. It can't be all that bad, can it?" She went to a small sideboard and poured him a brandy from a crystal decanter. "Here," she handed him the liquor, nestling her exquisitely rounded body down beside him. "Tell me."

"It's Annette," he began tiredly, his voice thin. "She's so headstrong. Why, she's behaving like a common—"

"Street girl," Matilda finished for him, unruffled.

"Yes, I suppose so. Oh Tilly, I don't know how to handle her. She threatened to leave. And then that damned son of mine—"

"Jensen?" She held a match to his cigar.

"Yes," he whispered harshly. "Jensen. He's always prying into things that aren't his business. I think he hates me, Tilly. I really do."

Matilda placed a warm, adoring kiss on Edward's

cheek. "Now, Edward. He's your son. I'm sure he doesn't hate you."

Edward groaned. "I wish I believed that. And I suppose I've made him that way. Why, he's absolutely driven. Oh, I suppose he's a fine businessman, but he's, well . . ."

"He's like you, I'll bet. Probably too much."

"Perhaps. I don't know. I just feel I've lost control over my children. They have no respect. None."

"You don't want Annette to leave, do you?" For the first time since Edward's arrival, Matilda's voice seemed slightly cool, even distant.

He looked at her carefully. "She's my daughter, Tilly. I don't want to see her harm herself or her reputation. Is there anything wrong in that?"

"No, Edward," she replied, wanting to ask him if that was the only reason he was so protective of his precious Annette.

"So what am I to do?"

"Give her a little freedom." Matilda glanced up into his face as her finger toyed with the chain of his watch. "She doesn't have a lover, does she?"

"Good God, I hope not! A beau maybe—"

"Now, dear, don't upset yourself so." She began to stroke his chest as she loosened the black lace covering her young breasts. "Relax, Edward. I'm sure Annette is too smart to, well, shall we say, to get herself in trouble."

"Oh," groaned Edward.

"There, now." Matilda freed her firm round breasts from the scanty lace. Taking Edward's hand, she placed it on her.

"You're so good to me," he murmured. "So good." He stroked her young, creamy flesh. As his breathing grew shallower and sweat formed on his brow, his touch became demanding. Soon, he forgot Annette's outrageous behavior, he forgot Jensen and the competition between them and he forget that day twelve years earlier, the day Cecile had left.

Chapter 8

The scene could have been taking place in any city in the Celestial Empire. The narrow streets were crowded, forming a kaleidoscope of yellow-skinned men and women intent on their own business, hawkers, paper lanterns, color. Lots of color: red lacquer, gleaming gold and brass, brilliant silk and satin embroidered robes, ivory carvings. The noise was overwhelming, a swirl of tinkling Oriental music, the excited jabber of Mandarin and Szechwan, cries, sobs, arguments, the muted clang of a gong.

This was Chinatown on a cool, misty night in November of 1890. The few white stragglers one might see on the streets were scarcely more numerous than would have been found in any open seaport in China itself, but they did exist. They were there to experience the exotic atmosphere and to taste the forbidden thrills of the Orient, namely opium and women. They were tourists and so they felt alien in this enclave of fabled seduction. They were a little bit afraid, a little tense and yet they enjoyed the feeling. It was an adventure.

Near the corner of Jackson and Powell Streets, on the edge of Chinatown but still within the range of Caucasian San Francisco, three men emerged from a noisy saloon into the murky darkness of the street.

Two of them were joking and laughing loudly, walking with very deliberate steps, their hats perched jauntily on the backs of their heads. The other man, obviously more sober, stood tall and broad-shouldered, his fair hair under his hat catching the light from the gas lamps. The light also showed distinctly his high cheekbones, the flat hollows of his cheeks, the shadow of his hooked nose and the dark pools of his eyes. He swung along the street with his two inebriated friends, but in a somewhat detatched manner, as if he felt he had to watch out for them.

"Hey, Rolf, old pal, what do you say we wander on over to the Lotus Den? Sure to be something goin' on over there tonight," one of the young men proposed to his tall friend.

"Great idea, Jerome!" chimed in his rowdy companion. "We haven't been there in ages!"

"You sure you two can handle the Den tonight?" asked Rolf quietly, smiling at the antics of his two friends. They seemed terribly young to him. In truth, however, they were both over thirty, very close to his own age.

Jerome stopped short, weaving on his feet. "Since when can't I handle the Lotus Den after a few rounds? Huh? Just tell me that, you sober old son of a bitch?"

"Sorry. Didn't mean to insult you."

"Apology accepted," said Jerome pompously. "So let's go. Come on, Lee."

The three men set off up the street, heading toward the brightly lit, colorful hills of Chinatown. Their progress was slow. Jerome and Lee kept tripping over unseen obstacles and then they had to wait as Lee disappeared into an alleyway to answer the call of nature.

Finally, they arrived at an inconspicuous doorway. Over it hung a brass sign with Chinese characters and a name in English: The Lotus Den. Jerome knocked. They waited. Soon, a small partition in a window slid open and one sparkling black Oriental eye examined them silently. The door opened and they stepped inside.

"Good evening, friends," said the owner of the sparkling black eye. "Welcome."

"Good evening, Madame Yin-May," replied Rolf soberly, removing his hat. "And how are you tonight?"

"Ah so, Yin-May busy, very busy as usual," she said, smiling widely, showing large, yellow teeth. Madame Yin-May was a big woman, very fat. She had a broad, sallow face and thin black hair that was pulled into a tight knot on the top of her head and stuck through with long golden pins. Her feet, to her undying shame, had never been bound, as she came from peasant stock. Large and broad, they were encased in delicately embroidered slippers. She wore long, ornate gold earrings. Her small black eyes glinted at Rolf. "You bring your friends again, Mister Rolf?" she asked.

"Yes, Madame. They couldn't stay away. Your girls are so beautiful, you know."

"Ah so, I know. Since new law passed, it very hard to get pretty Chinese girl these days, but we try." The smile shone again.

She led them into a large, smoky room filled with the sweet odor of opium. Several scantily clad girls lounged around, waiting dully for customers. They were Chinese and very, very young, some nearly children. In their quiet, bored repose, they all had a terrible sameness about them, a dead look that held in it no hope at all. A few men, white and Chinese, sat on cushions sucking on their pipes with the tenacity of drowning men hanging on to life preservers. In one corner of the room, under a flickering gaslight, a poker game was in progress.

"You wanna girls?" Madame Yin-May asked the three men, her smile now a grin.

"Damned right we want girls," slurred Jerome, leering drunkenly.

Yin-May's perpetual smile vanished. Giving Jerome a disapproving look, she turned to Rolf. "Your friends no talkee nice, I no let them come to Lotus Den, Mister Rolf. This place no dirty. This nice place."

"Sorry, Madame," said Jerome sheepishly.

"Okay, fella, you just be good." She shook a long, talonlike fingernail at him.

"They'll be good, Madame, I promise," said Rolf, a smile lurking at the corners of his mouth.

Imperiously, Madame Yin-May called out in Chinese, and several of the girls sauntered over, some of them so young that the hip-swinging walk they affected looked grotesque.

"Here my best girls, special for you, Mister Rolf," she smiled.

Jerome and Lee were surrounded immediately, dragged under by soft hands, perfume and practiced giggles. Rolf moved away from the girls, unable to get in the mood. The young girls sickened him; the despair on their faces depressed him. No, not tonight.

"Madame Yin-May, excuse me, who's in the game over there?" he asked. He always treated Madame Yin-May with great respect. She was a very powerful woman in Chinatown, having bought herself free from slavery many years before and having made a success of her establishment. She was also an astute businesswoman.

"Ah so, that is Fung Jing Toy. Your people call him Little Pete. And that is Tansy O'Neill and four friends of Blind Chris'." She shrugged her ample shoulders. "They no want girls, only gamble."

"Think they'd mind if I joined them?" Rolf asked. "I feel the urge for a little gambling myself." Unconsciously, his forefinger rubbed against his thumb, the age-old reflex of the professional card player testing the feel of the cards.

"Sure, okay. Why not? You can afford to lose?" The unwinking black eyes regarded him carefully even as her smile beamed wider.

"Madame Yin-May, I thank you for your consideration, but I can afford to lose. Although," he winked an eye at her, "I rarely do."

Madame's huge bulk leading the way, Rolf approached the poker table. The men playing were very quiet, their only talk low, muttered oaths, bets and raises. Their faces, except for Fung Jing Toy's, were absolutely expressionless in the typical manner of good players. Rolf could tell from the way they held their cards that these were no amateurs.

"Gentlemen, this Mr. Rolf Karman, a friend of mine. He wish play with you," Madame Yin-May announced.

Six pairs of eyes turned as one, examined him carefully and silently passed judgment.

"Sure," said an emaciated fellow, his voice thin and reedy. "There'll be a spot open at the table in a few minutes. We're playin' for high stakes, though, gotta warn ya."

"Mind if I just watch for a couple of hands?" asked Rolf.

"Suit yourself, Karman." He turned his back on Rolf and continued with the game.

Rolf watched the six men carefully, studying their various styles of playing, their expressions and the tiny, barely perceptible hand and eye movements that gave them away. It all came back to him in a flood of well-remembered impressions. And so he should remember. There had been a time, years before, when his very existence had depended on how well he read the men playing against him and on how well he knew the permutations and combinations of the fragile cards that held his fate in their impersonal dots of black or red.

He stood behind the thin man with the sunken, pale eyes and watched him play. Tansy, as the other men called him, was good. He never faltered, never gave anything away. He played conservatively and was always controlled. Little Pete, the Chinese, Rolf knew from his reputation as leader of the tong, the secret society within the Chinese community. He laughed too often, showing a gold tooth when he did and moaned and commented over his cards. But he played a slashing, aggressive game that belied his apparent silliness. His fingers were covered with rings fashioned of diamonds, rubies, emeralds, gold and silver. He wore an outlandish suit of chain mail, oddly enough, with a silk embroidered Chinese robe over it.

These two men would be his adversaries. The other four were types he'd played too often before. They thought themselves devastating players, but, in truth, it was the game of chance that controlled and devastated them. They were inconsequential, unless, of course, fate handed them an unbeatable combination.

Madame Yin-May was approaching, a long, thin pipe in her hand. "You like some opium, friends?" she offered, her golden earrings trembling in the flickering gaslight.

Little Pete took a few puffs, as did two of the other men. The rest, Rolf noticed, had tumblers of whiskey at their places, except for Tansy, who had only a glass of water.

"You like, Mister Rolf?"

"No thank you, Madame Yin-May." It was almost tempting to partake of oblivion again, but he knew better. He'd tried it once, years ago, and liked it so well that he'd tried it again and again. It had been hard to stop, but he'd had to. It had taken all his will power and the help of a good friend, but he had succeeded. Still, he remembered the sensation, the comfort, the ease of the drug. It would be too easy to fall under its spell again.

The men at the table had finished a hand and were leaning back for a minute, scraping chair legs across the floor, lighting up cigars, calling for fresh whiskey.

"Mind if I sit in now?" Rolf asked.

"Sure, get a load off," said the man sitting across from Tansy. "I'm through anyway. Done busted myself again. Think I'll have a woman with what I got left."

Rolf slid into the man's seat and anted a twenty dollar gold piece. The man to the left of Little Pete shuffled the deck and dealt five cards to each player.

Rolf looked over his hand. He had a pair of deuces. When he threw in three cards and got no help back, he grimaced and threw his cards down on the table. The play went around the table twice. Tansy's two pair, kings high, won the hand.

The play went on in the smoky room. Rolf forgot his two friends, forgot everything but the challenge of the cards. He didn't play often anymore, but when he did, his concentration was complete. There was an infinitesimally fine line between winning and losing, he had learned years ago, and he had developed the skill and judgment to be the overall winner.

He asked for a glass of whiskey and water—it gave him an aggressive edge. He won a few hands, lost a few. His winnings equaled his losses. Normal.

Then, finally, he was dealt a good hand: two

fives, two jacks. He threw one card in. He raised another twenty dollars and noticed Tansy O'Neill watching him speculatively, a cigarette dangling from his delicate pink lips, one eye closed to avoid the smoke that curled lazily up from the tip. The play went around once and then again, until everyone had dropped out but Rolf, Tansy and one of the other men. The pot was big, the atmosphere tense.

Then he heard Tansy's thin voice asking, "So you're Rolf Karman, the artist?"

What a strange time to make conversation, Rolf thought, or is it a deliberate attempt to break my concentration? "That's right," answered Rolf, meeting the pale, fishy eyes straight on.

"Play a damn good game," said Tansy.

"Thanks."

"I think we just might have an acquaintance in common, Karman."

"I doubt that," said Rolf coolly. What in hell did Tansy want?

"I might be mistaken, but I was sure I saw little Annette Tofler visit you the other day—for a long time." Tansy eyed Rolf victoriously, settled back in his chair and casually dropped a stack of silver dollars on the pile of money in the center of the table. "Raise you ten more."

The other man folded.

Rolf fought down a surge of anger. What in hell was Tansy doing, spying on him? Or was it Annette? It made no sense. But one thing was certain, it wouldn't do Annette any good if this got around. He'd find out later what O'Neill was up to. The man was dangerous, no doubt about it.

"Call," said Rolf smoothly. "You were mistaken. I don't know anyone by that name. You must have seen another lady."

Tansy shook his head, smiled his death's-head smile. "Sure as hell looked like the Tofler chippy." He laid his cards out triumphantly, two threes and two queens.

Slowly, deliberately, Rolf laid down his hand. Two jacks, three fives. He raked in the pile of money, noting Tansy's scowl of frustration from the corner of his eye. Lady Luck was with him now.

It was Tansy's deal. Rolf watched the man closely, trying to figure out what he had been after with his startling revelation. When his trained eye caught an odd motion, he focused even more closely on Tansy's cadaver-thin fingers. Sure enough, the man was dealing himself cards from the bottom of the deck! Obviously, he wasn't about to let Rolf win again. This was turning into a personal battle, the best way to ruin a good card game.

Tansy won a disappointingly small pot. The play went on. Madame Yin-May and the girls greeted men and went about their business, but to the men at the table in the corner, they might not have existed. The flickering gaslight cast strange shadows, illuminating Little Pete's ringed fingers, Tansy's pale face, the sweat-stained shirt of one of the other men and Rolf's hair, darkened with sweat on his forehead. Smoke drifted upward in trailing ribbons that lost themselves in swirling clouds on the ceiling.

Rolf won a small pot and one of the other men took the next hand. So the play continued. Once more, it was Tansy O'Neill's turn to deal. He gathered the cards in his long fingers and began to shuffle.

"I think we could use a new deck," ventured Rolf quietly, chillingly.

Tansy stopped shuffling instantly. He was as still as death. His pale, sunken eyes rose to meet Rolf's. "You tryin' to say something, Karman?"

"And a new dealer." His eyes met Tansy's, locked with them. There was hate in Tansy's gaze, cold, reptilian, unyielding hate. Rolf's eyes did not falter. The tension was as palpable as a San Francisco fog, as taut as a ship's mooring in a storm.

Tansy gave in. "Okay, sure. A game's a game, ain't it?"

Little Pete dealt, his parchment-yellow fingers flying, his gold tooth gleaming in the gaslight. The other men were strangely quiet, casting odd, questioning looks at Rolf and Tansy.

Rolf was dealt a pair of fours. He threw in three cards and got another four in return. He decided to bluff, to push O'Neill to the limit. The play went around several times. Most of the men dropped out. Tansy kept raising. He had the secret, satisfied look of a man with a good hand.

There must have been a thousand dollars in the pot. Finally, Little Pete dropped out, throwing cards down in disgust. Tansy called and began to spread his cards out in front of him, face up. His dainty pink lips slit open in a smile. He had a pair of sixes and a pair of tens. His hand reached out toward the pot. He glanced up at his opponent.

Rolf allowed himself the pleasure of a grin. He laid out his cards. Three fours. "Three of a kind beats two pairs," he said softly to Tansy. "I believe this hand is mine."

The hired cab rolled through the fog toward Rolf's lodgings at the Astor House. He had just dropped off Jerome and Lee, making sure they both got home without incident. He felt responsible for them, dazed as they were by opium, women and booze. After all, he was the one who had introduced them to the Lotus Den in the first place.

Under his elegantly cut frock coat, his shirt was still cold and clammy with sweat. It had taken some mighty smooth maneuvering to get him and his two friends out of Madame Yin-May's establishment without physical violence. Tansy O'Neill, furious over the outcome of the poker game, had been just barely able to restrain himself from challenging Rolf to a fight. Rolf almost would have welcomed the chance to take him on, but Tansy O'Neill was Blind Chris Buckley's man and it would have been foolhardy for Rolf to pit himself against the machine that ran San Francisco. So he extricated himself and his friends and left quietly, promising Yin-May that he'd return. All the while, Tansy had been standing in the background, quivering with white-hot fury. The hair on Rolf's neck had prickled as he left and he'd expected to feel a knife or bullet in his back at any moment. Things like that happened frequently in Chinatown.

The street was dark and foggy. Rolf could hear the cabby clucking to his horse. He settled into the back seat, free now to turn his attention to the matter of O'Neill's startling knowledge of his personal affairs. Why had the man been watching him? Rolf made it a policy to stay clear of business and politics. Had O'Neill been after Annette, then? But what on earth for? He wondered whether Annette knew about any of this. But no, of course she didn't. Maybe the whole family was under surveillance. Maybe the brother or the father was involved with Buckley. That would make more sense.

His mind wandered idly to thoughts of Annette. The girl was beautiful. She was very young, too, but that only made her more desirable. He could still feel the satiny skin, the warm curves and hollows under his hands. At least there had been no false modesty about her. Perhaps he had been cruel in taking her virginity, but it had been so easy. Better him than another man, he rationalized, someone ignorant and unfeeling who would have ruined her first experience with love.

He wondered just what Annette felt now about her first love affair. She probably hated him for what he'd said. It was better that way, so much better.

Chapter 9

When Annette's father tapped on her bedroom door and announced he was giving a party for her, it was the biggest surprise she had received since her return from Paris. "A party?" she replied, bewildered. She had felt certain that he had come to her room at this early hour to rage at her about the studio apartment.

"Yes. A homecoming party. In your honor. And you, my dear, may draw up the guest list yourself. I'm afraid I haven't the time to help. I will, of course, check over it, and perhaps Jensen will have some friends he wishes you to meet."

"Oh, Daddy," she cried in delight, "how wonderful! I mean"—she pulled on her robe and went to him, wanting to give him a hug—"I do love you so!"

Her father stiffened and pushed her away. Strangely embarrassed, he mumbled something and hastily excused himself from her room. Unperturbed, Annette called out her gratitude after him. As soon as he had closed the door, she began planning for the party.

It would be a ball, of course, followed by a midnight supper. She would invite hundreds of San Francisco's finest, including her father's business associates, Jensen's friends and her old school friends and their families. And there must be artists, all sorts of them, from the famous to the struggling unknown. It would be wonderful!

Annette spent the next two weeks preparing for the party, seeing that the house was properly clean, hiring musicians, selecting the menu. She had the invitations printed and either sent them by mail or, in some cases, had them delivered in person by Tom, their driver. Caught up in this whirlwind of activity, she was forced to send Bernard a note of apology for missing a sitting. Along with the note, Annette sent an invitation to the party. Bernard would understand. She sent many more invitations to local artists of all media, studiously omitting Rolf Karman's name from the guest list. Naturally, through his colleagues, he would hear about the party. Good, she thought wickedly.

Annette wondered what had prompted her father to give the ball. Two reasons occurred to her. First, it kept her busy and away from her painting and the studio. Second, no doubt he was hoping she would meet someone, an eligible friend of Jensen's perhaps, or the son of one of his business cronies. Annette didn't care. In truth, she was too excited about the party to dwell on his motives.

One night, soon after the invitations had arrived from the printer, Annette handed Jensen a stack. "Here. These are for your friends. I'm sure I don't know half of them."

"Blast it all, Annette," he complained. "I haven't the time to address all these." But when she pleaded with him, he capitulated.

"I saw the dressmaker leaving as I arrived home," he commented. "That makes the fourth time this week. Pray tell, what are you having the gown made of, diamonds and emeralds?"

Annette giggled. "No, silly, diamonds and

rubies—they go much better with my hair!" She tossed her auburn curls coquettishly.

The dress, although not made of precious gems, might well have been for all its cost. The deep blue silk shimmered deliciously under the light, flattering her alabaster skin, and the creamy lace skirting the bodice and inserted at the back of the fitted peplum was breathtaking. The bodice was encrusted with beading that glittered in the light and the skirt flared from the hips to the hem and sported a graceful train at the back. The gown was magnificent, elegant. Annette was immensely pleased with the work, even though her insistence on the deeply cut neckline had caused an argument with the dressmaker. Annette had the perfect corset to wear with the dress. The contraption could be pulled so tightly at the waist that a frailer woman might have fainted from lack of air. The stays under the bosom pushed her breasts up daringly high, forming two perfect mounds of white flesh above the lace.

On the day of the ball, Annette took a leisurely, scented bath in the late afternoon. Every detail had been checked and double-checked and all was in readiness. She couldn't think of a single person who had declined an invitation. Anybody who was anybody in San Francisco would be there. Surely, in the near future, when her name was etched on a brass placard at a gallery opening, everyone would remember her. How could they forget Annette Tofler, the belle of the ball. They'd be clamoring for her artwork. And the men who would watch in awe as she swept down the curving staircase would remember her, too. She would make certain of that.

For a fleeting instant, as she lazed in the tub, Annette wished she had sent Rolf Karman an invitation. It would have been wonderful to flirt with him for a moment and then turn her back on him, spirited away by some handsome gentleman who would pant over the bodice of her gown right under Rolf's nose. But it was too late, now. And probably just as well. After all, seeing him might upset her composure and she had vowed that if she ever laid eyes on him again, she would behave maturely and not like a silly, hurt child.

Vivian helped her into her underclothes, growling over the corset while Annette hung on to the bedpost, sucking in her breath and gasping for Vivian to tug even harder on the strings. When at last it was fastened, Vivian stood back, surveying Annette's tiny waist and overexposed bosom. "Disgusting! You look like a French whore for sure," she muttered.

"Exactly." Annette's almond eyes danced with glee.

Vivian slipped the blue silk gown over the girl's head and buttoned her into it. After it had been adjusted and smoothed to their satisfaction, Annette stepped into the matching silk slippers. Finally, she seated herself before the mirror. "A pompadour," she instructed Vivian, "and leave a few curls around my face, if you will."

Vivian fussed with the long mass of springy hair until it formed a full, richly curved bun on top of Annette's head. On each side of the girl's face and trailing down the nape of her neck were a few bouncing tendrils of auburn hair, framing her delicate features exquisitely. Annette dabbed perfume behind her ears and between the swelling mounds of her breasts. Around her neck, Vivian placed a single strand of diamonds with a large sapphire at the center. The sapphire rested against her white flesh just above her rich cleavage. The stone shimmered, drawing attention to her bosom.

Annette pulled on a pair of short white gloves, rose and stepped back to admire herself in the mirror.

She was delighted with herself and eager to make her entrance. She danced over to the window. The drive and the street below were already lined with shining black carriages. The drivers stood in a group and talked among themselves, no doubt anticipating the dinner that the Toflers would provide them according to social customs.

Annette turned away from the window, excited and impatient, wondering how much longer to wait before making her debut at the top of the staircase. Most likely everyone had arrived, but a few more minutes wouldn't kill her.

Finally, she sent Vivian to take a peek at the guests assembled below. "They're packed in like sardines, miss," the maid reported. "Go on, now. And have yourself a fun time, deary."

Annette did just that. She paused for a moment at the head of the wide staircase, just long enough to make certain that all eyes were on her, then began her slow, graceful descent. With each step, she felt more like she was entering into a fairyland, a dream. Below her was a colorful haze of elegance. Vaguely, she heard a few gasps break the ethereal silence that had fallen over the throng. She was a princess, a queen. These were her subjects, loyal and adoring. This was her night.

She arrived at the bottom of the steps. Dozens of richly attired guests flocked around her, the women exclaiming over her dress and her beauty, the men vying for a place on her dance card. Edward Tofler was there, too. However, he wasn't exclaiming over her as were the others. Instead, she slowly realized, he was frowning, his gaze resting on the daring bodice of her gown.

"How could you?" he choked in a low voice, drawing her aside momentarily.

"Oh, Daddy," she cooed, "look around you. Lots of the ladies are wearing low-cut gowns. It's the fashion now, you know." She spun away, undaunted, determined to let nothing spoil her evening. Her father was such a medieval prude.

The first strains of music drifted in from the conservatory, which had been decorated and cleared for the dancers. Annette was led into the tall, spacious room by Jensen, who had arranged in advance to claim her for the opening waltz. Along the way, she greeted friends and acquaintances and was introduced to many people she hadn't met. Each and every guest she spoke to looked her over speculatively, some with open admiration, others with less than approval.

"It's that neckline, my dear sister," Jensen commented, sweeping her onto the dance floor. "You certainly have your nerve."

"Don't I?" she winked, tossing back her head with a laugh.

They circled the candlelit, glassed-in room in a breathless whirl of music, color and finery. Annette could hardly believe how marvelous the mansion looked, so gaily lit and sparkling. To an onlooker, she and Jensen fit the scenario perfectly: he, dashingly handsome, and she, truly a princess, a fiery, radiant jewel. Men's eyes followed her every move, taking pleasure in the adorable tilt of her small chin, the proud upturned nose, the white column of her throat and the creamy mounds of her bosom beckoning to be touched, kissed, cherished.

Soon she was in another man's arms. He was a friend of Jensen's, he said, and his name was Theodore Crocker. Banking money, she guessed, feeling the slim man's arm encircle her waist longingly. He wasn't handsome, not at all, but she still laughed at his outrageous flattery.

"You're a treasure, Miss Tofler. A jewel. Why, I should call Jensen out for keeping you a secret. Will you marry me?"

Annette giggled. "Why, you embarrass me, Mr. Crocker." She blushed, feeling his eyes devour her décolletage.

"Please, I should hate to embarrass you, Miss Tofler. Forgive me. It's just that I'm overcome by your beauty. Might I speak with your father about calling on you?" he begged at the end of their dance. Before Annette could think of a clever reply, she was whisked away by another ardent young man who began the flattery anew.

One might think Annette would tire of the game, but she didn't. As her partners changed, her replies grew lighter, more flirtatious and daring. Yes, she thought as she whirled around the polished floor, they will most definitely remember me.

When the musicians took a break, Annette allowed her most recent escort, the widowed father of an old schoolmate of hers, to fetch her a champagne cocktail. The man was a railroad mogul named Roger B. Sutton. He was an impressively large man, trim and muscular for his age, which she guessed to be around forty-five. Peeking at his face from under the veil of her dark lashes, she was favorably impressed with his hair, curling mustache and long sideburns. Quite handsome, she decided. He too was panting over her, but not quite in the same dull manner of the younger men. This man was an accomplished rogue.

Handing her the champagne, he noted, "Lovely gown, Miss Tofler. It displays your charms quite adequately."

She blushed profusely. Was he teasing her, or was he serious? "Thank you," she murmured uncertainly.

"I've embarrassed you, and I had hoped not to.

You see, Miss Tofler," he smiled, "I am really too old to play childish games. If I admire something or someone, I approach on a straightforward path."

"Oh, I see," she said, wondering where he was headed.

"Yes. And I should like to see you again, Annette, if I might call you that. Perhaps you would visit my home some day."

"Your home?" Her surprise was not feigned.

"Come now, Annette. A woman of your bearing and beauty must have many such invitations. I believe in asking straight out, my dear. That way I'll know exactly where we stand."

"*We* stand nowhere, sir!" she cried with some shock. Turning to leave, she bumped straight into Bernard Maduro.

"Annette?" Bernard said questioningly, his eyes going from her to Sutton. "Is everything all right?"

"Yes," she lied, trying desperately to compose herself. Her eyes imploring, she added, "Isn't this our dance?"

Bernard glared at Sutton for a long moment before turning to lead Annette back onto the dance floor.

"Thank you," she said as they began to dance. "I did need rescuing."

"Sutton is a known womanizer. I suggest you tread lightly where he's concerned." Bernard frowned. "Did he insult you awfully?"

"No. I guess not. Not really. But he was terribly bold."

"And that's not to your liking, is it?"

Annette arched a dark brow. "What do you mean?"

"That if and when you decide to have an affair, Annette, I'm sure you will be the aggressor."

She froze. "How dare you . . ."

But Bernard smiled knowingly and Annette remembered, all too clearly, the time she had attempted to seduce Bernard and had been held firmly at bay. She began to dance again. "Very clever, aren't you?" She laughed a little. "And maybe, just maybe, you're correct. I should think it only wise of me to select my men and not vice versa. Why shouldn't the woman take the initiative?"

"My, how modern your thinking is, Annette. And one thing is for certain, I would never worry about you. You learn too fast," he laughed. "I think you'll do just fine with all your, shall we say, ventures?"

She smiled up at Bernard. If no one else in all San Francisco understood her, Bernard did. What a wonderful friend he was!

The dance ended. Annette allowed herself another champagne and stood chatting with Bernard and another sculptor, a friend of his, who must have been well into his seventies. Like Bernard, the man was a Marxist. They talked, and soon their shared philosophy began to bore her. She was definitely out of her league where politics was concerned, and only Jensen could make the subject less than dull.

The three of them were standing in the far corner of the room, near the punch bowl, where she was not very noticeable. She glanced around. Her dance card was full, so she knew that some young man must be looking for her, but her feet could use a rest this one time.

She caught a glimpse of her father in the crowd. He was deep in conversation with several older women and their husbands. Good. At least he was too involved to find her and begin a lecture.

Where was Jensen? she wondered, scanning the throng. Surely he was either dancing or swamped with chatty females, so he should be easy to spot. And then she saw him. He was standing at the other end of the large room, talking to an attractive blonde woman and a man who looked vaguely familiar. The man's back was turned, and all Annette could see of him was his light curly hair.

Light, curly. . . . She strained her eyes. Her breath caught in her throat. The dancers and passers-by maddeningly blocked her view, but finally she could see the man's head again. Yes. It did look like . . . But that was impossible! He hadn't been invited. Unless . . . unless Jensen had invited him. She had never dreamed . . .

"Excuse me," she said to Bernard and his friend abruptly, "but there's someone I must see."

The two men bowed. Annette smiled artificially, her mind consumed with the possibility that Rolf was there. She wove through the crowd in the conservatory, trying to see the stranger's face more clearly. It was frustrating to be stopped so often by acquaintances. She thought she would never find out who the man was. She felt as if she had been holding her breath all evening, and her bosom strained at the blue silk from the effort.

Rolf Karman, even if he was Jensen's invited guest, would not dare show up here, in her home. As she neared the trio, she got a clear glimpse of his face. It was definitely Rolf Karman. The unmitigated gall of the man!

In the midst of her anger, while she stood frozen, trembling with barely suppressed rage, she suddenly felt the light touch of a hand on her arm. She turned.

"Miss Tofler," said a very young man, "I believe I have this dance?"

Oh no! she thought. Putting on her most contrived smile, she said, "Oh, I'm so terribly sorry, but I have a terrible headache. Would you mind awfully if I sit this one out? I promise I'll save you a dance," she finished, praying he wouldn't detain her further.

"Well, if you promise a dance later," he grinned, "then I suppose I'll just have to wait. I do hope your headache gets better."

"Thank you." As quickly as she could, Annette made her way over to where Jensen stood, still talking to the blonde and Rolf. When she was nearly upon them, not knowing or caring what she was going to say or do, she recognized the woman. It was Eleanor Fairchild, a wealthy widow in her thirties who had a wicked reputation for engaging in lavish love affairs. Annette stopped. Her heart pounded furiously. Surely Jensen wasn't seeing Mrs. Fairchild. But if not, then Rolf must be! This was humiliating.

As if to confirm her suspicion, Rolf bent his leonine head and whispered in Mrs. Fairchild's ear. He was smiling. So he was here with her! Quite suddenly, Annette knew that she couldn't possibly face them. Never. She spun around, thinking to flee outside for a moment, when she heard her name being called.

"Annette!" It was Jensen's voice.

Without thinking, she paused, making it obvious that she had heard him. Under the circumstances, to run would be far more humiliating than to stay and acknowledge them.

Slowly, desperately willing a smile to her lips, she forced herself to turn back toward Jensen and walked as steadily as possible to the trio. "Oh, hello, Jensen," she managed to say. And then, to the gorgeous blonde, "Mrs. Fairchild, isn't it?" Good, she thought. By calling the woman Mrs., she had shown her to be much older than herself. It wasn't much, but anything helped. To Rolf, she said nothing, avoiding his dark eyes altogether.

"I see you have met Eleanor," remarked Jensen.

"Yes," Annette replied, "at a tea several weeks ago." Although she smiled more brightly, her insides were balled into a tight, sickening knot.

"And have you met my friend, Mr. Rolf Karman, Annette?"

She turned, finally, acknowledging him. "No," she lied uneasily. "I don't believe I have."

"Ah, but I've heard so much about you from Jensen," he taunted, an amused gleam in his eyes, "that I feel we already know one another."

Annette cringed inwardly. The nerve! The very nerve! Obviously, he had known exactly who she was when he had replied to her advertisement. Why, he had planned the whole, hideous thing.

"How do you do?" she murmured, wanting to scratch out his eyes.

"Yes," replied Rolf, "you are as lovely as Jensen described, if you don't mind my saying so, ma'am," he drawled rakishly.

"Why, thank you, Mr. Karman." This was too much! She turned to Jensen for help. Her brother, however, was smiling at Eleanor Fairchild and had not taken note of the whole embarrassing situation. At that moment she could have killed Jensen. And Rolf. And Eleanor Fairchild with her overblown charms.

"Miss Tofler," Rolf was saying in his deep voice, "if I might be permitted a comment?"

Annette glared her outrage at him through narrow, suspicious eyes. "Why, certainly," she almost hissed.

"I should think you would make an excellent model. Of course, I speak from the artist's point of view. Say, have you any interest in the arts?"

She detested him. "Why none at all," she replied, sensing that she had now caught her brother's rapt attention. "Frankly—Mr. Karman, wasn't it?—I find artists quite dull."

"Annette?" Jensen couldn't believe his ears.

But it was Rolf who replied, one corner of his mouth lifting with amusement. "Yes, to an adventurous woman, an artist might seem dull. Are you adventurous, Miss Tofler?" His mouth split in a knowing, infuriating grin.

"Quite," she countered, wanting to escape as quickly as possible.

Jensen took command of the conversation then, mercifully steering it away from the arts. She could feel Rolf's eyes burning into her flesh, judging her, making fun of her. Splotches of red covered her neck and shoulders. She knew she was reddening terribly, which served only to exacerbate her agitation.

Finally, gathering her dignity as best she could, Annette excused herself, begging the need to speak with an old friend she had just glimpsed among the guests. Once she had escaped, she let out her breath in a ragged sob. Grabbing a glass of champagne from a waiter's tray, she sought the seclusion of the garden to cool herself.

It was funny, she would think later, that she should run into Freddy Sims then, just as she was ready to cry out her rage in the shelter of the garden. It was funny and fortunate, because upon seeing him, she knew exactly how she would get back at Mr. Rolf Karman. She would show him how little he affected her. She would show him that she could have any man she chose. And to think, she had come out into the garden to weep, as if she were some spineless ninny.

"Annette!" Arabella Sims' brother exclaimed. "How wonderful to see you again!"

"Yes, Freddy." She tried to overcome the quavering of her voice. "It's been a long time. I don't think I've seen you since I was at school with Arabella."

"Too long." He crossed the garden path and took her hand, kissing it warmly. "I was hoping I'd see you alone tonight. Imagine my good fortune."

"Yes. I . . . I had a headache, and I thought I'd step outside," she tumbled over the words. "Why, Arabella tells me you have the most wonderful job at the *Examiner*. Are you a reporter?"

Freddy Sims tossed back his dark head and laughed. "Hardly, Annette. I'm on my way to a vice presidency!"

"Why, that's marvelous, Freddy. Truly." Her rage was beginning to abate at last. She looked up at Freddy, actually seeing him for the first time.

He was quite handsome, darkly so, in utter contrast to his sister's fairness. He had nice, soft brown eyes and a straight, even nose. He had thick sideburns, and he wore a mustache which curved downward, almost in a handlebar, at the corners of his wide, thin-lipped mouth. Yes, she judged, Freddy Sims would do just fine for what she had in mind.

"I know I missed signing your dance card," he said, "but do you suppose I might stand a chance?"

Annette laughed, lowering her lashes coyly, and led him inside the conservatory to the dance floor. They discussed old times together, days spent at school, and flattered one another in the light of their maturity. After the dance, Annette drank another glass of champagne, then another. Her head did begin to ache then, but not unpleasantly. She felt light, bubbly, flirtatious.

Freddy was the perfect foil.

She danced with several other men, too, and each one begged for more of her time. As she whirled, pressing her bosom against their chests, however, she thought only of Rolf's presence. He was still in the conservatory, still engaged in close conversation with Eleanor Fairchild. What poor taste he has, she thought, returning to Freddy's side. Surely Rolf Karman could do better for himself than that well-used creature who was draping herself around him disgustingly. But then, perhaps he couldn't do better, what with that rude personality of his.

"Freddy?" she asked sweetly. "Would you mind getting me another glass of champagne. I vow, I'm getting so thirsty!"

Freddy soon produced the punch, having had to fight his way back through the crowd of men surrounding Annette. It was a long time before he had a chance to speak with her privately. Finally he whispered close to her ear, "Do you really think all this champagne is wise, Annette? I mean, your head is bound to ache abominably in the morning."

"Oh, Freddy," she sighed, pressing the swell of her bosom against his arm, "don't be such a prude."

"Well . . ."

She lowered her eyes demurely. "You think I'm terrible, don't you?"

"Heavens, no! Why, I think you're just marvelous, Annette. Truly!"

She laughed lightly. Yes, Freddy was doing just fine. In fact, judging by the way his soft eyes never left her décolletage, he was doing better than fine.

Surely if Rolf could see them from where he stood, he could not fail to notice Freddy's infatuation. Perfect. It crossed her mind that she was doing Freddy Sims a terrible injustice by using him so blatantly. But what was the harm? Freddy was the envy of many a man there tonight, and in the back of her mind, she already was forming an idea of how to reward him. No, Frederick Sims would not suffer.

Annette spent most of her time before the late supper in Freddy's company. She took every opportunity possible to flirt with him and the other men who flocked around her, their eyes also fastened on the creamy flesh swelling above her gown. Even Roger Sutton ventured close to her again, asking if she might sit with him at supper.

Annette was about to refuse his offer by telling him she already had promised Mr. Sims, when her father interrupted them. "Annette, dear," he began, "I'm so sorry to barge in like this, but there is a matter I must speak to you about. Would you excuse us?" he asked her companions.

He led her through the crowd, steering her toward the library, his private domain. Annette was confused, wondering why he would want to speak with her so unexpectedly. What was so urgent that it couldn't keep?

He shut the door behind them, muffling the noise of the crowd and the musicians. "You've drunk far too much champagne," he began. "And your behavior. It's outrageous! How could you?"

Annette sighed and sank into a chair. First Rolf, she thought, and now this. "Daddy," she said softly, "I'm only having fun. It is my party—"

"Yes. It is. But that . . . that gown of yours. My dear, all the men are, well, staring at you." His face flushed and he turned his back to her. "You're too young to understand, Annette," he mumbled. "Men can be vile creatures—"

"Oh, Daddy, you're so protective. No one has touched me. I'm only having fun. Please don't scold tonight."

"Well," Edward shook his grey head thoughtfully, "just promise you'll stay away from men like that Sutton. He's no damned good. Terrible reputation! Things unfit to speak about in decent company."

"He is awful," she agreed, then rose, coming up behind her father. "I promise I won't have any more punch, Daddy. All right?" She encircled his waist with her arms, hugging him.

Edward froze, sputtering, "Our guests . . . we must . . . see to them." Hastily, he disengaged himself, crossed the room and opened the door.

"Daddy?" Annette said, bewildered. "Is something wrong? Are you feeling well?"

"Fine. I feel fine. We should join the others," he said gruffly, seemingly in a great hurry to be back at the party.

And then he was gone. Annette shrugged, vowing to make her father see a doctor as soon as possible.

She rejoined the guests, a trifle subdued, concerned over her father's health. She dined with Freddy on one side and Jensen on the other. Her father was nowhere to be seen. Perhaps he wasn't hungry at this late hour, she surmised.

Rolf, with Eleanor ever at his side, sat out of her view at the far end of another long banquet table. It was just as well, she thought. Seeing him might sicken her and she was already feeling the aftereffects of the champagne.

She toyed with her food while Freddy grew bolder with his advances. "You have the most wonderful eyes," he whispered in her ear. "In fact, all of you is too wonderful, Annette. You're a vision."

She smiled, blushing. "You're a terrible flirt, Frederick Sims."

"You drive me to it," he laughed. "Seriously, Annette, would you see me again if I were to call? That is, with your father's approval?"

She was about to answer when they were interrupted.

"I believe the music has begun again, Miss Tofler, ma'am. And this is my dance," came a hauntingly familiar voice.

She turned abruptly in her seat and looked up to see Rolf standing over her shoulder. Before she could stem her shock or find a proper retort, he had taken her hand and was helping her to her feet. Her eyes looked imploringly down to Freddy's, but he seemed resigned to her dancing with another. Didn't Freddy know this dance did not belong to this man? Couldn't he read it in her eyes? But now they were moving. Rolf was steering her back into the conservatory and other than cause a terrible scene, there wasn't a thing she could do.

Rolf swept her into his strong embrace, leading her through the steps of the waltz gracefully, expertly. She could feel his hand at her waist, its touch burning through her gown, searing her flesh. She didn't dare to look up and meet his dark, unreadable eyes. Her cheeks were flaming, she knew. It was the champagne, she told herself, feeling suddenly dizzy. When would the dance end?

"You realize, Annette," said Rolf finally, "that we have unfinished business."

She tossed her head back, meeting his cool regard with surprise. What could he mean?

Rolf laughed at her wide, hazel eyes. "I meant only that my painting of you is barely started."

"You cannot possibly believe I would come to your lodgings again." It was not a question. She looked around, seeking some mode of escape. Why didn't the musicians stop?

He tightened his hold, causing her to gasp with

outrage. "Perhaps we should strike a bargain," he suggested, "a strictly professional arrangement."

"Never!"

He laughed. "And so your ruffled pride wins out over your modeling career?"

"Oh, there are other artists, Mr. Karman. I can have any job I choose."

"Yes, perhaps you can at that," he drawled, his dark eyes resting on the swell of her cleavage. "But I should truly like to finish our work."

"I think this dance is over," she hissed.

The music had stopped. At last Rolf released her, noting that she seemed terribly flushed and somewhat faint. Perhaps he had pushed her a bit too far. Still, as she hurried away from him, he could not resist one last barb. "I think, Miss Tofler, ma'am," he said to her stiff back, "that our dance has just begun!"

While Annette sought the company of Frederick Sims, Rolf returned to Eleanor Fairchild's side.

"Quite lovely, isn't she?" commented Eleanor Fairchild, nodding in the direction of Annette. "And I have the most distinct feeling you two have met before." She smiled coyly, her white teeth gleaming.

In reply, Rolf laughed and placed an affectionate kiss on her pink cheek. No point in giving Eleanor ammunition, he thought to himself. She'd fire holes in Annette's back.

"Would you care for some fresh air?" he asked her, grinning, knowing that there was nothing in the world Eleanor would like more than to be alone with him.

They strolled out into the garden. The chill autumn air was refreshing. Toward the rear of the garden, near an iron gate, Rolf drew her unresisting body into his arms. Their lips met and locked in sweet passion. Eleanor's small breasts pressed urgently against the jacket of his black tuxedo, warming him.

She was the most experienced, most desirable woman he had ever met. The things Eleanor knew and did in the privacy of the bedroom would make a whore blush. She was wonderful, exotic. And when a man was lost in the throb of her flesh, he forgot all else.

This was Rolf's kind of woman. Squeamish virgins were generally not to his liking, for they demanded far too much. How he had allowed himself to bed Annette was beyond him. It simply had happened. From the moment his eyes had first devoured her youthful, naked body, he had known she was a virgin. After she had left his apartment, as he stood staring down at the blood-stained sheets, he had realized that his taking her had been inevitable, preordained. He had wanted her exquisite body ever since the time he had first spotted her with Jensen Tofler at the gallery opening. Later, by chance, he had met Jensen at a dinner party. Rolf had taken a liking to Jensen. As the two men conversed, Jensen had mentioned that his sister, Annette, was quite interested in art. He had even confided to him that Annette had rented a studio to pursue her career. Then Rolf had come across the advertisement.

He admitted to himself that what he had done to Annette verged on rape. Having used her innocence and naiveté against her, he had unreasonably thrown it in her face. Of course, the quarrel had been partially Annette's fault. He wondered whether she had meant the things she had said.

Well, he told himself now, while his lips traced a path across Eleanor's neck, at least his cruel words had turned Annette away from him. What else could he have done? Let her cling to him for months and see her miserable in the end? Fate, however, seemed to be insisting that he be entangled with the Toflers. Jensen had invited him to the ball, telling Rolf that Annette wanted to meet the artists of the area. And it had been worth showing up, if only to see the expression on Annette's face. She had carried it off rather well, after all. Quite a girl.

Now, if he could just win back her trust, on a purely professional basis, of course, perhaps she might let him finish the painting. They needn't be enemies.

As Annette made absent-minded small talk with a partner between dances, Freddy Sims moved in and placed a warm hand on her back. "Should I speak with your father about calling on you?" he asked hopefully as the new dance began.

Annette smiled up at him. Over his shoulder she could see Rolf reentering the conservatory with Eleanor Fairchild. The woman's color was high and her lips were red and swollen.

"No, Freddy," replied Annette, tearing her eyes away from Rolf. "I mean, I think Daddy might not approve. He's been so protective lately. I know what we can do," she said suddenly, lowering her voice to a whisper. "We can meet somewhere in secret."

"In secret?" he gasped, taken aback.

"Why, yes! Why shouldn't we?" She lowered her lashes. "Unless, of course, you don't want to . . ."

"Oh, my, of course I do! Surely you know how much! But in secret?"

"Yes. Or I shan't see you at all, I fear." She paused. "How would it be to meet in, say, Golden Gate Park? Near the entrance?"

"Why—"

"Say tomorrow?" she murmured, pressing close to him as Rolf and Eleanor approached. "At noon?"

"At noon," Freddy replied, his heart beating furiously.

The guests were beginning to leave, one by one wishing Annette well and thanking her profusely.

It was Eleanor and Rolf's turn.

Annette met the woman's eyes boldly, her confidence reinstated. "So nice of you to come, Mrs. Fairchild."

"A lovely party, Annette. Rolf and I enjoyed it so."

Suddenly Annette wanted to ask her if she had enjoyed the garden and Rolf's kisses, but that would be too unspeakable. "Do stop by for a visit sometime," she said instead.

"Thank you, I will."

"Good night, Miss Tofler," said Rolf, taking her gloved hand and kissing it lightly.

"Good night," she managed to reply, making sure she was leaning close to Freddy all the while.

And then Rolf, with Eleanor clinging to his arm, was gone.

Freddy was the last to leave. She walked him to the door.

"Are you certain about tomorrow?" he whispered.

"Quite." She smiled devilishly.

Sometime before dawn, Annette awoke, covered with a fine sheen of perspiration and struggling for air.

What a terrible nightmare, she realized, trying to grasp onto snatches of the dream. She had been dancing with Rolf, but not in the Nob Hill mansion. The place had been small, secluded—perhaps his lodgings. Slowly, Rolf had removed her blue silk gown, her stockings, everything, his hands burning a path down her flesh. She had wanted him desperately. And then the dream had shifted to the mansion's drawing room. Light had poured in through the window, streaking her naked body. Edward Tofler had been there, too, a gun in his hand. The cool metal had gleamed evilly. Rolf had moved between Annette and her father, shielding her. And then there had been a shot.

As she sat now in her bed, trembling, the dream refused to evaporate. It haunted her senses, filled her mind. Finally, she rose, went to the washstand and splashed cool water on her hot cheeks. When she felt calmer, more awake, she wondered at the dream. Why Rolf? And why her father, shooting at him? Or was it at her?

She returned to bed, mulling over the nightmare. It made little sense, save that Edward Tofler would no doubt shoot any man who came too close to her. That much, at least, was clear. But why hadn't she dreamed about Freddy? The incident with Rolf was over. It was Freddy who would be in danger if found in her embrace.

Eventually, as the morning sky turned a pearly grey, Annette managed to put the disquieting thoughts from her mind. In a few hours, she would be meeting Frederick Sims. He was young, virile, attractive. Envisioning him, she smiled to herself, imagining the things they would no doubt do in the seclusion of the park.

Her first sexual encounter had given her body much gratification, and now she knew what to expect. With Freddy, it would be even more thrilling. She liked Freddy.

She propped her head up on the pillows, a smile playing on her lips, her heartbeat increasing. Yes, she would thoroughly enjoy this meeting with Freddy. He would be a careful, considerate lover, and together they would reach untold heights of passion.

Chapter 10

Annette's eyes flew open. It was after ten in the morning! She couldn't remember exactly when she had fallen asleep again. It must have been sometime after daybreak.

She jumped out of bed. If she didn't hurry, she would miss Freddy. There was no time for breakfast. But that wasn't a major problem. What bothered Annette was what to wear. More than likely, she and Freddy would just take a little stroll, perhaps he would steal a kiss or two. There was another possibility, however. One thing might lead to another. It could happen. If she were overdressed, it would be quite difficult to manage her clothing.

Standing in the middle of her room in her virginal white lawn nightgown with the pale pink rosebuds embroidered on it, Annette blushed hotly. She could seduce Freddy. Easily. He was so obviously infatuated with her that it was possible, thinking on it, that she would engage in more than just a few kisses. But how far should she lead Freddy on? An impish smile tugged on her lips.

Finally, she selected a pair of black bloomers, which even Vivian had not yet discovered hidden in the drawer, and a matching black camisole. One petticoat would have to suffice. She couldn't, if she let Freddy get that far, be fussing with too many skirts. And certainly no corset! A garter belt and stockings, yes, but no awkward strings. Giggling to herself, she pulled on the underclothes, wondering how these things were done outside of a bedroom. Excitement of the unknown filled her.

Over her finest Paris lingerie, she chose to wear a yellow wool challis dress with a tight buttoned collar, long fitted sleeves and a slim skirt. This dress had no cumbersome bustle, as she had purchased it in Paris and bustles were on their way out there. Besides, she mused, it would be uncomfortable to stretch out on the grass, if she went that far, and have a bump pressing into her backside.

Suddenly she stopped. Why am I going to all this fuss, she thought, when I may not even choose to let Freddy near me? But he was attractive and seemed quite nice, too. Why not plan for any eventuality?

Sneaking out of the house was a simple matter. The servants were busy in the kitchen at the back of the mansion, and Edward and Jensen were still fast asleep on this Sunday morning. Vivian, too, was asleep, no doubt, as Annette had previously given her the day off. Most likely she would be home before anyone even realized she had left. If her father or Jensen noticed, she would say she had gone for a long walk to get rid of her headache from the previous evening's champagne.

The weather was ideal, cool and sunny. And so was the time of month for what just might happen, she recalled while walking to the California Street cable car stop. In Paris, modern women believed that if one engaged in an affair either right before or right after her time of the month, no unwanted pregnancy would occur. Of course, there was no proof of this, but many claimed it worked. The time had been right with Rolf, just after. And now, with Freddy, three weeks later, the timing was perfect again. How clever women are becoming, she thought as she climbed up onto the cable car. How very modern and clever.

Having hired a carriage from where the cable car route ended in the city's core, Annette arrived at the entrance to Golden Gate Park only a few minutes late. She paid the driver, confident that Frederick Sims would be there, and watched the carriage leave.

Several couples were strolling through the wide entrance, some pushing baby carriages. Others seemed to be young lovers, perhaps meeting secretly, she mused, like herself and Freddy. How romantic.

She saw Freddy coming toward her, a generous smile on his face. He looked like a thirsty man approaching an oasis. Her heart beat furiously. It was so exciting to meet this way, in secret, and the notion that she might get caught only added to the thrill.

"Annette!" he called, breaking into a run. "I can hardly believe you're actually here. Why, I must be dreaming."

"Oh, Freddy," her dark lashes fell coyly over her ale-colored eyes, "of course I'm here. Did you think I wouldn't come?"

"I couldn't allow myself to believe you would, Annette." He took her arm gingerly in his, as if he were a priest touching a precious Madonna. "I'd have died if you didn't come."

She smiled demurely, lifting her gaze to his soft brown eyes. Freddy was very handsome. He had such a nice face, well structured, with a fine, straight nose, a lovely, curling mustache and thick, brown hair which he wore neatly combed close to his head. His clothes were proper, a white shirt with a stiff collar and a dark pinstriped vest under a matching suit. Very proper, very businesslike. Hardly like Rolf, she thought smugly, with his ruffled shirts worn open at the neck exposing his chest indecently. Frederick Sims was a gentleman.

They walked through the black iron gate and along the winding, hilly path which led deep into the heart of the sprawling park. The grass and path were leaf-strewn, in the grip of autumn, and the leaves crunching under her button-up boots smelled delicious. She was intoxicated by the brilliance of autumn, the bright oranges, yellows and reds, the crisp air, the indigo blue sky which belonged only to this time of year. A bird chirped nearby. She felt heavenly, caught in a dream.

"You know, Freddy," she mused softly, "if I could succeed in capturing these colors on canvas, no one would believe it. People would say it was too sharp, too clear, far too overdone. That's why a wise artist does not try to reproduce the colors of autumn. They're just too, well, too beautiful to be real."

Freddy stopped and looked at her closely. "Why, Annette, you really are interested in painting, aren't you? Arabella told me you had studied in Paris."

"Of course I am," she raised an eyebrow. "Is there something wrong in that?"

"Oh, no!" he replied hastily, instantly contrite. "I think it's wonderful. Truly."

Her frown faded and she smiled. "I do carry on, don't I? It's simply that I have trouble convincing people of my intent."

"Your father?" he guessed.

"Yes. And Jensen is concerned, too. They just don't understand me."

"I do," he rushed to say. "I understand you, Annette."

She gazed up into his face. No, she thought, you

don't really understand me either, Freddy. You like me, a lot, but you don't really understand.

"Annette?" His voice was ragged. He studied her closely, longingly.

"Yes."

"Would you . . . Might I . . . I mean . . ."

"Yes, Freddy," she replied intuitively. "You may kiss me."

And then, much to her surprise because they were essentially alone, he looked around sheepishly.

"Perhaps," she suggested, slightly annoyed, "we should walk up into that stand of trees over there." With a nod, she indicated a nearby hill on which was a cluster of half-bared oaks surrounded by reddish brown bushes. She shrugged her shoulders. That should suit him, she thought.

Frederick looked stunned, as if he couldn't believe she would suggest such a thing. Perhaps he really was a gentleman, too much so.

"Well?" Annette didn't even try to conceal the impatience etched in her voice. "Are we going to just stand here, Freddy?"

"Oh!" he gulped, his cheeks flushing. "No, of course not. No. I just . . ."

They veered off the path and began walking through the grass. "Do I shock you, Freddy?" she asked, then realized how callous she sounded. But really, she wasn't a virgin or anything, and his silly game seemed terribly immature to her all of a sudden. Nothing a man and woman might do together was wrong.

"Oh, my sweet Annette." He stopped and pulled her close to him. "If only you knew how perfect you are to me. If only you knew the things I dreamed all last night." He kissed her, hard, giving rein to his desire.

At first Annette was truly shocked. The force of

his demanding mouth hurt her, made her want to pull away. But then his kiss softened and she could feel her heartbeat throbbing in her breast which was pressed close to him.

When at last he released her, Annette was breathless. Yes, she wanted him. It wasn't just Rolf's touch which could set her senses on fire, she realized. She wanted Frederick Sims, wanted to feel his warm flesh pressed against hers, wanted to feel him inside her, possessing her, bringing a wonderful release to her thirsty flesh.

Her eyes darkened to smoky topaz. "Come." She led Freddy up through the bushes. Leaning her supple back against a tree, she whispered, "Kiss me, Freddy. Kiss me."

"Oh, Annette! If only you knew . . ."

"I do know." She came up on tiptoe to meet his mouth, placing her arms around his neck.

For a long moment, Freddy merely kissed her, his arms locked around her small waist. Then he tore himself away and looked down into her closed eyes. "Annette," he breathed hoarsely. "Oh, Annette. I don't know if I can hold myself back. You drive a man wild!"

She wanted to cry, "Don't hold back!" but that would have been too forward, too shocking. Instead, she drew his head down to hers again. This time she kissed him, passionately, pressing her firm breasts against his pounding chest, her body answering for her.

Either Freddy must have understood her intent or was now unable to hold himself in check, for his hands sought the mounds of her bosom, clawing at the unyielding yellow fabric.

Annette groaned, wanting to feel the pressure of his fingers against her naked flesh. Why didn't he unfasten the buttons on her bodice? Should she? Finally, be began to fumble wth the tiny, awkward pearls, but they were slippery in his trembling fingers.

Well, she would just have to help him. Why should she feel embarrassed? She pulled away slightly. "Here," she laughed weakly, "let me, Freddy." As deftly as possible under the circumstances, she undid the buttons. Now only her black camisole stood in the way.

Freddy drew in a quivering breath at the sight. Reverently, he cupped her large firm breasts in his hands. Finally, after some awkward tugging on the bodice of the camisole, her breasts sprang free above the lace.

Annette felt somewhat ridiculous then, leaning against the tree trunk with her yellow dress half off her shoulders, hampering the movement of her arms. Her camisole had slipped uncomfortably down nearly to her waist and Freddy's eyes and hands were devouring her naked breasts. If only she were free of the dress altogether. But how was it done? How did other women manage gracefully under similar circumstances? Was the man supposed to help her, or was she to shed her clothes herself? After a few moments, she whispered, averting her eyes, "Perhaps I should get out of my dress, Freddy."

"Oh!" He drew back, surprised. Maybe he hadn't expected her to be so bold, so forward, to go so far with him.

Shrugging inwardly, Annette eased her arms out of the dress and let it fall in a yellow circle around her feet. Now she was standing there with only her petticoat, bloomers and camisole to cover herself. The camisole was, of course, still halfway down to her waist.

"You're so beautiful." He seemed unable to move.

She lowered her eyes. "Could I lie down on your jacket, Freddy?" she asked, wondering why she was the one who had to suggest it.

Turning scarlet, Freddy quickly shed his coat and spread it out as neatly as possible on the cool, rough ground. Annette eased herself down onto it, immediately uncomfortable. Freddy followed suit, taking her into his arms, stroking her bosom heatedly, his weight too heavy for her against the hard earth.

When he did no more than exclaim over her beauty and fondle her sensitive nipples, she decided, calculatingly, to ease down her petticoat. This was not too difficult, save that she had to squirm awkwardly under his oppressive weight. Now if only she could free herself from the bloomers. And what on earth could she do about her boots? Leave them on? How obscene! Still, there would be no unbuttoning them, not in this predicament. If only it had been summer and she'd worn slippers.

Uncertain as to how to proceed, and with Freddy seemingly lost in the charms of her bosom, Annette whispered, "Would you help me with my bloomers?"

He drew back. "Annette," he choked, "are we . . . are you really going to let me . . . I mean, are you sure?"

"Yes."

And so Freddy helped her then, breathing heavily, exclaiming over her beauty as her full nakedness was exposed to his hungry eyes. She lay there, waiting, still clad in the garter belt, her hose and boots, but ready for him nonetheless.

Freddy's hand stroked her flat stomach, moved lower. Groping inside the garter belt, he found her secret, soft flesh. "Oh, God, Annette! Oh God!" he moaned.

Quickly then, he undid his suspenders, unfastened

his pants and eased them down. He wasn't going to take them off, she realized, seeing his trousers hanging limply around his knees, his member hard and swollen, perched above her ominously.

If she hadn't been breathing so hard, waiting for the exquisite moment when he would drive himself deep into her pulsing body, she would have laughed at their ludicrous appearance. But as it was, she closed her eyes, saying only, "Yes, Freddy, yes!"

She opened her slim legs to him, arched her back, felt his hips touch her inner thighs between the straps of the garter belt. Her abdomen twisted in knots, waiting, crying out to be pierced. God, how she wanted to be taken, plundered, ravished, fulfilled! She knew now. Rolf had taught her.

Then, mercifully, he found the right place and slowly entered her. She clung to him, arching and grinding her hips. He withdrew quickly, entered again, each thrust more rapid than the last until she was writhing with pleasure, her body demanding release.

Abruptly, Freddy cried out. It was so fast she couldn't believe he was already shuddering above her. She twisted and moaned beneath him. He fell against her, sweating and panting.

But no! she thought frantically. He can't be done! She wasn't fulfilled yet! "Oh Freddy," she sobbed, begging. "Please, don't stop now!"

"I . . . oh," he breathed, then began to move inside her again, but it was not the same. There was no urgency, no driving rhythm.

Annette closed her eyes, tried not to think, only to feel. She thrust up against him, working hard now for release, perspiring. She moaned, reaching the height, cried out, moaned again and fell back against the hard ground.

It was over. She had been fulfilled for the second

time now. For a fleeting moment, she allowed herself, while struggling for air beneath his weight, to compare the two men. Her conclusions were not to her liking. She drove the thought aside.

Freddy was whispering, moving away. "Annette, oh Annette! Can you ever forgive me?"

"Forgive you?" She sat up, watching him pull his pants back up hurriedly. "For what?"

"For taking your virginity. I'm so . . . such a beast! Please, say you forgive me?"

Her virginity? But he couldn't actually think . . .? She began dressing, too. What should she say to Freddy? Should she lie or tell him the truth?

Her silence, however, only drove him to greater depths of remorse. "I knew you'd hate me," he was saying.

"But I don't hate you," she exclaimed then, redoing the buttons on her dress. "It was wonderful, Freddy. It wasn't your fault."

"Yes, it was. I forced you." He put his head in his hands.

Annette pulled his hands away, forcing him to meet her eyes. "It was not your fault, Freddy," she said firmly. "I wanted it, too."

"How forgiving you are!" he cried. "I don't deserve it, Annette. I'm a brute. And of course we'll be married at once—"

"What?" The word exploded from her lips.

"I want to marry you, Annette. Surely you can't think I would let you face this shame alone."

She could not believe her ears. Suddenly, unthinkingly, she laughed.

"Annette," he soothed, trying to take her in his arms. "I know you're upset now, but as soon as we're married you'll feel better. Things like this happen. It wasn't your fault."

This was too much! She had to make him understand, put a stop to this insane talk of marriage. "Freddy," she said, sobering, "I don't want to get married. It's very, very sweet of you to ask, but no. I'm not ready yet."

"But," he sputtered in disbelief, "your virginity!"

She had better tell him. If she didn't, God only knew what he might do or the guilt feelings he would suffer later.

She got up and took his hand, leading him down the hillside. "Freddy," she began, "you'll think I'm terrible, no doubt, but you did not take my virginity. I've been with a man before."

He froze in his tracks. "You weren't a virgin?"

She smiled up at him weakly. "No. I wasn't. Honestly."

A heavy silence fell between them as Freddy digested this new information. Finally, he said, "It doesn't matter. I want to marry you anyway. Truly, Annette. I love you so."

Was there no putting him off? "No, Freddy," she said firmly. "There will be no marriage. I don't love you. When I do marry, it will be for love, when I'm ready. Not now."

A great sadness filled his soft brown eyes. "But I love you!"

Annette squeezed his hand. "There is a difference between love and lust, Freddy. I don't think you love me any more than I love you. Don't you see?"

The revelation was so clear to Annette that she was stunned at her own mature reasoning. It was not clear to Freddy, however.

"What if . . . if there is a child? Please, Annette, you can't go through this alone."

"There will not be a child. And Freddy, for God's

sake, you must understand that I don't want to be married yet. I have a dream to fulfill first. I'm too young. I want to live all I can before settling down. Do you understand?"

Freddy studied her for an endless moment. "You baffle me, Annette," he muttered finally. "But I think you really are serious. I don't quite understand all this, but . . ."

"You will, someday. Women are changing, Freddy. There will come a time when we will have equality with men. When that happens, we will be free to do as we choose."

"But that's shocking!"

"Yes," she replied, musingly. "Isn't it?"

Annette let herself back into the house only to be met by a thundering voice.

"And where," shouted her father, the chandelier in the hall tinkling, "have you been?"

"Daddy," she caught her breath, "you frightened me."

"Where have you been!"

"You needn't shout at me," Annette protested. "I merely went for a long walk. It's a beautiful autumn day."

Edward Tofler let out his breath in a low whistle. His face was still splotched with anger. "By God, you'd better not be lying to me."

"Daddy," she frowned, "where else would I have been?"

"I don't know. Meeting someone, for all I know."

Annette feigned shock. "Meeting someone?" she cried with indignation. And then a mental picture seized her mind: Freddy, standing above her, his trousers sagging in loose folds at his knees. "How could you say . . . how could you even think such a horrible thing!" She swept past her father, her skirt rustling in contrived anger, a smile lurking just under the surface as she mounted the stairs.

Chapter 11

The December light in her studio was beginning to dull. Annette sighed and put down her palette. This was the first oil she had attempted since her return from Paris, and it was giving her a lot of difficulty. The painting, she had thought from time to time over the past few weeks, was like a baby that didn't want to be born.

It was a simple enough picture, just a vase of dried grasses. Monsieur Cormon had always told her that a still life was good for discipline, and although she would have preferred to paint puppies or alley cats or dray horses, she had decided to follow his advice. Accordingly, she had picked some tall, golden grasses and brought a delicately beautiful Chinese vase from her room at home. She had set the arrangement on an old black velvet skirt she'd found in her closet. It was a striking subject, but on canvas it had somehow lost all interest and become humdrum.

She stood back and cocked her head, studying it. Perhaps she should mute the Chinese design on the vase so as not to take away from the overall effect. Or, on the other hand, perhaps she should make it bolder and the center of focus. How was one to know? She wished her scrawny instructor were standing at her shoulder, scolding in his rapid-fire French. He would know what to do. Experience was required, failures as well as successes, she decided. But was that enough? She was terribly afraid that it took an inborn sort of knowledge that only the true artist possessed, and not the ordinary person. The thought chilled her.

She could ask Bernard. Yes, he would very likely give her good advice. His eye was critical, yet accurate. She'd have to drop by his studio, maybe tomorrow, and ask him to come over.

As she cleaned up the brushes and paint, Annette was pensive. Would she someday have a sudden breakthrough, an illumination? Or would she work for years, slowly improving until she was satisfied? She guessed that an artist was never quite satisfied. No matter how well something was portrayed, it could have been done better.

She paused and stood in the center of the small room, examining her painting again. It lacked life. Her technique was fine. There were no real mistakes, but the study evoked no emotional response. It lacked the heart-gripping sensuousness of the great masters. Any moderately talented painter could have done it. It was not the work of a true artist.

Sighing again, Annette sank into one of the paint-spattered chairs and cupped her chin in her hand. When, *when* would she be able to do something good? She'd had two affairs, posed for a sculptor, suffered the agonies of humiliation with Rolf and scaled the heights of happiness at her ball. Wasn't that experience enough? Should she go out and seduce someone else? The game was beginning to pall. How much living and suffering must she endure to fulfill herself as a person? What exactly did she have to do to become a great painter?

Sometimes her quest for living, for suffering, as

Cormon had put it, seemed almost too comical. Here she was, trying to grab life by the tail, while other people, like Vivian and her experience with the miscarriage, had life and suffering come to them so easily.

If only I were older, she mused, angry at herself for being only nineteen. Even Freddy Sims, in his letter to her last week, had made mention of her youth. He had said, ". . . and so I shall wait for you, Annette. Upon thinking about your words that day, I realized that you are indeed too young for marriage. You must sow your wild oats, my love. And I shall wait . . ." If only Freddy knew how close to the truth he had come. But as for waiting for her—he would have a long wait. She had replied to his letter at once. With as much kindness and consideration as possible, she had made it clear that there could never be a marriage between them and that, in fact, she might never marry anyone. It was better to make a clean break so that no one suffered overly long. It was only fair to Freddy and also to herself.

She took off her smock, cleaned her hands and put on her fur-trimmed coat. Locking the door carefully behind her, Annette slowly descended the stairs of the building to the lobby. She could hear the hubbub coming from Coppa's restaurant, right next to the lobby. It was always full of young artists, talking, gesticulating, singing, eating, drinking. Oh, how she'd love to join them, to go in and sit down, order a coffee, nod to acquaintances. She'd pictured it all many times. "And how is your latest masterpiece coming, Annette?" they'd ask her. She'd smile benignly, knowingly, sweep a graceful hand. "Oh, it's always difficult, you know." They'd hang on her every word, ask when her next show would be and who had given her the latest huge commission. It would be wonderful.

A lady, however, did not go into a restaurant

alone. Even with her liberated ideas, Annette did not quite have the nerve. Maybe she'd get Bernard to take her.

Just as she was on her way out the door, she heard the desk clerk's voice call to her, "Miss Annette!" She went to the desk. No matter what time of day she was there, the thin clerk, she still didn't know his name, was at his post. She'd begun to wonder if he ever went anywhere else. Maybe he ate there, slept there. Maybe he was glued to the floor behind the desk. "There's a letter for you," he was saying. He handed her a white envelope.

"Thank you," she replied automatically, sticking the letter in her reticule. She wanted this time to herself, wanted to think some more about her painting and puzzle things out. It was probably another artist wanting a model. That was wonderful, of course, but she didn't have the time to take on another job now that she'd begun working herself.

The ride up the hill on the cable car was always one of her favorite times. There was a marvelous view of the steep drop of the hill, dotted with houses and steeples, then the dark, wind-touched bay and the towns gracing its opposite rim. She loved the busy jumble of buildings, the color of the trees that showed in masses around the buildings. And, too, one could sense the throbbing progress of San Francisco, with its new skyscrapers going up downtown. The constant clatter of building, the noise from the heavy traffic, the yells and barks and whinnies and creaking wheels all combined into one cheerful symphony of sound.

It was a grey, stormy day in early December. Great, towering, dark clouds were rolling in off the Pacific. It wasn't raining yet. But it would.

Annette got off at her stop and walked the few blocks home, pulling her coat tightly around her against the rising wind. At least she didn't have to worry about facing a quarrel with her father when she got home. Somehow, since the last big fight they'd had around the time of the ball, he'd given up trying to control her. He seemed distant these days, absent-minded. She was worried about him. He was acting oddly and his color wasn't good. Poor Daddy, she thought, it's as if something is eating away at him. But what? My painting? She couldn't imagine that was serious enough. Maybe he misses Mother after all these years. Maybe he feels lonely in his old age. Whatever, it made her life so much more comfortable not to have to fight him at every turn that she almost welcomed his silence.

When she got to her cheerful and sweet-smelling room, glowing warm and rosy, she remembered the letter in her reticule. Almost indifferently, she took it out, opened the envelope and slid out the note. The moment she had unfolded it, something struck her. It was the handwriting. Her eyes raced to the signature. My God! It read, "Sincerely, Rolf Karman." Quickly her eyes flew over the few boldly penned lines.

> Dear Annette,
> I wish, firstly, to thank you for inviting me to your ball and supper. It was an enchanting evening.

Ha! she thought, he knows full well that I never invited him and that I didn't want him there.

> And secondly, I want to remind you again that we have unfinished work to complete. I am in need of a model to finish my painting and you, my dear, have not fulfilled your obligations as a model. On a strictly

professional basis, I would like you to continue your sittings until the painting is done. If you so decide, I will expect you next Tuesday at ten o'clock in the morning.

Of all the nerve, she thought. He expects that if he just snaps his fingers, I'll come running. Well, Mr. Rolf Karman would have to be disappointed. She could never, never put herself in such a position again. Why, the man was disgustingly arrogant. She had made a dreadful mistake in having anything to do with him. So, she'd just chalk up her error in judgment to experience and not make the same mistake twice. Deliberately, she crumpled up the paper and dropped it in her wastebasket. So much for Rolf Karman.

Dinner that night was very quiet. Jensen was home, but Edward still had not returned by the time the meal was served.

"Where is Daddy?" asked Annette, spooning up the chocolate mousse.

"Said he had some work to do at the office and not to expect him."

"Again?"

Jensen shrugged. "Perhaps he finds our company distasteful."

"Jensen!"

"Well, he certainly seems to be avoiding us lately. In my case, it's just as well."

Annette stared into space, thinking again that there must be something wrong with her father. She turned her golden gaze on Jensen. "Is the business in trouble? Something like that?"

"Not that I can tell. In fact, it seems to be booming."

She frowned pensively. She had given a lot of thought to her father's behavior since her return from

Paris and to the things that seemed to upset him so. Her painting, of course, was one. But there was another subject that caused him to either lose his temper or grow strangely pale and distant.

"Then it's Cecile." Annette spoke the words firmly, decisively.

Jensen's head snapped up. "What?"

"He's heard from Cecile and is afraid to tell us. She's in some sort of trouble."

"Ridiculous. What makes you think he even cares about her?"

"Oh, things." Annette tapped the rim of her wine glass with a fingernail. "He gets extremely upset whenever her name is mentioned."

"That's absurd." Jensen wiped his lips with a napkin. "That man cares nothing about anything but himself and his business. His children have always come in a poor second. And so did his wife when she was alive."

"I'm not so sure," Annette mused. "It's got to be either Cecile or my painting."

"Don't overestimate his concern for you. Once he saw that he'd lost in his little bid for power, he gave up, that's all."

"Perhaps."

"Well," Jensen pushed his chair back from the table, "I'm off to the opera tonight."

"With friends," she asked, "or a special friend?"

"With friends," he emphasized the word. "The women in this town bore me. They're all exact replicas of their mothers and each other. Dull. Empty-headed."

"Surely there must be a few."

"Well, if there are, I haven't found them," laughed Jensen ruefully.

Jensen went out, leaving Annette alone in the huge, hushed edifice. She wandered aimlessly around the downstairs for a while, then climbed the broad staircase to her room. After changing into a dressing gown, she dismissed Vivian for the night and propped herself up in bed to read.

It was only a few minutes before she realized that her mind was not comprehending the words. She put the book down. Outside her window, she could hear the howling wind and the slashing rain. It was a real winter storm.

Restlessly, Annette moved to the window. After searching the wet darkness and finding nothing there, she turned away. The crumpled ball of paper in the wastebasket caught her eye. Reaching down, as if directed by some external force, she picked up the letter and smoothed it out. Magnetized, her eyes rested on the words, ". . . not fulfilled your obligations. . . ." Her lips drew together in a tight line. She knew he was deliberately baiting her with those words, hoping to reel her in by challenging her courage and pride. She knew that instinctively. At the same time, she knew she'd hate for him to think she was a coward, afraid to face him. She didn't like to leave a job undone. It was just part of her personality, she guessed, but it galled her not to finish something she'd started. Rolf Karman had hit on a sore point. And his very arrogance, while angering Annette, made her want to conquer it at the same time.

"I just might go and surprise the bejesus out of him," she whispered to the storm-tossed night, to the rose damask walls of her room. "I just might go."

Strangely enough, Annette was even more nervous about her impending visit to Rolf's studio this time than last. Of course, in one way, it was understandable after what had occurred between them. She had an awful time deciding what to wear. The peasant outfit would not do. Dignity should be the keynote, she decided. She'd wear her most elegant clothes, even if they were more difficult to remove. Perhaps her attire would inspire respect in Rolf. That he was utterly lacking in respect for her irked her no end.

Once or twice, in an introspective mood, it had occurred to her that her behavior with him had not warranted his unqualified respect. But he didn't have to make it so obvious. He had completely refused to play the social game, and it had caught her off guard. Well, this time she'd know better. She'd know just how to treat him—with cool, lofty condescension.

Annette decided on a well-tailored suit she had bought in Paris. It was a fine soft wool in a glorious shade of mauve. The jacket was short and fitted, the skirt slim and clinging in front, draped and bustled in back. The jacket was decorated with swirling arabesques of jet beads and there was a cunning little hat to match, which was trimmed with black feathers. She turned in front of the upright mirror, narrowing her catlike eyes at her reflection. Yes, she looked infinitely poised and dignified. He'd be sure to notice.

At ten o'clock sharp, she stood in front of the Astor House. Outwardly, she was studiously calm. Was he expecting her? She wondered just how sure of himself he was, or how sure of her. She wondered, too, whether she was doing the right thing. Still, even if she was misguided, she was determined not to let him have the last word.

Her heart pounded drumbeats in her ears as she climbed the stairs to his suite. She took a deep breath, squeezed her eyes shut for a moment and knocked. The sound rang in her ears. She waited. Maybe he'd left, had forgotten her or something. Maybe she wouldn't have to face his mocking smile, the dark eyes that pinned her down as if she were a butterfly, his intimidating air of self-assurance.

But no, he was there. She heard the handle turn, saw the door begin to open. She steeled herself for his first sarcastic remark.

"Annette," he said calmly. His face was perfectly still, concealing anything he might feel. "Come in."

She felt somehow let down. It was as if nothing had ever happened between them, as if they were old friends or acquaintances. It was all so casual, so matter-of-fact. There were none of the innuendoes of the previous visit, none of the nervous thrills, the unexpected pauses, the uncomfortable looks. This was all business. Perhaps his letter had been perfectly serious and straightforward.

She undressed behind the curtain and took her place on the bench, resuming her pose. He did not touch her. They could have been working together like this for years.

Rolf spoke little, only an occasional request to move a hand or leg. He busied himself with the brush, a frown of concentration on his brow. Annette felt as if she weren't really there. It might have been a statue he was so assiduously painting.

She watched him closely, attempting to understand the extraordinary fascination this man evoked in her. He was in his usual working outfit, an open-necked white shirt with the sleeves rolled up. The shirt was an elegant one, with tucks and ruffles down the front, but he wore it as if it were a castoff. His tanned, golden-fuzzed chest was visible where the shirt was open and she watched the corded muscles of his forearms working under his smooth skin.

The man was undeniably attractive in a bold, savage way. His high cheekbones shadowed his dark eyes and the flat planes of his cheeks caught the light with a kind of silken gleam, setting off the strong, square line of his jaw. Even the carefully tended mustache above his wide, curving lips was attractive, and the sun-streaked, rough hair invited straying fingers to run through it.

He was working with complete concentration and didn't notice Annette's rapt perusal. Once he turned away from her to reach for something, and the muscles of his back and shoulders, tensing, pulled the thin fabric of the shirt tight. Her breath caught in her throat at the pure masculine beauty of his body.

She felt an unbearable tension building up within her. She had done him a favor, after all, coming here like this after his unspeakable rudeness. And he'd never even said thank you. She might as well have been a complete stranger, a woman off the street, someone he didn't know or care about at all. Merely a model.

Well, that was what he'd proposed. A business arrangement. Then why did she feel so annoyed, so unappreciated? Something had to happen or she'd burst with frustration.

"Isn't it time for a rest?" she asked finally. "I mean, you've been at it for so long."

He looked at her. It took him a moment to focus his attention on her as a live person. "Yes, perhaps this is enough for today," he answered slowly. "I've accomplished quite a lot."

Languidly, Annette unfolded her limbs, stretching. Damn it, she wanted some reaction from him: anger, mockery, laughter, anything but this cold disinterest. His eyes, analyzing her body so closely, had raked paths of hot lava over her as he'd been painting. And yet he seemed indifferent.

Ignoring the sheet, Annette moved to the alcove

where her clothes were. An idea struck her. She began to dress slowly, leaving the curtain wide open. He couldn't help but notice now.

First the bloomers, edged in Belgian lace, then the sheer silk stockings, slowly, stretching out one curvaceous leg at a time. She sneaked a look from under the veil of her lashes. Was he watching? No, he was cleaning his brushes! She slipped into the silk petticoat, the black Parisian camisole, the corset. It took a few minutes to get the corset on properly. The contraption went on so much more easily when Vivian helped her. She looked up. Still he was busy, not noticing her. Any other man would have been panting at her feet by now.

Annette pulled on her blouse, a purple silk with ruffles, and buttoned it excruciatingly slowly. As she was getting into her skirt, she marveled at his lack of attention. What kind of man was he, anyway? How many women had he brought up here, seduced and discarded? Did Eleanor Fairchild visit him here, sit for him perhaps? Make love in the same bed on which she had lost her virginity? My God!

She looked up, struggling with the hooks she was trying to fasten. Had he forgotten she was there? She spoke the words almost before they had formed themselves in her mind. "Rolf, excuse me, could you help me with these hooks? I just can't seem to . . ." Annette was afraid to raise her eyes to meet his. She kept fumbling with the hooks that were at the back of her skirt, but it was useless. She couldn't even begin to do them up. Sensing his approach, Annette felt her breath catch in her throat. Her heart was pounding. His nearness was so disturbing that he could have been a jungle beast, dangerous and just as intimidating. As Rolf moved toward her, his form blotting out the light, Annette felt like a small animal caught in a trap. A trap of her own making, her frenzied mind shrilled silently at her.

"Back here?" he asked quietly, putting a large hand on her waist and turning her around so that her back was to him.

"Yes," she whispered, barely able to keep herself from leaping at his touch.

His hands worked at the fastening. She held her breath, afraid that if she took a gulp of air, her skin might press against his fingers. The idea of touching him seemed somehow unbearable. Annette could feel his breath on her back, between her shoulder blades, like a knife poised to violate her flesh. His familiar scent filled her nostrils, a uniquely masculine odor. He was so close, so close. Then he was turning her back around, his hands scalding her arms. A faintly sardonic smile curved his lips. "There," he said, holding on to her arms for the barest fraction of a second too long.

Now, she thought, now he will bend his head down and kiss me. Surely he will, right now. Her eyes began to close, inviting him. But he didn't.

Later, as she rode home in a hansom cab, Annette went over and over the scene in her mind. She prayed Rolf hadn't seen through her, seen her desire, naked and unmasked. Annette could only hope he hadn't noticed her quivering, her half-closed eyes, her quickened breathing.

Annette's response to Rolf filled her with shame and anger and self-loathing. She wondered how she could have behaved like that. Thank the stars Rolf, at least, had had the sense or control or disinterest to go no further.

She was quiet at dinner, on which Edward commented, and quietly pensive later in her room. A singular thought invaded her mind. Was she falling in love with Rolf Karman? Was that the explanation for her reaction to him, for the weakness of her flesh when he was near? Was that, really, why she had returned to his studio? Was this unsatisfied, turbulent feeling called love?

Chapter 12

It was a rare occasion when Jensen met Annette for lunch. Usually, he was far too busy at Tofler Transport to lunch in leisure and often these days he didn't even slow down for a quick bite in the middle of the day. Today, however, was an occasion. He had just sewn up the huge army contract which had run into endless snags in the previous weeks. Even Edward Tofler had given up hope of an agreement. It was Jensen, and Jensen alone, who had persisted in wading through the miles of bureaucratic red tape to acquire the proper signatures.

Annette was delighted that her brother had chosen her to celebrate with, for she was certain he had far lovelier women with whom he could have dined. She dressed in her finest day gown, an elegant green silk with a high ruffled collar and long leg-of-mutton sleeves. The hat perched on top of her auburn ringlets was made of the same silk and sported sleek chartreuse feathers which streamed out from behind.

"You look ravishing, my dear sister," exclaimed Jensen as she swept into his office. "Absolutely beautiful."

"Oh, go on now." Annette laughed and sat down

carefully in the chair beside his desk. "Where's Daddy?"

"Our father," he announced with a touch of sarcasm, "has not been in this office for three days now. I don't suppose he's at home now, is he?"

Annette frowned. "No. At least, he wasn't there when I left."

Seeing the worry on his sister's face, Jensen rose from his desk and placed a reassuring hand on her shoulder. "Don't fret. I'm sure there's a logical explanation for his behavior of late." He helped her to her feet. "Now let's go to lunch. Where would you like to eat?"

"Anywhere," she answered distractedly. "Perhaps he's away on business? Or maybe . . . Do you suppose he might have a lady friend?"

Jensen raised a dark brow. "A lady friend? Now, who would take an interest in our pompous, domineering father?"

"Oh Jensen, don't be cruel. He's not so bad. And besides, he's rich," she added mischievously.

"Humph."

They ate a leisurely meal at the United States restaurant. The establishment had a saloon on one side, filled with men drinking their business lunches, and a handsomely decorated dining room on the other side. The dining room was a blend of dark woods, leaded glass, red velvet chairs and an abundance of flowing ferns. It was a perfectly proper choice of restaurants for a young couple. San Francisco society had taken to dining out frequently. It was the very latest thing to do, an opportunity to show off their fashionable clothes, their gay and carefree spirits and their newest romantic companions. Mingling with this fashionable crowd were the poorly dressed, self-consciously intellectual Bohemians.

As Annette and Jensen were finishing their meal with cups of steaming coffee, their appetites pleasantly satisfied, Annette spotted a familiar figure. He was on the other side of the open double doors that led to the saloon, leaning one elbow on the polished bar surface.

"Why, that's Bernard Maduro."

"Who?" asked Jensen, glancing up.

"An artist friend of mine. A sculptor."

"Looks it," Jensen smirked, noting the man's casual shirt and shabby, loose jacket.

"Oh stop, now." Annette rose. "Would you mind if I spoke to him for just a moment?"

"Well . . ." Before he could stop her, his sister was already halfway to the doors. She tapped the dark-haired man on the shoulder.

"Bernard," Annette said, smiling.

He turned and grinned as he took in her rich attire with a sweeping glance. "Why, Annette," he exclaimed, "you look wonderful!" And then, "What on earth are you doing in a saloon?"

"Oh!" she laughed, seeing the men's heads turn in her direction. "I'm lunching with my brother next door. Did you think I'd taken to drink?"

"No." He looked around quickly, seeing the avid attention Annette was receiving. "Say," he lowered his voice, "I don't suppose you'd like to come over again sometime and see the finished sculpture?"

"Oh, yes!" she cried in delight, her hazel eyes sparkling. The men's hearts throbbed. "Could I see it now, today?"

"Well . . . what about your brother? Does he know about your modeling?" Bernard nodded to where Jensen sat, a frown creasing his handsome features.

"He knows some," she hesitated. "About my studio, anyway. I can walk him back to Daddy's office and then meet you here."

"Well, I suppose it would be all right. But I'll watch for you outside. Don't come back here alone."

"Why, Bernard!" Her tinkling laughter filled the air delightfully. "You're such a gentleman."

Annette did walk Jensen back, promising to hire a cab home. Then she walked straight back to the saloon and met Bernard as arranged. After she saw the sculpture, which was truly a beautiful, bold work of art, she persuaded him to come with her to the Montgomery Block to see her canvas.

Mounting the steps to her studio, she paused. "It's a terrible painting, Bernard," she said, frustrated. "I'm just lost."

"Well," he chuckled with understanding, "let's just take a look at it. I'll wager it's not all that terrible."

And to Bernard, it wasn't. He held the canvas of the weeds in the Chinese vase up to catch the light. As he studied it, twisting it this way and that, Annette worried her lower lip with her teeth and wrung her hands expectantly.

"Umm," he responded noncommittally.

"Well?" She held her breath.

"Not bad." Bernard set the canvas back onto the easel. "Not bad at all. In fact," he turned toward her, a smile playing on his fine lips, "it's good, Annette."

"Oh? Really? I mean—"

"It's good, I said. Not great." He glanced around the small room, his eyes coming to rest on the Chinese vase. He walked over and picked it up. "See this clear blue here?" He held it up to the light. "You've missed how the sun strikes it, illuminates it."

Annette furrowed her brow. "But then there would be too much focal point. Cormon said—"

"Yes, I know," Bernard interrupted. "The Impressionists of France try not to direct the eye on any one aspect of the painting. But your style and lines are clearly different. You see, it's as if you've missed the climax of the painting. Your style is more defined than that of the Impressionists and frankly, I like the daring lines you apply far better." He paused, studying her momentarily. "I think, Annette, that if you let your hand go, you may very well make a fine artist. This still life is good, natural. How long did it take you?"

"A week," she replied, her spirits brighter. "Do you really think I have possibilities?"

"Most definitely. Although," he added, "I'm a sculptor, not a painter, and my eye is not as trained as some."

Nevertheless, Annette respected his criticism. Bernard did have a good eye. Once he'd pointed it out, she'd realized immediately that the blue in the vase needed to be enhanced. It was odd, but she'd toned it down purposefully, thinking the light on the vase took away from the overall effect. Why hadn't she left it the way it was? She wondered whether she would ever have the eye to see her mistakes.

They talked for a while longer. Finally, Bernard left, promising to visit her at the same time the next day at the studio to see her corrections.

Annette buttoned on her smock and mixed her colors on the palette, carefully squeezing deep indigo blue next to the white and dabbing at the colors until she felt they were mixed correctly. She walked over to the canvas, cocked her head to one side, then returned to the tubes of paint and added a touch more white.

"There," she said, pleased with the color which was much bolder than what she'd used before. With a heavy, daring stroke, she slashed away the dull blue with the new sunlit color. Yes.

She applied a thick, raised cross stroke. Even better.

The next day, she awaited Bernard's arrival with a pounding heart. Was the canvas really improved? She thought so.

When he finally arrived, agonizingly late, she pushed him over to the easel sitting in the light that poured in through the window. "Well?"

"Beautiful. Bold and beautiful, Annette. It's so much better."

She beamed. "I'm thinking of doing a waterfront scene—a few buildings, run-down of course. And the water, maybe a boat moored . . ."

"Yes?" He eyed her carefully.

"Would you walk down there with me? I've got to do a sketch first. I shouldn't go there alone."

"To the Barbary Coast, Annette?"

"Yes. Oh, please, Bernard. Please?"

"Really, Annette. I mean, if it were just me. But you. Well, you're so lovely. It's not a good idea."

"Please?"

"Well, damn. All right. But tomorrow, in the middle of the day."

She threw her arms around his neck and kissed him full on the lips.

"Hey there," Bernard pulled away sharply. "No more of that! I'm only human, after all, my dear."

She laughed. Her cheer dissolved. "Bernard?" she raised her hazel eyes to his dark ones. "If you want, well, we could. . . . Never mind."

A smile tugged on his lips. "Could what?"

"You know . . ."

"I swear, Annette," he began, "you are a caution! But to be entirely honest, yes, I would like very much to sleep with you and I think you're ready. But I also admire you as a colleague. Let's both think on it. Anything is possible," he winked.

"Yes. Anything . . ." She returned his smile impishly.

The next day, as they strolled down toward the Barbary Coast just after the lunch hour, Annette thought about how very dear Bernard had become to her. And, yes, she would very much like to bed him, but perhaps he was right. Perhaps they should get to know each other better and decide just exactly how they felt about each other. There was loads of time for other things. It was fun to tease him, though, and he seemed to take her flirtation lightly, with good humor. If only all men were so easy to be with. If only Rolf, for instance, had not shut her out so coolly and calculatingly, treated her as if she were a child. Frederick Sims with his double standard would never understand her either. Yet, she mused, there was no love between her and Bernard, only kinship and understanding. What would it take to have friendship and camaraderie with a man, and love, too?

They walked, arm in arm, into the heart of the infamous Coast. Even at this early hour, sailors swayed drunkenly on street corners, swearing, laughing, picking up blowzy, short-skirted chippies, fondling them in public. The saloons and gambling houses and brothels were already busy, their doors wide open, the proprietors luring the customers into their havens with outrageous, exotic tales.

For fifty years, San Francisco's docks had been the port of entry for the American West. All of the necessary staple goods had found their way through her harbor and into the consumers' hands. It was a throbbing, vital port. Those who had not found their way over the snowcapped barrier mountains to the great Pacific coast had come by ship through the protected Golden Gate and made their lives on the hilly shore. The docks themselves swelled with warehouses.

Some of the original wooden structures had survived, but most of the buildings were made of brick or stone. All of the warehouses contained cargoes from the world over. Situated a block from the lapping shore were the infamous gambling houses, brothels and saloons which had given name to the Barbary Coast. They attracted the worst sorts.

Annette took in the scenes with delight, giggling, pointing, noticing that there were other well-dressed couples visiting the Coast. Obviously, it was a tourist attraction, so there was nothing wrong in her being there. She hadn't known.

Bernard smiled at her observations, noticed how many seamen watched her with keen interest, their tongues wetting their lips. Annette Tofler could do that to a man. She was perhaps the most desirable little wench he had ever encountered. She was quick witted, too. Not much escaped her eye. Even when she observed her surroundings silently, she was digesting, learning, questing for knowledge. What an unusual woman. What a perfect mate she would make someday for the man of her choosing.

While they took in the sights, sounds and odors of the Barbary Coast, he laughed to himself ruefully. He would not bed Annette. No. If he were to allow himself that, he would be forever under her devilish spell—forever hopelessly in love with this young, vital, exquisite woman. After all, he mused as he watched her suck on a fresh oyster at an open-air bar, he had seen, sculpted and agonized over her flesh. He knew what forbidden charms she possessed without having actually tasted them.

Down by the waterfront, where the steamers, ferryboats and schooners rocked gently against their moorings, where incoming and outgoing cargoes littered the damp, wooden docks, Annette pulled out her sketch pad. Artfully, she stroked in charcoal, reproducing with great alacrity the exotic scene.

Bernard saw her safely back to the California Street cable car, promising that they would venture around the city again someday. Annette kissed him good-bye excitedly, her cheeks rosy from the fresh air and the thrill of adventure. She could hardly wait until they met again and toured the city's secrets.

"Can we go to Chinatown?" she begged as she climbed into the car.

Bernard shook his head, amused. "Yes."

"Oh! When?"

"Day after tomorrow." He waved good-bye. "Same time, you little vixen!"

That night her father was home for dinner. Edward Tofler looked better than he had in weeks. He told his children that he had been out of town on unexpected business and Annette scolded him for not letting them know, for worrying them.

As she mounted the curving staircase to the second story, she was pleased with the way the dinner had gone. For once, her father had been pleasant, not asking her too much about her days or prying into her activities. Once, he had asked her if she was still painting. When she replied affirmatively, he said little, save that she should keep Vivian with her when she ventured out to the studio. Annette was quite shocked at the mention of her studio without an attendant lecture. She wondered if perhaps he had spoken to someone about her career and received advice favorable to her. Perhaps it had been a business acquaintance with a daughter, someone like that. At any rate, she was pleased.

That night before retiring, Annette worked on a final sketch of the waterfront scene which she would begin to put on canvas the next day. When Bernard joined her at the studio for their jaunt to Chinatown on the following day, she could seek his opinion on her format. It was wonderful to have someone look at her work with an honest, critical eye. It helped immensely. If only there were someone else. A second opinion would be even better. A painter, a good one, would be perfect.

But, she remembered only too clearly as she snuggled under her rose satin quilt, there was only one good painter in all of San Francisco whom she knew well enough to ask. Rolf Karman. And she'd be damned if she would ever ask his opinion.

With Bernard Maduro as her guide, San Francisco and its exotic districts unfolded before Annette's eyes. She tasted the life of Chinatown. Daring to enter a "crib" once, she commented on the sweet smell of opium and the dark, secret atmosphere. She developed a taste for the Oriental vegetable dishes served in the tourist restaurants. And all the while, she sketched avidly with her charcoal.

Almost daily now, she met with Bernard to spend the afternoon touring the city. On clear days, they would walk the pulsing streets. Whenever the December fog settled oppressively over the city, she would treat Bernard to lunch at one of the fine restaurants where they would chat for hours. He did most of the talking. He told her about his poverty-stricken childhood, about his hopes that Marxist socialism would cure the ills of the poor people of the world.

Often these days, Annette wondered whether she and Bernard would ever sleep together. Certainly the opportunity was there. She began to envision him naked, his slim, muscular body pressed to hers. Although smaller in frame than Freddy or Rolf, he was attractive. She sensed that he would be an excellent lover, could imagine him molding her flesh with reverence as if she were precious sculpture.

One sunny, clear day as they strolled down to the waterfront area, Annette ventured to ask, "Do you ever think about me at night?"

Bernard stopped, surveying her with his eyes. She was dressed in a dusty rose velvet dress with a matching cape, and her small hat was dangling from her slim hand. Her auburn curls caught the sun and danced with fire. Her ale-colored eyes were wide with expectation and her mouth was parted ever so slightly, the full lower lip promising secret delight. She was a vision. With a mere word, she could bring a strong man to his knees.

"Sometimes," he admitted. "But I've decided to spare myself the torture."

Her eyes widened still more. "The torture?"

Bernard chuckled softly. "Yes, my dear. The torture. You see, I fear the results of following my desire. You are quite a tempting morsel, Annette. I'm not at all sure I could resist locking you up and keeping you all for myself."

"Oh, come now, Bernard. You're teasing."

He did a strange thing then, and it frightened Annette a little. Taking hold of her shoulder roughly, he drew her toward him without care for the passers-by who stared in their direction, whispering. "Do you love me, Annette?" he demanded.

She was stunned, first by his manner and then by his question. "I . . ."

But whatever she was going to answer died on her lips as she suddenly became aware of another presence beside them.

"Good afternoon," came a hauntingly familiar voice. She stood frozen, speechless, locked in Bernard's firm hold. The tall, fair-haired man smiled. "Haven't seen you in quite a while, Bernard," he drawled smoothly. "How have you been?" Pointedly, he ignored Annette; she might as well not even have been there.

"Quite well." Bernard collected himself and dropped his hands from Annette's shoulders. "I say, do you two know one another? Rolf Karman," he said politely, "this is Miss Annette Tofler."

Rolf raked her boldly, leisurely, with dark, unreadable eyes. "Yes," he remarked easily, "we have met before."

Damn him! her mind shrieked. How dare he treat me so casually, so arrogantly!

She drew her glance quickly from his and focused her attention on Bernard. "Why, don't you remember, *dear*?" Bernard shot her a look of surprise but she didn't care. "Mr. Karman and, what was her name? Oh, yes. Mrs. Fairchild. They were at my ball. Jensen," she glanced again at Rolf, her heart threatening to burst, "invited Mr. Karman."

"Oh," muttered Bernard, plainly confused by Annette's manner.

"Yes." Rolf's smile faded. "And don't forget, Miss Tofler, that you have been modeling for me. Haven't you told Bernard?"

Annette was as shocked as if she had been slapped in the face. How could he? What sort of man would insult her in front of a friend? He certainly didn't have to mention that she had modeled for him. Not that she was ashamed of the fact. It was the way he had thrown it in Bernard's face. What a beast he was.

The awkward moment stretched out endlessly for Annette. Her hands gripping her sketch pad were white. She felt her face prickle with color as her eyes fixed on the pavement, unseeing. No one spoke. How could she save the situation? What must Bernard think of her now? She looked desperately up at Bernard, who gazed at her with amazement and then close speculation.

When he finally spoke, he kept his voice under tight control. "No, Rolf, she never mentioned a thing. How unlike you, Annette." His eyes pinned her to the spot.

Annette swallowed, felt the red splotches on her face deepen. "I . . . It didn't seem important at all, Bernard," she murmured. "And besides, I've finished modeling for Mr. Karman."

"Oh?" said Rolf, apparently unruffled.

Annette shot him a hateful look.

He continued, bent on having the last word and delighting in the embarrassment he was causing Annette and Bernard. "I shouldn't think, ma'am," he began again, deliberately, "that the job is finished when I still need you for one last sitting. And I might mention that you have, shall we say," he hesitated slightly for effect, "been paid already."

"Oh!" she gasped, swaying involuntarily against Bernard. This was the final humiliation. If Bernard had missed Rolf's hidden meaning then, of course, he would think she had taken money from Rolf and left a job incomplete.

She forced herself to gain some measure of control. Gathering her courage, holding on to whatever shred of dignity Rolf had left her, she lifted her eyes to meet his with courage. The tears threatening to spill over onto her hot cheeks turned her eyes to molten gold.

Rolf met her eyes knowingly. Leisurely, he dropped his gaze, letting it travel over her accusingly. After a long, agonizing moment, he bowed mockingly, glanced casually at the two of them and turned away. "Good day," he said simply, leaving at last. He strode away down the street confidently.

Annette drew in a deep, quavering breath as she watched him round the corner. Hatred blazed in her eyes. "I detest him!" she cried with outrage. "How could he . . .?"

"Calm down, Annette." Bernard placed an arm around her shoulder.

"But," she looked up into his eyes, "you don't really understand. He's so rude, so arrogant. He's just so horrible."

"And," Bernard added, lifting one eyebrow, "you slept with him."

The tears spilled over. Rolf had been so obvious, intimating that she had already been paid, raking her body with his eyes. The bastard. How could she explain to Bernard? What should she say to him? "It . . . it just happened . . ."

"A poor choice of lovers, I'd say, Annette."

"Oh, Bernard," she sobbed, "are you disgusted? Do you hate me now?"

"I'm merely jealous, Annette."

"Jealous?"

"Yes. You see, I've known Rolf for some time, my dear, and I've always respected him. I must tell you honestly that now I respect him even more for taking what I haven't the nerve to take. You, my dear." He paused, looking down into her surprised face. "After witnessing that little scene just now, Annette, I think that you may feel more for Mr. Rolf Karman than you would like to."

"No!" she cried, her throat closing over the word. "No . . . I don't . . . I can't . . ."

"Are you ever going to go back to finish sitting for him?"

"Heavens no! Besides, he was just saying that to be rude. As far as I know, he doesn't need me anymore."

"I see." Bernard looked thoughtful. He took her arm and led her down the street, back toward the central city. "Another thing," he said, "is that I do believe Rolf may like you a little more than he's letting on. Perhaps you two are playing a game."

"We are playing nothing!" she defended quickly. Still, as Bernard left her at the studio, promising he wasn't angry and being ever so understanding, Annette wasn't so certain. Perhaps she and Rolf really were playing out a little game. Each time their paths crossed, they were like actors on a stage. Keeping their true feelings hidden deep beneath the surface, they read their lines as if from a sheet of paper. It was all such a farce.

Bernard, who was quite observant, had said that Rolf seemed to like her more than he was letting on. But Rolf was seeing Eleanor Fairchild. Besides, why would he hide his true feelings if he cared a whit about Annette? She thought about the way Rolf had looked at her on the street. His deep brown eyes had ravished her body as if she were a chippy. Annette couldn't help but wonder why he would look at her so accusingly if he didn't care something about her. How dare he insult her in front of Bernard! And what could make him think so ill of her?

When the answer came to her, she felt as if she had been splashed in the face with a bucketful of cold water. Because she had so freely given him her body, Rolf now thought she was no better than a common, cheap whore. And she had actually toyed with the notion that she might love him! What a stupid, naive little fool she had been. If ever Mr. Rolf

Karman came near her again, she would tell him exactly what she thought of him.

Suddenly, Annette could not wait to see him again.

Chapter 13

Jensen studied the papers in front of him. They presented a problem in logistics: how to transport a load of fresh produce from the central valley to Chicago. Automatically, his mind began to sort out details, possibilities, relevant information. He scribbled notes on a piece of paper, consulted railroad timetables, checked on the availability of Tofler boxcars and teamster's outfits at either end, calculated gross weights. Just as he was filling in the last details on the shipping order, Ned poked his head into Jensen's office.

"Excuse me."

"Sure, Ned. What's up?"

"A ragged little urchin just ran into my office with a note for you. Said a lady paid him to deliver it." Looking vaguely disapproving, Ned held the note by a corner.

"A lady? Hmm." Jensen pondered. There weren't any ladies he could think of who would send him a note at work. Annette, perhaps? Ned handed the note to him. The white paper was creased and smudged, probably by the grimy little hand that delivered it. He opened it up and glanced at the unfamiliar handwriting.

Dear Jensen,

I know this will be a terrible shock, but I had to make my presence known to you. Please, please forgive me for doing it this way. I want to see you so badly. Can you meet me in the Mermaid restaurant down by the harbor on Friday at noon?

I beg of you not to tell Annette or Father of this note. I will explain when I see you. If you do not choose to come, I will understand and will wish you the best always.

Your loving sister,
Cecile

"My God," whispered Jensen. He read the letter again slowly and carefully, trying to assimilate the news that his long-lost sister was alive and nearby. He wondered how she could possibly think that he wouldn't meet her. She must be afraid that they were angry with her. How odd that Annette, not long ago, had thought that Edward might have heard from Cecile. How close to the truth she had been.

His mind went back over the day, twelve years before, when his beloved elder sister, Cecile, had disappeared. He remembered the terrible quarrels that had gone on between his mother and father for weeks after she'd left. Edward had been haggard and subdued and his beautiful, gay mother had locked herself up in her room. Jensen had heard her sobbing through the thick, oak door that for the first time in his life was closed to him and his little sister.

His loving, warm-hearted mother had died soon after, of a broken heart, he'd always believed. Somehow, the boy had known it was his father's fault.

Jensen ran a hand through his light brown wavy hair. Resting his forehead on his hand, he studied the note once again. He would honor her request that he tell no one. Friday was only a few days away. Soon he'd find the answers to his questions.

He suddenly wondered whether he would recognize her. It had been twelve years since he'd seen Cecile. He'd been eleven, she'd been fourteen. He tried to conjure up an image of her, but it was vague and indistinct. He remembered her as tall. But, of course, he'd been shorter then, so perhaps his impression was wrong. She had been slim, with thick, wavy hair the color of honey and big, soulful, velvety brown eyes. She'd looked very much like his mother, whereas Jensen and Annette favored their father's side of the family.

He was worried that Cecile was in trouble of some sort. Had she been in San Francisco all these years, hiding from them? He pictured her old, haggard, gaunt and starving. Perhaps she had a child or children, ragged, snot-nosed brats. Or perhaps she had a swollen belly and no husband. Maybe she needed his help, which he'd gladly give, but why had she decided to contact him at this particular time? His brain whirled with possibilities. He rubbed his eyes and tried to stem colliding thoughts. He'd just have to wait.

The Mermaid restaurant was on Market Street, one block from the harbor. It was a pleasant looking place, not a sailor's flophouse or dance hall as Jensen had feared, but a brick-fronted, narrow edifice that sported an elegant brass mermaid above its door.

Jensen took a deep breath, pushed open the door and stepped inside. He paused for an instant while his eyes grew accustomed to the dimness. How would he know her?

Scanning the small dining room, he saw several nautical looking types, a few businessmen and several middle-aged women seated around a table, giggling over their lunch.

The maître d' was approaching him. Should he ask for Cecile? Was she known here? Or should he take a table and wait for her to find him? He hesitated. "I'm meeting someone here," he finally said.

"Of course, sir. Would you care to sit by the window?"

"Yes. Thank you." The man led Jensen to a secluded table in a corner, next to a many-paned window that overlooked the busy street. Jensen ordered a glass of beer and said he'd eat later.

Impatiently, Jensen craned his neck around to search the rest of the dining room. There were no single ladies. Drumming his fingers on the table, he sipped his beer. He pulled his gold watch out of his waistcoat pocket. It was 12:10.

Where was Cecile? Maybe she wasn't going to show up. Maybe she'd become frightened and run away, or maybe something had detained her. It even occurred to him that the note was a hoax.

He picked up the menu and began to read it idly. The fare appeared to be excellent. There was abalone, crab, all sorts of fish and shellfish. At least he could have a good lunch.

"Jensen?" A soft, gentle voice, still familiar after all the years, spoke close to his ear. His nostrils caught a whiff of sweet scent. A gloved hand rested lightly on his shoulder. He heard a rustle of fabric and then she was standing in front of him.

He rose from his seat. "Cecile," he breathed.

"Yes. It's me," she said simply.

Now he could really look at her, take her in. She

was tall and stately, beautiful. Her eyes were huge and soft and sad, her hair a burnished golden brown, her skin the same alabaster white as was Annette's. She was wearing a beautiful, slightly foreign looking dress of deep royal blue and over that, a short fur cape. She looked ravishing.

"Oh, it's good to see you," she said. "You don't know how good." She looked undecided, ill at ease.

Jensen took a step toward her and enfolded her in his arms. "God, Cecile! Welcome home."

Her face broke into a wide smile and she stepped back. "Let me look at you. Oh, you're all grown up!"

"Well, of course. What did you expect?" he grinned.

They sat down, both of them all smiles.

"You look wonderful," Jensen told her. "I had all these awful thoughts. I thought you might be . . . well . . ."

"I can imagine. But, as you can see, I'm fine." She hesitated a moment. "I'm married now. To a wonderful man named Luke Bogarde. He's Australian—"

"So that's where you've been all these years! My God, Cecile, I have a million questions to ask."

"I'm sure you do, but first, how is Annette?" Her soulful brown eyes grew hazy remembering her younger sister.

"Annette! She's something. Wants to be an artist. She flaunts all sorts of modern, liberated ideas in Father's face and gets away with it. She's fine. She's wonderful. She's got the men of the city at her feet and doesn't give a hoot about any of them."

"She always was artistic. Good. She sounds like she'll make something of her life. I'm glad she can stand up to Father. I never could. And how is the patriarch?"

"Oh," Jensen's face lost its animation, "he's fine. Annette's been worried about him lately. She thinks he's been working too hard."

"And Mama?" Cecile's face was apprehensive.

Jensen paused in shock. Of course, how could she know? He put a hand out and touched Cecile's. "Cecile, Mama died. It was years and years ago, right after you . . . left." His voice was gentle.

Her reaction was strangely calm. She looked down at his hand covering hers on the table. "I guess, somehow, I knew." She lifted her head and met his gaze staunchly. "I'm not sad. Really, I'm not. Maybe it was even better."

"What on earth do you mean?" Jensen was puzzled. "Mama was such a happy person."

"Oh, never mind. I don't know," said Cecile quickly.

Jensen looked at Cecile's beautiful face, her fine clothes, the lurking sadness in her eyes. "Tell me about your husband. Where did you meet him? And when? Do you live in Australia? Do you have any children?"

"Wait!" Cecile laughed. "One at a time. Let's see. Luke is a tall, handsome man. A ship captain. He's quite a bit older than I am. We live in Sydney, but I've traveled with him a few times, to places like Singapore and Hong Kong and Djakarta. This time he had to make a trip to San Francisco, so I decided it was time I came back."

"How did you meet him? How in heaven's name did you get to Australia?"

Cecile's eyes had a faraway look. "You know, I can't remember exactly where I met Luke. It must have been right after I left San Francisco, because I can't even remember not knowing him. I was on his ship, alone, and he was kind to me." Cecile stopped. A frown creased her brow and her eyes grew distant and opaque. "It's hard to explain, Jensen, but everything before that is hazy. I can't remember. I've tried and tried over the years, but it's all sort of a nightmare. Snatches, images. Something happened, but I can't remember."

"My God, Cecile, what happened? Why did you run away?"

She turned a dark, tormented gaze on Jensen. "Oh, I don't know. Something. Daddy and Mama fighting. I don't know. But I had to go away. I had to."

Jensen patted her hand soothingly, realizing that she was becoming distraught. "Never mind, Cecile. It doesn't matter now that you're home."

"Jensen, I can't stay. Luke will be here for a few more weeks on business, then we'll be sailing back. My home is in Sydney now, with Luke. I only came because I had to find something." She paused, searching for words. "Something I'd left behind here, a part of myself. Maybe only memories. I don't know."

"Will you come home and see Father and Annette?" Jensen asked gently.

"No! Oh, I couldn't. Wait!" She held out a hand as if to stop a physical assault, then took a deep breath. "I'm not ready, Jensen. I don't know if I ever will be. I'm afraid." She shivered delicately.

"Afraid of what?"

"I don't know. Oh, I don't know!" Her eyes filled with tears. "If I knew, I wouldn't be afraid."

"It'll come to you sometime, I'm sure," Jensen reassured her.

"Maybe. I'm not even sure I want to know anymore. There are things buried in the human mind that are better never brought to the light of day." Cecile laughed nervously. "Oh, just listen to me. Luke says I'm always too serious and you can see he's right." She smiled tremulously, the curve of her lips quivering a little.

"Are you happy, Cecile?" Jensen asked softly.

"Yes," she replied, but her tone was pensive.

"You don't sound quite sure."

"I am. I love Luke and he loves me. But," she got that faraway look in her eyes again, "there's something missing. A small part of a puzzle, something that stands between us. That's why I had to come back." Her brown eyes met his beseechingly.

Jensen thought it best to change the subject. "Won't you come up to the house and have dinner with us? Or can we meet you and Luke somewhere. We'd love to know your husband. He's part of the family now."

"No, please, Jensen. Give me some time. I'm not ready yet. Maybe—"

"But Christmas is coming up soon. Wouldn't you like to spend Christmas with your family? You'd be more than welcome, and Luke, too."

"Thank you. I'll think about it. But it might be rather uncomfortable for all of us."

"Don't be silly."

"Let it rest, Jensen. I have to think."

"All right. But you can reach me any time. We'll meet again, soon. Okay?"

Cecile smiled. "Of course."

"Good. That's settled then. Now let's eat. I'm hungry."

Lunch was pleasant, relaxed. They spoke of old times, of childhood memories, of Jensen's career and Annette's painting, of Luke's family in Sydney and their life there.

It was a happy interlude for them both but, although Cecile spoke easily and with poise, Jensen detected a sadness in her manner. She was not quite the whole, happy child he remembered.

They promised to meet again, but set no date. She left first. He watched her graceful, gliding walk as she left the restaurant, saw her walk past the window where he sat and wave timidly to him. She disappeared down the street toward the waterfront where her husband's ship lay at anchor.

It had been a very curious meeting, indeed, Jensen decided, walking back to his office. He would have a devil of a time keeping the news to himself, too, especially after what Annette had said. It was as if she'd had some sort of intuitive sense that Cecile was near. Odd.

That evening, Jensen was to dine with some friends and then go to the theater to see a new play just in from New York. Annette was going out with that poverty-stricken artist that she was seeing so much of lately. She certainly was hanging around with strange, Bohemian types, but Jensen guessed that was supposed to be artistic, at least in Annette's mind. The fellow seemed decent enough, Bernard something or other, but Jensen hoped his sister was watching out for herself. Those sensitive, intense, Mediterranean types could be terribly volatile.

Damn! Now he had two sisters to worry about. Why couldn't he have a nice, dull, ordinary family with nice, dull married sisters whose husbands would do the worrying?

He instructed Tom, the driver, to take him to the Poodle Dog restaurant where he was to meet his friends, then dismissed him. He'd get a ride home with one of the fellows after the theater. It was a chilly, damp night. The ubiquitous fog rolled in over the downtown area, clinging to the buildings, crawling through the streets as stealthily as an ancient ghost. It cloaked everything, eerily muffling the sounds of horses' hooves and wagon wheels, blurring the halos of the gaslights.

Jensen pulled his stylish chesterfield coat closed over his impeccable black evening clothes as he walked to the restaurant. Entering it, he was met with warmth and light and gaiety, quite a contrast to the damp, close winter night he had just left. His spirits rose instantly. Now he was in his element. The maître d' knew Jensen and greeted him respectfully. He led him to the table where his friends were already gathered, each wealthy young man in the dazzling black and white of formal attire, each red cheeked, laughing, drinking from the magnum of French champagne that sat in a silver bucket by the table. They were secure in their exalted positions of wealth and privilege. They were the heirs of San Francisco's enormous wealth and power and they knew it. And now, while they had the youth and health and time to enjoy life to the fullest, they were determined to take advantage of the pleasures that were so readily available to them.

"Hey, Jensen, you're late!" called one of his friends, seeing him approach through the crowd.

"What kept you, buddy?" shouted another.

"Christ, keep it down!" Jensen laughed, sitting down in the empty chair. "You'll get kicked out of here on your derrières it you're not careful." A platter, strewn with empty oyster shells, sat in the center of the table, the parsley all pushed aside, the lemon quarters squeezed to limp husks.

"Have a glass of bubbly." One of the fellows poured him a glass, sloshing champagne over the rim, and handed it to him, dripping. Grinning, Jensen flicked the sweet, wet stuff off his fingers and drained the glass in one gulp. His friends cheered as he plunked the glass down on the table, empty.

"Let's eat," said his friend. "We've been waiting for you to show up, Jensen. The crab sounds good tonight."

"No, the roast beef is better, by far," said another.

An argument ensued upon the relative merits of crab and beef. The young men took sides, laughing, joking, shouting, swearing. These were the eager young moments of comradeship and the love of life's bounty. It was starting out to be a superlative evening.

When they were finished, the table was littered with stained napkins, empty crab shells, spots of wine, half-filled coffee cups and cigarette and cigar butts. The satiated group of men sat back in their chairs, young, muscular legs stretched out in front of them under the table, sipping their brandies and puffing on cigars.

Just at that moment, the precariously poised bedrock plates under the city decided to shift. The heavy crystal chandeliers in the Poodle Dog shivered, and some of the candles on the tables fell over, starting tiny fires that were quickly put out. The floor heaved ever so slightly and the window frames rattled. Then it was over. A few people, tourists no doubt, cried out and rushed to the doorways. One woman fainted.

The young men at Jensen's table laughed, however, doused the flames and puffed on their expensive cigars while waiters nonchalantly swept up the broken glass.

"That wasn't bad," Jensen commented, blasé to the core.

"Hardly noticed it," laughed a friend.

"Well, we'd better get going to the theater," one of the young men said casually.

Grunts of agreement met his words.

"Jensen, you're the most sober of us all. Be a pal and go hire a hansom for us. We'll settle up here," suggested one.

Groaning with humorous lament, Jensen rose. "You'll have to pay my share then," he chuckled, his cheeks flushed from the wine, his light brown hair slightly mussed. "This is a chore worth payment."

His remark caused a chorus of moans and wails and friendly curses. He shook a facetious fist at the group and made his way unsteadily toward the door. To his right was the staircase that descended from the upper floor where, gossip had it, the nabobs met with their paramours in elegant, curtained seclusion. Jensen stopped and put a hand out to steady himself against the curved mahogany banister as a wave of giddiness swept over him. The room whirled in a pleasing kaleidoscope of bright color. A man and a woman came gliding down the staircase above him. He raised his eyes blearily, but curiously, ready to assess the kind of people who took advantage of the Poodle Dog's special upstairs rooms. It was a portly, middle-aged gentleman in well-cut evening clothes leading, on his arm, a lovely apparition. Jensen peered closer. He went rigid. My God, it was his father!

Edward was staring at him now, open-mouthed, pale. Jensen's wine-blurred gaze flew to the woman. Who was she?

Jensen's heart constricted in shock. He felt a cold wave of bitterness wash over him. Instantly, he was sober. The woman—no, girl, for she looked no older than seventeen or eighteen—was dressed in an expensive, shimmering blue gown. Her figure was exquisitely voluptuous and very young. But it was at her lovely face that Jensen stared, frigid with a kind of horrified rage at his father.

The girl looked exactly like a portrait of his mother. No, he realized, she looked even more like Cecile.

Chapter 14

January 17 was a busy day for Annette. It was Jensen's twenty-fourth birthday and she had planned an elaborate dinner with a many-tiered cake to follow. It would be the first time the Tofler family had dined together since Christmas, since either she or Jensen or Edward had been absent from the house in the evenings.

She had spent most of the afternoon in the kitchen, preparing for dinner, icing the cake, directing the cook and getting hopelessly underfoot. It was fun for a change to be busy around the house when she had spent so much time of late either touring San Francisco with Bernard, lunching out, or painting in her studio. It was time for a break, a domestic one.

Flour-smudged and grease-stained from the hours spent in the kitchen, Annette went upstairs in the late afternoon to take a long, relaxing bath. By the time the menfolk arrived home from the office, she was dressed in a flattering coral gown and already had dismissed Vivian for the evening.

Annette greeted them both in the drawing room, where the atmosphere was warm and relaxed. Jensen was his usual self—humorous, carefree, full of inside stories about the city. Edward, too, was in a pleasant mood that evening. Annette found it heartening to be with her family under such happy circumstances. It was quite late before they walked, laughing and cheerful, toward the dining room where earlier Annette had placed a gift on Jensen's chair.

On the way through the hall, however, the knocker sounded at the front door, disrupting their mood.

"Oh, bother." Annette frowned. "Who on earth would stop by at this hour?"

"I'll get it," offered Jensen, hoping to preserve the good mood of the occasion.

Annette and her father continued on toward the dining room, leaving Jensen to handle the late caller.

Suddenly, they were stopped by Jensen's voice. "I don't believe it!" he gasped.

Annette froze, spun around. For a moment, confusion played across her features as she stood staring at Jensen, who was embracing a lovely, statuesque, golden-haired woman. The woman was tantalizingly familiar, yet Annette was positive she had never seen her before. Who could it be?

Jensen was drawing the woman inside with a rush of words, taking her coat. And then Annette distinctly heard him calling her Cecile.

Cecile? It seemed impossible, but the woman Jensen was leading toward them must be their sister! It must be Cecile. Annette's heart skipped several beats.

"Cecile." The word escaped Annette's lips in a whisper. Slowly, she moved toward the woman, tears welling up in her eyes. "Oh, Cecile." She embraced her sister, clinging to her in disbelief.

"Little Annette," Cecile was murmuring, stroking her auburn curls with a loving hand. "How very beautiful you are."

"Oh, Cecile! Is it really you? Is it really—" Annette began to cry, unable to release her sister. "I never thought we'd see you again!" She turned her head then, searching for their father. "Daddy! Can you believe it? It's really Cecile!"

Edward stood fixed to the spot, his face contorted, ashen, his hands hanging limply at his sides. "My God," he muttered. Then, "It really is you! But you look so much like . . . like . . ."

"Like Mother." Jensen smiled at Cecile, looked from her over to Edward and back. It must be a great shock to his father. Cecile was so like their mother that it must have seemed to him that his wife, Elizabeth, had returned from the grave. No wonder Edward was so pale.

Cecile finally disengaged herself from Annette, who stood wiping at her tear-stained cheeks, her eyes filled with wonder and love. "Father," Cecile said, walking slowly, hesitantly toward him.

Edward Tofler did a strange thing then. Instead of meeting Cecile halfway, he hung back, his hands balling into white fists at his sides. "So you've come back," he muttered distantly. "After all these years."

"Yes, Father. I've come back. I was hoping to stay for a while."

"Oh, yes!" cried Annette. "We'll never let you leave again. Never!" She moved toward her sister, taking her arm, leading her into the dining room. "You must tell us everything," she bubbled, unaware of Edward's mute horror or Jensen's pensive gaze resting on their father. "It's Jensen's birthday," Annette was rushing to tell her, "and you're going to celebrate with us." She looked over her shoulder toward Jensen. "Isn't this the most wonderful present in the world?"

"I know. I remembered," Cecile said softly.

"Yes." Jensen tore his eyes from his father and smiled. "It is truly wonderful." He caught Cecile's eye momentarily and saw that his sister wasn't going to mention their previous meeting. She was here, however, and that was all that mattered for the time being.

It was an hour before Annette finally let up on her questioning, and then only because Jensen insisted she stop grilling Cecile about the past. Annette must be deaf and blind, he thought, if she can't sense the tension in the room. Edward had not spoken at all since Cecile's arrival and Cecile pointedly steered away from Annette's questions about her life before Australia.

Cecile did, however, become animated when describing her life in Sydney with Luke Bogarde. "He's a wonderful man, Annette," she said, blushing slightly. "He's terribly big and handsome, and sweet, too. So good to me."

"But where is he? Why didn't you bring him?" gushed Annette.

Cecile lowered her eyes. "He has business in San Francisco and lots to do on the ship. He . . . he just couldn't make it here tonight."

"But aren't you living on the ship with him? I mean, are you really going to stay with us? Here?"

"For a time, Annette. I'd like to live here while Luke is so busy." She glanced at their father. "Is it all right?"

"Of course," he mumbled, ringing for the dinner plates to be cleared, mopping at his damp brow. "You always have a home here, Cecile."

Annette watched her father, finally realizing how terribly quiet he had been all during the meal. And why couldn't Cecile remember anything about her life here? Had she really forgotten, as she said she had, or was there something else? And why didn't she ask about their mother? Did she know?

Knitting her brows, Annette looked from Edward's strained face to Cecile, who was quietly studying her hands, to Jensen who seemed to be lost in thought, his eyes fixed on their father.

It all seemed very strange to her suddenly, like a mystery she had once read, where the characters were hopelessly ensnarled in their own secret lives, revealing nothing to one another. The plot had thickened ominously until, in the end, their secrets had unfolded one by one, each affecting the other like the box within the box within the box . . .

Shaking off the unsettling mood, Annette forced herself to smile again. "Wait until you see the cake, Jensen. And aren't you going to open your present?"

"Oh," he said, picking up the neatly wrapped box which he had set aside and forgotten. "Now what can this be?" He shook it, laughed teasingly, forced himself to play Annette's game.

"Daddy and I picked it out for you. What do you think it is?"

"A new robe?"

Annette giggled. "No, silly. The box is too small. Now be serious." She winked at Cecile.

"A new gold watch?"

"No."

Jensen tore off the wrapping and shook the small velvet box. "A ring?"

Annette frowned. "How did you know?"

"What else comes in a small, black velvet box?" He opened it and found a handsomely set diamond in a large gold band. "Extraordinary!" he breathed.

"Don't you recognize it?" asked Annette, dying to tell him.

"Well, no."

"It was Grandfather's," she said quickly. "Daddy and I had it reset for you!"

Jensen smiled broadly. He rose, came to Annette and kissed her lightly on the cheek. "It's marvelous, little sister. Thank you." Then to Edward, "You really shouldn't have."

"Always meant to give it to you, Jensen. But it was Annette's idea."

Of course, thought Jensen. Everything he had ever gotten out of his father had been given somewhat grudgingly. No doubt, it would be the same way with the business. Whenever Jensen took the initiative at the office, Edward, when he was around at all, would criticize him in some way.

The tension between them grew palpable. Why did it always have to be this way? Annette wondered. She only wanted her little family to be carefree, happy, especially now that Cecile was home. Why was there always this tension between them?

She glanced at Cecile. Yes, her sister sensed it, too. She seemed nervous and was squirming uncomfortably in her seat.

Annette rose. "Come on, Cecile," she smiled, "let's get dessert ready. It will be such fun," she added, trying desperately to remain bright.

When they were alone in the pantry, lighting the candles on Jensen's cake, Annette said, "It truly is wonderful to have you home."

"Yes," replied Cecile faintly, "wonderful. Listen, Annette," she said in a moment, "there's something I've got to tell you. I saw Jensen some weeks back. Before Christmas." She placed a reassuring hand on Annette's arm. "I'd have told you, dear, but I've been so confused since my arrival. Perhaps I'll explain later, if I can."

"You saw Jensen?"

"Yes. I sent him a note. I asked him to keep it a secret, Annette."

"Oh." Annette looked at Cecile thoughtfully. "Then you know about Mama?"

"Yes. Jensen told me."

"I was wondering . . ."

Cecile laughed weakly. "Come on. We'll chat later. Right now there's wax dripping all over the cake!"

"Oh!"

After the long meal, although it was quite late, Annette insisted on tucking in her sister. She sat on the edge of Cecile's old four-poster. "You get a good night's sleep and tomorrow we'll have such fun!" Annette touched Cecile's hand. "And I'm sorry if I wore you out with all those questions. It was thoughtless of me."

"That's quite all right, Annette. Really. I wish I could answer more of them. It's just that my past—before I met Luke, that is—is so hazy."

Annette rose and turned down the flame on the bedside lamp. "Cecile?"

"Yes?"

"Can I meet Luke someday?"

"Of course you will. Soon. I promise." She smiled into the dimness. "And Annette, I want to tell you how delighted I am to have such a lovely little sister. I mean it."

Annette finally retired, but found sleep slow in coming. The evening had been too exciting. When Cecile had walked through the door after twelve years, it was like having a dream come true. She wondered whether her sister would stay in San Francisco and whether her husband would stay, too. Why had Cecile taken so long to come home? What was in her past that had kept her from returning, that had forced her to flee in the first place? She had so many questions.

Not long before dawn, Annette was awakened by a piercing scream. It took her a moment to realize that the cry had come from the bedroom next door, from

Cecile's room. She leapt out of bed and flew to her sister's side.

"Cecile!" Annette shook her sister's shoulders lightly. Her skin was damp. "Wake up! You're dreaming!" Cecile moaned and twisted her head on the pillow, still in the grip of the nightmare. Annette reached over and turned the lamp up, chasing the shadows back into the corners. "Cecile," she said more gently. "It's me, Annette."

Jensen rushed in. He stood over the bed, his face etched with worry.

"Annette? Jensen?" Cecile sobbed. "Thank God! I . . . I had this terrible nightmare. It was awful!" She covered her face with her hands and shook her head, moaning hopelessly.

Annette put her arms around Cecile, cuddling her, rocking back and forth gently. "It's all right. Jensen and I are here now. It's all right." She looked up at her brother. Yes, he was as worried as she.

Finally, after a long spell of sobbing, Cecile was able to respond to Jensen, who was trying to make sense of the nightmare. "Tell us, if you can, what happened in your dream," he coaxed softly.

Cecile kept her face hidden in the fold of Annette's gown. "It was Father . . . and Mother. They were quarreling. It was awful!"

"Do you remember what they were fighting about?" asked Jensen with infinite care.

"No. No. I always have the same dream," she wept, "and I think it has something to do with me. I don't know!"

"There, now," soothed Annette, still rocking her sister in her arms. "We won't talk about it anymore. I'll stay with you if you want."

"Oh, please? Will you?" Cecile looked up at Annette, her face wet with tears. "Please?"

"Of course I will." Annette glanced at Jensen and nodded toward the door. "Now you lie back down," she told her sister, "and everything will be all right."

Annette never did get back to sleep. Cecile was restless. She cried in her sleep, never at peace, and the unexplained fear that gripped her kept Annette fully awake. And then too she was dying to talk to Jensen, but in private. So many frightening questions filled her mind, and she sensed that only Jensen could provide the answers.

"Go right in, Miss Annette," said Ned. "I'm sure Jensen won't mind."

"Annette?" Jensen looked up from his papers. "What on earth are you doing here? And at this hour?" It was only ten in the morning and it had been a long night.

Annette closed the office door behind her and sat down purposefully in front of her brother. "We must talk, Jensen. I want you to be straightforward with me. I'm grown up now and I want some honest answers."

He studied her for a long moment. "All right. Ask."

"It's about Cecile. Why did she leave?" Annette came right to the point.

"I don't know."

"Jensen," she became irritated, "I want an honest answer."

"I honestly don't know. I think it had something to do with Father, but that's only guesswork on my part. And that's all I can tell you."

"What about Mama and Daddy? Do you recall them quarreling?"

"Yes. It was awful. Right before Mother died."

"Then Cecile was gone already?"

"Yes, I suppose so. It was a dreadful year. It's hard to remember now."

"Jensen?" She drew her winglike brows together in a frown. "Didn't you think Daddy was behaving awfully strangely last night?"

"Quite."

"He seemed, well, terribly ill. He was so quiet at dinner. And then later, when Cecile had the nightmare, why didn't he come to see if she was all right?"

"I don't know."

"Is he here now, somewhere in the building?"

"No. He left the house early and hasn't been here yet."

"Where does he go?"

"Look, I don't know the first thing about his activities!" Jensen exclaimed with exasperation. "All I know is that he's been neglecting the business lately and our associates are getting worried."

"Oh, Jensen," she cried, aghast, "is the business going to fail?"

"No. I've been meeting with some people lately and I think things are getting ironed out. It will be fine."

Annette was pensive for a time. "Just one last thing," she ventured at last. "Can you take a guess as to why Cecile really left?"

Jensen directed his gaze beyond Annette. "Only Cecile can tell us that."

She left the office completely unsatisfied with the answers Jensen had given her. There was only one thing left to do. She would have to search Cecile's memory. But that, Annette sensed, would not be at all easy. Cecile was on the verge of some sort of a breakdown. The thought sent chills up and down Annette's spine. She had never seen a person go mad, but she had heard stories. Cecile fit the mold. Annette was certain that her sister's sanity was at stake, and that the key to her recovery was in the past. Something had happened to Cecile twelve years before that to this day was eating away at her like a dread, terminal disease. And then, to add to her worry, there was the matter of their father's strange behavior.

Jensen sat at his father's desk, tapping the tip of his pen against his teeth. It had been a most unusual two days. Among the many questions plaguing his mind, one stood out. What had Edward Tofler done to drive his daughter away and cause the untimely death of his wife? The answer eluded him like a breeze on calm waters.

There were several possibilities. Perhaps Cecile had a weak mind and Edward had pressured her beyond endurance. Or perhaps there was a mother-daughter jealousy that the family had been unable to resolve. But there must have been some specific incident, something so traumatic that his elder sister had blocked it out of her mind. Could it be possible. . . ? But no, that was too hideous to consider. Jensen strove to drive the sick notion from his thoughts.

He cleared his mind and looked down once again at the stack of disorganized papers on his father's desk. How could things be so misfiled? And where was that bill of lading that had been troubling him just before Annette had arrived? It had something to do with a shipment of peaches to Seattle. That would have been perfectly ordinary except for the time of year. And there was another thing about it that bothered Jensen. The company transporting the fruit was called Pacific Growers. Jensen had never heard of that company. It didn't seem possible that he could have missed knowing about the very existence of a grower with such a sizable shipment.

Jensen was still brooding over the question when

his father finally arrived, banging open the door to his own office. "What are you doing at my desk?" he bellowed, slamming the door behind him.

Calmly, with self-assurance, Jensen looked up from the papers. "I'm putting things in order here. Which is more," he added pointedly, "than you seem able to do lately."

"Why you little. . . ." Edward took several steps toward his son. "How dare you!"

Jensen rose, meeting the challenge. The time had come. "I dare," he said between clenched teeth, "because I'm taking over the company."

"What!" Edward came to an abrupt halt. He grabbed the back of the chair in front of him for support and clutched his chest.

"You heard me. And I've got the backing. I've been working on it for weeks."

"No."

"Yes, my dear father. I'm afraid you've become nothing more than a figurehead here. And I might add that you have only yourself to blame. If you had been here more often," he went on relentlessly, not caring that his father's face was grey, that his hand still clutched at his chest, "instead of spending your time with that trollop of yours—"

"Leave her out of this!" Edward choked.

"All right. I will. That's your business. But it seems to me that you made your choice a long time ago. You traded the transport business for your little paramour."

"You . . . you can't just take over!"

"Oh, but I can. In fact, I have almost completed the takeover. It's too late to stop me. If you try the business will surely fail." Jensen sat back down and folded his hands in front of him. "Don't destroy yourself, Father," he said smoothly with deliberate care.

"Accept things the way they are. It's time anyway, and you know it."

Edward Tofler finally sank into the chair opposite his desk. His son's desk now. He groaned inwardly, sensing the impossible. Defeat. "But you haven't the experience, Jensen. You'll lose everything. Everything."

"No I won't. I'm smarter than you've ever given me credit for. There are some things, however, that you had better explain to me about this file here." He tapped the papers on the desk with a steady finger. "For instance," he intoned, "who are the Pacific Growers, and why are they shipping a boxcar full of peaches to Seattle in December?"

Chapter 15

The slim, well-dressed man rose half out of the chair behind his huge gleaming desk. His face pinched with anger, he stabbed the air in front of him with his long finger as he spoke in a low voice throbbing with fury. "You'd damned well better find Tofler or your reputation around here won't be worth a plugged nickel! That's what you're paid for, isn't it, O'Neill?" His voice turned ominously soft and smooth.

"Yes, sir." Tansy O'Neill squirmed under the man's cold scrutiny, even though he knew his employer really couldn't see him. He'd seen the man's rages before, directed toward others, and had no desire to be the target of one himself. "I'll find Tofler. It's just that I need a little time. Don't worry, I know where he hangs out." The dead looking eyes shifted from the desk to the tasteful velvet drapes in the dim room. Because his employer was blind, O'Neill always had the feeling that he could see inside him with a sight unknown to normal people.

"That man owes me and I want him to pay. Nobody gets away with double crossing Blind Chris. Nobody." The man's voice was filled with the certain knowledge of his own power and it made Tansy shift restlessly from foot to foot. "You do whatever it takes.

I can't let this go on. Tofler's no good to me anymore, but I want payments. Do you understand? An eye for an eye."

"Yes, sir."

"Find him. Soon. I am not a patient man."

Tansy turned and left the dim, thickly carpeted room. He swallowed convulsively, his Adam's apple bobbing in his skinny throat. Why did Blind Chris always make him feel so damn shaky? That man had a way about him. Tansy knew Blind Chris would get anybody who crossed him. Eventually, he would—no matter who it was. That's why Tansy had to be so careful. He had his own little thing going that Chris didn't know about and God help him if his boss ever found out.

As Tansy left the Snug Café he took a deep breath of fresh, cool air. But of course Buckley would never find out. Who would have the nerve to tell him? Nobody. Tansy had seen to that.

Now, however, he had a more immediate problem. He must find Edward Tofler and extract payment from him for messing up his end of the deal at the railroad yard. The Tofler Transport offices were the place to start. If Edward wasn't there, the son no doubt could be persuaded to reveal his father's whereabouts.

Edward Tofler shifted his bulk in the mussed bedclothes. It was very late. He must have slept the morning away. And no wonder, after all that brandy last night. He put a hand to his head. It ached with a dull, thudding pain and his stomach felt queasy. He'd have to stop the drinking, but that son of his had given him a damned good reason to tie one on. Of all the nerve! He'd do something about Jensen as soon as he felt better. That young whippersnapper was full of himself. Well, he'd find out soon enough.

"Tilly," he called.

"Yes, Edward." Her sweet, youthful voice reassured him. It wasn't every man of sixty who could keep a young thing like Tilly happy. She was beautiful, too. There was something about her he'd been unable to resist from the first moment he'd seen her in that dance hall.

Matilda Grueter entered the bedroom, smiling. She was carrying a cup of coffee and the morning paper. Leaning down she kissed Edward's bristly cheek. "Good morning, honey bun."

Edward fondled one of her ripe breasts. Tilly laughed lightly and sat on the edge of the bed while he sipped his coffee and opened the paper.

January 22, 1891. "What day of the week is it, honey?" asked Edward absently.

"Thursday, silly," she cooed.

His brow puckered. The date rang a bell somewhere in his mind. If only his head would stop pounding, he'd be able to think more clearly. It seemed there was something he had to do . . . "Oh my God," he breathed, remembering. Thursday. It was Thursday. Too late. He'd forgotten. The Chinese girls, the railroad cars! Too late, too late!

"What is it, honey bun?" asked Tilly in her little-girl voice.

"Nothing," he muttered, pushing her away and heaving himself out of bed. "I've got to go out."

"Can I come?"

"No!" He took a deep breath, repented of his harsh tone. Lord, it wasn't her fault. "No, lovey. This is business. You'd be bored."

"Oh, all right." Tilly pouted becomingly but Edward wasn't watching. He pulled his clothes on hastily and disappeared into the bathroom. She heard water splashing furiously.

He rushed back into the sitting room, his eyes wild. "Where's my coat?" he barked.

Tilly got it for him, slipped it on his heavy shoulders. How oddly he was acting, frightened and in such a hurry. She'd never seen him like that before.

He gave her a perfunctory peck. "I don't know how long I'll be. Some important business I neglected."

Edward tried to forget his lurching stomach and aching head as he stumped down the stairs and out onto Oak Street. No cab. Damn! He'd have to walk until he found one. There was no time to wait. And him with his chest pains, too, on top of it all. He'd go to the railroad yards first, see what had happened. Then he'd have to figure out how to deal with Buckley. He shivered. God, that man was cold. He'd never forgive or forget. And after that last time. . . . Well, that hadn't really been his fault, but still, it looked bad.

How could he have forgotten? Stupid old fool! He'd been drinking, crying in his brandy about his son's perfidy when he should have been out taking care of business. He'd have to pay more attention from now on. Buckley was a dangerous man, much too dangerous to cross.

Edward Tofler forced his bulk to move even faster down Oak Street. There was a pained, intent expression on his pale face.

"I'd like to see Mr. Tofler," said Tansy.

"Which one?" asked Ned coolly.

"Edward Tofler."

"He's not in."

"Then his son."

"Out to lunch." There was a trace of satisfaction in the secretary's voice. He did not like Tansy O'Neill, not one bit.

Tansy looked at Ned coldly for a moment, then

turned and stalked from the office, his head bobbing on top of his skeletal frame.

He hailed a cabby and directed him to the Tofler mansion on Nob Hill. "Is Mr. Tofler in?" he asked the dignified butler.

"No, sir. Neither Mr. Tofler is in."

"Will Mr. Edward Tofler be returning soon?"

"I really couldn't say, sir." The butler's impassive face gave nothing away. It could have been a stone wall.

Damn! Was Tofler already in hiding? Had he run? Or was he merely dallying with his whore? The last possibility was the most likely. Tansy started off down the hill, his long, skinny legs eating up the distance. He'd walk. That would give him time to think of some way to make Tofler suffer for this wasted day, this wild-goose chase.

Tilly, still in her dressing gown, sat in front of her mirror and rubbed the oily rouge onto her cheeks. She had considered changing into a dress and her new furs and going shopping, but Edward had been too upset when he'd left. If he came back and she wasn't there, he'd be furious. She'd better stay home then. Later, she'd send out for some supper, on Edward's credit, of course, and they'd have a cozy meal by candlelight.

There was a knock on her door. Could that be Edward already? Perhaps he had forgotten his key. She rose, pulling her pink satin dressing gown around her full breasts, and went to open the door. It was not Edward. Tilly gasped, startled by the man who was standing on her threshold. He was tall and as thin as a cadaver, but it was his face that frightened her. His face, with its bruised purple eye sockets, its cold expressionless eyes, its fleshless, beaklike nose and the incongruously pink lips, made her think of death. He was smiling politely, which made him seem even more gruesome.

"Is Mr. Tofler home?" asked the stranger in a reedy voice.

Tilly thought quickly. Certainly Edward didn't want anyone to know about her.

"Mr. *who*?" she asked innocently, letting the pink satin robe fall tantalizingly away from her throat.

The pale eyes did not waver. "Edward Tofler."

"Why, you must have the wrong address. I live here alone. I don't know any Mr. . . . uh . . . Tofler, although there is a man in the downstairs apartment."

The man pushed past her rudely and entered the room. Snatching a cigar butt from an ashtray, he thrust it close to her face. "Whose is this then, Miss Grueter? Yours?" His voice was thin and hard and sarcastic now. "Come on, where's Tofler? Don't try to lie to me. I know everything about you and that old man."

Tilly's mind whirled in terror. Who was this horrible man? Why did he want Edward? How did he know about them? "I told you I don't know any Mr. Tofler." She tried to sound calm.

Suddenly the man grabbed her arm, yanking her around. He pushed his face close to hers. "No more fooling around. I need to see Tofler and quick," he hissed, digging his fingers into her soft white arm.

"I don't—" Her words were cut off by a stinging slap to her face. She could feel the searing imprint of his hand and a spot inside her mouth where her teeth had cut her lip.

"Tell me, you stupid slut!"

The man hit her again, this time on the side of her head, making her ear ring. She opened her mouth to scream but a hand clamped over it. She was afraid she'd suffocate. Her head spun sickeningly.

"Tell me . . . now." The man's voice was quiet

and menacing. He took his hand away from her mouth.

"I don't know. He went out and didn't tell me. Please! Don't hit me again! It's the truth!" She shrank away from the man in dread. Now she recognized the look in his cold eyes: it was death itself. Words tumbled out of her mouth in a panic. She had to keep his hands from her. "He goes away, sometimes for days, never tells me. He goes to bars sometimes and drinks. I don't know where. Really I don't! Please, I'm telling the truth!"

"Okay lady, shut up." The man was silent for a moment, thinking. Tilly couldn't move, could scarcely breathe. The taste of blood was in her mouth and the side of her face throbbed.

He fastened his eyes on her, grinning. His smile chilled her to the bone. His pink lips were stretched over his teeth, making him look even more like a skull. "I know how to get Tofler to show up. I know just how to handle this."

Chapter 16

Annette had a date to meet Bernard at eight in the evening at Coppa's restaurant in the Montgomery Block. She was able to plan these evening escapades because Edward rarely had been home for dinner since Cecile's arrival. Even when he was, he retired immediately after the meal and was not seen for the rest of the night.

She felt at ease when she entered Coppa's and greeted jolly, rotund "Papa." She was even comfortable as she sat down at a table by herself because she knew Bernard would be there in a few moments. Often he was already there, waiting, his shy yet knowing smile curving his lips, his dark, limpid eyes lighting up at her appearance. It felt good to be in the same noisy, smoke-filled room with all the other artists of San Francisco, to feel the camaraderie, to belong. It also was good to be away from the mansion. Everything there was so unsettling of late.

On this particular evening she had arrived a bit early, so she had a few minutes alone to enjoy the fellowship of the place. She nodded and smiled to a few acquaintances, writers who rented rooms upstairs or other artists whom she'd seen in the halls on her way to her studio. Her escape was incomplete, however, as her mind was still on Cecile, the long-lost sister whom she barely remembered. Cecile had been back now for quite a few days and Annette found herself worrying about her more and more. Cecile was pale and she never slept well. Her story about not remembering why she had run away was bizarre. As for their father, Edward had been even more taciturn since Cecile's arrival on the night of Jensen's birthday. Annette was puzzled. She had talked to Jensen about these things, but he had been no help whatsoever. She suspected that he knew more about Cecile's past than he was letting on. It was all so unsettling, so strange.

She glanced around Coppa's, sipping at a steaming cup of tea. It was such a relief to escape the tension in her home. Although she had a great desire to help Cecile and to find out what was wrong with her father, sometimes the problems crowded in on her and she simply had to get away for a few hours.

Bernard was a great help. He was someone uninvolved with the Tofler problems with whom she could talk. And he was a constant reminder of her chosen career. He helped her with her painting and introduced her to people in the world of art, affording her the opportunity to learn. It was exciting. For a few short minutes of the day she could pretend her only problem was to reach her goal as an artist.

If only Bernard would get here, she thought, her eyes fixed on her cup of tea. Whenever she had too much time to think, Cecile's face would pop into her mind, worrying her. And Edward's face would appear too, pale, tense and distant.

"What are you looking so thoughtful about?" interrupted a familiar voice.

"Oh, Bernard!" Annette looked up, a smile coming easily to her lips. "It's just my sister. I told you—"

"Ah, yes, the enchanting but slightly unhinged Cecile who can't remember anything."

"Bernard! She's miserable. Something terrible is going on at home and Jensen and I don't know what it is. Please don't make fun of her." Annette's straight, dark brows drew together like wings above her golden eyes.

Instantly Bernard sobered. "I'm sorry. It's just that when people are rich, I cannot conceive of them being unhappy or beset with problems."

"Well, we do have problems!" Her full lower lip gave the barest soupçon of a pout. "We bleed. We hurt. Believe it or not, we even die like you ordinary mortals!"

Bernard's expression was one of rueful admiration. "I'm beginning to realize that."

"Good."

He put out a slim olive-skinned hand whose tiny creases were as always filled with plaster dust and covered hers. "I apologize. Truly. Now, on to happier things. Where am I to take you tonight? Florence's Dance Hall where the women wear no tops, I've been told, the Golden Dragon Saloon which is really an opium den, or just Wing Ho's restaurant for a cup of tea? What'll it be?" His brown eyes danced with merriment.

"Oh, let's just take a little walk. I love the crowds on the streets. We'll see what looks interesting and drop in, all right?"

"Sure, whatever you want." He leaned across the table and winked at her. "I've been to all those places anyway."

"I'm sure you have, Bernard, you old reprobate, you!" she laughed.

She had suggested a walk because Bernard couldn't afford to hire a cab and he hated for her to pay. Walking had become a routine by now in spite of the winter weather. She thought he was ridiculously sensitive about his poverty. To her, money was merely something you used to get what you wanted. To Bernard, however, it was satisfaction, status, success, everything he desired in life. Through Bernard's eyes, she was beginning to see what life could be like without money and she found it somewhat exciting. In her eyes, it represented the unknown, the exotic, the challenge. But Bernard spoke of poverty as if it were some dread, disgusting disease that everyone must work to stamp out. He thought that somewhere, somehow, sometime, someone would discover a cure for poverty.

It was a chilly night in late January. Stars spangled the sky, a scattering of fiery gems. Annette drew in the cold air cheerfully. She was well bundled up in an ankle-length, fox-fur coat, its long red fur just a shade or two lighter than her hair, and wore a matching muff and a round pillbox hat. Even her high-buttoned boots were made of a new kind of material that was waterproof. Bernard, however, shivered in his old wool jacket and thin-soled shoes lined with newspapers.

Once Annette had chided him for being silly when he refused to let her buy him a new topcoat for Christmas. He had been furious. She had learned the hard way that his pride was immense. He always paid her, punctually, for every hour she sat for him. Even though she was ashamed to take his money, he forced it on her. She had promised herself to bring him one of Jensen's old coats, but she had forgotten. Now, having dragged Bernard out into the damp winter night, she was ashamed again, this time at her cruel thoughtlessness. She could not bear to see an animal or a person suffer, not from the cold or anything else she could prevent.

"Are you cold?" she asked, hesitant.

"No, I'm fine," he answered, looking at her thoughtfully in the darkness of the street. "Don't worry about me, Annette."

"Oh, but I do. Here." She slipped her hand through his arm and pulled him close, snuggling up to his slim body. "Is that warmer?"

"Much," he said insinuatingly, a dark eyebrow raised.

Annette felt better. They strolled toward Chinatown watching the sailors, the street nymphs and the young men out carousing. It was beginning to look familiar to Annette. She loved it all, except for the beggars who held out their half-frozen, dirty hands to her. No matter how many times Bernard scolded her, she still insisted on dropping coins into those thin, heart-wrenching hands. Afterward without fail, she would receive a lecture on the ills of the world, on poverty and the need for people to believe in socialism. Bernard's philosophy was still an enigma to Annette, but silently, trying to understand and learn, she listened.

They passed a saloon brimming over with drunken men, its steamy windows hiding all but the sustained roar that emerged into the cold night. Annette tried to imagine what it was like inside. She thought it must be terribly exotic and wished she could go in.

As they neared Chinatown the atmosphere underwent a subtle change. The buildings grew more closely crowded together and were dotted with hundreds of tiny, high balconies. The background noises were different. The people, as if touched by a magic wand, became short and slight with yellow skin and black eyes, and most of them were dressed in the dark blue jacket and pants of the coolie. It was like entering another world, crossing the ocean in an instant. The people even walked differently. Their movements were more contained than the loose American stride and they kept their eyes lowered. Fewer women were on the streets. And somehow one never saw a rich Chinese. Annette wondered if they were all in hiding.

Annette and Bernard stopped outside an elegant restaurant that was obviously meant for tourists. Its double teak doors were surrounded by a lacquered, carved archway featuring dragons, exotic foliage and beautiful Chinese pagodas. On the upper balconies stood valuable vases full of plants and flowers. Bernard and Annette huddled in the cold and read the menu, which was absolutely mouth watering.

"What on earth is bird's-nest soup?" asked Annette. "And shark-fin soup?"

"I have no idea," admitted Bernard. "Chinese delicacies, I suppose."

"Let's go in and try them," pleaded Annette.

"I've eaten," replied Bernard glumly, recalling the bread and cheese that had been his dinner.

"So have I, but so what?" She hesitated. "Look, I'll pay this time—"

"I'm not hungry," he replied stiffly.

"Oh, never mind," Annette said quickly, embarrassed.

"I'm hoping to get a big commission next week," Bernard added loftily, "and then I'll bring you here and we'll celebrate."

"Oh, wonderful, Bernard!" Annette cried. "What is the commission?"

"Oh, it's something for the Hearsts. It's for their garden, actually."

"That's fantastic!" She was genuinely thrilled for him. "Maybe I can talk Daddy into ordering something from you."

"Annette, I don't want charity." His tone was chilling.

"Good heavens, it wouldn't be charity! Why, Jensen just bought one of Rolf Karman's paintings. It's hanging in the parlor. I'd rather look at something of yours."

"Why? Is his painting bad?"

"Well, no, it's not bad, it's . . . oh, forget it. You know what I mean." She moved away from the lighted facade of the restaurant, the night shadows enveloping her.

Bernard followed, his wry smile hidden by the darkness. She was awfully young, he thought, ridiculously, gloriously young. My God, to be like that again! He could allow himself to pine and suffer over her if he wasn't careful, but he wouldn't. He knew better. She was too strong willed, too competitive, too desirous of experimentation. Bernard knew himself. What he needed was a spare, ascetic woman, one who could share his Marxist beliefs, a helpmate. Annette, though undoubtedly exciting and provocative and sensually satisfying, would not be a help to Bernard on his chosen path.

As they strolled slowly up a hill, Annette pointed out various things that she noticed: a particularly well casted brass Buddha in a shop window, a bright silken scroll embroidered with birds and flowers, an exquisitely embroidered robe, an incense shop from which wafted pungent odors. They turned a corner, stepping out of a circle of light that pooled under a gaslight.

A gabble of angry Chinese erupted from behind the dark facade of a nearby building. A mangy cat slunk around a corner. They heard a scrabbling noise somewhere near them.

Bernard turned his head to glance behind them and then suddenly, terrifyingly, Annette felt a man's hands close on her. With one arm around her waist he nearly lifted her off her feet as he clamped his other hand, foul smelling and grimy, across her mouth.

She tried to scream and reached frantically for Bernard. A big man was standing over him with something dark and long and thick in his hand. The next glimpse she got, Bernard was crumpling as if in slow motion. He seemed to fall forever, his slim body suddenly boneless. As she watched horrified, he thudded to the dark pavement and lay motionless.

Kicking and twisting she fought the arms that gripped her, but they only squeezed tighter, cutting off her breath. She was being pulled backward, away from the untidy heap that was Bernard. In her frantic attempt to break free, she was aware of nothing but those iron bands that choked her, the rasping sound of her own breath, the frightful pounding of her heart, the muttered oaths of her captor when she succeeded in biting his hand. He drew back his arm and slapped her hard on the side of her face. Her ears rang and tears spurted from her eyes.

"Hey, don't hurt her!" she heard the big man say. "The boss'll murder us. No marks, he says."

"The bitch bit me!" howled her captor. "No hoity-toity society bitch does that to me!"

"Aw, shut up," grumbled the big man, and then they were silent.

Annette was pushed and shoved along shadowy streets and alleys. She'd lost her muff, her hat was falling off and her hair was tumbling into her face. She went without fighting now, realizing there was nothing she could do. Her ribs ached and her breath came in short, tearing gasps.

Finally they stopped in front of an anonymous door in an alleyway, the back door of one of the buildings that faced Grant Street. The big man knocked in a pattern—three short raps and two long. The door opened immediately and a rectangle of light spread onto the damp pavement. The silhouette of a huge, fat woman filled the doorway. She had a strange round knot on the top of her head and long gold earrings dangled from her fleshy earlobes.

"Ah so, this is girl for Mr. O'Neill?"

"Yeah. Quick, get her the hell out of sight. Where's Tansy?"

"You ask me 'please,' sirs."

"Yeah, sure. Please, Madame Yin-May. But you better hurry," answered Annette's captor.

"Come in, okay?" Yin-May ushered them into a narrow hallway.

Annette took it all in, her eyes wide with horror. She was having some kind of heinous nightmare, like one of Cecile's. Soon she'd wake screaming and someone would comfort her.

Madame Yin-May led them along the dim hall past several closed doors. Opening a door at the end of the hall, she gestured inside. Annette's captor shoved her through the doorway. She stopped short, clinging to the doorframe. A flight of stairs led down into stygian darkness.

"Get down there, bitch, before I push you," hissed the man.

"Easy," cautioned the big man. "Get a light."

"Light on top step, sirs, okay?" came Yin-May's voice. "I go now. Business very heavy tonight."

"Sure, go ahead. We'll find Tansy later." The big one reached down, found a kerosene lantern and lit it with a long wooden match.

"What are you doing with me?" quavered Annette. "Why are you doing this?" It was the first time she'd dared to speak since her kidnapping and her voice emerged far braver than she felt. She cowered against the wall away from the two men.

"How the hell do I know? I follow orders. Tansy says snatch the Tofler chippy, I do it. Now shut up and get down there!"

A big hand pressed against the small of her back and she stumbled down the rough wooden steps into a murky cellar. The kerosene lamp her captor held showed dust and shadows and cobwebs. Then Annette saw a wooden bench, a rough table and two chairs. A couple of moth-eaten blankets lay on the bench and a stub of a candle was stuck in its own wax on the table. The walls of bare rock were damp with condensation.

Sickened, horrified, Annette shuddered. "What do you want? Is it money? My father will pay you well to return me. He's rich." She tried to sound calm and self-possessed. Her eyes roamed the room and she cringed inwardly at the sight of the leaking walls, the dust and cobwebs, the splintered bench. She was surrounded by decay.

The big man laughed, showing broken yellow teeth. "Your father? Why, he's the one they're after!" He and his partner turned, climbed the stairs and stepped into the hall taking the lantern with them.

"No!" screamed Annette, her nerves completely jangled. "No! Don't leave me here! What do you want?"

But the door was closing. Now there was nothing but cold, stark blackness. Her sob hung in the air, desolate, frightening her with its feebleness. She was standing in the center of a dark, cold room, unable to see anything. She wanted to scream, to run, to beat her fists against the walls.

Mercifully, after what seemed an eternity of terror, her good sense began to take over. Stay calm, she told herself. They said you weren't to be harmed.

They're keeping you for something, for someone . . . this Tansy, whoever he is. Gradually, the thought fortified her. If only they had left her the lamp! It was the darkness that was unbearable. It closed in on her with unseen terrors, tiny sounds that were magnified out of all proportion.

Stretching her arms out in front of her, Annette walked slowly in the direction of the stairs. After what seemed a long time, her hands touched a cold, slimy wall. She recoiled in horror. Groping to the left and then to the right, she eventually located the stairs and began to climb, one hand on the wall. When her hand encountered the door, she felt around for the door handle. She tried it. It was locked. Quietly, not knowing who might be outside the door, she worked at the handle, pushing and pulling, trying to loosen the door. It was useless.

After a while she gave up and made her way back down the stairs. She began to cross the room to where she thought the table was, thinking that there might be some matches near the candle. She wanted to hurry, but the blackness was heavy with shadows and every step filled her with dread. She was afraid that at any moment she might collide with something unutterably horrible. Knocking her shin against one of the chairs, she let out a sharp cry that echoed again and again in the clammy cellar. Shaking, she sat down in the chair and felt all over the table top for a match. She even ran her hands over the grimy floor to see if any had dropped. Nothing.

Hugging her arms around her body, she decided there was nothing to do but wait. She designed a painting in her mind, every line, every brush stroke, every dab of color. It helped to keep her sane in the suffocating darkness.

Time was strangely disjointed. Annette had no

idea whether an hour or three hours had passed. She must have been in this hellhole for most of the night by now. Why didn't someone come to rescue her? Even the sight of that horrible man who had thrown her down here would be welcome!

Images of Bernard filled her mind. Was he dead? And if he were only unconscious, wouldn't he freeze to death or get pneumonia before somebody found him? If only she'd brought him that coat! Suddenly she was overcome by a terrible, useless regret.

She wondered what the big man had meant when he said they were after her father. Just who were "they"? As these questions whirled in her brain, she fought to keep her wits, to put fear out of her mind, to wait without wondering.

When the door opened at last her first reaction was to recoil from the light. Then she leapt to her feet.

"Miss Tofler?" came a thin, high-pitched man's voice.

"Yes, who is it?" she asked, having to lick her dry lips, force her throat to make the sounds.

A lantern descended the stairs. The figure behind was still bathed in shadows. "Tansy O'Neill, at your service," came the disembodied voice.

He put the lantern down on the table. Light touched the shadowy man and she could finally see him.

She couldn't help but stare. He was tall and emaciated. His face was like a skull, all bones and dark, sunken eye sockets, and his clothes hung limply on his skeletal limbs. His mouth, however, was pink and soft and her eyes were drawn to the eerie smile she saw there. It frightened her even more than the darkness.

"Sorry those apes left you in the dark," offered Tansy. "That wasn't supposed to happen."

She averted her eyes from his smile. "What do you want? My father has lots of—"

He cut her off. "I know your father and I know how much money he has. That's not it." He eyed her greedily, reached out a thin white hand to fondle a strand of her tousled hair. "Now I know what Karman was after. He ain't no fool."

"Karman! What do you mean?" Annette was shocked. Did this whole thing have something to do with Rolf? And how did this Tansy know?

"Nothing, honey. Now, I'll tell you all about what's going on here." He sat down on a chair, arranging his scarecrow legs in front of him, and moved the lantern so that it cast light on them both. "Sit down." He gestured at the other chair.

Annette sat hesitantly.

"It's like this. Your daddy has been mucking up lately. And my boss don't like it 'cause he loses money every time it happens. Last night a shipment of Chinese girls, an illegal shipment, that is, was bound for Seattle and the railroad car wasn't there. Your old daddy messed up. It was his job to have the car there. Them poor heathen girls milled around the railroad yard until they were found out and shipped back to the harbor. Now that cost my boss a lot of money and he's mad."

"I don't believe it! Let me talk to this boss of yours. Who is he?" Her stomach lurched sickeningly at Tansy's story.

"Chris Buckley."

"Chris . . . Blind Chris Buckley?" she choked, horrified. But her father wouldn't deal with a man like that. He just wouldn't. "No!" she cried. "You're lying!"

Tansy O'Neill laughed shrilly. "Why else do you

think we'd have you here? Use that pretty little head of yours."

Oh God, she thought in mute terror. Was he telling her the truth? Could her father actually be dealing with these beasts? Was it possible? But even as her mind recoiled from Tansy's revelation, Annette had no choice but to believe him. It was true. It had to be. Why else would she be here? Now she knew the worst. Her father was dealing with that criminal. It explained everything. She was silent, unable even to think.

Tansy continued, his cold, deathly grin still on his face. "So naturally your daddy has to be disciplined. We get his daughter, he gets another car set up, has more girls shipped to Seattle and everything's fine. Little Annette is returned to him, safe and sound."

"And if he doesn't?" Her voice emerged in a sick, weak whisper.

"He will."

"What if something happens? What if he can't?"

"He damned well better!" snarled Tansy.

"What are you going to do with me meanwhile?"

"You stay here." He nodded and closed his eyes, grinning. "But with a light, of course."

"I see."

"There's one little thing you have to do for us." He pulled a creased, dirty sheet of paper from his pocket and a stub of a pencil. "You write down what I tell you so your daddy'll know we really got you."

"What do I say?"

"Just write that we have you and to do like we say or you're done for. Then sign your name. And no tricks."

Annette wrote the note, her hand trembling so badly that she wondered whether her father would recognize it as her own handwriting.

Tansy took the paper, folded it and put it in his

pocket. "Thank you, Miss Annette Tofler," he replied sarcastically. "Now you better damned well hope your daddy takes enough time off from Tilly Grueter to see to this business." He gave a short, harsh laugh.

"Tilly?"

"Your daddy's fancy woman. Why you should see her. 'Bout your age, she is. Real pretty. Don't you know anything?" He laughed again and ran lightly up the stairs, closing the door behind him with a sharp click.

Annette put her head down on her folded arms and cried, her body shaking convulsively with sobs. After a while she sat up, dried her eyes and wiped her nose on a hanky she found stuffed in a pocket of her fur coat.

She had plenty of time to digest all the new information she'd just learned. It all made sense now. So Edward had a mistress. Of course. That's why he'd been gone so much. And his dealings with Blind Chris Buckley. Maybe, she guessed, everyone dealt with him. Maybe they had to.

She wondered then if Jensen knew. He might have been lying to her when he'd told her Edward was above dealing with Chris Buckley. But one thing still puzzled her. How did Tansy know about her and Rolf Karman? Her face flushed hot even in the cold, dim basement. How many other people knew?

Then it occurred to her that she would be missed soon. Even if Edward wasn't home, Jensen would worry about her. And Bernard! If he was still alive, he'd tell the police. But no, Blind Chris owned the police. Everyone knew that. They wouldn't help. But maybe Jensen would know what to do. Maybe he'd find her anyway.

As the hours passed slowly, endlessly, Annette's spirits seesawed. One minute she was sure her father would meet their demands and have her safely out of there by morning; the next minute she was just as sure something would go wrong and she would be left in this hellhole to rot forever. Her muscles grew cramped and chilled. Her mind raced. She couldn't even begin to sleep. She walked up and down, up and down, thinking, planning, wondering. At last she sank down onto the hard wooden bench and curled up with the filthy blanket over her. She dozed, started, dozed again. The cold made her muscles ache. She dreamed in snatches, saw Bernard, her father, Cecile, then, oddly enough, Rolf Karman's roughhewn face.

She woke. The kerosene lamp had gone out, but from above her through a blackened window a dim light reached into the cellar. It was morning.

Suddenly she heard a noise behind her. It came from the corner under the stairs. She turned. A large wharf rat regarded her unblinkingly. Then it disappeared into the dark shadows. She yelped in fright, her heart pounding, her hands clutched to her chest.

And then she heard another sound. Her overwrought nerves gave way. She jumped up and screamed.

It was only the door opening at the top of the stairs. A crack of light spilled into the cellar and gradually widened. They were coming to rescue her!

Madame Yin-May appeared in the doorway. She was tugging at something. The figure of a slim girl appeared behind her, a Chinese girl dressed in black pants and a black, quilted Chinese jacket. Obviously terrified, she was resisting the fat woman's grip. Her shining black hair was caught up in a long pigtail at the back of her head and it swung around her face as she pulled back. Madame Yin-May shoved the girl unceremoniously down the stairs. She bumped against the wall, lost her footing and fell.

Annette heard her cry of fear. She jumped up, ran to the stairs and helped the Chinese girl to her feet. The girl was so small and fragile that her bones were mere matchsticks. She was young too, perhaps Annette's age. Her pale, ivory face was dirty and streaked with tears and her huge black eyes were wide with terror. She stood trembling in the dank cellar, looking at Annette.

"Do you speak English?" Annette asked cautiously. "Why are you here? Did they hurt you?" She stopped, afraid she was frightening the girl even more. "My name is Annette. I'm a prisoner here, too." She spoke very slowly, enunciating each word carefully.

The beautiful Chinese girl looked back at her with a kind of sad dignity, her tilted black eyes wondering. She smiled a tiny, gentle smile that seemed to light up the dark cellar. "My name is Su Ling," she whispered in lilting, accented English.

"Oh, I'm so glad to have someone to talk to! It's been so terrible. Why are you here? What do they want from you?"

Su Ling shrugged her thin shoulders. A wise, tender smile touched her lips. "Me? They wish to sell me."

"Sell you?" cried Annette. "My God!"

"It's done all the time. My father lost the battle, he was killed, my sisters taken. Me they sell." She spoke as if she were remarking on the weather.

"Battle? What battle?"

"In China, near Shanghai, where I live. Many months ago."

"They sent you from China? How do you know English?" Annette was beyond amazement. The world was not the tidy little place she'd thought. Even Bernard's Marxism seemed naive in the face of Su Ling's story.

"I go to Christian Father's school. My family very modern. That's why my feet are not bound." She looked down at her delicate, narrow feet that certainly looked small enough to Annette. "That's why no man in China wants me. But here the men don't know better. They don't care if a woman has big, ugly feet."

Annette gave a little laugh. She felt so much better. At least she wasn't alone anymore. She even felt a little hungry and thirsty.

The door opened again. Madame Yin-May's round face appeared. As if she had read Annette's thoughts, the woman brought in a tray containing a teapot and two cups. She set it down on the rough table. "Very good tea," she said. "Okay? You drink tea all up. Make you feel better."

"What about something to eat?" Annette cried, almost frantic. "We'll starve to death."

As if she hadn't heard Annette's outburst, Madame Yin-May repeated, "Drink tea all up." She turned and climbed the stairs in an amazingly agile manner for a woman of her girth and years and closed the door in the two girls' surprised faces.

Chapter 17

Jensen rubbed his tired eyes and checked his pocket watch once more. It was fifteen minutes to two. "Damn," he muttered rising from his desk. He went to the window and looked out over Third Street. Where were Annette and Cecile? They were supposed to have met him for lunch at noon and it had been Annette's idea in the first place.

Only yesterday morning she had said, "Let's take Cecile to lunch tomorrow and then go shopping. It might cheer her up."

Where were they? He paced back to his desk and then to the window again. Perhaps Annette was angry with him for not coming home last night. But good Lord, her behavior hadn't been much better of late. Besides, he had made the appointment for dinner and a card game with his friends several nights before. She wasn't his mother, after all. Last night had been perfectly innocent. It was just that his friends had kept him up all night long. As he thought it over, he realized it couldn't be that. Annette wouldn't care. She wasn't angry, she was just plain late.

It was two fifteen before Ned rapped on the office door and announced Jensen's sister.

"At last," grumbled Jensen, thoroughly annoyed.

Cecile entered the office, alone.

"Where's Annette?" asked Jensen gruffly, unintentionally venting his anger on Cecile.

"She's . . . Oh, Jensen!" His older sister suddenly began to weep. "I don't know!"

Cecile was exceptionally upset. This was more than her usual nervousness. She was clearly overwrought. "Come now," he soothed, going to her. "She's probably gone off somewhere with one of her artist friends. Don't look so worried."

"No! No, I'm sure she never even came home last night! I waited all morning. She's gone!"

Jensen fell silent, his brows knitted together. "You're sure she didn't come home last night?"

"Yes. Vivian said so, too. Her bed was untouched. We're all so upset!"

Now that was odd, thought Jensen. Very bizarre, even for Annette. She had always been home at night, always. And lately, since Cecile's return, Annette had been spending more time around the house than usual. This was strange indeed.

He led Cecile back to the outer office. "Ned, see that my sister gets home safely." He put his arm around Cecile. "Now don't you fret. I have an idea where she may be. It's nothing to concern yourself over. Believe me, when I get her home, we'll all give her a good tongue lashing. He tried to smile cheerfully.

"Are you certain she's all right?"

"Yes, Cecile. Now go on. And don't worry." He kissed her on the cheek reassuringly.

Jensen had no trouble finding Annette's studio at the Montgomery Block building. Once he had slipped the clerk five dollars, he was most helpful. He led Jensen upstairs himself, "Just to be sure you're really Miss Annette's brother," and let him in with the passkey when she failed to answer the door.

Jensen glanced briefly around the small room and was surprised by the excellent quality of Annette's paintings. She wasn't there. On the way back to the lobby, he thought to ask the thin desk clerk, "I say, do you know my sister's friend, Bernard Maduro? I believe that's his name."

"I do, sir. He often dines in Coppa's restaurant."

"Would you know where he lodges?" Jensen asked.

"Now that, sir, I wouldn't know."

A dead end. Where on earth could Annette be? This wasn't like her at all. Jensen walked out onto Montgomery Street. The biting wind slashing off the bay chilled him. He paced the street, turning his coat collar up against the damp cold. Who would know where Maduro lived? Who were some of Annette's other friends in the artistic community? Did she know anyone in the upper crust of that circle, someone with whom he could check? Someone at the Bohemian Club, for instance?

Bernard Maduro was an up and coming sculptor, so perhaps someone at the Astor House knew him. Who knows, he might even live there. It was worth a try. By God, Jensen thought, as the stinging air nipped his cheeks, when he found Annette he was going to throttle her!

As he purposefully walked the few blocks to the Astor House, he cursed Annette many times over. When he found her he was going to put an end to her shenanigans once and for all. This business of her traipsing around like a common chippy was going to stop. And to think how worried Cecile was! Why would Annette do such a heartless thing?

Jensen was disappointed to discover that Bernard Maduro did not reside at the Astor House. "No, sir," said the clerk, "there is no one with that name here."

Frowning, he turned to leave. An idea occurred to him and he stopped. "Rolf Karman lives here, doesn't he?"

"Why yes, sir."

Bernard Maduro knew Rolf Karman, Jensen recalled. Fortunately Rolf was at home. Obviously, however, Jensen had come at a most inopportune time. He had knocked on the door, been greeted by Rolf warmly then shown inside. Then it had turned awkward.

Eleanor Fairchild, with whom Jensen was acquainted, was standing half naked in Rolf's studio room, with only a scanty sheet for covering.

"Eleanor is modeling," explained Rolf easily, an amused grin touching his lips.

"Oh," replied Jensen, nodding politely at Eleanor who looked much like a woman disturbed in the throes of love: flushed, swollen-lipped, blonde hair tangled to her waist.

Still, Eleanor seemed unconcerned. She returned Jensen's greeting and moved toward a curtained alcove. "I suppose we should call it a day, Rolf," she cooed lightly.

"Yes," he agreed. "Same time tomorrow?" Rolf led Jensen back down the hall to a surprisingly tidy sitting room.

Jensen stood in the center of the room, facing Rolf. "Sorry," he shrugged. "I had no idea you were . . . entertaining."

"Enertaining?" Rolf laughed, a deep, amused sound. "Well, yes, Eleanor is quite entertaining, but she actually was modeling. That is," he winked, "when you knocked."

Jensen relaxed. "That makes me feel a little better."

"And besides," added Rolf, "I can't think of anything quite as pleasantly unexpected as a visit from you. Perhaps we should paint the town red tonight. It's been a long while, my friend."

"Yes. It has." Jensen sank into a chair. "But I'm afraid this is business, Rolf. It's about Annette."

"Annette?" Abruptly Rolf's handsome features darkened. A frown settled over his brow. "My God, is she all right?"

Jensen pushed aside his surprise over Rolf's strong reaction to the mention of his sister. "I'm not sure." He paused, studying Rolf's face once more. The man seemed truly concerned. Now that was odd. "She's missing. Since last night it appears. The only person I could think of she might be with is—"

"Me," interrupted Rolf, his eyes meeting Jensen's levelly.

Jensen fell silent measuring the tall, fair-haired man standing before him. Yes, he reasoned suddenly, Annette would be fascinated by a carefree, rakish type like Rolf Karman. How stupid he had been not to have seen it before. At her party Annette had danced with Rolf. And they had conversed earlier in the evening. It had been a tense conversation.

Rolf was speaking. "Judging by the look on your face, Jensen," he said tightly, "I'd say I let the cat out of the bag."

"Yes. I'm afraid you have." He felt sudden anger flare within him.

"You were going to mention someone else, weren't you? Perhaps Annette's dear friend, Bernard." Rolf went to the door and closed it for privacy.

"Yes. I was going to ask you if you knew where he lived. I had no idea that you, well, that you knew Annette quite so well." His tone was stiff, artificial.

Rolf smiled thinly. His dark, unreadable eyes rested on Jensen for a long moment. "I'm not ashamed to say that I do know your sister . . . quite well. If you wish," he paused, shrugging, "to make this a matter of honor . . ."

"Honor!" Jensen leapt to his feet. "Annette's missing and you speak of honor!"

Rolf remained motionless, the smile fading. "You're quite right, Jensen. We must find her first. And then . . ."

"And then," Jensen finished for him, "you both have some explaining to do. If she's been . . . seeing you, I hold you fully responsible. You are the man, the one with experience."

"Annette," drawled Rolf, eyeing Jensen with laughter in his eyes, "would hate to admit that."

"What in hell are you driving at?" asked Jensen angrily.

"Nothing except that your baby sister has her own ideas of what she wants."

"And she wants you?" sneered Jensen. "A man of no background whatsoever? A cracker? A gambler? Don't be ridiculous. She's just experimenting!"

With sudden agility, Rolf's hand was on his arm, forcing Jensen around to face him. Shocked and angry Jensen pulled away, ready to come to blows.

"Oh!" came a cry from the door, freezing the two men like statues.

"Eleanor," Rolf growled, dropping his hand from Jensen, shaking off the sudden loss of control. "What are you still doing here?" He walked to a small sideboard and poured a brandy. Looking over his shoulder toward Jensen, he poured another.

"I was just leaving," she murmured timidly, looking from one man to the other. "Well," she faltered, "I'll see you tomorrow." She reclosed the door.

Rolf picked up the brandies and walked back to

Jensen. "I'm sorry," he said levelly. "I shouldn't have mentioned anything about Annette and me."

Jensen was still furious, his hands trembling at his sides. He studied Rolf for a long, pregnant moment. Damn the man, he thought silently. Just how far had he gone with Annette? What exactly did he mean by quite well? And he had admitted it so openly, so coolly!

After taking the brandy and draining the glass with a long gulp, Jensen spoke. "My only concern at this moment, Rolf, is to find Annette. I must admit," he paused glaring hotly at the painter, "that I should very much like to call you out, but it will have to wait."

"As you like," drawled Rolf dryly. "And I should hope you'll allow me to assist in finding her. Whatever you choose to believe, Jensen, I do care about your sister."

"I'll accept your help, but only because you know the crowd Annette associates with far better than I."

Rolf strode to the door. "We should check Maduro's place first, then."

Silently, they walked through the growing cold of the late afternoon to Bernard Maduro's apartment house on Powell Street. It was only a few blocks. At the entrance to the building, Rolf stopped. "Perhaps you should go up alone," he stated unemotionally, "as Bernard and I aren't getting along too well lately. I'm sure you understand."

"An argument over my sister, no doubt," said Jensen grimly.

"Yes. A while back I ran into them down near the Barbary Coast. I'm afraid I overreacted to the situation."

"I see," replied Jensen, averting his eyes. "I'll be down shortly then, with Annette in tow, I hope."

Neither Bernard nor Annette was there, however. Jensen checked with the landlady. No, she hadn't seen Bernard for a couple of days.

Once back out on the street, Rolf suggested to Jensen that they might check at the police station.

Jenson froze. "You don't think . . ."

"I'm not thinking anything. I only suggest we check. It can't do any harm." Rolf's tone was deep and reassuring to Jensen.

The police station was back toward the center of the city, but still only a few blocks. Again they walked. The darkness increased, and the damp air seeped through their warm woolen coats. The tops of the tall buildings were still bathed in a pearly pink glow as the sun slid farther below the Pacific horizon. The alleyways they passed were now shadowy and forbidding, threatening danger to those who dared to enter. Now and again, like red spots of light, the eyes of a rat stared unblinkingly out from the dimness, sending a chill up Jensen's spine. Occasionally at night and particularly on this night, the fun-seeking city lost all its charm for Jensen. There were too many thefts, rapes, kidnappings—the infamous shanghai routine. It was a dark jungle where evil could lurk under the canopy of fog in the dim, secret alleyways between tall buildings. Annette might well be lost in this jungle, alone and terrified.

"Bernard Maduro or Annette Tofler? Let me check for you," said the burly Irish sergeant on desk duty at the police station. He climbed down from his tall wooden stool and disappeared through a swinging door to the rear.

Returning several minutes later, he climbed back up onto his lofty perch. He held a paper in his hand. "Seems this Bernard Maduro was found last night in an alley off Grant Avenue in Chinatown."

"My God!" whispered Jensen, anxiety washing over him.

"Take it easy." Rolf led him over to a stiff-backed wooden chair, then returned to the sergeant. "Is Maduro alive?" he asked calmly, under his breath.

"Alive? Yes. He's at the Sisters of Mercy Hospital. But it says here that he's still unconscious."

"And Annette Tofler? Any report on her?" Rolf held his breath.

"Nope. Just this Maduro fellow."

"Thank you, Sergeant."

Rolf gave Jensen the news as he led him back outside into the shadowy night. He hailed a carriage as the hospital was some distance away on Van Ness Street. "At least Annette isn't in the hospital," he reassured Jensen, trying to remain calm and collected. "And there's no way of telling whether she was in Chinatown with Maduro in the first place. Let's just wait and see if he's conscious yet. There's nothing else we can do. Take it easy, Jensen." Rolf patted him on the arm as the carriage rattled through the patchy fog along Van Ness Street.

"Oh God, Rolf," Jensen moaned, "what if she was shanghaied?"

"Come on now, Jensen. First off, those kidnappings only occur on the Barbary Coast, not in Chinatown. And secondly, only seamen or curious, stray young boys are shanghaied. Now quit speculating. Let's just wait and piece this puzzle together as best we can. All right?"

"All right." Jensen took a deep breath of the damp, chill air. "And Rolf, I want to thank you for this support. Annette's very dear to me. I'm sorry I lost my temper earlier."

Rolf smiled tightly. "Whatever else you may believe, Jensen, she's very special to me also."

A white-clad nun led the two tall men to Bernard's bedside in the long charity ward. Bernard looked like death itself, but it turned out that he'd regained consciousness for a brief spell several hours before. The nun now felt certain that he would recover and thought it likely that he would be able to talk to them.

She touched Bernard's arm lightly. "Are you awake, Mr. Maduro?"

Bernard opened his eyes slowly. Squinting, he looked up at the gaslight. "Where . . . where am I?" he groaned.

"You're at the Sisters of Mercy Hospital. Don't you remember? You were struck on the head?"

"Yes, from behind." Pausing, he seemed to search his memory. "Annette and I were—"

"Annette!" cried Jensen.

Rolf placed a restraining hand on Jensen's shoulder. "Let's take it slowly," he suggested quietly. He leaned closer to Bernard. "It's Rolf Karman, Bernard. Annette's brother and I are looking for her. Have you any idea where she might be?"

"Rolf?" Bernard turned his head toward him, grimacing with pain.

"Yes. Rolf Karman. About Annette?"

"We were walking," Bernard said faintly, beginning to slip under again. "In Chinatown. I got slugged from behind. Annette? I don't know." His head fell back on the pillow and he dozed off.

"Oh, God!" Jensen moaned. "But why?" With an effort, he gathered himself together. He left instructions for Maduro to be moved to a private room and assigned a full-time nurse. At the mention of his name, the white-robed nuns scurried to comply. Why, the Toflers could donate a whole new wing if they wanted!

The two men walked back to the carriage. "Mason Street," Rolf instructed the driver.

"Home? Why?" asked Jensen, frowning, trying desperately to think.

"Because it sounds like a kidnapping, Jensen. Why else would Bernard have been found alone if it was robbery, for instance, or some other thing? And if it is a kidnapping, you can expect a ransom note. All we can do is wait."

The carriage pulled up in front of the Nob Hill mansion. Rolf paid the driver and the two men rushed up the marble steps.

"Jensen!" cried Cecile, swinging open the door. "Have you found Annette?"

"No. Not yet."

Cecile looked at the tall, handsome man following Jensen into the hall. "I'm Jensen's sister, Cecile," she introduced herself.

"Rolf Karman, ma'am. I'm a friend." He took her hand and squeezed it reassuringly. "Might I ask if there's been any letter delivered today?"

Cecile thought for a moment. "Why, yes," she remembered, "late this afternoon. It was addressed to my father, though."

"Where is it?" asked Jensen, alarmed.

Cecile went to the hall table and picked up a sealed letter. She handed it to Jensen. It was addressed to Edward Tofler and she told them it had been hand delivered. "Is it about Annette?" she asked in a trembling whisper, her hands twisting in the folds of her dress.

"I don't know," replied Jensen, tearing open the seal.

Rolf suggested to Cecile that she might pour them both a brandy. There was no point in having this delicate woman hear the contents of the letter without proper preparation. When Cecile had disappeared into the drawing room Jensen went to the lamp and began reading. The handwriting was a terrible scrawl.

> Tofler,
>
> I have your daughter and I'm sure you know exactly why. If my demands are not met. . . .
>
> You have fouled up the shipment of women to Seattle for the last time. This mess cost us plenty and new girls are hard to come by. The next shipment will be at your expense and at your leisure, as I will hold Annette until the boxcar leaves Oakland safely. If any authorities interfere, either police or railroad inspectors, well, Tofler, so much the worse for Annette.
>
> Contact Tansy when the boxcar is ready.
>
> Chris.

With it was Annette's short note, scribbled hastily.

"Dear God!" The letter slipped from Jensen's fingers and fluttered to the floor. "Seattle," he muttered, "Pacific Growers, of course!"

Rolf picked up the two sheets of paper, scanning their contents for himself. Cecile reappeared then, carrying a silver tray with two brandies.

"Is it about Annette?" she asked, swaying on her feet.

Rolf took the tray from her and set it down on the hall table. She looked from one worried face to the other. A tear slid down her cheek.

"Jensen," said Rolf, "would you mind if I handled this?"

Cecile looked both dubious and frightened, but

Jensen nodded affirmatively to Rolf. "Rolf will explain it all to you," he told her, his voice distant. "It's all right, Cecile," he added, forcing a smile. "You go on up to your sitting room with Rolf. He'll tell you everything." Jensen reread the letter and Annette's note, tossing down the brandy in one quick gulp.

Rolf found Jensen in the drawing room when he returned a little while later. "Your sister is with Vivian," he told him, shedding his heavy overcoat and going to stand near the fireplace. "I told her only that someone had taken Annette for ransom, that she was perfectly fine and soon would be safely home."

"That's good." Jensen rubbed his hands before the leaping flames. "Cecile's quite weak. Hasn't been well lately. Thank you for handling it." He looked at Rolf vacantly.

"She does seem frail. But what about your father? Shouldn't he be told?"

"The almighty Edward Tofler?" spat Jensen. "And who do you suppose got Annette into this mess in the first place? I've been so blind not to see this coming!"

"What exactly," asked Rolf slowly, "is going on with this shipment of women, anyway? I assume they're Chinese."

"Yes. Apparently my esteemed father has been providing boxcars for Chris Buckley to ship these women to various destinations. Like cattle. Lately, I've been suspicious that something like this was going on."

"Perhaps your father, then, should handle this."

"God, no! Never!"

Rolf was taken aback by the vehemence in Jensen's voice, but said nothing. If Jensen wanted to explain, he would.

"You've got to understand that my father has all but destroyed his family. Oh sure, we've got money.

Some say the world is at our feet. But Edward Tofler has turned into a sickness that's eating away at us all. Even Annette." Jensen went to the sideboard and poured another brandy. "Right now Edward Tofler is no doubt with his little trollop. Tilly something or other." He faced Rolf from across the room. "You should see her, Rolf. Why, she's not much older than Annette. It's disgusting."

Rolf nodded silently.

"He can stay with her and rot, for all I give a damn. I'll take care of my sisters and to hell with Edward Tofler."

"All right," agreed Rolf finally, his hand smoothing the neat mustache above his lip thoughtfully. "Would you allow me a suggestion?"

"Of course."

"First off," Rolf gazed down into the glowing embers, "I think you should know . . . let me correct that . . . you have the right to know . . . that I care very deeply for Annette. More than I should. I was her first lover, Jensen. I pursued her, perhaps deceitfully, but she's been a thorn in my side ever since." He lifted his gaze from the fire to meet Jensen's eyes levelly. "I'm telling you this because I want you to know that anything I suggest is for her safety and that alone."

"Do you love her, Rolf?"

Rolf shrugged and laughed ruefully. "Love? I've never been in love, Jensen. And I honestly don't know if I ever will be. What's more, Annette thoroughly dislikes me. Isn't that a switch?" Again he laughed. "At any rate, I think you should send a message to Buckley. Let him know you're working on the so-called ransom."

"No!" Jensen balled his fists at his sides. "I won't deal with him. Tofler Transport is my life now. I can't deal with a criminal like him. Don't you see that I'd never be free of his corrupt machine if I did? I'd end up a ruined shell just like him."

Slowly, deliberately, Rolf chose his words. "I didn't suggest that you actually go through with a deal. Just stall him, for Annette's sake. Look," he said purposefully, "we can assume she's being held in Chinatown somewhere. We have an edge there."

"The police! We could—"

"No. The police are in Buckley's pocket. They won't help. We'll have to do it on our own."

"You're right, of course. No police." Jensen raked a hand through his thick brown hair, mussing it.

"Get a message to Buckley. Tell him you're working on the details for the shipment. Tell him something convincing that will buy us a little time."

"Yes. I'll do it. But Rolf," Jensen reminded, "I can't deal with him."

Rolf studied him for a long moment. "What if we can't locate her ourselves? Chris Buckley doesn't bluff."

"I know, I know." Jensen looked away, tormented. "We'll just have to cross that bridge when we come to it." Suddenly his young face contorted. "Do you think Buckley would harm her?"

"No. Not if we act quickly."

"But . . . in other ways? My God," he moaned, "she's so young, so beautiful."

Yes, thought Rolf grimly, she is young. Hadn't he himself been unable to keep his hands off her beautiful flesh? What man could resist a woman like Annette?

Unbidden, Tansy O'Neill's face rose to Rolf's mind. As Chris Buckley's henchman, he was no doubt involved in the kidnapping of Annette. Tansy was a vile man capable of any atrocities against those who crossed him. Rolf recalled the card game at the Lotus Den, Tansy's sunken eyes boring into his own. The man was vicious and what was worse, Rolf suspected, quite insane.

"What if. . . ? Rolf tried to keep the thought from entering his mind but was unable to. What if Tansy took a liking to Annette? What if those cadaverous fingers touched her beautiful flesh? Images filled his mind. He fought desperately against them. He mustn't lose his tight control. Not now. He wouldn't think about it, he couldn't.

A vile, sick taste rose to his mouth. He forced it down. "We can't worry about that possibility, Jensen. We can't allow ourselves to. Remember this, if Annette is returned to you harmed in any way, then surely Buckley knows you'll seek revenge."

"Yes. Yes, you're right. He wouldn't dare."

"All right then," said Rolf, determinedly pushing aside all thoughts about Annette's present danger, "write the message and send it over right away."

"And then?"

"And then we start at the beginning. We go to Chinatown."

A knock at the front door interrupted them. Both men stiffened. It was late, too late for a caller. Perhaps it was someone with word of Annette. Jensen arrived at the door only a pace ahead of Rolf. He swung open the heavy door, worry lines creasing his brow. His hand trembled in anticipation. He had expected a policeman or a messenger, but surprisingly, there was a young woman standing in the portal, the hood of her long grey wool cape hiding her features.

"What?" Jensen murmured as she stepped into the shaft of light from the hall lamp. Suddenly he recognized her. "How dare you come here!" he exploded, but then, just as abruptly, he fell silent. It was his father's mistress, yes, but some of his anger abated as he noticed her condition. She had been beaten, not too severely, but enough to blacken one eye and bruise her full lower lip. Had Edward Tofler resorted to this?

"I demand to see Edward!" she cried shrilly.

"He's not here." Jensen remained standing in front of Rolf, barring her entrance to the house.

"He's in terrible danger!" the young woman continued frantically. "I must see him! I waited and waited, but he didn't come. I've looked everyplace else I could think of."

"I already told you. He's not here. In fact," continued Jensen bitterly, "you should have a better notion of where he is than I do."

"I'm so frightened," moaned Tilly, oblivious to Jensen's obvious distaste for her. "He beat me up! He said awful things! And I really don't know where Edward is. He goes to different saloons. Men's clubs, sometimes. I don't know where he is!"

"Who beat you up?" asked Jensen quickly.

"That man, that awful skinny man!" cried Tilly. "He wanted to find Edward."

"I should imagine that my beloved father is quite fine," Jensen answered deliberately. "No doubt he's drunk somewhere. You see, when they couldn't find Edward Tofler, they took his daughter instead."

"What?" Tilly gasped, confused.

"My sister, Annette, has been kidnapped. When you find your dear Edward, tell him that! Tell him the danger he's placed his daughter in!"

"Oh Lord, but we must find Edward and tell him!"

"You find Edward!" spat Jensen. "I couldn't care less where he is or what kind of state he's in."

"But that man will find him and—"

"It's his fault Annette is in danger. When you locate him, or when he comes crawling back to you, tell him that. And tell him that I'll handle this. Tell him to keep out of it." Jensen felt a restraining hand on his arm and realized it was Rolf.

"Listen," began Rolf softly, "I think this young lady should be on her way home. It's late. Have you a cab?" he asked, looking past her into the darkness.

Tilly Grueter looked from one masculine face to the other. "Yes," she said, "I hired one to find Edward. It was quite expensive. In fact, I had to see a doctor, too. I don't have the money for these things. I'm a poor girl and it seems to me that since it was his fault I got messed up in all this . . ." Defiantly, she stood her ground on the doorstep, her swollen cheek only too evident as she let the hood fall back.

"Here," growled Jensen, peeling off a bill from a roll of money in his pocket. "This should cover your expenses."

"Pretty uppish, aren't we?" hissed Tilly. "If your father—"

"Good night, ma'am," Rolf offered, hoping to end the scene as quickly as possible.

Holding her chin erect, she whirled away into the chill night as Jensen all but slammed the door on her retreating form. Raking a tired hand through his thick hair, he turned to face Rolf.

"Mercenary little thing, isn't she?" commented Rolf.

"My father deserves her."

They walked back toward the drawing room where Jensen slumped into an overstuffed chair facing the hearth. "You know," he reflected, "I used to think my father was the strongest, smartest man walking the earth. Then, as I got older, I made up excuses for him. . . ."

"And now?" Rolf prompted quietly.

"Now? Yes, well, now he's merely an empty hull of a man. A has-been. God, how I loathe him!"

Chapter 18

After two days Annette was no longer sure how many hours or days had passed in the horrible cellar. Sometimes it seemed that only a few minutes had drifted by and then again it seemed that she had been locked in forever, her former carefree life of freedom a distant dream.

Dreams. She had been having the most curious dreams. Her mind floated when she slept, twisting and turning in a labyrinth of colors and images that were beautiful but terrifying and frighteningly vivid. Sometimes she dreamed she was home in her rose-colored room and it seemed appropriate to be there. Then she would wake up to the cold, dank cellar and that too would seem quite appropriate. Faces swam in front of her eyes. Some were familiar and some strange, with staring eyes and mouths forming alien words that somehow she was able to understand. Su Ling was having odd dreams, too and the two girls had discussed it several times.

During the day they were both lethargic. Slumping on the hard bench, they spoke desultorily of their past lives, or of when they thought they might be let out of the cellar. In Su Ling's case, that would be when Madame Yin-May found a buyer willing to spend a fortune on a virginal Chinese girl of good family. Su Ling was very curious when Annette confided to her that she was no longer a virgin. Annette described the act of love in detail and then the men. They laughed till they could hardly breathe over her escapade with Freddy Sims and then they drifted into more dreams and were quiet.

It was a strange interlude. After the initial day of hunger and some pleading on Annette's part, they were fed twice a day, usually by one of the two men who had captured Annette or occasionally by Madame Yin-May. There was usually rice, a few vegetables or fish—certainly not enough to sustain one human life, much less two—and always, without fail, the pot of warming, fragrant tea. The steaming pot of tea was the focal point of their day; they awaited it with hungry desire. They would drink it slowly, savoring every sip, pretending they were not in a filthy dungeon. And then they would feel drowsy and content and would fall silent again.

Annette began to feel she knew Su Ling very well, better than anyone she'd ever known. They confided their most cherished dreams and hopes to each other. Annette spoke of her painting and Su Ling of her desire for peace and security, a husband and many children. Su Ling was a brave girl. She never cried or complained, but accepted her fate with seeming equanimity. She would go with the *tao*, she explained, but Annette never quite grasped what the *tao* was. Still, she respected and liked Su Ling more and more.

They spoke of their families. Even when Su Ling described her father's death her voice did not falter. It was the *tao*, she said. One must accept it. She spoke of her brothers and sisters, described them as life's warriors, handsome and brave and intelligent. Her life had been serene and lovely. In turn Annette described her father, Cecile and Jensen. She found herself growing eloquent over her brother's attributes.

"He's very handsome with light brown wavy hair. He has hazel eyes like mine and a lovely dimple in the middle of his chin. Jensen's very smart and knowledgeable. He knows everybody. He's kind and sweet and he'll make a wonderful husband someday. But he says all the girls in San Francisco are boring." She sighed, remembering. "Oh, how I wish he were here now!"

It must have been toward the end of her second day in the cellar, for she remembered only four pots of tea, when Tansy O'Neill banged open the door and descended the stairs. Annette leapt to her feet. Surely her father had ransomed her! The dank room spun crazily; her ears rang.

But Tansy's face was white and drawn and angry. "Your damned father ain't around and your brother got the note!" he snarled. "He says he can't arrange things yet. He needs time, he says, till tomorrow!"

Annette cowered back, afraid he was going to hit her.

"He's just playing for time. I know it." He turned his pale gaze on her. "So you'll set here some more."

"I . . . I'm sorry," was all Annette could think of to say. She tried desperately to gather her wits, but the damp cellar seeed to have done something to her. Her brain was addled. "I know he'll do it. Please . . ."

"He better! Or your pretty little neck'll be wrung like a chicken's!"

She felt the blood drain from her face and she went cold all over. He'd do it. She knew he would. Oh, Jensen, she prayed, please get me out of here!

Tansy was furious. He raved, stalking on stork legs up and down the room, cursing, waving a fist under her nose. The two girls sat cringing on the bench, wide-eyed. He was a madman. He stopped, panting, and eyed Annette. "You been causing me too much trouble. I should kill you now and be rid of you."

Annette thought furiously, fighting the fog that was seeping into her mind. "You can't do that," she said calmly. "Blind Chris wouldn't like it."

"Chris Buckley ain't in charge of this deal. I am. He don't know everything that's going on. He's blind!"

"But he's your boss. You have to do what he wants, don't you?"

"Ha!" Tansy whirled on her, his eyes glaring like white fire in their circles of purple flesh. "He don't know everything, like I said." He closed one eye chillingly and looked at her. "For instance," he gloated, "he don't know that I'm collecting protection money from half the cribs in Chinatown. He don't even know they exist!"

At least, Annette thought, she'd gotten him onto another subject, one less dangerous to herself. She'd play him along. "That's awfully clever of you, Mr. O'Neill, but won't someone tell Chris?"

"They're scared to. After all, I'm the one who does his dirty work. You know what'd happen to anyone who crossed me?" Pushing his gaunt face close to hers, he drew a hand across his throat, grinning as he did. "That's what'd happen. Easy as cutting butter!"

She shrank away from him, sickened. He was a madman, a cruel, fiendish madman! But he held her life in his hands and Su Ling's, too. Surely, she thought, there must be some way of appealing to him, to whatever small amount of compassion he might possess. How could he treat them so cruelly? Anger touched her suddenly. "Can't you at least feed us some decent food?" she cried.

Tansy laughed wickedly. "Hungry, are you?" He took a step toward her. "And what would I get in return if I decided to let you have some more food, Miss

Tofler?" His pink lips split into a lascivious smile as his hand reached out to grope the bodice of her dress.

Annette's first reaction was to recoil, but then she realized how foolish it would be to further anger Tansy O'Neill. She closed her eyes. It wouldn't hurt to let him touch her. Maybe a touch would buy them food. It wouldn't hurt . . .

Abruptly, shockingly Annette felt a stinging slap on her cheek, snapping her head to one side. Her eyes flew open in horror.

"You bitch!" hissed Tansy. "I wouldn't touch that cheap body of yours if you paid me!" he sneered.

A flood of emotions engulfed Annette. First she was ashamed of letting this horrible man touch her and then she was confused. What did he mean by calling her cheap? Most men desired her. Why was he different? Surely he must want her, too and was simply trying to humiliate her by calling her cheap.

Annette turned to Su Ling, who was holding out her frail arms for comfort. Oh God, Annette thought, am I strong enough to survive this? How much more strength do I need to go on living, to keep from slumping onto this cold, damp floor and giving up? Oh please, God, she prayed mutely, please help me to endure this.

Tansy watched the two women for a few minutes and then spun away, kicking the bench over. "Enjoy yourselves, ladies," he spat.

The two girls fell against each other and eventually sank into a half-dozing state, waiting for their next pot of tea. Time stretched out infinitely behind them and in front of them. They were suspended on an island that floated without direction. It was difficult for Annette to isolate one thought, to hold it in her mind and complete it rationally. Her mind darted confusingly, then came to rest on beautiful, brightly colored illusions.

Something nagged at the back of her mind constantly, like an elusive dream she could not remember but knew she'd dreamed. It irritated her, but when the tea came, she forgot. It was much later when she finally caught hold of the idea and forced it to stay put in her mind. They had to escape.

There was no way out except for the door at the top of the stairs. That would have to be it, then. But how? She thought hard. It was desperately difficult work. Only one person at a time brought their meager food or tea and then, for a minute, the door was left open. If she could somehow incapacitate the person, they could dash out the door. Thank God she knew where the outside door was. But how was she to incapacitate the person? Hit him on the head, she decided. But with what?

Slowly, Annette rose and began to examine the few articles in the cellar. The table was too heavy, the chairs too flimsy, the bench too big. She looked around, never realizing that Su Ling was watching her, puzzled, her black eyes following Annette's every movement.

She lifted everything, mumbling to herself, shaking her head. Once she sat down and stared into space, forgetting what she was doing. Then she jerked upright again, her eyes darting around the cold cellar.

She had it. Purposefully while she still had her wits about her and keeping the object in focus at all times, she went to it, hefted it. Perfect. The chamber pot would do nicely.

Slowly, she drifted back to the bench and sat down next to Su Ling.

"What you doing?" asked the Chinese girl.

"I just had the most wonderful idea," Annette

suddenly laughed foolishly. "How we could get out of here, you and me." It sounded so ridiculous, even to her own ears, that she had to giggle again.

"How?" Su Ling's black eyes were serious, but a smile lurked at the corners of her delicately full lips.

"Hit the guard on the head when he brings us our food and run away!" Annette's stomach heaved with laughter at the thought.

Su Ling began to laugh too, holding her tiny hand in front of her lips politely, her black eyes sparkling. In all her life, Annette had never felt closer to another human being. Su Ling, foreign as she was, understood Annette as no one ever had before. They were like one person.

And like one person, they giggled and laughed until the sun went down and Annette had to light the candle with one of the matches the guard had left them. Madame Yin-May brought their supper, a bowl of unseasoned rice. She also brought them another pot of tea. Eagerly, they waited for the fat woman to leave, then poured their precious cups of tea and sipped from them. They forgot to eat, forgot the clammy walls and smelly darkness, even forgot the rats.

Madame Yin-May appeared the next morning. A wide smile curved her mouth and her heavy gold earrings swung jauntily. "Man coming to see Su Ling tonight," she said for Annette's benefit, then spoke in Mandarin to Su Ling.

The Chinese girl replied something incomprehensible, but even to Annette's ears it was utterly scathing. Turning pale with anger, Madame Yin-May stepped forward and slapped Su Ling with all her weight behind it. Then she lumbered up the stairs muttering to herself and slammed the door.

Su Ling stood still in the center of the room, holding a hand to her cheek. Her black eyes were clear and filled with deadly hate. "That woman is very low," she finally said. "A peasant. She knows my father owned thousands like her."

"What did she say?" asked Annette.

"Oh, just what some man would do to me." Su Ling shrugged. "She's jealous. No man wants her!"

"This is awful! Why hasn't Jensen gotten me out of here?" The enormity of her situation struck Annette with full force. Her head cleared for the first time since . . . since when? Yesterday? The day before? "Look," she turned to Su Ling, "when Jensen comes, I'll ask him to buy you. He'll do it. Then you can go home with us. Of course, that's what I'll do!"

Su Ling looked at her sadly. "So nice of you, but now Madame Yin-May never will agree. She wishes to sell me to an ugly old man who will beat me."

"Jensen will pay more than anyone. I'll ask him to! Don't you see?"

"Annette, I am only one Chinese girl. There are hundreds other ones in the city. Will your Jensen save us all? Why me only? That would not be fair."

"Fair? My God, Su Ling, if we can save even one, that's something, isn't it?"

The girl was silent.

Annette went to her and shook her fiercely. "We have to escape!" She clutched her head between her hands. Why had she been laughing before? "It's not funny!" Now she had Su Ling's attention. "This is my plan. When one of the men comes in, today, before you get sold, I'll pretend to cozy up to him, to like him. You understand? Then, when I have his attention, you hit him on the head with that." She pointed a slim, imperious finger at the object. "But you have to hit him hard. Hard! You understand?"

"Yes, I understand, but it won't work."

"Why not?"

"You already tried that with Tansy O'Neill. It didn't work then."

"Well listen, Su Ling, not all men are like O'Neill. Believe me, I know. It will work. It has to."

"Then there is another problem. The men upstairs will see us."

"That's something we have to risk."

They picked at their rice, drank the sweet, fragrant tea and dozed some more. Annette dreamed of her childhood, saw her mother again, smiling, beckoning, her face full of love. Annette smiled happily. "Mama," she whispered.

A door opened somewhere and her mother glided gracefully out into a garden riotous with blooms in vibrant, brilliant color. It was so beautiful.

"Wake up!" shouted a shrill, angry voice. "You stupid twit!"

Tansy O'Neill was shaking her shoulder. Blearily, Annette looked up at him. Why had he interrupted her beautiful dream? It was so much lovelier than reality. She wished she could close her eyes and drift back into the garden, but it had evaporated.

"What in hell is wrong with your stupid brother?" yelled Tansy. "Don't he give a damn about his sister?" He waved a piece of paper in front of her face. "He says he needs another day! Tomorrow, he says. Well, it damn well better be tomorrow. That's all he has—twenty-four hours!"

Closing her eyes, Annette tried to retreat into her vision, but it wouldn't come back. She squeezed her eyes tighter, wishing. Suddenly she felt Tansy's hand on her arm, shaking her like a dog would shake a rat. She let out a fearful cry.

Su Ling leapt to her friend's aid, trying to drag Tansy off her, but Annette's perception had grown dim. He struck Su Ling with the back of his arm as if he were swatting a fly and she fell backward to the floor.

But he had let go of Annette. He stood over her, panting, his pink lips drawn back from his teeth. Then, abruptly, he turned and was gone.

"You're right. We must escape," said Su Ling coldly, picking herself up from the floor. "Next time they come with the food."

But strangely enough the next time it was Madame Yin-May who brought their tray and a big guard was standing at the top of the stairs by the door. Their plan wouldn't work for two reasons. First, Yin-May wouldn't be susceptible to Annette's advances and second, they couldn't knock both people out at once.

When the dim light of day was completely gone, Su Ling lit the candle. Annette sat on the bench, idly staring at her dirty fingernails. She reached up and touched her stringy hair. She was becoming a hag, she realized, and it didn't even matter.

She felt Su Ling's hand grip her arm, breaking her trance. "Shh!" hissed Su Ling. "Listen!" A key was turning in the lock. Who was it? Madame Yin-May again or the man? Both girls held their breath. The rectangle of light widened. A figure was silhouetted in it.

It was Tansy O'Neill and he was alone. It seemed to them both that he took hours, days, to descend the stairs. Annette was amazed to see that he was carrying a large tray. There was food on it, mountains of hot, fragrant food! She wasn't quite sure whether she should believe her eyes. Why would Tansy O'Neill bring them this glorious tray of food?

Su Ling remained in the background, a thin, frail shadow, while Annette, holding her breath, took a step forward into the flickering halo of candlelight.

"Looks pretty tempting, don't it?" taunted Tansy.

"Yes," Annette whispered in reply, not meeting his gaze. She was beginning to feel uneasy and remained suspicious. She wrapped her arms around herself unconsciously.

"Maybe I was a little harsh with you yesterday," Tansy began, his eyes devouring Annette's body. Then he pulled his gaze away from her and directed it toward Su Ling. "You go busy yourself in that corner over there," he nodded into the shadows, "while Annette here thanks me for this food." His pink lips formed a sick smile.

"No," Annette whispered in sudden, terrifying realization. "No!"

She backed away from the patterned light, shaking her head in denial. Tansy pounced on her so swiftly that Annette barely had time to raise her hands in defense. First she was reeling away from him and then she was imprisoned in his arms. Tansy's hands pulled at her clothes, groped at her flesh.

Annette tried to scream, but his flaccid pink lips covered her own, transforming her cry into a muffled sob of revulsion. Horror washed over her as she felt the bulge of his crotch through her skirt. Gasping for breath, she pushed him away in panic. A terrible claustrophobia gripped her. Her stomach was churning with nausea and she heard herself whimper.

All at once his fierce grip slackened and his hands dragged downward over her breasts, slipped to her hips and down her thighs. With a groan, he sagged to the floor. Annette staggered back and nearly fell. She saw Su Ling standing across from her, paralyzed, her huge black eyes wide and unblinking. The chamber pot lay on the ground by the man's head, which was wet and dark with smeared blood.

"Come on, Su Ling!" cried Annette, tearing her eyes away. "Let's go!"

But Su Ling stood rigid and unmoving, mesmerized by the scene before her. Annette grabbed her arm, yanked her toward the stairs. "Quick! Run!"

The Chinese girl snapped out of her trance. She looked around her wildly. When she saw Annette, she opened her mouth to say something, but no sound came out.

They ran like frightened deer up the stairs and out into the brightly lit hall. They both stopped short, panting furiously. No one was there.

Annette pulled Su Ling toward the far end of the hall. She thought her heart would burst. If they were caught. . . . Her muscles, unused to moving, felt weak and stiff and wouldn't react properly. She stumbled down the hall. It seemed so long, miles and miles. She could hear Su Ling gasping behind her.

The door! The door! There it was! She shoved against it, and cold, damp air filled her lungs. She lurched forward and ran, dragging Su Ling after her into the black, terror-filled night.

The cold was beginning to penetrate Rolf's bones. It was pitch dark already, even though it was only seven o'clock. That was good. No one would be as likely to see them. He shifted his position, leaning his other shoulder against the wall. Jensen fidgeted beside him. They were both exhausted. Rolf hoped they would be able to do something if the time came.

They had spent the whole day and the night before dressed as poor sailors, hanging around the bars, opium dens and cribs of Chinatown. They pretended to be sailors on leave, looking for a poker game with Tansy O'Neill. They told people they'd heard he ran the best games in town. They were very careful, always pretending to be drunk. If O'Neill or Buckley got wind of anyone asking too many questions, they'd be more likely to harm Annette.

Rolf knew it had to be Tansy O'Neill who had kidnapped Annette. Jensen had told him that Tansy had come to his father's office several times. Besides, Rolf knew Tansy had followed Annette at least once, because at the poker game he'd bragged about seeing her go into Rolf's apartment. It only made sense. Tansy was Buckley's leg man. He carried out Blind Chris' orders, did all the dirty work.

Rolf and Jensen had found out that Tansy was frequently seen at several places in Chinatown, seeing to his protection racket and running his poker games. Every tidbit of information they'd gathered pointed to three places where Annette might be hidden. They had spent hours watching each of the other two places and Tansy had not been around.

That left the Lotus Den. Rolf didn't dare go inside, even in disguise. It would be too dangerous. So they'd settled themselves to watch, positioned on the corner of the alleyway where they could see both the front and back doors. No one of interest to them had entered or left since five o'clock.

"If this doesn't work," Jensen whispered, "I'll have to give in tomorrow. I'll have to do what he wants. He won't let me stall anymore."

"Let's not decide just yet. We've got all night. And," Rolf added, "what makes you think he'll return her even if you do pay up? Kidnappers have been known to take the money and still. . . . Well, you know what I mean."

He heard Jensen's muffled oath. "I'd pull this city apart stone by stone to get him if he did that," vowed Jensen. "He knows better."

"I hope so." Rolf's voice was grim.

They fell silent, peering tiredly out into the foggy night. Several men knocked at the front door, were allowed access and disappeared inside. Tansy did not appear. An hour passed. The two men stomped their feet to get the blood flowing, blew into their cold fists and jammed their hands into their dirty pea jackets. The tension mounted. Both knew this was their last chance. They had no more leads to follow.

Suddenly the door onto the alleyway banged open, spilling light onto the damp cobblestones. Two thin, dark shadows fled down the alley in the opposite direction, away from them.

"What?" Jensen gasped. "My God, those were women!"

"Come on," growled Rolf. He ran down the alley after the two fleeing figures, Jensen right behind him. Their feet pounded on the hard stones. They came to a dark, deserted corner. Two slim, darting shadows caught Rolf's eye beyond the next building. He ran toward them.

"Annette!" Jensen called.

They gained on the two figures. Rolf glimpsed a white, scared oval of a face turn toward him over a shoulder. The face turned away and the two figures fled around a corner. They were gone.

"Annette!" gasped Jensen. "Wait! It's me, Jensen!"

Rolf rounded the corner and found himself in a blind alley. Huddled up against the brick wall at the end of the cul-de-sac were two people. Wide, terror-stricken eyes stared up at him, like does about to be shot. Their chests were heaving and four white hands clutched at each other.

He plowed to a halt, breathing hard, and moved toward them cautiously, as one would approach a wild animal. He spoke slowly, softly. "Annette, it's me. Rolf. I won't hurt you. You're safe now. Jensen is here, too."

Yes, one of them was Annette. He recognized her dark red hair. The other person was perhaps a young boy, for he wore trousers. The frightened face was Oriental, delicately beautiful.

Annette pushed the boy behind her and stood up, facing Rolf's advancing figure. She snatched a loose board from the garbage-littered ground and waved it threateningly. "Go away!" she cried. "Leave us alone! I'll kill you!"

She was the image of avenging fury, all wild hair and staring eyes. Rolf stopped short. She was so brave, so beautiful in her wild state. His heart went out to her. Cold hatred filled him. What had Tansy O'Neill done to turn a gently bred society girl into this creature?

Rolf held her brother back with an outspread arm, afraid that Jensen had not had time to assess the situation. If either of them were to rush forward now, Annette's nerves might snap. Rolf ripped off his sailor hat. He stepped forward. "It's Rolf, Annette," he repeated. "And Jensen. We're here to help you."

"Jensen?" Annette's voice quavered. She wanted desperately to believe. "Rolf?" She looked from one to the other through the darkness, confused, scared.

What had her captors done to her? Slowly, ever so slowly, she lowered the board. Rolf waited, hardly daring to breathe. He held out his hand. "Take my hand, Annette. I want to help you, to take you home."

Falteringly, she held her hand up to her throat, searching his face as if she didn't trust her own eyes. "Rolf?"

"Yes, Annette. I'm here to take you home."

"Home?" She appeared curious. The savage look had gone out of her eyes and now they were dull and dazed. Tentatively, her eyes never leaving his face, she held her hand out to him.

Chapter 19

Annette dreamt she was in a boat. Sometimes she was alone, sometimes with Su Ling. The river down which the boat floated was gentle, rocking the vessel lazily, water lapping softly against its edges. Around each bend a new scene drew her attention to the distant banks. Each was pleasant; some were exotic. The colors were brilliant. Trees were so green that they glowed like emeralds; the sky was such a dazzling blue that it hurt the eye. Even the animals on the banks were brightly colored. Once she saw an orange horse grazing, which raised its huge red eyes to her passing.

But something in the dream was quite wrong. In the dark recesses of her mind, she knew that around several more bends lay a waterfall whose crashing mountain of water cascaded into a bottomless ocean. Jensen stood on one of the peaceful banks, waving at her, calling for her to come in, warning her that it was too dangerous. Around the next curve was a crowd of people and among them was Rolf. He was holding a long rope. But when he threw the rope at her, the crowd grew furious and hauled it back to the bank.

As the vessel rounded yet another curve, Rolf shrank from sight. Annette looked down to discover that she was naked. Strangely her father was in the boat with her, his eyes fixed on her flesh accusingly. His mouth moving in slow motion, he told her that she must go the way of Cecile, over the waterfall, to be plunged deep into the watery abyss below.

Annette's heart beat furiously. Perspiration covered her naked skin in a fine, glistening sheen. She opened her eyes and screamed.

"It's all right, Annette. You're safe." The disjointed words came from Rolf's mouth. But how did he get into the boat? And where had her father gone?

She squeezed her eyes shut. Then she felt a new sensation, a hand on her forehead. Now she was lying down in the boat and the hand turned suddenly cold, pressed her down further. Desperately, she rolled away, moaning.

"Wake up, Annette." It was Rolf again.

"The ocean!" she cried through parched lips.

"Yes, Annette. I hear it too."

"No! We're going to die!"

"It's below us. We're all right."

It seemed to Annette then that Rolf was lying in the bottom of the vessel with her, holding her, the sleeve of his shirt grazing the tops of her naked breasts. She thrashed away. She wept. Finally, she lay spent in the crook of his arm, accepting their fate, ready to plunge into the deathly darkness below.

For two days and nights Annette continued to dream, jolted awake and plunged back into nightmares. Several times she sensed Rolf and Jensen somewhere nearby Once she was certain that Cecile had risen from the deep waters and was calling to her. Occasionally the rocking of the vessel would make her violently sick. Rolf would wipe at her mouth with a damp towel while she tried to explain their peril, looming ominously nearer with the meandering of the river.

On the third morning she sat up and stared straight ahead, her eyes wild and wide open. She screamed. Somewhere nearby a door banged open. Suddenly Rolf was there, but not in the boat. This time he was standing in a doorway of a room. But then, where was she?

"Rolf." She formed the word through cracked, trembling lips then fell back onto . . . a bed. Yes, she puzzled, she must be on a bed.

Rolf sat down next to her and the mattress sagged under his weight. His hand stroked her arm carefully. "Thank God you're awake," he was just able to choke out.

His lips brushed her damp brow and his hands wandered in the tangled mass of her hair. She tried to speak. "Where am I?"

"In my cottage. We're on the western side of the peninsula, on the ocean."

"I hear the waves."

"That's right, below us, crashing on the rocks. It's safe, though. And Jensen is here, too."

She relaxed. A cold, sick perspiration covered her. A thought struck her. She turned her haggard eyes to Rolf. "Bernard! They hit him."

"He's all right. He had a bad concussion, but the sisters tell us he's doing well now." His voice was calm and reassuring.

"And Su Ling?"

"Here with us. She's fine, Annette. And she's worried about you. Would you like to see her?"

"Yes, please."

It was comforting to see Su Ling. The girl was thin and pale, dressed in a much too big man's robe, but she looked well. Su Ling was smiling, but too many unanswered questions crowded Annette's mind and she was unable to communicate.

After Su Ling left, Jensen visited the small, wood-beamed bedroom and kissed Annette tenderly on the cheek. She heard Rolf whispering to Jensen at the door before Jensen left. Then she was alone again with Rolf.

She ate soup later and managed to keep it down. Afterward, with Rolf's help, she took a bath in a tub which had been set up across from the bedroom.

If Annette hadn't been so weak, she would have been embarrassed. Rolf carried her to the tub, lowered her naked body into the warm water and ran the soap over her flesh and into her hair. As it was, she let him minister to her. His hands, she thought as they traveled over her, should bring an arousing response as they had before. This time, however, she felt nothing but a terrible weakness.

When she was finished, a strange man came in silently and removed the tub of water. She drew back in fear. Who was he? The man was Oriental, but he seemed different from the Chinese on Grant Street. He was squat and stocky and his eyes were mere slits in his yellow face. Although he nodded to her politely, she was frightened of him. In fact, most everything was frightening to her.

"This is Igurashi Nakamura, my manservant," explained Rolf gently, seeing her fear. "He's been with me for years. When I'm in the city, he stays out here and looks after things."

Annette's anxiety subsided. She gave a weak smile to the man who bowed in return and then left silently.

As the day went on, she gradually grew accustomed to the Japanese man's presence. He moved efficiently and always silently. He rarely spoke, but his round, somber face grew familiar to her.

That evening after dozing, she ate once more and felt somewhat better, less drained. She asked Rolf a few questions and said she wanted to see Su Ling and Jensen again.

"If you're sure you feel up to it." Rolf scooped her up, still wrapped in the blankets, into his strong arms and carried her into a small, warm living room.

A fire blazed in a large hearth in the center of the room, which was high-ceilinged and supported by dark, rough beams. The walls were white and partially covered with paintings, most of which showed Rolf's touch. The wood furnishings were crude but comfortable, covered with deep, velvet cushions of burgundy. The floor was wood also, made of wide, polished planks, and there was a round braided brown rug in front of the fireplace. Everything in the comfortable room was cast in the orange-red glow of the fire.

It might have been a room in a hunting lodge, she thought, except for the tall potted plants which filled the otherwise empty corners. There were many ferns and two palms stood near a window overlooking the sea. It was an odd combination, she decided, but quite nice.

Jensen and Su Ling were there, sitting together on a deep couch. They greeted Annette warmly, glad to see her up and about. Nakamura came into the room, silent and stolid, and served everyone tea.

"Cecile came to visit," said Jensen, leaning toward her chair, which Rolf had placed near the fire. "It was yesterday. I sent her a message to let her know you were all right and that sister of ours was here within the hour."

Annette smiled and looked over at Su Ling. "How are you feeling?" she asked weakly.

"I am much better than you. I was sick only for one day. But you worry us so!"

"Sick, yes," mused Annette. "But from what?"

Rolf, who was standing near the hearth, looked from Annette to Jensen and then back. "You and Su Ling were drugged," he told her carefully. "Opium, I'm afraid."

Annette gasped, her hand flying to her breast.

"But it's over now," he added quickly. "And you're recovering just fine. I promise."

"It was the tea, then. Yes." Annette's eyes searched Su Ling's. The girl nodded. "But why would they do such an awful thing?"

It was Rolf who answered. "To keep you two quiet, no doubt. How in God's name you ever managed to plot that escape of yours is beyond me!"

"Annette is the one who made the plan. She is very brave."

Annette lowered her eyes. Su Ling gazed at Annette in admiration. "We just had to get out of there."

"I'm sorry it took us so long to find you," said Jensen. "We had to be very careful."

"Both of you," she remembered suddenly, "were in the alley?"

"Yes. We were watching the Lotus Den when we saw the two of you running." Rolf ran a hand through his light, curly hair. "It's lucky they didn't find you first."

"Yes. It was." Annette curled her bare feet under her for warmth and wrapped the rough blanket more securely around her shoulders. She glanced at Jensen. "What about the ransom?"

"No. You've got to understand, Annette, I couldn't let myself fall into their trap."

"I do understand. And I'm glad you didn't. The things they wanted were too horrible to contemplate." She fell silent and gazed into the mesmerizing flames. "Where is Father, Jensen? Does he know?"

"No. Our dear father hasn't been home at all since your abduction. And Cecile has been worried half out of her mind about you both. I'm not at all surprised that she showed up here."

"I'm glad she came, Jensen. I'm worried about her, too." Annette yawned. The brief visit had tired her already. She still felt dizzy and occasionally it seemed as if the orange glow in the room flared brightly. It must be an effect of the opium. She wondered whether the hallucinations would ever go away.

"Perhaps," observed Rolf, "you ought to retire, Annette. You've been through quite an ordeal, and this must be a strain on you."

"Yes," agreed Jensen. "You get a good night's sleep. I'll be back early in the morning."

"But why can't I go home? Su Ling could come too."

"Let me explain," said Rolf as he again scooped Annette up into his arms. "Chris Buckley will want some kind of revenge for your escape. Jensen naturally is not going to give in to him and until we can think of some way of appeasing Chris, well, it's just better that you remain here." He carried her into the bedroom.

"Will you be here all the time?" Her hazel eyes looked imploringly into his as he carefully placed her on the bed.

"Yes. I won't leave you. I'm afraid the opium may cause you occasional hallucinations. And Su Ling, too. I'll be right here if you need me."

Annette glanced around the room. It was definitely Rolf's own bedroom. She looked back to him, her eyes shining and wide. "This is your room?"

"Yes." He laughed. "But I've been sleeping on the couch most of the time."

"And the rest of the time?"

Dodging her question, Rolf replied, "Under the

spell of opium, there's no telling what a person may do. Most of the time you feel drowsy, lost in a dream world. But there may be times when you might confuse a dream with reality."

"How do you know so much about opium?" she asked thoughtfully.

"I had a very bad experience with it once, Annette. I'm ashamed to say I let it control my life for a time. It was stupid of me."

"How did you stop?"

"I wanted to. A friend helped me. It was a long time ago."

"And now you've helped me," she whispered almost to herself.

"Yes."

"And I suppose you were in this room with me a lot at night."

Rolf knew exactly what she meant. A smile gathered on his lips. "I did sleep next to you, Annette. You were delirious."

"Oh." She closed her eyes, unable to keep them open a moment longer. "I thought I dreamt it."

A week passed before Annette regained her strength enough to help in the kitchen or bathe herself without Rolf's constant assistance. It became humiliating having to endure his protection as if she were no more than a child. And Su Ling was no help, either. Jensen, who spent most of the afternoons and evenings there, took up all of Su Ling's attention. Funny, Annette thought, but it almost seemed as if he came to see Su Ling, not herself.

The most curious part of the ordeal for Annette, however, was Rolf's constant, close proximity. Even when he wasn't helping her dress or combing her hair, he was ever watching her and pampering her. When she did manage to do things for herself, such as reaching up into a cupboard for a tea mug, Rolf's eyes were always on her. She could feel him staring at the fabric of her white blouse as it stretched across her breasts or at her hair, which tumbled loosely down her back.

It seemed silly. After all, he had seen her quite naked, so why the sudden interest in her now that she was clothed? It was unsettling, too. She had thought Rolf had no interest in her anymore. Hadn't he made that plain enough the last time she had been at his studio?

Rolf read to her in the late afternoons and in the mornings he would allow her to watch as he sketched in the sunny studio off the living room. Sometimes he would look up from his book or sketch pad, catch her eyes on him and smile thoughtfully.

He was such a handsome man, Annette often found herself thinking. He belonged to the outdoors with his tanned skin and his sun-streaked hair that curled slightly over his casual shirt collars. But his eyes, a contrast to his fair complexion, held Annette's interest the most. They were such dark, unreadable pools that she often felt slightly intimidated in his presence. Throughout those days with him, she came to know his face well. Sometimes she longed to reach out and trace a finger over the flat plane of his cheek and up along the curved, generous ridge of his nose. She studied him silently, just as she knew he was studying her.

The firewood ran out and one afternoon Rolf brought her a warm cape. "Would you like to get some fresh air while I chop the wood?" he asked.

She was delighted to be outdoors again. The cool air laden with sea spray was invigorating. The sun, riding low over the blue Pacific, stretched gentle winter fingers across the sea and touched Annette as she sat watching Rolf swing his axe.

The cottage, sitting high above the rocky coast, was called Devil's Cove after the small inlet below. Rolf had bought the land from an old Spanish estate and built the five-room house himself. He told Annette that it had taken him three years to complete.

Now she looked down from their lofty perch at the rock-strewn shore below. Devil's Cove. She thought of the painting she had seen at the Golden Gate Gallery, remembered the dynamic brush strokes, the thundering waves, the grey, ominous sky. Yes, Rolf had captured it exactly. A spurt of jealousy shot through her. Suddenly she wanted to sketch.

She rose from her seat on a log. "Rolf? May I borrow your sketch pad and some charcoal?"

He sank the axe head into a log and wiped at his brow with a muscular forearm. "Of course you can."

Annette tried to draw in the lines of the coast and finally gave up. She turned her eye onto Rolf. Yes, she was certain she could capture the flexing of his strong, corded muscles, the tensing of his thighs, his naked back, broad and sinewy. He, in himself, was a work of art.

She began to draw. Several times he looked up from his task and caught her eye. He smiled indulgently. Once he ventured to ask, "Would you like me to take off the rest of my clothes?"

Annette blushed and lowered her eyes, concentrating on her sketch. If only he'd quit teasing, she thought. Her work that day, she decided objectively, was good. Animal and human forms were her forte. She was indeed capturing Rolf in this setting.

At last he was finished. "Listen, Annette," he said, breathless, "I've cut far more wood than I intended. Do you mind?"

She laughed lightly and gave him back some of his own. "Now how do you suppose I felt, modeling for you, cramped up in that position for hours!"

"Ah," countered Rolf, mopping the sweat from his neck and chest, "but I gave you a massage, didn't I?"

So he did remember, she thought in amazement, blushing profusely. He remembered that day. Now, for the first time since she'd come to the cottage, she flirted back, batting her long eyelashes coyly. "Why, Rolf," her voice was husky, "I thought you had forgotten." And then, "If you'd like a massage, though, I suppose I do owe you one."

Rolf's smile faded. He pulled on his Irish fisherman's sweater over his head. "You know, Annette," he began, "you're not the same girl who came to my apartment that first day."

"Oh?" She felt an expectant flutter in her stomach.

"You've changed. You're older, somehow. Perhaps it was that terrible ordeal at the Lotus Den. I'm not sure."

"Perhaps it was you, Rolf," she dared to whisper. "Perhaps you taught me that life—that living, I should say, is not a silly game." She was surprised at her own gravity and by the significance of her statement. How childish she had been that day in his apartment! She had been willing only to take, not to give.

"Perhaps," he commented.

They walked back into the cottage, Annette insisting that she help carry some of the wood. Once they had stacked up enough to last at least a day, she went back outside and picked up the sketch pad. Her drawing was good enough to put on canvas and it would be excellent, she was sure.

Jensen arrived in time for dinner, laden down

with boxes of food and more clothes for Annette and Su Ling. Annette's clothes were from her wardrobe and highboy, but she noticed that Su Ling's were new. Jensen was beginning to amaze her. Had he shopped for them himself?

She listened to the news of the city, which had come to seem terribly remote, and to a report of how Cecile was getting along. They all decided that Cecile should come and visit, but they were also concerned that Jensen or Cecile might be followed. They had no way of knowing how far Buckley's machine would go to seek revenge.

The question seldom came up, but Annette knew that Jensen and Rolf were still working on a solution. It hardly mattered anymore, however, for she was growing accustomed to living in the cottage with Rolf. She really could not imagine leaving.

"I picked up your mail," Jensen told Rolf over dinner. Annette suddenly wondered how Rolf could be away from his painting for so long. Eventually he had to go back into the city and so did she.

But as she and Su Ling dried the dishes later that evening, she realized that this was only an interlude in her life. No doubt she was making much more out of Rolf's teasing and attention than was real. He had no romantic interest in her; she must remember that at all times. She also knew that to try and seduce him would be useless and would result only in her own humiliation yet again.

Rolf was reading his mail in the studio when Annette, wiping her hands dry with a towel, appeared in the doorway. "Anything interesting?" she asked.

He looked up from a letter. "Annette," he said soberly, "I've got to go into the city for a couple of days."

Her heart sank. She smiled. "A commission?"

He was silent for a long moment. "No," he said finally. "Personal business, I'm afraid."

She knew instinctively that Rolf was holding a letter from Eleanor Fairchild and that he was going to see her. She didn't have to ask. Besides, it was none of her business, she told herself firmly, feeling tears near the surface. She turned to leave.

"Nakamura will be here with you."

"That's fine." She left the room quickly.

Annette purposely lingered in bed the following morning and Rolf left quietly. She busied herself around the cottage, straightening, dusting and otherwise getting in Nakamura's way. Late in the day, Su Ling placed a hand on her arm while they were working in the kitchen.

"You are very sad, Annette?"

"No."

"You like Rolf much, I think. He likes you, too."

Annette put down the wooden spoon she was holding. "Su Ling, you already know that Rolf took my virginity. But that was all there was between us. There's nothing more to it."

"You aren't lovers now?"

"No. He sleeps on the couch."

"I see." Su Ling averted her dark, oval eyes. "Jensen asked me to live with him."

"What?"

"He wants to get me a place of my own and visit me. I said yes."

Annette was quiet for a long while. Although it had been obvious that Jensen was enamored with the lovely girl, Su Ling's news came as a surprise. "Su Ling," she said at last, "you should be married. You deserve a fine husband. Jensen wants you as a mistress."

"Yes. I know. That's all right with me," Su Ling answered with firm resolve.

Annette knew then that the girl would accept Jensen's offer, seeing it as fated, ordained. She would never try to change her destiny, for the *tao* beckoned.

Neither of the girls saw Jensen standing in the doorway. "She told you?" he asked Annette, startling her.

"Yes."

"Well?"

"I won't interfere in your life, Jensen," replied Annette thoughtfully. "You have never interfered in mine."

"Thank you."

That night, alone in Rolf's bed, sleep was a long time coming. Annette thought about Jensen and Su Ling, who had disappeared into the other bedroom together some time earlier, and about Rolf Karman. A while back, late last autumn, she had asked herself whether she loved him. It seemed an eternity ago.

Well, she thought in the darkness, do you love him? Her answer came in many ways: she loved the way he moved in easy, lithe strides; she loved his sense of humor and his strength; she loved the way he looked at her quietly, measuring her with those unfathomable eyes. Yes, she loved many things about him, but did she love him for himself?

Shortly after dawn, Annette went into Rolf's studio and set up a clean canvas. She would have to wait until much later in the morning when the light was better to mix her paints. She hoped Rolf wouldn't mind, but no doubt he was too busy to think about such a small thing.

She drank the tea Nakamura brought her, made her bed and took a bath. She drove the thought of Rolf and Eleanor together from her mind by envisioning the colors she would combine to capture the scene she had in mind. She planned to paint a woods scene, using the bright colors she had seen when she and Rolf were outside on the previous afternoon. In the painting, but not as the focal point, she would place a young woman sketching with great concentration. At first Annette had thought to try to capture Rolf's form on canvas, but then she realized with utter clarity that, emotionally speaking, she herself had been the center of yesterday's scene. The girl Annette planned to capture would come alive on the canvas. She might be a bit sad, but she would be alive. Annette knew she could do it.

By late afternoon, Annette was ready to paint life into the girl, to give her features, as she had the surrounding trees and rocks. The next day she would begin working on the finer details, on the pine needles, the scars in the rock, the late sun striking the scene from the west. Finally she would paint in the expression on the girl's young face and then deepen the shadows until the canvas as a whole grabbed the eyes and held them captive.

She cleaned the brushes and sagged wearily into a hard wooden chair. It was late. Nakamura had already prepared dinner. Annette was exhausted. It was a satisfied exhaustion, however. She had worked hard and the results were pleasing. To be sure, if Bernard saw it, he would find fault here and there, but she knew he would like it. It really was good. What a wonderful, gratifying feeling!

Annette fell into bed that evening certain that sleep would come quickly. But it didn't. No matter how hard she tried to rid herself of thoughts of Rolf and Eleanor, she could not. What did thirty-year-old Eleanor Fairchild possess that she herself did not? Was it maturity that attracted Rolf? Did he want a woman closer to his own age?

The questions and comparisons tormented her and made her feel small and inadequate. She felt so alone. She wanted desperately to be back home, safe in her rose damask room with Vivian near at hand. She wept silently into her pillow. Annette hated to cry, it was so demoralizing, so female. Why had she let herself come under Rolf's charm in the first place? This was all her own fault.

"I hope you're enjoying yourself, Rolf Karman!" she raged into her pillow.

Swollen-eyed and spent, Annette fell asleep at last. She didn't hear the horse trot up or the front door open, nor did she awaken when Rolf entered the bedroom. It wasn't until she felt the mattress sag that she opened her eyes and flew to a sitting position.

"It's me, don't be frightened," came that low, haunting voice.

"Rolf?"

"Yes, Annette. I'm back."

"But, what are you doing?"

"I think you already know the answer." His whispering voice sweetly caressed her ears. "I had to come back. I have to know, Annette."

Know what? she wondered, her heart beating furiously, the darkness holding them both in its spell.

"Will you have me?" he asked then, his hand touching her hair so gently that she wasn't sure if he was real or imagined.

"Yes," she answered into the darkness. Why did he need to ask at all? Didn't he know?

She went into his arms then. His mouth sought hers. Her breasts beneath the filmy nightgown were pressed flat to her body as he embraced her, devouring her. This was different from the first time. Rolf was like a starving man, a primitive who was taking her flesh to his in a mindless moment of passion.

His hands tore at the delicate cloth of her gown until she was free, naked. He hadn't even unclothed himself fully, just pulled his shirt open enough for her to feel the curling hairs on his chest rough against her soft flesh.

"God, Annette! How I want you!" he cried. His hands explored her flesh, stroking it, kneading it.

She had grown thinner during her ordeal. She felt his hand search the hollow of her stomach, the curve of her hip, sending shivers of delight up her spine. The steel band of his arm encircled her waist and he rolled her over on top of him. The buttons on his open shirt scraped across her breasts. She moaned.

"God . . ." He stopped abruptly. "Am I hurting you?"

"No," whispered Annette. His hands molded her breasts, brought them to his mouth where he savored each taut nipple until she was gasping.

Still, he wouldn't relent. She began to writhe above him, her hips moving, ready to receive him. She felt like a volcano, ready to erupt from the pressure building up deep within her. And still his hands played with her pulsing flesh, his mouth teasing, nipping, driving her half-mad with desire.

It hadn't been at all like this before. She never knew . . .

He lifted her weight, bringing her to a sitting position above him. He rose also, then eased her over backward onto the mattress with her knees in the air. Surely he would take her now!

But he didn't. His hand found the throbbing spot between her legs and caressed it. Annette moaned and twisted, calling out his name, begging mindlessly for release.

Then, to her shock, instead of stretching his body above her, his head bent and his mouth touched her. She cried out and tried to push him away.

"Let me have you, Annette. Let me show you how it can be."

She protested. His head bent again. Her words of shame and confusion died on her lips as his mouth sought the secret, inner flesh of her thighs.

Her body began to react with a will of its own. Her hips gyrated instinctively. Soft, uncontrollable sounds of pleasure escaped her trembling lips as the pressure in her belly became unbearable. Her senses spiraled upward, piercing a heaven she never knew existed. She rode high on wave after wave of raw sensation until she was moaning and spent.

Rolf let her rest for a moment, then opened her legs once more with his hands. "That was just the beginning, Annette," he whispered into the darkness. "Now you are ready for me."

But she couldn't! she thought wildly. She was too drained, too weak. Still, she let him gain entry slowly, her body throbbing with each tiny push. Finally, he drove himself deep into her womb and she cried aloud, her back arching to meet his thrust. For some time he filled and emptied her body, slowly, inevitably, each thrust renewing her strength until her hips rose and fell in rhythm with his. Her desire began to build again and words of wonder and passion spilled from her lips.

His mouth found her breast and his tongue circled her nipple, bringing her exquisite pain. She felt the wave of pleasure building again deep within and rode on its mounting crest. Her hands kneaded and raked at his broad, sinewy back until she was crying aloud once more. She felt him thrust so deeply within her that she thought her body would surely split in two.

Rolf groaned, his arms crushing her to him, his

body shuddering above hers until they lay together silently, exhausted, flesh locked to flesh. She fell asleep.

A short while later they began to whisper in the darkness, still holding each other. "I didn't expect you back," said Annette, "until tomorrow." She wanted to ask him if he had been with Eleanor Fairchild and why he had come home early. But she didn't. Perhaps she really didn't want to know the answer.

"I came home," he placed a gentle kiss on her nose, "to be with you." Rolf laughed lightly then. "I couldn't stay away."

"You're teasing me!" she protested.

"It's true, though. And now, after our little romp tonight," he squeezed her affectionately, "I suppose I'll have to marry you!"

"Oh, Rolf, stop teasing!"

"But I'm quite serious, Annette. I'm not such a cad as you may think. I'm duty bound to ask for your hand."

"Duty bound?" she echoed.

"I've said it wrongly. I *want* to marry you. What do you say, lovely little thing? Will you have me?"

In the darkness, Annette's eyes widened in surprise. She focused on tiny specks of dancing, imaginary light on the ceiling. Duty bound. Yes, he would think that. But did he really want to marry her? Did he love her?

Her heart pounded in the still night. To be married. And to Rolf! The notion was both thrilling and frightening at once. How could she know what was right for her and for Rolf, too?

"Well?" His voice spanned the inky darkness.

"I . . . I don't know. I haven't thought about marriage, Rolf. I . . . I've been thinking only about my painting . . . a career."

"You can have that, too."

She thought for a long moment. Was it possible for her to do both? And what about a family? How could she paint if she had babies? Was she ready for such a commitment?

"Come on now, Annette. Surely you can answer yes or no."

Rolf the gambler. Rolf the womanizer. Did he love her? He had never spoken of love to her. Oh, certainly he lusted after her, and she after him . . . but love?

Duty bound. That was more like the truth. One did not base a marriage on duty, at least not her marriage! Suddenly she could see herself holding a baby while Rolf waved good-bye on his way to his studio or to Eleanor Fairchild. And Annette's career? It was gone, lost in the bustle of married life.

Her heart sank. She swallowed hard, feeling the pressure of his arm against her breasts. "I don't think I'm ready yet, Rolf," she whispered miserably, a lump growing in her throat.

Rolf was silent for a long moment. When he did speak, the words emerged slowly, pensively, severing the tension between them. "All right, Annette. If that's the way you want it, I won't ask again."

My God! she thought frantically. What have I done? Why? Was a career that important? Could it be that she was fooling herself, that she had turned Rolf down because she feared his domineering ways? Or could it have been simply because he no doubt just had come from Eleanor Fairchild's bed?

Annette felt tears burning hotly behind her eyelids. She let out a quavering breath and ran a finger down Rolf's arm along his long, corded muscles.

"I told you it was all right," he said quietly. "I do understand you, Annette. Perhaps you're right. You may not be ready for marriage." He kissed her forehead and then her lips, his tongue thrusting into her mouth.

Suddenly he broke off the kiss. "You see, Annette, I am a passionate man and perhaps, for us, this will be enough. You have made your choice."

Painfully, his mouth possessed hers again.

Chapter 20

Jensen's horse trotted toward home without any guidance from him. He barely noticed, for his mind was possessed by memories of the time he'd just spent at the house on Devil's Cove. It was, in a way, a charmed place where everything was more beautiful, more real than in the outside world.

Funny, he'd come to think of everything beyond Rolf's house as the outside world. It was as if nothing had any significance except within that house. When he asked himself why, the answer jolted him. It was Su Ling. She was strong, yet at the same time as slim and fragile as a baby bird. To his eyes, she was beautiful beyond belief and as graceful and lovely as a spray of spring blossoms. She was utterly fascinating.

Her story outraged him, filled Jensen with disgust for the entire human race. He felt very protective of her. He had only known her for a little over a week. It hardly seemed possible that in such a short time he had grown to care so much for her.

Jensen started and looked up. His horse had stopped in front of the stable door and was waiting with equine patience for him to dismount. He rang for the groom, handed the horse over to him and walked to the house.

The mansion seemed more than usually empty these days. Luckily Cecile was still there or Jensen would have been utterly alone. As far as he knew, Edward had not been home for days. It was obvious that his father was at Tilly Grueter's. Why was it, he wondered, that ever since Cecile had arrived, Edward had all but withdrawn from life?

Jensen's anger flared. The man, no matter how pitiful, would have to face what he'd done. And there was still the problem of Tansy O'Neill. Jensen's lips curved in a grim smile as he entered the Nob Hill mansion. Annette had saved him a lot of trouble by her courage and good sense, but O'Neill would soon be back, demanding restitution, holding it over Jensen's head. It was not unlikely that Jensen himself was in danger.

Annette and Su Ling were safe, thank God, but Jensen was worried about Cecile. She wasn't ready to go back to her husband yet. She kept insisting that she had to find something, an elusive, missing piece to a puzzle which she felt she was coming closer to every day. Jensen had been so concerned about Cecile's safety that he had asked Ned from the office to move into the carriage house and keep an eye on the mansion when he himself wasn't there. He'd also cautioned Cecile and the house staff to keep every door locked at all times. Jensen wished that Cecile would go back to her husband's ship or that Luke Bogarde would stay with her on Nob Hill, but she had refused to consider either idea. Odd, very odd. He wondered whether there might be some problem between Cecile and Luke.

Jensen tossed his hat onto the sideboard and took his gloves off. Lost in thought, he slapped them against his thigh as he entered the drawing room. Cecile was not there. He rang for the butler, Henry, who told him that she had gone out for a drive with Ned that afternoon and was expected back shortly.

Jensen went into the library and sat in front of the fire, stretching his long legs out to warm them. He considered the problem of his father. Edward had to be confronted with the results of his dealings with Blind Chris. Jensen's mind simply could not accept the fact of a man sliding away from the consequences of his deeds. He was too young to accept injustice. If his father wouldn't come home or to the office, Jensen would have to track him down at Tilly Grueter's, wherever that was.

Jensen rose with a sense of determination and rang for Henry. The middle-aged butler appeared, staid and dignified as usual. "Yes, sir?"

"Please call Tom in here. I'd like to see him, Henry."

"Certainly, sir."

The coachman arrived promptly and stood respectfully, hat in hand, while Jensen paced the carpet in front of the fire. "Tom, I know this is touchy, but I need your help." He stopped and fixed his gaze on the man. "I must know where my father has been going lately. I am quite aware that he probably told you not to tell anyone, but matters are quite serious now and I must see him, immediately."

Tom paled. "I'm sure I don't know, sir."

"Hogwash! I'll bet every servant in this house knows more about my father's mistress than I do." He paused, watching Tom shrink. "You see, I know already."

The expression on Tom's face would have been comical if Jensen had not had so much on his mind. The coachman was worried, relieved and embarrassed all at once. "I guess it won't do no harm then, sir. She lives on Oak Street. Number 925." His eyes could not meet Jensen's, but fled over the young master's shoulder and then down to the floor.

"That'll be all, then, Tom. And thank you. I'll drive myself in the buggy. Please get it ready."

Mumbling, Tom scurried out of the room.

As this was one of the first free afternoons Jensen had had in days, he took the time to tend to a matter which had been on his mind for some time. On the way to Oak Street, he stopped at the Sisters of Mercy Hospital. Bernard was asleep, he was informed by the nun, but was coming along nicely. "He'll be well enough to go home in a few days. And," the sister in white added, "he said to thank you very much for the private room, but he's moved back into the ward."

"What?"

"Says there's no need for him to be treated better than his brothers."

"His brothers? What on earth did he mean?"

"I believe," the nun cast her eyes down, "he meant the poor folk." She turned and glided silently down the antiseptic hall as if on wheels, leaving Jensen to puzzle over her strange words as he left the white corridors of Sisters of Mercy Hospital.

The house on Oak Street was charming and brand new, with a narrow front and wood sides. It even had a shingled, round tower on one corner and there were carved gingerbread decorations on the front porch. There were three apartments in the building. Miss Matilda Grueter lived in the topmost one.

Jensen knocked, steeling himself for the interview. It wouldn't be pleasant. Although he felt more self-confident these days and was no longer under his father's thumb, still, facing the old man took a lot of courage. His father, whether right or wrong, still could intimidate him. This time Jensen was determined not to let that happen. He would not back down.

The beautiful young girl who had come to Nob Hill on that terrible evening when Jensen had received the ransom note answered the door, her face no longer bruised or swollen. Again he was struck by her uncanny resemblance to Cecile. When Matilda Grueter saw Jensen, her large brown eyes hardened, giving her a predatory look.

"Is Edward Tofler here?" Jensen inquired.

"Why, yes." Her answer was reluctant.

Brusquely he pushed past her and entered a cozy, fire-lit room. His father was slumped in a deep overstuffed chair, looking as if he hadn't slept in weeks. There were dark circles etched beneath his eyes.

When he saw his son, Edward started and the color drained out of his face. A cone of ashes dropped off the end of his cigar and onto the floor. "Jensen! Have you received word about Annette?"

"Yes, Father, but we have to talk." His hazel eyes burned into Edward's. "In private."

Edward glanced tensely at Tilly. His heavy jowls quivered. "Tilly, dear, could you go into your bedroom for a few minutes? I promise it won't be long."

Tilly pouted but went. Her door closed, clicking loudly in the silent room.

With great effort, Edward rose. He appeared shorter now to Jensen, diminished.

"Annette?" asked Edward again, breathlessly.

"She's all right. We found her," Jensen replied tersely.

Edward sank back into his chair, trembling. "Thank God." He looked up at Jensen. "Did Fallon find her?"

"Fallon? Who's that?"

"The detective I hired. He said he was on her trail yesterday."

"Detective! You fool! Buckley could have found

out. You put her in even more danger. I told you to stay out of this!"

"I had to do something. I couldn't very well look for her myself. They came after Tilly, you know." Edward began to whine. "Poor sweet Tilly. She told me about the kidnapping of my baby. I just had to do something."

"Well, Annette got away on her own, no thanks to you. She's with a friend. She's going to be all right."

"Thank God," Edward whispered.

"Yes," ground out Jensen, "thank God your ineptitude and greed didn't cost Annette her life. And don't try to lie your way out of this. I know all about your dealings with Buckley and the Pacific Fruit Growers." His tone was scathing.

"I had no choice. You don't know Buckley. You don't understand about business."

"One always has a choice," countered Jensen without a trace of compassion. And then he saw his father as he really was, the veneer with which Edward Tofler faced the cruel, hard world suddenly stripped away. He was merely a sick old man who was afraid of his son's youth and strength.

"It's just too bad Annette had to suffer for your mistakes." Jensen glared at his father. "How can you live with yourself knowing that? Luckily, it turned out all right. But not through any of your doing."

Edward barely heard him. He was rocking back and forth, almost moaning to himself. "My Annette! Oh my God, how could I? Annette. My baby." He stopped and looked up at Jensen, his eyes red-rimmed and full of misery. "My children, my children," he groaned. "Every one of them. And now Annette. She was the only one left. Now she'll hate me, too. Oh God, my children!"

Jensen watched, repulsed. His father was disintegrating in front of his eyes. What drivel was he moaning? God, the man sickened him. Still Jensen felt a sort of disgusted pity for him—and a tiny clutch of fear, too. Watching his father fall apart was an eerie reminder of his own mortality.

He spun around wanting only to get away. He couldn't bear to be in the room. It reeked of vileness, of illicit knowledge, of sickness. Edward Tofler was a doomed man. He didn't even matter anymore.

All the way home, Jensen could hear his father's miserable groaning, his nonsensical words. Exactly what had he meant? By the time he pulled up to the ornate brass gate on Mason Street, he felt drained and disgusted.

A strange, booming voice from the sitting room fell on his ears as he entered the front hallway. He quirked a questioning brow at Henry who had come to collect his hat and coat.

"Mr. Luke Bogarde and Mrs. Cecile Bogarde," replied Henry, pokerfaced as always.

"Luke?" Surprised, he strode into the sitting room. Cecile and a man were bent over an old photo album, one which showed the Tofler children when they were young. Cecile was pointing and laughing like a young girl. The man had his arm around her and was looking over her shoulder.

"Cecile?" Jensen murmured.

"Oh! I'm so glad you're home, Jensen. I brought Luke back with me today." She regarded her husband fondly. "Luke, this is my brother, Jensen. Jensen, this is my husband, Captain Luke Bogarde."

The man straightened. He was immensely tall, a brawny man with a barrellike chest and was clothed in a navy blue captain's uniform with brass buttons and gold-fringed epaulets. His grin was wide and infectious. He had twinkling blue eyes, a large nose and a well-kept beard that was streaked with grey. He held out a huge hand.

"Glad to meet you, Jensen. I've 'eard so much about you," he boomed, his Australian accent resounding strangely in Jensen's ears. His hand folded over Jensen's, covering it completely.

"Welcome to San Francisco, Captain Bogarde," replied Jensen.

"Luke, me boy, we don't stand on formalities down under. First names only."

"Well then, Luke." Jensen was slightly overcome by the big man's exuberance. "Will you stay for dinner?"

"Can't. The boys'll tear the ship apart if I leave 'em too long. Sailors, you know. Same the world over." He winked at Jensen. "I keep a tight ship. It's the only way."

"I'd imagine. Well, will we be seeing you again?"

"Probably. But I've been fearful busy here, arranging contracts and such like." He turned to Cecile, his voice softening. "Honeybee, will you be coming to see me soon again?" His blue eyes caressed his wife's face.

"Oh, yes. Tomorrow, if you like. Now that Annette's not here, it's so quiet." She went to the Australian, put her arms around him, laid her cheek against his broad chest. As tall as Cecile was, the top of her head came only to her husband's chin. "Bye, dear."

"Bye, honeybee." Luke bent his grizzled head and gave her an embarrassed peck on the cheek. Sadness lurked in his bright blue eyes as he embraced her. "Take care."

When he left, the room seemed suddenly empty without his bulk and his resonant voice. Cecile looked sad, too. Tears brimmed in her big, velvety brown eyes. Fleetingly, Jensen wondered exactly what the relationship was between them. It was obvious that they loved each other, so why couldn't they be together?

By mid-February, there was already a softness in the air that presaged spring. Annette awoke, sensing the beam of light that touched her closed eyes. She stretched and turned, automatically reaching out to touch Rolf's bare shoulder. He was there, warm, strong and comforting. His body was a bulwark for her, a barrier against the terrible dreams and fears that still haunted her from time to time. She loved the smell of his skin, the strength in his long, ropelike muscles, his rough, curling hair streaked by the sun, the tickling hairs on his legs and the awesome power of his hands which were, nevertheless, so very gentle with her.

She could submerge herself in this man. The power he held over her frightened her a little. She lay utterly still, lazily content, her body curled against his, basking in his presence.

Rolf stirred and turned to her, then drifted into sleep again. She looked at his face as if for the first time, although it was now as familiar to her as her own. No, she realized, more so, for she had watched it ceaselessly for days and days.

Annette finally slipped out of bed and walked naked to the window. The waves hurled themselves against the rocky coast, fell back and hurled themselves again, unendingly. Today the sky was cobalt blue, the sea a sparkling quilt of diamonds and sapphires. Far out, a whale's spout punctured the horizon. Wonder seized her with a serene hand.

"Annette?" Rolf's sleepy voice called to her.

"Here."

"Come back to bed. You must be cold," he teased.

"Not this morning," she laughed. "I'm going to paint this morning. Out on the rocks. Look at it! It's glorious out there!" She pirouetted across the room smiling.

Rolf pretended to be grumpy. "Painting! That's all you think about now."

"Come on, get up. We'll have Nakamura serve us breakfast on the patio."

"We'll need overcoats," he growled.

"So what? Come on, Rolf, please."

He couldn't deny her anything. Especially not when she leaned over him naked, her pale skin gleaming luminously, the rosy tips of her breasts brushing his bare chest, her auburn hair in wild abandon, her golden eyes imploring and full of merriment.

"Please?"

He pulled her onto the tumbled bed, kissed her full, moist lips, then rolled her over until he lay on top of her. "All right," he said finally, kissing her again. "You win." His lips lingered on her neck.

"Rolf." Her voice was breathless, throaty.

"We'll both paint this morning," he promised. "I'm a man of my word."

But she was already beyond leaving. Deep within her the embers of passion began to glow and she felt that familiar ache inside. Her breathing became shallow and rapid. As his lips nibbled on her neck, her throat, her shoulder, her breast, an urgent tingling surged through her. She heard his low, hoarse chuckle as he realized that she had changed her mind. She thought his weight might crush her, but it was sweet to feel the length of his taut body stretched out on top of her.

He rolled over again and now she was sitting

astride him, writhing with desire. He lifted her up, guided her onto him. Her dark hair fell forward and veiled her face as they moved together in a concert of ecstasy. She felt the crescendo approach, inevitable, yet just out of reach. Closer . . . closer . . . and then it broke over her. She cried out, consumed by sensation, fulfillment, glory.

Later in the morning, Annette set up her easel on the rocks above Devil's Cove. She began a sketch of the stunted pine, the rocky coast and the sky. When she was at last satisfied with the sketch, she put down the charcoal and mixed a few colors on her palette. If this painting turned out well, she promised herself, she would never, never sell it. It would be hers to study, to remember, to love. Concentrating, her full lower lip caught between her small white teeth, she did not hear anyone approach above the muted roar of the waves below.

"Miss Cecile," she heard Nakamura say.

Annette started. "Oh!" The man was always creeping up silently behind her. Once Rolf had joked about buying Nakamura a new, squeaky pair of boots. "Thank you, Nakamura," she said when he had announced her visitor. He bowed and glided away.

"Cecile!" she cried, turning to greet her sister. "I'm so glad you came." They embraced warmly.

"I sneaked away and took the cable car downtown. I was very careful. I changed cabs twice and even walked the last mile," Cecile recited. "I must admit I felt foolish."

Annette laughed. "Better safe than sorry!" She pulled on her sister's hand. "Come look at this. What do you think?"

There was a little color now on the canvas. The rocks were done in dark browns and grey and there were brighter, sun-splashed strokes over the water.

"Wonderful!" exclaimed Cecile.

"Oh, you'd say that even if you didn't think so, wouldn't you?" asked Annette with a worried little frown.

"No, really."

"Oh, never mind. I'm glad to see you anyway. How are you?"

"Fine. And you?"

"Wonderful!" Annette grinned. But the smile faded as she noticed her sister's expression. "You're not fine, are you? Tell me." She sat down, cross-legged, and patted the ground beside her. "Sit here and tell me, Cecile."

"It's awful of me to come and cry on your shoulder, especially after what you've been through," Cecile began, "but I have to talk to someone. Jensen's so busy these days with . . . well, with . . ."

"Su Ling," Annette calmly filled in. "I'm quite aware of that and it doesn't bother me in the least. Now, tell me what's the matter. That's what sisters are for. Now that I have a sister again, I want to hear everything she has to say."

Cecile sank down beside Annette, her full skirt billowing up around her. She patted it down. "It's Luke. And me." She hesitated. "I came back to San Francisco because something wasn't right between us." She glanced at Annette. "I mean, we love each other. Really, we do. It's just that"—she turned her face away, a blush staining her cheeks—"I don't truly enjoy him to . . . touch me. I know it's wrong of me. God knows, Luke deserves a woman who can respond to him, but I can't." Her soulful brown eyes were filled with confusion and an equal measure of torment. "I've tried and tried. I love Luke. I love to hold him and kiss him, but then when he wants to . . . Well, I let him, but I don't feel anything. It's like I'm dead." She looked imploringly at Annette. "It isn't like that with you and Rolf, is it?"

"No, it isn't, Cecile," Annette replied soberly. "It's wonderful for me."

"I know. I could tell just by looking at you. And I don't know why I'm so cold. But it has something to do with why I ran away, with the things I can't remember. I just know it does!"

"Poor Cecile," murmured Annette.

Cecile shook her head, making her honey brown curls bounce. "I went to see Luke yesterday. We thought maybe not being together for so long would help. But when he touched me, I just couldn't!" Tears stood in her brown eyes. "Oh God, he deserves better than me! He deserves a whole woman!"

"Now, don't say that! If you love each other—"

"We do! That's why we're both so miserable. Don't you see? I can't go back to Sydney with him like this. The answer is here somewhere and I have to find it! Oh, what's wrong with me?"

"Shush. Nothing's wrong with you that can't be cured. We'll think of a way." Annette stroked her sister's glossy hair. "If only Mama were alive, I know she'd be able to help you." The words were uttered quietly, as if to herself. "Look," Annette advised, "we'll lick this thing. We'll find out what it is, or was. It's like a mystery story and we'll just follow the clues."

"You make it sound so easy." Cecile's voice was tearful. "You're so sure of yourself, so strong."

"You should have seen how weak and helpless I was a couple of weeks ago when Rolf brought me here. You wouldn't have said that then," replied Annette ruefully. "It's so much easier to sound sure about somebody else's problems."

"You always were a cheeky little girl." Cecile

tried to smile through her tears. "You make it sound simple."

"No, not simple, perhaps. I'm still a little off balance myself at times. Life is a strange affair, isn't it? You never know." Annette gazed at the horizon unseeing. After a long moment, she turned back to Cecile and her ale-colored eyes snapped back into focus. "We are going to find out what happened if I have to turn the whole household upside down and question Daddy until he's blue in the face! Then you'll be able to love your Luke like he's never been loved before. I promise you that."

"Oh," sighed Cecile. "I hope you're right."

The sisters visited for a while longer. When Cecile was gone, Annette picked up her palette again and brushed on a few strokes of color. They did not please her. She put the colors down again. It was no good. Her mood had been broken. She wished Rolf would come and joke with her, cheer her up, but she knew he'd gone to the market for some groceries.

She sat on the rocks, gazing out over the immense, swelling plain of the water, following it till it merged with the sky. Within that even, sparkling blanket of the ocean's surface Annette knew each wave was born, crested and died. It was the same with the world of people. Viewed en masse, they were just a crowd of nameless, unimportant faces. Yet each man, woman and child lived, suffered and died, his pain as real to him as hers was to her.

It mattered. Every wave, every person, every drop of water had its own meaning, its own reason for existence. And so did Cecile's life and so did her own.

Annette sighed, rose stiffly from the ground and began to gather her art supplies together. She'd been hiding away here at Devil's Cove for too long. Her idyll had to end. Real life, with all its pain and glory, beckoned. Rolf could not protect her from herself anymore.

She heard his beloved, familiar voice as she entered the back door of the house. He was calling to her, his slight drawl elongating her name in a way she had come to love.

"Here I am, Rolf," she answered, following the sound of his voice.

His arms were full of groceries: a bag of flour, coffee, a sack of beans, a brown-wrapped ham. She took one of the bundles and looked at him carefully, as if seeing him for the first time. His affection for her shone in his dark eyes.

"Rolf, my dear, dear love, I have to go home now," she said at last.

The happy smile was wiped off his face, replaced by a sober expression. Unhurriedly, he turned and set the packages down, stood with his broad back to her for an endless moment.

Annette's eyes grew moist. She felt torn. She wanted to run to him, tell him of her love, comfort him, and yet at the same time she wanted to push him, force him to prove himself to her. Yes, she admitted to herself, she wanted him to beg her to stay, to say he couldn't live without her.

But he didn't. "Yes, of course, you have to go home. You're much better now. But, my dear, it's safer here. We still don't know what O'Neill might do." His dark eyes held hers, but they were unreadable once more, heavy-lidded and somber.

"I thought of that." Her eyes slid away from his, disappointed by his practical approach to the matter. "But I also wondered why O'Neill couldn't find this place if he really wanted to. Why, he could have had Jensen followed any number of times."

"Yes, he could have," agreed Rolf, his dark gaze level.

"Well, then, your argument holds no water. I shall have to go."

"Yes, I suppose you do. But why, pray tell, did you decide so precipitately? What brought it up?"

Annette took a deep breath. She'd try to be as honest as she could. If they were ever to mean anything substantive to each other, the groundwork had to be laid now, brick by painful brick. "Lots of reasons. Cecile came again today. She needs my help badly and she had no one else to turn to. I promised her I'd help."

"By doing what?" His wide mouth was a straight line on his face, the deeply indented grooves running from his nose to its outer edges giving him a harsh look.

"I'm not sure. Something. She's my sister, Rolf. I have to try." Annette turned and walked to the big window and stared out at the breaking waves. "And then there's you and me. I'm not sure about us, Rolf." She turned to him, begging for understanding, the words wrenched from her. "I'm worried that you could overwhelm me, that I'd be afraid to compete with you and your talent. Then I'd hate myself forever for not doing what I wanted. I have to try first, don't you see? I have to try and maybe fail, or I'll never know." She stood silently, her hands at her sides, afraid to go near him or touch him, afraid that she'd be lost in a maelstrom of love and desire if she did.

Rolf was silent, a tall, shadowed figure, his eyes expressionless black pools.

"And then," Annette continued, looking down at her hands twisting together in front of her, "there are other problems, things you haven't decided about yet." She was too embarrassed to continue.

Rolf gave a short, cold laugh. "Why not let me worry about my other problems, Annette? I'd say you have enough of your own."

Was he rejecting her, then? She felt as if a dagger were being twisted in her gut. Not once had he asked her to stay or told her he loved her. And now he'd turned hard and sarcastic. If only he'd say something to her—a word, a glimmering of understanding or belief in her.

But he remained silent. When he broke the quiet it was only to say, "I'll drive you home tomorrow morning then. I only hope to hell Tansy O'Neill doesn't get his hands on you again." His anger lay just beneath the surface of his words.

Annette straightened her shoulders. She wouldn't cry or carry on in front of him. If she couldn't take his love with her, then she'd be damned if she'd abandon her dignity to him as well.

Annette smiled at him, which took immense willpower. "Don't worry, Rolf. I'll be very careful."

She turned to the window again and stared sightlessly out over the sparkling Pacific. Yes, she thought, she would have to be careful where Tansy was concerned, but she knew exactly how to take care of him.

Chapter 21

On her first morning home Annette rose early, surprised at the luxury that surrounded her. She saw with new eyes the rose damask boudoir in which she'd grown up. And yet, she thought wistfully, something important was gone from her life. She felt empty and alone.

Vivian didn't allow her to feel that way for long, however. As she bustled into Annette's room early carrying a breakfast tray, she was unusually talkative. Her frizzy red hair kept popping out from under her lace-edged cap as if she'd stuck it on in a hurry.

"Oh, Miss Annette, and weren't we all just out of our minds with worry! You're looking all right though. A little thin, maybe." Efficiently, she set the breakfast tray down on Annette's lap, pulled the drapes, arranged things on the dresser. "I'm so glad you're home."

"Thank you, Viv. I'm glad, too." She cracked the top off a soft-boiled egg, spooned some up and took a sip of coffee and a bite of toast. "I'm going downtown early this morning, Viv. I need something very smart to wear."

"You're not going to that studio again, are you, Miss Annette?"

"No," she laughed, "not today. I have something rather more important to do."

"Am I to accompany you, miss?"

"No, but it won't take long."

Vivian looked at her suspiciously, but went to the closet and selected a few outfits for inspection. Annette chose carefully, for she had to feel absolutely perfect that day. She was a woman of wit and strength, invulnerable, equal to anyone in the business world—at least she intended to appear that way.

"Ah, that's the one." She pointed with a triangle of toast. "The black taffeta."

Vivian held up a suit of stark black taffeta, tailored almost like a man's suit except for the shorter, more fitted tunic. There was scarcely any bustle, only a plain, sweeping skirt. The tunic had a high, severe neck with many buttons and was meant to be worn without a blouse. The unrelieved black would make her feel as if she were in mourning, severe, businesslike mourning.

She dressed quickly, pleased with the effect. She looked older, a little pale, but utterly sure of herself. Her golden eyes blazed commandingly out of her white face. A small black hat and diamond stud earrings completed her very proper outfit. She dabbed her most wildly expensive Parisian scent liberally on her neck and wrists. It was vital for this particular job she had to do.

Jensen was just leaving as she arrived downstairs. "Glad I got to see you before I left for the office." He kissed her cheek. "My, you look smart today." He smiled warmly. "Good to have you home again. By the way," he grinned sheepishly, "I probably won't be home after work. I may be quite late, so don't wait for me."

"Su Ling?" asked Annette.

"Yes. I promised to stop by. She's so lonely, poor

thing. I hate to think of her alone all day in her new apartment."

"Oh, go ahead and admit you can't stay away from her for a second," teased Annette.

"And another thing," he studied her attire for a moment, "if you plan on going out, promise me you'll keep Tom with you at all times."

"Oh, I will," she lied smoothly.

"By the way, I think I have a plan to appease our friends."

"Oh?"

"Yes, but don't you worry about it, Annette. You've been through enough already." Jensen grinned again and dashed out to the waiting buggy.

Annette shook her head ruefully. He was like a boy consumed with puppy love. Amazing. Her cool, sarcastic brother, who found the belles of high society boring, was insanely in love with a poor Chinese orphan.

It was too bad she'd had to lie to Jensen, but she knew exactly what she was doing. She rode the cable car down California Street, sitting erect on the seat, tensely anticipating the execution of what she had planned for the morning. Carefully she put all thoughts and regrets over Rolf aside. Instead, she went over and over the things she would say, the logic of her arguments. It was foolproof. Still, she admitted, she was afraid. But she had to do it. It was the only way out for all of them.

She had a few blocks to walk when she got off the cable car. Striding resolutely and looking straight ahead, she concentrated on her forthcoming task. Her black taffeta skirt swished reassuringly against her legs.

Her heart pounded as she approached the corner of Kearny and Washington Streets. She found the sign reading "Snug Café" and pushed the door open. A few men sat in the front barroom, eating pickled eggs and snacks with mugs of beer. The bartender was drying glasses with a big white towel. To the last man, they all turned and looked her over with keen interest. She felt hot and awkward as they continued to stare. Boldly she walked to the bar, ignoring them as best she could. "I would like to see Mr. Buckley," she announced calmly.

The bartender was a big man with an oversized lantern jaw. He smiled, showing gaps in his teeth. "Got an appointment?"

"You might say so. Tell him Annette Tofler is here to see him."

"Just a minute." The bartender gave her a thoughtful, sweeping glance, then disappeared into a back room. When he re-emerged a moment later, there was new respect on his face. "This way."

She followed him down a short hall. He opened a door, ushered her in and closed it. She was in a large, ornately decorated room. A huge desk sat between two tall windows that were draped in rich maroon velvet. A carpet covered the floor, soft and thick. The room was very dim, the drapes drawn. Oddly, Annette noticed, the desk top was clear, not a paper on it.

"Miss Tofler?" A well modulated voice greeted her from across the room.

Then she noticed him sitting in a chair at the desk. The room was so dim that she hadn't seen him at first. It was Blind Chris Buckley, the ruler of the city's political machine. He was slender and dapper, dressed beautifully in a pinstriped navy blue suit, a high, starched white collar and a neat white cravat with a diamond stickpin. A charming smile was displayed on his lips, but the atmosphere in the room was chilling.

"Yes, I'm Annette Tofler." Her voice sounded strange in the big room. It echoed a little.

"Please sit down, Miss Tofler, then tell me what's

on your mind." He was still smiling. With a slim hand he gestured to a chair as if he could see it.

When she was seated, she examined his face closely, particularly his eyes. They were half closed and expressionless, but otherwise normal looking. Was he really blind?

"Yes, it's true. I am blind," he said as if reading her thoughts. "Everyone wonders, so I tell them right off. Now, what's on your mind, young lady?"

Annette drew a deep breath. "I have an offer to make you, one that is to both our advantages."

"I'm always willing to listen. But why does a beautiful young lady come to me with an offer? Why not her father or her brother?"

"How do you know I'm—"

"Beautiful?" Buckley laughed. "A woman who wears that sort of perfume has got to be beautiful!"

"Oh. How perceptive of you, Mr. Buckley," replied Annette nervously. "As for why I'm here, well, my father is very ill, and my brother doesn't have the information to make a deal with you."

"And you do?"

"Yes."

"Go on." His tone was level, noncommittal.

"First, I want you to know that I am absolutely serious about everything I say. Also, in return for the favor I will do you, I must have your promise that Tofler Transport will be left alone, and me and the rest of my family, too. My father has retired, and my brother has taken over the business. And Jensen will not deal with you."

Chris Buckley leaned back in his big, squeaking leather chair, tented his fingers and smiled easily. "A tall order, Miss Tofler. My dealings with your father have been very lucrative to us both." He paused. "You must have quite a tidbit to dangle in front of me to ask such a thing."

"I do." Her voice was hard and cold.

"Before we speak of that, I wish to apologize for the, ah, inconvenience caused you a few weeks ago. There was nothing personal involved, I assure you. I think Mr. O'Neill got carried away. He tries too hard sometimes and becomes a bit overzealous. However, the breach of contract on your father's part must still be righted. It was a firm business agreement."

"I think we can take care of that. My information will allow you to recover more than the money you lost through my father's failure to supply your boxcar."

"How so, young lady?"

"One of the men in your organization is cheating you, Mr. Buckley."

"Pocketing a few extra tips here and there? That's only to be expected." He waved a disdainful hand.

"Rather more than that, I believe. I was told that he's collecting protection money from half the cribs in Chinatown because you don't know they exist. He bragged about it, in fact. Even alluded to your . . . infirmity."

Buckley was silent. A scowl covered his face. His fingers tapped impatiently on the polished surface of the empty desk top. "Do you have proof?" he questioned her.

"Check at a place called the Lotus Den. It's on Grant Street. I'm sure you'll find all sorts of interesting things going on there." Annette held her breath. Her whole plan depended on his reaction. If he knew already, or if he didn't care, then her hopes would be dashed. Suddenly, her whole plan seemed childish, absolutely ridiculous.

"The Lotus Den," Buckley contemplated the

name. "Who is the man that is doing all this stealing from me?"

"I'll tell you when I have your promise that there will be no reprisals against my family or the business."

Silence. The dim room seemed to pulse with an evil life of its own. Annette could almost taste it—a suffocating fog that confused the senses, leaving one off balance and unnerved. She waited, her stomach tied in knots, her heart pounding.

"Tell me," he offered at last. "If I like what I hear, we'll have a deal."

Annette silently drew in a long breath. Should she show her hand now? "Tansy O'Neill," she replied confidently.

A low oath spilled from Buckley's lips. Half rising from his chair, he leaned forward on his desk. His eyes stared sightlessly at a spot just over Annette's shoulder. Inadvertently, she shrank away from him.

"You'd damned well better be right, Miss Tofler, or you'll wish you'd never heard of Blind Chris Buckley!" he ground out the words through clenched teeth. "I don't take very well to troublemakers like you."

"It's the truth. Find out for yourself." Annette rose, struggling desperately to stay calm. Waves of powerful hate radiated from Buckley's figure, striking her with terrifying force. "I think our arrangement will be satisfactory to us both. Thank you so much for your time, Mr. Buckley." She began to back away from him toward the door. She found herself smiling inanely, even though, of course, he couldn't see her. She felt for the door handle behind her, twisted it and let herself out into the corridor. Then she quietly closed the door. The image of Buckley, crouched over his desk like a wild beast over his prey, refused to leave.

She fled through the bar and out into the street, into the fresh air and glittering sunshine of the spring day, back into the normal world of people who laughed and cried and felt fear. She felt as if she had just left the realm of Hades where darkness holds sway and evil overcomes all.

Su Ling handed Annette a translucent porcelain cup filled with fragrant Chinese tea. "That was a very bad thing you did, to go to the blind white devil. Your brother is very, very angry with you." The Chinese girl's ivory skin glowed with new beauty now that she had fully recovered from her ordeal. She wore a brilliantly colorful satin jacket with a mandarin collar over a pair of matching trousers. Her gleaming black hair was piled intricately in coils on top of her head and a spray of apple blossoms had been tucked into it. She had the presence and dignity of a very great lady, a princess of the Celestial Empire.

"It had to be done, Su Ling," returned Annette. "You know it."

"Now tell us again what it was you said to him," Cecile interrupted, setting down her teacup.

"I merely told him that Tansy was cheating him. Very simple. We're all fortunate it worked." Annette took a dainty bite of an almond cookie.

"Still, Jensen will never forgive you. When he found out, he came here in a terrible rage," Su Ling shook her head. "He almost frightened me." Her big black eyes widened at the memory.

"Oh, don't be silly. He was just angry that I'd put myself in danger. Men are always like that. He's already calmed down. Don't worry. Jensen never stays mad for too long." Annette smiled, recalling Jensen's impotent fury at the story of her meeting with Buckley. "His bark is worse than his bite."

"Pardon?" asked Su Ling.

"It's just a saying we have," explained Cecile. "It means he sounds angrier than he is."

"Oh, I understand now."

The three women were sitting in the parlor of the flat on Telegraph Hill that Jensen had rented for Su Ling. It was a pretty place and Su Ling had added many Oriental touches that made it absolutely charming. On this warm March day, the sun streamed in through the bay window overlooking Lombard Street, splashing across the bright, embroidered silk curtains and low, brass inlaid teak tables.

The women were silent for a while, sipping their tea. Annette just had to ask the question. "Are you happy, Su?"

The Chinese girl turned suddenly somber, her eyes thoughtful, considering. She met Annette's eyes at last. "I go with Jensen because all ladies need a man when their family is gone. I am not so foolish to think I can live by myself. I have nothing but my family name now. In Shanghai that was worth very much, but here," she spread her hands, palms up, "I am nothing at all." Then she smiled, slowly, secretly, tucking her tiny hands back into the loose sleeves of her jacket. "But I like Jensen now very, very much. He is a good man. He is good to me. I am very happy."

"I'm so glad," Annette smiled. "Jensen seems happy, too. I've never seen him like this before. I think he's in love with you."

Su Ling flushed and looked down at her lap. "He tells me that, too." She looked up at her two visitors, serious again. "But I am only a concubine. I will never be the number one wife of Jensen." She sighed. "I guess that is better than being the concubine of a bad, ugly man." She paused again. "But in Shanghai I had many suitors. Rich, young men that wanted me to be their wife. I was taught how to be a good wife, to run a big house, keep watch of the expenses, have babies, order food. Here I can do little." Her tiny, birdlike hands fluttered at the small apartment. "He won't let me."

"It will work out, Su Ling. Jensen will take care of you. I know it," commiserated Annette, sorry for Su Ling's predicament.

"Never mind. I am happy. Jensen is good to me. He doesn't leave me sad one minute. He told me we can go on trip to China to find my family, if anybody is still alive." Her delicate face brightened.

"China! How wonderful!" cried Cecile. "I've been there with Luke, you know. It's a fascinating place."

Su Ling poured more tea. The ladies chatted easily as the afternoon waned.

Annette looked at the gold watch she wore on a chain around her neck. "Lord, it's late! We'll have to go now, Cecile."

"Oh, goodness, I told Luke I'd come by the ship for dinner! What's the time?"

"Nearly five-thirty." Annette turned to her Chinese friend. "Thank you for a lovely afternoon. We'll come again soon."

They stood at the door, ready to leave.

"Do you see Rolf?" asked Su Ling suddenly. "You have not mentioned him today."

"Well, you see," Annette wasn't sure what to say, for she wasn't at all sure about Rolf these days. He hadn't called on her since he'd driven her home and that had been over a week ago. "We've decided not to see each other for a while," she said tentatively.

"American ladies always make big problems with men. If you love a man, you should be with him. It's easy," Su Ling scolded, her head cocked to one side.

"Not quite so easy," replied Annette dryly.

"No, not a bit," agreed Cecile.

After Tom took Cecile to the docks to meet Luke, Annette had time to think about her sister as she rode home. Cecile was still troubled. Her relationship with Luke was strained and uncertain. But there was a new element to Cecile's distress now. Luke was winding up his business and was talking of going home in a few weeks. Cecile was terrified, for she couldn't leave until she found the answers she needed for her future happiness, nor could she bear to send Luke home without her. Annette felt completely helpless.

Back in the Nob Hill mansion, Annette went quickly to the conservatory where she'd set up her easel. She'd taken to working at the house now and had given up the studio. There was no longer any reason to hide her painting from her father since he was never home and didn't seem to care anyway.

She'd been working on a canvas for several days and had a new idea to try before the sun went down and the light faded. She threw on her smock, squeezed a few blobs of color onto her palette and studied the half-finished work. It was a painting of Moor, one of the matched pair of horses that pulled the Tofler carriage. He was standing in his stall, looking at something, his ears perked forward. Annette had been having trouble capturing the proper dull sheen of the black horse in the dim stable. It had eluded her for days, but now she thought she had it. She dabbed lighter color on Moor's haunches, neck and chest. Yes, it was better, much better. She'd made a breakthrough.

If only Rolf could see it, she thought. He'd be proud of her. Perhaps one day he would see it. Perhaps. She missed him dreadfully but still, she needed this time. She'd been painting like a fury since she'd been home and her work was better than it had ever been. There was a new significance to it that surprised her. She had learned how to construct her paintings or, at least, could figure it out after several tries. She wasn't always sure when something was right, but she knew now when it was wrong.

There, Moor was finished. Tomorrow she could work on the background. Images kept crowding into her mind these days. Already she had several more ideas for paintings. It was terribly exciting.

She left her brushes to soak, hung the smock on a hook and ascended the stairs to her room. God, she was tired. Perhaps a nap before dinner. No, she remembered something else she had to do. She went into her room and sat down at her writing desk. Pulling out a piece of pale blue stationery with her initials at the top in gold, she began to write.

> Dear Bernard,
>
> I was so glad to hear from you last week and to know that you are well. I feel so much at fault for everything that happened, or at least that my family was at fault. Let us thank God that you recovered.
>
> Yes, I am well. As for happy, well, I am content at least.
>
> My painting is coming along fine. I would love for you to stop by and see my work. Your opinion is always appreciated.
>
> It was thrilling to hear that your notoriety, as you call it, has brought you a lot of work. I am glad to have been a party to your success, although I'm not sure I'd do it again!
>
> My very best to you always,
> Annette

There. She folded the letter and was about to put it in the envelope when she heard a noise in the hall outside her room. Was Jensen home? No, he was going to Su Ling's tonight. Cecile, then. But she was visiting Luke.

The door to Cecile's room opened, then shut quietly. How strange, thought Annette. Usually Cecile taps on my door first. Oh dear, what if she's had a terrible quarrel with Luke and is too miserable even to talk to me.

Annette rose. She'd go and talk to Cecile. Her sister was much too troubled to suffer in silence. She needed Annette's help or at least her understanding.

When she reached her sister's door, she decided against knocking. In her despair, Cecile might pretend she wasn't there. Annette opened the door.

The heavy drapes were drawn, and there was little light in the room. Pregnant silence filled the large space. Annette waited for her eyes to adjust to the semidarkness. Her head tilted expectantly. Where was Cecile? She glanced around the room and the shadowy sight that met her eyes was so stunning that for a moment she stood paralyzed, her hand still on the door handle. She couldn't begin to comprehend what she saw.

"Daddy," she whispered.

Edward Tofler stood motionless, as if in a trance, next to Cecile's bed. He was holding a pale blue silk nightgown that belonged to his oldest daughter up to his cheek. He stared at Annette, but she knew he wasn't seeing her. His mouth worked soundlessly and she could swear she saw tears running down his cheeks. He was rubbing the garment against his face,

"Daddy," said Annette again, moving toward his shadowy figure, her hand extended.

Then Edward Tofler saw her. He moaned and clutched the nightgown more tightly. "I had to come back. I just had to."

"But, Daddy, I don't understand," Annette whispered, placing a hand on his arm.

As if it had seared his flesh, Edward jerked away from her touch. The nightgown slipped from his hand and floated to the floor at his feet. His eyes followed it, wide and full of terror.

"Daddy?" Annette repeated, unable to comprehend the scene before her. "What's wrong?"

A deep, throaty groan escaped his lips, a sound more animal than human. "No one ever understood." Frantically he whirled, pushed past Annette and fled from the dim room.

Unthinkingly, she reached down, picked up the nightgown and folded it carefully, her eyes riveted to the doorway through which her father had just disappeared.

Chapter 22

Rolf simply could not concentrate. He threw down a paint-splattered rag in disgust and stalked to the window of his Astor House studio. Frustration was eating away at him.

Damn that girl! He'd sent her notes, not once, but several times. They remained unanswered. Was she teasing him, trying to find out how far he could be pushed? Or was she genuinely not interested in him anymore?

Her image was never far from his thoughts. He could see her so clearly in his mind's eye. He could see her naked, posing in front of that very window, or flirting outrageously at her ball, or clinging to Bernard's arm, her face cold with outrage. He could see her as a raving fury, threatening him with a raised board in a Chinatown alleyway, or moaning and delirious as she fought the spell of opium at Devil's Cove. He knew her body as well as he knew his own. Damn her!

He'd already decided he shouldn't pursue her. She was nervous and needed room. But his patience was wearing thin. Angrily, he paced the large room.

Another thing remained unfinished, too. It bothered him, ate away at his self-respect. Tansy O'Neill.

Oh yes, he knew about the deal Annette had

made with Buckley. My God, that girl was brave and smart and, at times, absolutely unfathomable. But Rolf had his own score to settle with O'Neill. The man had dared to lay his filthy, corrupt hands on Rolf's woman! It was as simple and primitive as that, and although Rolf considered himself a civilized man, he couldn't stand by and allow O'Neill to get away with it. It just didn't sit well with him.

Abruptly, he stopped pacing and grabbed his overcoat. Jamming a tweed wool cap on his blond head, he strode out of his suite and down the stairs.

It didn't take him long to find Tansy O'Neill, only an hour or so of making inquiries in various bars along Market Street. He pushed the swinging doors of the Hornet's Nest Saloon open and entered the smoky room that reeked of unwashed sailors' bodies and stale beer.

Scanning the noisy crowd in the saloon, Rolf pushed up to the bar and, for effect, shouted drunkenly for more grog. There, at one end of the long bar, he saw Tansy's heronlike frame leaning negligently against the gleaming wood.

Rolf's heart began to pound. He was excited, expectant, every muscle taut. He pushed his way through the boisterous throng, his eyes glued to the skeletal figure that lounged against the bar, unknowing, uncaring.

"O'Neill."

"Yeah?" asked the man, eyeing Rolf with contempt. "Karman, ain't it?"

"Yes. I want to talk to you." Rolf's voice was as flat and emotionless as slate. Inside, however, was a boiling rage.

"Sure. What's the problem?" Tansy gave Rolf a chilling smile and looked him up and down with a measuring glance.

"Outside, O'Neill." Rolf jerked his head toward the swinging doors.

Tansy's face hardened. His Adam's apple bobbed convulsively. "You crazy? You wanna fight?"

"Yes."

"Anything to oblige," he smirked. "Bet it's over that Tofler dame, ain't it? A piece of sweet flesh Karman, but no chippy's worth fighting over."

"This one is."

"Come on, then." Tansy shrugged eloquently and turned his back as if to walk to the doors, then spun around and lashed out at Rolf with lightning speed.

The crowd drew back to make room. They were accustomed to barroom brawls. Two of the men hauled Rolf to his feet. He stood dazed for a moment as the circle around him and Tansy cheered them on.

Shaking his head to clear it, he focused on Tansy who stood facing him, a cynical grin splitting his pink lips.

"Come on, Karman," he hissed. "You been askin' for it a long time."

Suddenly Rolf saw everything through a red haze. He went into a kind of trance, a state of being where only destruction existed. His muscles obeyed automatically, instinctively. He'd had to fight often enough during his hard, loveless boyhood.

All at once hands were on him, many hands, and voices were shouting. "Hey, stop now! You nearly killed the man! Enough! Pull him off!"

The hands wrenched him away from Tansy's inert form as if they were Lilliputians struggling with a giant Gulliver. Giving a roar, Rolf shook them off. He stood, crouched like an animal, breathing hard. A red ribbon of blood trickled from the corner of his mouth.

"Hey, take it easy, fella. You got him good," ventured a grizzled old miner. "He ain't goin' nowheres."

His head finally cleared and Rolf looked about him. He saw Tansy's body on the rough wooden floor. A hint of a smile tugged at Rolf's lips. He wiped away the blood with his forearm. "No, I guess he isn't," he said, appeased at last.

It was a glorious spring day in the bay area, clear and bright. The soft sea breeze touched the hills and tenderly kissed the buds on the oak trees. Spring in the city was Annette's favorite time of year. It was a time of rebirth. Trees and flowers blossomed. New foals stood on long, spindly legs. The delightful chirping of birds in their nests enhanced the serenity of morning.

Buildings were sprouting up in the downtown area, altering the skyline above the blue bay. Homes popped up by the dozens spangling the city hills. They were fresh and clean looking with their large bay windows, tidy flower boxes and gingerbread trim painted in pastels.

A faint promise of summer was in the air. Annette could feel it as she sat in the garden working at her easel, filling a canvas with spring's gentle colors. The warm sun bathed her shoulders.

Soon it would be lunch time and she would join Cecile in the conservatory. They would chat, perhaps plan an afternoon of shopping. Cecile seemed happier since Annette had returned, but she was far from peaceful. The sisters often discussed the past, delving into their childhoods and sharing fond memories of their mother, Elizabeth. Both women were pleased with Jensen's new role as adoring companion to Su Ling. Secretly, they wished he would marry the beautiful Chinese girl, in spite of the social stigma attached to mixed marriages. Their father, they had decided, would not dare object. How could he when he was barely a member of the family anymore? In fact, since

Annette had seen him that day some weeks past in Cecile's room, none of them had heard from him. It was as if he didn't exist.

Still, Annette refused to be depressed. They all knew where he lived now. If he was happy, well then, for his sake, she would be happy, too. It was only Jensen who became angry at the mention of Edward Tofler, so Annette and Cecile seldom spoke of him when Jensen was around.

Satisfied with the morning's work, Annette cleaned her brushes, took off her smock and joined Cecile for lunch.

As she sat down across from her sister, she noticed a formal looking envelope resting on her plate. "What's this?"

Cecile poured them each a glass of wine. "It looks like an invitation. It was hand delivered a short while ago."

Annette opened it and pulled out an embossed vellum card. After scanning its contents, she lifted her eyes to meet Cecile's. "It's from Rolf," she said quietly, her pulse racing. "There's an opening at the Golden Gate Gallery for his new works. He signed the invitation himself."

"You'll attend, of course."

"I don't know. It's been so long. I don't know if I can bear to see him again."

"Oh, Annette, please! Go. You know you want to," implored Cecile.

"Yes. I do. But it's so hard. Don't you see," tears sprang to her eyes, "we aren't meant for each other? He doesn't love me, Cecile. Not at all."

"You don't know that, Annette. He did ask you to marry him, after all."

"I told you why I couldn't!"

Cecile frowned, unconvinced. "Because it was his

duty? I don't believe that for a minute. As for his mistress, that's a farce, too. Why, everyone knows Mrs. Fairchild sees many men. Rolf can't be seriously interested in her."

Annette mulled over Cecile's words. "But he doesn't love me."

"Do you love him?"

"Yes. I suppose I have all along, Cecile."

"Then you can make him love you, too."

"Rolf can't be made to do anything, least of all love me. I told you, Cecile, he wants me in only one way."

Cecile dished salad greens onto their plates. "Go to the opening, Annette. See him again. He did send you a personal invitation, so he must want to see you again very much. And he's sent all those notes."

"I don't know. Perhaps. But if he thinks he can lure me into his bed again, well, I won't do it. I can't. I die inside everytime I think about him. No, if I go at all, I'll have to avoid him entirely."

The opening was a week away. Annette tormented herself for the full seven days until the very afternoon of the showing. First she was definitely going, then she wasn't. She vacillated between the two alternatives, sometimes crying, sometimes laughing for her silliness.

It was two hours before the opening when Cecile came into her bedroom. "Aren't you dressed yet?"

"I'm not going." Annette sat at her dresser, running a brush through her long ringlets, coiling them absent-mindedly around a slim finger.

Cecile walked to the wardrobe. "It's quite warm today." She opened the doors. "I think this low-cut yellow gown would do fine. It enhances your waistline and bust." She took it out and shook the folds loose.

"I'm not going."

"Oh, yes you are!"

As it turned out, the lemon yellow dress did flatter Annette's slim waist and high, full bustline. The chest panel and neck were made of sheer, cream-colored lace. The sleeves were full and long, trimmed at the cuff in the same delicate lace. The full bust tapered down to a tiny waistline, a small bustle and a full, draped skirt. The material was a very light voile that shimmered deliciously in the light. It was an afternoon dress suitable for a princess. Oddly enough, Annette had purchased it only a few days before at an exclusive dress shop on Kearny Street. When Cecile had asked her where she was planning to wear such a beautiful dress, Annette had shrugged her shoulders. "I don't have the faintest idea."

Vivian arranged her hair into a pompadour and placed a small, cream-colored straw hat on the full bun of her hair.

"You both are wasting your time," Annette complained, irritated with the two women fussing over her. "I'm not going!" She parked herself on the bench in front of the pink satin dressing table and folded her arms obstinately.

Tom drove Annette to the Kearny Street gallery. She instructed him to wait right in front of the place as she wasn't going to stay but a minute.

Annette mounted the steps and entered the long, spacious room, which was already brimming over with people. She greeted a few friends, sipped a glass of champagne and tried desperately not to look around the room for Rolf.

She had just decided to take a quick look at his works and slip away when she felt a hand on her arm. She froze.

"Why, Annette!" came a familiar, honey-sweet voice. "How nice to see you again!"

Annette let her breath out in a long, calming

whoosh. "Hello, Arabella. Nice to see you, too." Inadvertently, her eyes traveled around the room for a glimpse of Rolf.

"Why, don't you just look wonderful! That dress! You simply must give me the name of your seamstress." Arabella Sims batted long, pale lashes. "Why I'm so excited," she rushed on breathlessly, "but of course you've heard? Freddy is marrying that lovely Collins girl, Jessica. Isn't it just too marvelous?" Arabella's breath fanned Annette's cheeks conspiratorially.

"Yes, I did hear the good news. I'm very happy for Freddy. He deserves a fine wife." Bored, she casually scanned the large room once more.

"Come now, Annette, are you happy? I mean really happy?" Arabella leaned even closer. The light in her eyes faded and was replaced by sly amusement. "I mean, I should think that after Freddy dropped you—"

"Freddy dropped me?" gasped Annette, her attention drawn to Arabella fully now.

"Why, yes. Everyone knows," whispered Arabella smugly. "Why you poor thing."

"Listen, Arabella," replied Annette coolly, "I really do want to see Mr. Karman's works. If you'll excuse me?"

But before Annette could leave, she heard the girl's voice at the back of her neck. "I just bet you do want to see Mr. Karman's works!"

Annette would have spun around and uttered a scathing remark except that she would not allow herself to rise to the bait. No doubt everyone in San Francisco knew about her affair with Rolf. So what? Let them gossip.

She continued walking away without a backward glance. She stopped in front of a group of his paintings, a few she had seen lying haphazardly around his house or studio and others she had watched him work on. Already there were "Sold" signs placed on a couple of them. Rolf was doing quite well for himself.

But where was he? Why hadn't she caught at least a glimpse of his tall form in the crowd? Annette tried to keep her attention on the paintings, forcing herself to look interested.

She walked on. Her heart was beating far too quickly, she knew, and she was beginning to feel hot and closed-in as she neared the far wall. There were so many people. A few she recognized, but most were total strangers.

It was odd, she thought suddenly as she stood in front of a commanding mountain landscape, but hadn't it grown awfully quiet at this end of the room? And then, too, it seemed as if people were staring at her, whispering behind their hands. But perhaps she was only imagining it.

She kept her back to the throng. The last time she had been here, with Jensen, she had wanted people to stare openly at her, to admire her. Now, however, she felt inexplicably uncomfortable, so much so that she wanted to leave, and quickly.

Forcing her feet to move on, she stepped up to the next painting, another landscape. It looked like the Russian River north of the city. It was good, bold and dynamic. All of Rolf's works struck the eye that way. People loved him. They bought and traded his finer pieces and awaited his showings eagerly.

If only she could do half as well. One day, perhaps

Where was he? She turned sideways, affording herself a view of the crowd. Rolf was still nowhere in sight. Perhaps he wasn't there at all. But she had been right about one thing: people definitely were staring at her.

Annette turned and walked to the other end of the gallery. Her nerves were raw. She was so wrapped up in thought and so on edge that at first she failed to see the large painting on the wall before her. Nor did she notice the many eyes following her progress around the room, silently mocking her.

How dare Rolf not even show up! And if he was here, he was making himself deliberately invisible. Was this some sort of beastly punishment because she wouldn't fall at his feet? Well, if so, she decided, she would simply turn around and leave. She would show Mr. Rolf Karman!

Lifting her delicate chin, ready to make her exit, Annette was shocked into immobility by the sight before her eyes.

"It's . . . it's me," she whispered unthinkingly, her heart squeezing in her breast. "My Lord!" In front of Annette and the obvious center of attraction was the very canvas for which she had modeled.

She stood mesmerized, glued to the spot. Her hand flew to her bosom as if to stop the furious beating of her heart. The painting was exquisite, intense. The brilliant colors leapt from the canvas hypnotizing the eye.

Annette's one thought at the moment was that the painting reminded her of Botticelli's *Aphrodite Rising from the Sea,* which she had seen at the Uffizi Gallery in Florence the summer before. In the old painting the fascinating goddess stood almost nude on a salmon pink seashell which floated enchantingly on the ocean. Annette adored Botticelli's painting and frequently thought about it.

And now here she was, although not floating on the sea. Instead she was most certainly naked and sitting in repose on the rocks along the shore. Violent waves crashed, sending spouts of spray and foam into the air while grey, angry clouds scudded overhead indicating a storm in the making.

It was Devil's Cove. There was no mistaking the setting. And she was the woman. Her hair streamed behind, too long, the wind tearing at the wild auburn mass. Her body sat proudly erect in the violent storm, defying nature, glistening with sea spray from the surging waves.

There was no doubt that Rolf had painted her as an elusive, radiant goddess. A love goddess, perhaps, for her slightly pouting lips were full and sensual and the large, expressive eyes implored, beckoned, sought fulfillment.

Rolf had captured it all: her mind, her body, her very soul. Without embarrassment or shame, Annette viewed the painting critically. No matter the artist or the model, there was such depth of feeling to it that adoration and, yes, even love radiated from the canvas. It couldn't be mistaken or missed.

She forgot her surroundings, held willing prisoner by the awesome painting. Her eyes traveled around the canvas from the bold, slashing strokes of the ocean, to the forceful clouds, to the enduring rock. But always the eye settled back onto the girl, beautiful, unearthly and unattainable.

And this, her mind acknowledged, was the way Rolf viewed her! Had he asked her here to see this? She saw a small placard on the right hand bottom corner: "Not For Sale." He was keeping it, then, for himself.

The throng eddied and flowed around Annette as she stood there, oblivious to all, staring at the painting. She cared not at all that everyone in the gallery knew who the fascinating goddess was, that they were gaping at the glistening, naked body on the canvas, turning their eyes on Annette, comparing. None of that mattered to her.

What mattered was that Rolf, through his painting, was conveying a message to her. But was she reading it properly?

"Good, isn't it?" The spell shattered and she spun around to face the owner of the low, faintly sarcastic voice. Of course. It was Rolf.

He stood next to her, his dark eyes giving away nothing, his mouth tilted slightly at one corner in mockery or amusement. Or was he laughing *with* her at the whole, crazy thing between them? Annette's eyes, full of confused wonder, held his.

"Well? Do you like it or not?" Rolf drawled. He was standing in a relaxed pose, his hands on his slim hips, in a finely cut suit of pale grey. The white collar of his shirt contrasted sharply with his tanned skin. Once again, Annette was struck by the incongruity of his rough, untamed face and the richness and style of his attire. He certainly had an enthralling way about him. He was so handsome, so compelling.

She swallowed. "I like it. It's quite good." Her eyes slid away, back to the painting. "But who, may I ask, is the model?"

Rolf tossed back his leonine head and gave a deep laugh. "Still the little tease, ma'am? You haven't changed."

"Is that so terrible?" she asked, controlling the tremor in her voice only with great effort.

"I wouldn't have you any other way." The curved, sensual lips beneath the mustache widened into a grin.

"Have me, sir?" she quipped, flashing him a coy, irresistible glance.

"Do you have any doubt that I will?"

Annette's breath caught in her throat and suddenly she saw the faces around them, caught the eyes shifting away uneasily. Trying desperately to ignore

Rolf's question, his taunting grin, those dark, unfathomable eyes that seemed to strip her naked, Annette took a step toward the entrance. "Would you see me out?" She managed a weak smile.

"But, of course, ma'am." Rolf held her arm lightly under the elbow and steered them through the crowd. His touch, featherlike as it was, still felt like a caress. It sent shivers up her spine. Would there always be this between them? Could there be more?

As they passed through the staring crowd, Annette stole a look at Rolf out of the corner of her eye. His strong profile reminded her of a general on an ancient Roman coin. Then she noticed a half-healed cut on his lip, hidden by his mustache.

She stopped short. "What's that?" she asked. "Have you been hurt?" She pointed a slim, gloved finger at his lip.

His hand went up to touch the spot. He smiled, a secret, lazy smile. "A certain Mr. O'Neill gave me that."

"Rolf!" she cried. "Has Tansy been after you? Oh, my God!"

Rolf laughed. "Don't fret, my dear. Tansy O'Neill, when I last saw him, wasn't after anybody."

"What have you done?" she whispered.

"I beat the tar out of him," Rolf answered flatly.

"But he wouldn't have done anything. I took care of that with Buckley."

"Well, I took care of it in my own way, Annette, and it gave me great pleasure."

"Did you really beat him up?" she asked, wide-eyed.

"Sure enough."

"Good," she declared. "I'm glad." Then she was silent, walking proudly next to Rolf through the crowd that parted silently as if in awe of them. At the head of the wide, marble staircase leading down to the street, Annette stopped. "I can find my way from here, Rolf. Thank you."

He took her gloved hand. "Try your wings, Annette. I'm a patient man. But just remember that you have made a nest already." He bent his fair, curly head and kissed her hand.

She was speechless. He had said so much to her while saying so little. Did he really want her as a wife, or did he mean only to bed her as a mistress? And love, what about love? He had never said the word.

"Good-bye, Annette—or should I say, *au revoir*?"

"Good-bye, Rolf. I enjoyed the showing." Unexpectedly, tears filled her eyes. She had to get away. She had to think.

He released her hand. "*A bientôt* then, Annette."

Gathering her skirts, she descended the steps majestically. Rolf, she knew without looking, was still at the head of the staircase, watching her. His dark eyes pursued her in her mind.

The hour spent in the gallery spun around in her thoughts as the carriage climbed the steep rise of Nob Hill. She sat erect, unseeing, recalling each and every word and glance that had passed between them. She isolated them, analyzed them, savored them. Rolf still wanted her, she concluded. He hadn't forgotten the sweet bliss they could bring to one another. He was even, admittedly, waiting for her to return to the so-called nest.

One question remained unanswered, however. Did he love her?

Chapter 23

The sun was high overhead. Despite the coolness in the air, it was fully spring. Lying on a warm southern latitude, only the strange perversity of her geographic position and the winds keep San Francisco cool all year round. The acacia and laurel trees were bursting into full bloom. The birds sang. Apple blossoms, roses and all the flowers of the carefully tended Nob Hill gardens had come to life once more.

In the late afternoon of that day Cecile Tofler was walking in the garden. She should have been enjoying the glorious day but she was not. Her hands were clasped behind her back and her head was bowed as she followed the flagstone path.

Her recent unsettling conversation with her sea captain husband rang in her ears. He'd begged her to forget her useless search for, as he put it, some sort of Holy Grail, and come home to Sydney with him. And although she loved him, she couldn't, not yet. Something mysterious and subtle but crucial held her there, as the tiny, invisible strands of a spider web hold its defenseless prey. Cecile could no more walk away from the dark, brooding secret that sat poised at the center of the web than could a defenseless gnat. And so she suffered, unwilling to hurt her husband, yet unable to do as he desired, held in a disconsolate limbo.

Hearing something, she lifted her head. It was the conservatory door closing. Someone was rustling in the shrubbery beside the path.

"Annette? Is that you?" she called. "How was Rolf's show?" There was no answer. Puzzled, she began walking toward the sounds. Perhaps one of the servants was looking for her. Perhaps Luke had come back to tell her he'd stay.

But it was her father she nearly bumped into where the path curved sharply around the sun dial. "Father! Oh, you surprised me. I thought it was Annette."

"Cecile." He said nothing else, just gazed at her for a moment. He looked ill, thinner and quite grey. His ruddy cheeks had faded and his jowls were no more than empty flaps of skin. Even his hair seemed thinner. He looked old.

"Yes, Father?"

"No one was in the house. Henry told me you were in the garden." He appeared ill at ease. His eyes blinked rapidly and his fingers twitched, scratching at empty air. "I haven't really talked to you since you've been home." He was silent a long time, unable to go on. "I meant to, though," he continued at last. "Really I did. I wanted you to know how happy I am to see you again, my child. But I've been sick lately."

"Are you all right, Father?" Cecile extended a hand as if to support him, but he waved it away.

"I'm all right. Well, perhaps we should sit down. I'm not at all well to tell the truth."

They walked to a wrought-iron bench nearby. Edward sank onto it thankfully. His chest heaved as if he had run a mile.

Cecile waited. What could he want to say to her?

He made her nervous, this near stranger. This sick old man who was her father was someone she didn't know at all, or rather, someone she didn't really wish to know. She tried to concentrate on the trilling of a bird in a tree. It reminded her of Australia, of home.

Edward was talking in agonized bursts of speech. "I know why you ran away so long ago, Cecile. I know, and your mother knows. And deep down inside, you know, too. That's why you've come back, isn't it? To remember. That's it, isn't it?"

A cold hand of fear clutched Cecile's heart. She rose. "Don't upset yourself, Father. I don't know what you're talking about. And Mama's dead." She turned as if to leave, but his hand grasped hers and pulled her back.

"No, wait. Don't go. I must talk to you." Distraughtly, he rubbed his hands through his thin grey hair until it stood up wildly around his head. "I must, I must. And I never can do it right. I only do things that make all of you hate me. You hate me, don't you Cecile?" He looked at her with rheumy eyes, begging her to forgive him.

"I don't hate you, Father. Now may I go?"

He laughed then, a sad, stricken laugh. "I'll tell you where your mother is. Then will you stay and listen?"

"I know where she is. She's buried in the Hill of Peace Cemetery with the rest of the Toflers. I visited her grave."

He laughed again. The sound shivered down Cecile's spine. "Your mother is alive, Cecile. What do you think of that?"

"Father, you'd better go inside. I think we should send for the doctor. You're not well."

"I'm not crazy! Not yet. Listen," his hand plucked

ineffectually at her sleeve, "she's alive. Elizabeth's alive. I swear it. The grave and headstone were my idea, so nobody would know . . ."

Cecile sank down onto the bench, her face drained of blood. His words rang in her ears but they made no sense.

Edward was still talking as if a dam had broken within him. "She's alive. It's true. And nobody ever knew except the sisters. Because I gave them so much money for their chapel every year."

"Sisters?" asked Cecile weakly.

"The Franciscan sisters in Santa Rosa. The convent. That's where she is. They send me a report every year." He looked at his daughter beseechingly. "They say she's doing well. She's happy. You know how religious your mother always was."

"Yes." Cecile was stunned. She could not grasp the meaning of Edward's words. It was too bizarre. She looked up at him slowly. "But why? Why?"

Edward seemed to shrink, to fold in upon himself. "It was better that way. After you disappeared, she had a breakdown. A nervous breakdown. I had to do something. I had to! She wasn't alive. She wasn't dead. I had to do something with her. She's better now, they say."

The haze surrounding Cecile parted for a moment. Anger filled her. She turned on her father. "Then why didn't you tell us? Why did you lie? What happened to her! How could you let Annette and Jensen think all these years. . . ?" The haze swirled. Cecile put her face in her hands. Streaks of colored light flashed in front of her closed eyes. *It was dark in the room, so dark.*

When she felt her father's hand on her arm, she drew back as if she'd been burned. "Don't touch me!" she screamed.

Silence hung over the garden. It was as if one of the notorious fogs of the city had descended, but the sky was still blue and the sun still shone.

Cecile gasped, afraid of the ominous memories that began to creep into her mind, chilling her. She tried to push them away.

"I'm sorry," Edward said. "I never wanted to hurt you. I loved you so much. You're my daughter, my first-born child. So beautiful. You were so beautiful. And you looked just like your mother."

Cecile stared at him, horrified. Images beat on the closed door of her memory. *The room was so dark. She was in bed. There was a noise in the darkness. The hair on the back of her neck prickled in the blackness.*

Edward held out a trembling hand and touched her skirt. "Cecile, my daughter. Don't you understand? It was only because I loved you so much. I never meant to hurt you." He touched her cheek with his age-spotted hand. "You were so lovely."

At his touch the memories leapt upon her like a pack of wolves, ravaging, tearing. "Oh my God!" she cried. "It was you! I remember!" She sprang to her feet, cast a wild eye around her and fled toward the house. Edward cried out at her words and reached for her, but she was already gone.

"Wait," he whispered to the empty garden. "Wait." He got up and followed his daughter's disappearing form. "Cecile. Please listen. I only loved you. Is that so awful?" He lurched down the path with heavy, lumbering steps. His breathing grew more labored, his hand went unconsciously to his chest where his heart pounded fiercely. "Wait, Cecile," he panted, still running. "I'm sorry! I'm sorry!"

Then he felt a white-hot searing in his chest. He slowed, gasped, slumped to the ground. There was a blinding light in his head, then darkness descended and the terrible pain was gone.

When the carriage stopped in front of the familiar brass gate on Mason Street, Annette was still perplexed. Her heart told her that Rolf loved her and her body yearned for what he could give her, but her head refused to accept the evidence as truth. And, she told herself, even if he did feel something for her, it was only the same physical need that she felt. Rolf didn't really need her. She was afraid he didn't even respect her. She was a plaything to him, that was all. She wouldn't allow herself to fall into the tender trap he so carefully had set.

But her heart leapt as she remembered the painting and the adoration she'd seen in it. Could she have been mistaken? Which was the truth? She was being pulled to pieces by her love and her fear and her yearning for some kind of answer.

Time was what was needed, she finally decided. It would take a good while for her to know Rolf better. In time she would know whether he would continue to pursue her, or whether he would lose interest in someone who did not fall into his bed as she so unwisely had done. Still, was she cheating herself of happiness?

She walked to the front door and slowly let herself in. As she handed her wrap to Henry, she idly asked him where everyone was.

"Miss Cecile is in the garden, miss, and Mr. Jensen is in the sitting room. Your father also came in, not an hour ago."

"Daddy? Oh, where is he?" she asked, delighted at the prospect of seeing him again.

"I have no idea, miss."

She practically ran into the sitting room. "Jensen? Did you know Daddy's here? Henry just told me."

"Oh," Jensen commented cynically, arching a brow, "so he's deigned to pay us a call? He's probably in his room, packing some clean clothes to take to Tilly's."

"Jensen! You've been nearly as bad yourself lately!"

"Humph!"

"It's true. Where's Cecile, then?"

"Out in the garden, I think. I'm not sure."

"I'd like to talk to her. I need some advice. Everything's turned so confusing." She sat down on the overstuffed sofa, took off her straw hat and fiddled absent-mindedly with the ribbons on it.

"Rolf?" asked Jensen sagely.

"Yes. He's—"

Her words were cut off by a terrible cry that stunned them both. It came from the back of the house. They froze, looking at each other blankly.

"What was that?" asked Jensen, getting to his feet.

"Somebody screamed. Is it an earthquake? What is it?" cried Annette.

They both ran toward the sound, but it was not repeated. Nor did they hear the rumble of a tremor or feel any vibration. Jensen reached the conservatory first and dashed through the room to the double doors that led out to the garden. Annette followed, her heart thumping unmercifully. Henry was right on her heels.

In front of her, Jensen skidded to a halt. Annette couldn't see around him. Frantically she pushed him aside. "What is it?"

Cecile was standing in the middle of the path, her eyes as big as saucers in her white face. She was staring down at something on the ground . . . a pile of clothes or something.

Annette went cold all over. Her legs nearly gave

way. She reached out for Jensen, felt his strong hand grasp hers. It was curiously cold, so cold.

Her father was sprawled on the ground. He looked so inert, so empty, that she knew without a doubt that he was dead.

Chapter 24

There was so much to be done in arranging a funeral. It was such a grief-stricken, frantic, horrible time that the customary three days stretched out unendingly in their misery.

Cecile, Jensen and Annette stuck together during the ordeal of the first terrible day. The house brimmed over with well-wishers, friends, acquaintances and business associates. They came and went steadily, unhurriedly, as if in a slow-motion nightmare. Jensen handled the funeral arrangements with such calm deliberation that several times Annette wanted to scream at him for being so cold. But she couldn't. Deep down she knew that Jensen would never mourn his father's passing. And who could blame him?

Cecile, on the other hand, was most upset. She was unable to talk much about the terrible thing her father had done to her. "It's past . . . over," she told Annette weakly on the afternoon of Edward Tofler's death. "I don't want to think about it just yet. I've told you all I can. And then there's still Mama to think about."

Together, the three children had decided to wait until after the funeral was over to search out their mother. Jensen and Annette had then discussed briefly the things to which Edward had confessed and decided, for Cecile's sake, not to mention them again.

For Annette, however, it was hard to push aside the horrid thoughts about her father. She had loved him, but now his memory was forever tainted. She wished she could talk to someone about it. She needed to sort it out, to understand it. She needed to find comfort in someone's embrace. But there was no one, certainly not Jensen or Cecile.

Luke Bogarde arrived the day after Edward's death in answer to a note from Jensen. At first, Cecile had hidden her face in shame and refused to see him. However, after much persuasion, Annette finally had convinced her that it was best to tell him now so that she could put it behind her once and for all. Still, Cecile could not face Luke herself. She begged Annette to explain everything to him.

Reluctantly, Annette agreed. She joined Luke in the privacy of the drawing room. They conversed for a few minutes and Annette found him quite likable.

And then she began, casting her eyes downward. "Cecile asked me to speak with you in private about a very delicate matter."

"Aye," he groaned, "I knew there was something amiss. Is she all right?"

"Cecile's fine. Really. It's about our father, Luke, and something awful that happened many years ago." It was so difficult to think about the incident, much less speak of it, that Annette thought she might not be able to get the words out of her mouth.

"I feel you must tell me, lass. I can tell it's not going to be easy, but I sense it 'as something to do with my wife."

"Yes. It does, Luke. Perhaps if I just tell you outright—"

"Aye. You do that." Luke rose from his chair and paced the floor. "Go on now."

"Father," she gulped, embarrassment staining her cheeks, "went into Cecile's bedroom once many years ago . . . and he . . . he . . ."

Luke came quickly to her side and knelt down next to her chair. "Stop now, lass. I think I understand. Yes. Makes all the sense in the world. No wonder," he sighed. He rose. "Where's my wife?" The words were wrenched from his throat.

"In her room—up the stairs and to the left. Go to her, Luke. She needs you."

An hour later Luke found Annette in the kitchen, instructing the cook as to what should be prepared for the many visitors.

"She's coming home to Australia," Luke told Annette, smiling grimly. "We're going to be just fine now. After the funeral and after she sees her mother, we'll be setting sail for home."

"I'm so glad. I really am so happy for you both." And she was. It was for the best. Surely Cecile could have a normal, healthy marriage now, especially with a man as big-hearted as Luke.

That evening there was a whirlwind of activity in the Tofler mansion. Visitors kept coming in a never-ending stream of grim faces and murmured condolences.

It must have been at around six in the evening, when Annette was pouring tea in the drawing room, that she heard Jensen's raised voice coming from the entrance hall.

She excused herself from the guests and went to see what was going on. Jensen stood in the doorway, barring the entrance, facing a very lovely, though a touch overdressed and made-up young female.

"How dare you show your face here!" Jensen thundered.

"I've every right. Edward and I were to be married and I can prove it," the voluptuous young woman countered.

"Oh?"

"That's right. And I'm going to get what's due me. It's all on paper with my lawyer, Mr. Tofler," she hissed.

"Is it really?" Jensen drawled. "And tell me, Miss Grueter, who would your lawyer be? Some quack who'll get half of what he can cheat my family out of in your behalf?"

"How dare you!"

"But of course I suppose my father even pledged on paper to marry you and your lawyer has it all documented. Am I correct?"

"That's right." The woman stood her ground, a smile on her full lips.

"Then I suggest you go ahead and sue, Miss Grueter."

She looked at him dubiously, the smile fading.

Annette viewed the whole scene from a few steps behind Jensen. At first she couldn't understand why her brother would tell the woman to sue, but then she realized that their father could not possibly have promised marriage. The whole thing was a hoax on this awful woman's part, for Edward Tofler was still legally married to Elizabeth.

How clever Jensen is, thought Annette as she watched the woman leave with an indignant swish of her skirt. Edward Tofler's mistress had no right coming to their home and threatening them. She deserved the snub.

All evening Cecile mechanically greeted people and received their condolences. Jensen remained controlled and matter-of-fact, his true feelings for his father showing plainly. Annette watched her brother and sister as if they were giving a theatrical performance. And she was, too. There hadn't been enough time to think about her father's death or the confessions he had made. It was too soon. The truth had not yet settled in. She wished the funeral were over and all the well-wishers gone. It was all too polite, too much of a farce.

At around eight in the evening, Cecile came into the drawing room with a note for Annette. "Rolf's man is waiting for your reply."

Annette read the note quickly and looked up at Cecile. "Rolf read about Father in the morning paper and wants to see me. Should I go? I mean, perhaps I shouldn't leave right now under the circumstances."

"Go to him," advised Cecile. "You're all done in today. We all are. Jensen and I can wrap things up here."

"I don't know. I do want to see him, especially now. But nothing between Rolf and me is resolved, Cecile." Annette paced the floor uneasily. "Yesterday I thought he might feel something for me. Today, I don't know."

"Then go and find out."

Annette did indeed take Cecile's advice and joined Nakamura in the carriage provided for her. Rolf, the dour Nakamura told her, was waiting at Devil's Cove. For a few moments as the horse clopped along, she wished she had refused. It seemed all Rolf had to do was snap his fingers and she would miraculously appear. But then she remembered her thoughts of earlier that day, that she would love to have someone close to talk with during this horrible ordeal, someone to hold and comfort her.

Rolf was waiting for her in the living room. A fire

crackled in the hearth, staving off the chill of the spring night. He took Annette's cape and tossed it unceremoniously onto a chair. "You came." His dark eyes met hers measuringly as he stood towering over her. "I wasn't certain you would."

"I wanted to talk to someone, Rolf. This last day has been too awful."

"I'm sure it has. You loved your father, didn't you?" He led her over to the familiar couch.

Annette felt warm and safe in the small cottage she had come to know so well. It seemed right for her to be there alone with Rolf, sitting comfortably in front of his fire. She could confide her inner thoughts to him far more easily than to Jensen or Cecile under the present circumstances.

"Yes, Rolf. I did love him. I miss him already." Her eyes filled with tears. Funny, she thought, but there had been so little time for tears.

"What happened, Annette?" He wrapped his strong arm around her shoulders and drew her against his firm chest.

"He had a heart attack. In the garden. It was so horrible . . ." Annette's voice cracked. Hot tears rolled down her flushed cheeks. Rolf held her carefully while she sobbed. She had been holding it all in since the death. It was time to cry now.

Sometime during the outpouring of her sorrow, Rolf drew a patchwork quilt around her legs and curled her into a ball on his lap. It felt so wonderful to be in Rolf's embrace. If only she could stay forever and never return to Nob Hill—to forget about her sister's plight and Jensen's calm acceptance of her father's death. Neither of them could ever understand her love for their father. But Rolf did.

He kissed her damp brow and tenderly pushed aside the stray auburn tendrils of hair from her face.

He provided a hanky for her, then a fiery brandy. All the while they never spoke.

An eternity later, the brandy warming her stomach, Annette stopped crying and sat up. Sniffing, her lashes spiked with tears, she found herself pouring out the whole story of what her father had done. Rolf listened silently to the rush of words, as if he were a priest hearing a confession.

". . . it was twelve years ago when he drove Cecile away. It must have been hideous for her. How could he do such a vile thing to his own daughter?"

Rolf placed a quieting finger to her lips. "It happens, Annette. Just because you've never heard of such things before, doesn't mean they don't exist."

"But God! It's too ghastly to believe that Daddy would—"

"All types of men, Annette, are capable of the deed. It does happen. Every day. It was an evil deed, but it doesn't mean that your father was an evil man. He wasn't well."

"But I loved him," she whispered.

"It's all right to love him and his memory. Your relationship with your father was quite different from Cecile's."

"Yes, it was. But recently he wouldn't even hug me anymore. Nothing."

"Since Cecile's return?"

"Well . . . yes, I suppose so, and even before."

Annette told Rolf about their mother and their desire to visit her after the funeral. "We have to," she explained. "Even if Mama is awfully sick still, we must let her know we care for her, that we love her."

"That's reasonable."

"It will be so strange to see her."

"I should imagine."

They lapsed into a comfortable silence, gazing at

the flickering patterns of the fire. It was good to be with Rolf, just to sit with him quietly.

"By the way," Rolf drawled lazily, "did you hear the news about Tansy O'Neill?"

"What news?" she asked casually.

"He got shanghaied by the captain of the *Unicorn* and is on his way to Bombay."

"How do you know that, Rolf?"

"It's common knowledge down on the waterfront. The *Unicorn*'s captain owed Blind Chris a favor, so Chris finally decided what to do with O'Neill."

"I hope he never comes back," she uttered fervently.

"If and when our friend returns, he'll be a new man," laughed Rolf.

While Annette took comfort in Rolf's attention, the hour grew late. They were interrupted by Nakamura some time after midnight. "Will you desire the carriage, sir?" he asked Rolf with a little bow.

Rolf lifted an eyebrow and looked questioningly at Annette. It was her decision.

"I'll stay the night," she murmured, her hazel eyes averted from his face. Why shouldn't I? she asked herself. I want him. I'd die if I had to leave him now. And if he doesn't love me? That doesn't matter either, not tonight.

Annette knew, in spite of the fact that she planned to sleep with Rolf that night, that when she returned to Nob Hill the next day, her life would be forever altered. There would be no room for Rolf in her life, not until she either succeeded or failed in her goal. She must at least try. And she needed time to come to terms with her father's death and with the awful things he had done to his family. Annette needed to heal, to become whole once more. In any case, she could never be sure of Rolf's feelings for her.

But tonight would be hers. She would not deny herself the pleasure of his lovemaking. It might be the last time he would hold her in his arms, make exquisite love to her.

They were alone once more. Rolf rose from the couch and stirred the dying embers of the fire with a poker. Annette sighed, sinking into the comfort of the couch. She could see his muscles flex underneath the white shirt, the hard lean cords of his legs as he stooped before the hearth. He was such a handsome, virile man, so self-confident and mature. A man like Rolf knew what he wanted from life and took it, then enjoyed it unashamedly. She would like to be afforded an equal opportunity to know herself and find her role in life. Unfortunately, women were seldom given the chance.

The red glow of the embers struck the flat plane of Rolf's cheek and the hook in his generous nose, setting them off from the rest of his face. The thick hair that curled to his shirt collar shone with gold. He was so strong in every way. Was that why he still frightened her a little? she mused. Could it be that she feared he would sap her strength if allowed too near? If so, then she was fooling herself with the questions about his relationship with Eleanor Fairchild and the sincerity of his marriage proposal to herself. Perhaps she wasn't holding back because she was afraid that he felt duty bound to marry her, but because she feared losing herself in his commanding presence.

Rolf came back to the couch and sat beside Annette again. All her thoughts and questions evaporated.

"Warm enough?" he asked.

"Umm." She nestled close to him, savoring his masculine scent.

Rolf kissed her on her neck bringing his hand up to stroke her bosom through the thin material of her dress. Annette turned her head lazily, seeking his mouth. When she felt the response of his lips, she gave a content, feline sigh.

The kiss grew in intensity until they were locked in an ardent embrace, their hands exploring each other in the heat of mounting passion.

"Let's go to the bedroom," Rolf suggested, his breathing irregular.

Annette looked at him slyly. "No. Let's stay right here. It'll be fun."

Chuckling at her impishness, he began to unfasten the buttons on her dress. Slipping it down, he uncovered the soft swell of her breast above her scanty chemise. "I see you like black," he observed, his eyes devouring the delicious sight of her white bosom above the daring Parisian lace.

"Don't you like it?" she teased, wriggling out of the top half of her dress.

"I do admit it excites me. But it's a good thing I was the first one to savor your charms, ma'am, or I'd think quite little of your virtue seeing you in this flimsy thing." With deft fingers he untied the ribbons on the chemise, drawing aside the material until the high, perfect contour of her bosom was exposed to his scrutiny. "Still, I doubt I could resist." He toyed with her pink nipples until she moaned with pleasure.

Suddenly his hands fell away. His dark eyes grew thoughtful as he met her confused gaze. "Tell me, Annette," he began in a tone far more serious than before, "how is it you have not become pregnant? I must confess that I fully expected, after your long stay in the cottage, that you would come to me with news of a child."

A mischievous smiled played on her lips. "I have my ways."

"You don't do anything dangerous?"

"No! It's quite simple. A woman needs only to know what time of month she is in and pregnancy can be prevented."

"I see. You're quite clever, aren't you?" With one hand he began to tease her breast again.

"Quite," she sighed.

Rolf's mouth sought her lips, then the hollow at the base of her throat while his hands slowly freed her of all her clothing. He stroked her soft curves, lingering on the dark triangle of her womanhood until she gasped.

He freed himself from his own clothes. Then taking her hands, he showed her how to pleasure a man until she was touching him of her own volition.

Rolf pressed her down into the soft cushions. Rising above her on his elbows, he parted her thighs with his legs. His eyes held hers in the firelight for a long moment, and then he thrust himself deep within her body. Teasing her, he withdrew. She twisted frantically beneath him, crying for release. He thrust again. Each time the torment became more exquisite, more aching, until at last her senses soared. Her nails raking his back, she cried out in a whirlwind of pleasure, then collapsed, exhausted beneath him.

Twice more during the long night Rolf took her to the heights and back. Both times he positioned her body in a new and exotic way. It caused her to blush, but nonetheless she craved more. Annette had never imagined love could be made in such a variety of positions. It seemed naughty, but it secretly thrilled her to comply with his suggestions.

Afterward he told her simply, "I must possess you in all ways, Annette. Allow me at least this much."

She would have allowed him everything, anything, for in the morning she would be in possession of herself again. Perhaps forever.

It was true, Annette thought, cuddled warmly in his arms as dawn streaked the sky with pearly fingers, Rolf controlled her whenever she let him too near. She was powerless against his strength and manhood. And yes, it scared her, shattered all her perceptions and hopes.

She knew she must get away from him, love or no love, or surely she would never find herself, but remain hopelessly lost forever in his compelling presence.

Chapter 25

They got off the ferry in Sausalito early in the morning when the birds were just waking and the sun was an orange ball beyond the bay and over the hills to the east. Jensen drove the carriage himself. This was a family journey and only his two sisters were with him.

They passed through the tiny village of Sausalito and on through lush farmland that was green now with the season's onrush. They drove over hills covered with grape vines just beginning to sprout from the thick, gnarled stocks. The carriage rolled along the winding, dusty road through San Rafael, Ignacio, Petaluma—Spanish towns whose names were reminiscent of Old World aristocracy and the area's first settlers.

They had lunch by a stream outside a small farming village. They didn't talk much, each considering his own thoughts about their trip. It was an awkward time and they were all glad to climb into the carriage and get under way again. The last few days had seethed with activity, what with the arrangements and the funeral. There had been so much to do. Now they had the leisure, too much, perhaps, to contemplate this new piece of knowledge that had burst into their lives like a thunderbolt.

They were each afraid to voice their questions

aloud. Was their mother insane? Would she even know them? Why hadn't she revealed herself to them? Would their arrival disturb her peace?

In the early afternoon they came to a road marked with a rough, wooden sign: "Franciscan Sisters of Santa Rosa." They drove up the long driveway lined with stately eucalyptus trees whose characteristic odor scented the air sharply. The convent itself was a low, sand-colored adobe structure with a tall, square bell tower to one side. It was a squat, solid building, featureless on the outside but for black iron grilles on the few windows, a red tile roof, and a large, heavy wooden door.

The three Tofler children looked at the convent, looked at each other and descended from the carriage wordlessly. The mother superior would be expecting them, for Jensen had written to her several days before.

He pulled the long chain and heard a faint tinkling from inside the thick walls. A small door opened in the large one and a sister dressed in a white habit poked her head out.

"We're the Tofler children. We've come to see our mother, Elizabeth."

"Oh yes. Mother Superior would like to talk to you first. This way please."

They were led down a hushed, bare corridor. The sister knocked on a door and was told to enter. They found themselves in a large, airy room with a view of the graceful arcade surrounding the interior of the Spanish-style building. A handsome, elderly woman sat across from them behind a dark wooden desk.

"You are Jensen Tofler?" she asked.

"Yes, Mother Superior. And these are my sisters, Annette and Cecile. As I said in my letter, we wish to see our mother."

The woman rose and stepped out from behind her desk. The three Toflers knelt for her blessing. There was an aura of holy strength about the woman. It was awesome. "I know about the past tragedy in your lives and why your mother is here," began the mother superior. "Frankly, it was the best thing your father could have done at the time. For him to have kept all of you in ignorance because of his shame, however, I cannot condone. Still, perhaps it was the best he could do, may his soul rest in peace.

"I want to tell you a little about your mother's history here. By the way, she is now called Sister Teresa." The mother superior sat down at her desk again and looked sternly at the three of them. "Your mother was in a state of complete collapse when she was brought here. She could barely talk. She nearly died. I think she wanted to die. But the Holy Father comforted her and she recovered, although she is not very strong. Perhaps He saved her for this very day. You must realize, however, that she would not be able to bear a tearful reunion or any emotional upheaval. It would leave her sick for days. I felt you should know this before you saw her. It would be a shame for all our patient efforts over the last twelve years to go to waste."

"We'll be very careful," promised Jensen.

"Will she know us?" Annette quavered.

"I am sure she will, although she has her good days and her bad days. But she has spoken of you three so often that I almost feel I know you myself." The mother superior smiled for the first time and it lit up the room. "Go out to the arcade, I'll send her to you."

She showed them outside to the cool, tree-shaded walkway encircling the courtyard of the convent, which was filled with palms and flowers and a fountain in which a bird splashed playfully. It was a beautiful, peaceful scene, yet the three were filled with trepidation as they waited. Annette, perhaps, was the least anxious, for she remembered her mother only as a vague, comforting presence. But Cecile and Jensen were very nervous. What would she think of them? Had she been told that Edward was dead? Did she wonder why they had never been to see her? What would she think of Cecile's return?

A lone figure in a white habit walked toward them, slowly, tranquilly. Her head was bowed devoutly, her hands folded within the loose sleeves of her habit. The graceful, swaying walk reached back over the years and tugged at their memories.

"Mother," whispered Jensen.

The figure drew closer, striped alternately light and dark by the pillars of the arcade. Her face was still hidden.

Cecile took a step toward her mother with a muffled cry. Pain and love showed in her face, each vying for control. Annette stood back, feeling she had not as much right to Elizabeth's notice since she recalled so little of her mother.

The figure in white raised her head. She was radiant and smiling, with a serenity that went beyond mere happiness. "My children," she said simply. "I'm so happy to see you, all of you."

Jensen bent and kissed her on the cheek. She held him close, stroking his hair. Cecile, too, joined them and the three of them embraced. Elizabeth stepped forward. "Annette, come and kiss your mother. Did you think I had forgotten you?" She held out her arms. "My baby."

Annette went to her slowly, moisture blurring her vision. "Mama?" Then she was enfolded in her mother's arms and all four were laughing and talking at the same time.

"Come, let's go sit down and let me look at you. I never knew I had three such beautiful children." Elizabeth led the way to a stone bench on the edge of the courtyard.

She gazed at them endlessly, stroking their cheeks, her own eyes sparkling. "Now, we need to get down to more serious matters," she said at last. "Mother Superior told me that Edward is dead."

"Yes, Mama, a week ago. He had a heart attack," said Jensen.

"Poor man, I feel no personal loss, but then I had not loved him for so long. Still, he was my husband for many years. I forgave him long ago for what he did." She turned to Cecile, a vague frown shadowing her features. "Are you well, my daughter? You seem troubled. Your father—"

"I know, Mama. I finally remembered what he did to me." Cecile looked away. "I ran away and went to Australia, Mama. I forgot everything, until last week."

"Your father told you?"

Cecile looked down at her hands. "Yes. That's how we found you. He told me everything."

Elizabeth put her long white hand on Cecile's. "You see, he did confess at last, even against his own will. God spoke through him. And you, Jensen, you are well?"

"Yes, Mama. I run the business now, and not too badly at that," he grinned.

"Annette?"

"I'm a painter, Mama," she said proudly. "I'm working very hard and hope to have a showing someday when I'm good enough."

"Yes, you always were artistic. Oh, my dear Lord,

I haven't even asked—am I a grandmother yet?" she laughed.

"No, Mama, not yet," smiled Jensen. "However, Cecile's married to an Australian sea captain, a very good man, and Annette, well"—he winked at her—"she may be married before long to a dashing, famous painter."

"I am not going to marry Rolf," protested Annette, "contrary to what all of you think!"

"And I am madly in love with a wonderful girl," continued Jensen quietly, "but she is Chinese." A silence fell over the group.

After a moment, Elizabeth spoke. "Do what your heart dictates, my son, and try not to pay too much attention to the opinions of others. God will guide you." She looked adoringly at each of them, her beautiful brown eyes, so like Cecile's, clear and bright. "Now my life is complete. For so many years I had wished to see you again. And yet I was afraid, afraid of what your father had told you about me. And I have always been burdened for having left you to fend for yourselves. I am a weak, sinful woman. I have prayed for you every day of my life here."

"We never knew you were here," explained Annette. "Daddy told us you were dead."

"I see. Well, he was trying to protect himself. I understand his motives. But now you are here and all so well and so beautiful! And my poor Cecile had to bear the brunt of it all." She stroked Cecile's cheek with her cool, white hand. "But now you're all right again."

Cecile smiled shyly. "Yes, I feel like a new person. I remember everything now and it no longer haunts me. I'm free. My father did at least that for me."

"Even the misguided can be instruments of good. Does not the Lord Jesus tell us that?"

"Yes, Mama," the three answered obediently, remembering the Bible readings she had given them as young children.

They talked on and on until the shadows of late afternoon lay across them. A sister came silently and tapped Elizabeth on the shoulder.

"It's time for evening prayers," Elizabeth excused herself, rising. "I must go. But, my children, please keep in touch and know that I pray for you every day." She kissed each one of them in turn, then turned and walked away. The sister led them to the entrance and bade them farewell.

They left silently, full of peace and wonder. They had lost their father and found their mother all in the same week.

Jensen had made arrangements for them to spend the night at a country inn in Santa Rosa. It was a whitewashed, Spanish building that had its own small winery next door. The dining room served only its own wines, proud of the local California vintage.

Annette and Cecile were given a spacious room hung with crimson velvet drapes. There was a canopy over the huge, antique bed. They washed, dressed and went down to dinner just as the sun was setting over the green, rolling hills. A stout Spanish matron and her tall, slender husband ran the inn. Since there were few other guests, the couple welcomed the Toflers gladly and lavished attention on them. Señora Mendoza served them a tasty meal of spicy saffron rice and chicken, home-baked bread and the first strawberries of the season. She also brought them a bottle of their finest red wine, which the señora explained was made from the cabernet sauvignon grapes that grew on their own hillsides.

Jensen raised his glass of ruby wine and proposed a toast. "To the three of us!"

They drank.

"To our mother," added Cecile.

Annette had never seen her sister look so alive and happy. She was a different person from the troubled, high-strung girl she had known for three months.

"Can we leave early in the morning?" asked Cecile eagerly. "Luke will be waiting. He'll want to know how everything worked out. He's been so patient with me. I vow I don't know how he could have borne it all these years!"

"He loves you, that's how," laughed Annette.

"I guess so." Cecile smiled radiantly.

They drank again. The soothing wine made them red-cheeked and talkative. Señora Mendoza beamed on them as she bustled around the dining room.

"I'm considering marrying Su Ling," began Jensen, a trifle pompously.

"Good," Annette commented tartly. "She deserves a proper marriage."

"It won't be easy," observed Cecile, "but if you love her—"

"I do. And I think my position is secure enough now that no one would dare ostracize us."

"She'll be snubbed, and then there are children to think of." Cecile pointed out.

Jensen got a faraway look in his eyes. "I have considered that, but you know, I have a feeling that someday in the not too distant future there will be so much intermarriage in California that no one will care anymore. I'm only the first pebble in the avalanche. Our children will be a combination of the very best of two cultures. They'll be very special."

"And will you visit China?" asked Cecile.

"Yes, when I train someone I can trust to run the business while I'm gone. Maybe Ned."

"When you do, you must come to Sydney and visit us too. You'll love it."

"I will." He laughed. "Here we are making plans for years ahead! Maybe Su won't have me."

"She will." Annette had no doubt.

"And you, little sister?" asked Jensen suddenly. "What are you plans?"

"Oh, I'll paint. Someday, if I'm good enough, I'll have a show and see what the world thinks of me. I won't rest until I've accomplished that much, at least."

"You'll succeed, I'm sure of it." Cecile smiled. "Anyone with your talent and single-mindedness simply has to. But what about Rolf?"

"Rolf?" Annette frowned. "I don't know. I'm not ready yet. I need time." She looked up and tried to smile brightly. "I'm not at all sure Rolf and I could ever get along. He's so domineering. He frightens me sometimes. I feel that he overpowers me, erases my individuality. Why, I'd only be Rolf Karman's wife. I wouldn't be Annette Tofler at all."

They fell silent, each lost in private thoughts. Cecile and Jensen had bright futures to look forward to, but Annette felt oddly troubled. Her future should seem rosy to her, now that she could concentrate on her painting. Somehow, though, the idea lacked the excitement it once had had. Perhaps, she thought, it was because there was no one with whom she could share her success.

Chapter 26

As spring took hold in San Francisco, the days and evenings grew steadily warmer. Ladies donned their brightly colored muslins and linens and stylish, beribboned straw hats adorned their heads. Shoppers were more numerous on Kearny Street and restaurants set up tables with colorful umbrellas outside under shade trees for the enjoyment of their patrons. Chinatown's many fascinating shops were festooned with colorful paper lanterns, with Chinese sausages ornamented with colored bits of paper, and tourists milled about, sampling the exotic foods. Below, on the Barbary Coast, the saloons, gambling houses and brothels were filled to overflowing with seamen and in the confusion, young boys still disappeared, shanghaied. The crime rate soared as the mild weather brought people from all walks of life back out onto the streets. Blind Chris Buckley didn't mind, however, as the fee for protection rose in accordance with the number of crimes committed.

It was early May. Summer was just around the corner, and not too long thereafter it would be a year since Annette's return from Paris. At times she felt it had been a year of achievement and great advance in her painting, but there were also times when she was discouraged and felt certain that she was an utter failure as an artist.

Still, she worked diligently, often from morning's first light until the last rays of the sun died in an orange glow across her canvas.

Cecile had gone back to Australia with Luke a few weeks past. Annette missed her sister. It seemed to her that just when they had found each other, her sister was gone again. At least, she told herself, Cecile was a far happier person than she had been before. The sisters had promised to write each other often and Cecile also had assured Annette that she would come to San Francisco the next time Luke did. Perhaps with children, Cecile had added, and then she had blushed and smiled shyly. The thought comforted Annette; her sister was not lost to her.

Jensen was not at home as much as he would have liked to be. He was terribly busy at the office and took occasional business trips which kept him away from the city for several days at a time. The Tofler Transport Company, the elegant Nob Hill mansion and one half of Edward's monetary holdings belonged to Jensen now. Annette and Cecile had been left the other half of the fortune, which was to be divided equally between them. It was a vast amount, so large that it hardly mattered to Annette. She was happier for Cecile, who was going to buy Luke a new house in Australia and a new, finely crafted vessel which could hold three times the cargo of his present one. And still Cecile would have a tremendous sum to invest wherever she chose.

Annette was not alone in the great, elegant edifice however, for Su Ling was there to keep her company. Jensen and Su Ling's wedding had been small but tasteful. Newspapermen had been invited and almost to a man, they had written favorably of the new Tofler bride. Some of their accounts had included glowing descriptions of the girl's exotic beauty and noble bearing. Reading the papers on the day after the wedding, Jensen had been wryly amused. "I wonder how they would have reacted to our marriage had I been less prominent and wealthy?" It was undeniably true that Jensen Tofler's union with a Chinese girl was the object of much gossip, but never to his face. People simply wouldn't dare.

Gossip about Annette's long stay at Devil's Cove had died down, for since then she had become all but a recluse. She now spent most of her time in the mansion, painting. The inner circles of San Francisco society had never gotten wind of Edward Tofler's perversion, as only the family and Rolf knew the truth. Wisely, the servants had been kept in the dark during the ordeal. Annette had a feeling that the butler, Henry, guessed the truth, but if he did he never said so.

Su Ling, much to everyone's delight, was pregnant. She and Annette figured it must have happened before the wedding. The notion made them giggle like schoolchildren. Jensen, when he found out, beamed proudly and started treating Su Ling as if she were a fine porcelain doll who would break at his mere touch. Once, Annette overheard Su Ling saying to her husband, "Jensen, I won't break like glass! I won't take a separate bedroom. I don't want to sleep alone!"

Everything at the Tofler house appeared to be in order. Everything, that is, but Annette's life, which presently was without direction. The paintings, everyone told her, were excellent, but what did a few servants and her brother and sister-in-law know about art?

So she painted and agonized and painted again. The number of completed canvases grew and grew.

They were strewn haphazardly around the conservatory, leaning against chairs to dry. Those that were incomplete had been placed against the walls, waiting for final touches or, in some cases, a burst of inspiration.

Occasionally a canvas would come up entirely different from the others. Annette attributed the brighter colors and vague images to her past opium dreams, which had had a lasting effect on her and on her work.

More often than she would have liked, Annette thought about her father. Her memories of him were mixed. Some were quite pleasant and some so hideous that they made her dizzy and nauseous. She began to wonder whether his memory ever would cease to torment her. There was no one with whom she could discuss her father. Vivian, of course, was ignorant of what had occurred between Edward and Cecile. Su Ling also knew nothing about the past nightmare. As for Jensen, his animosity toward his dead father was so great that she certainly could not talk to him. And so the questions in her mind went unanswered. She painted.

She tried never to think about Rolf. That, however, was quite difficult, for once a week or more a note would arrive from him, hand delivered by Nakamura. Of course she always read the notes, and they always said more or less the same thing.

> Dear Annette,
>
> I should like very much to see you. Recently I ran into Jensen and he tells me you see no one save him and Su Ling and that you spend your days painting. I worry that you have locked yourself away from the world and perhaps I am partially at fault.
>
> In spite of your father's death, life does go

on. And as for your painting, you certainly cannot always create from memory alone.

If you would allow me to visit, I feel certain you would not regret it.

Yours, Rolf

Annette had yet to reply to any of his notes. She felt she couldn't, not until her life was in order. Rolf, she reminded herself time after time, would smother her. Still, her heart pounded furiously at just the touch of his handwriting under her fingers. If only she were a success. If only she could heal the wound her father had left her. If only everything would fall into place in her life, then maybe she could find room for Rolf. But would he still want her? Or was his apparent concern merely friendship on his part?

It was a rainy afternoon in early May and Annette was forced to stay inside and paint in the conservatory. She had felt sick that morning and the dreary day did nothing to lift her spirits. The painting she was working on frustrated her. Something was wrong with the shading and she was at a loss as to how she could correct it. Nothing was going her way.

Vivian's Irish lilt reached her ears all the way from the entrance hall, disrupting her concentration. "You'll not be disturbin' her!" Vivian's voice came nearer. "She'll be furious, I tell you! Now stop!"

Angry now, Annette tossed her brush onto the palette and rose. What on earth was going on? Couldn't Vivian handle anything?

Then she saw him silhouetted in the doorway leading to the conservatory. It was Rolf. Even at this distance, there was no mistaking the way he carried his tall, well-proportioned frame. As he strode toward her, his lithe grace reminded her of a jungle creature stalking its prey.

"I'm sorry," he was saying, "but I'll be damned if you think you can put me off so easily by ignoring me, Annette." His tone was angry, but she glimpsed softness in his eyes. In spite of his harsh words, she knew he was glad to see her. And that deep, lazy voice. How could she have forgotten the slight Southern drawl behind his insolent, controlled tone?

"Well? Are you just going to stand there gaping, Annette? Haven't you anything to say?"

"You haven't given me a chance, Rolf. I guess I'm just surprised to see you."

"Indeed? Did you think I'd stay away forever?"

"I . . ."

"Or have you found someone else to entertain you!" The moment the words were out, Rolf could see his mistake.

Annette drew away shocked, her hazel eyes wide, her hand going to her breast. "What a high opinion you have of me," she returned icily.

Rolf raked a strong hand through his hair. His expression grew gentle. "I'm sorry," he confessed uneasily. "I don't know what made me say that. I suppose it's just because I've been worried about you. You infuriated me when you wouldn't answer my letters or allow me to see you."

"So you just barge in here and shout at me?" asked Annette incredulously. She sat back down on the stool and folded her arms across her smock.

"That's right. Why not? This behavior is not like you. I truly am worried and I want to know what's going on."

Annette sat in pensive silence for a long moment. "I really haven't felt like seeing anyone, Rolf. Everything has changed so much."

"You mean since your father's death." It was not a question.

"I suppose so."

"Then let me help, for God's sake. Be fair, Annette."

"I need time, Rolf. I told you that. My life is in such turmoil. Nothing seems to be going quite right. And my painting . . ."

Rolf glanced around the room for the first time. "There's nothing wrong with your painting." Only a moment before, his face had been creased with anger, but now it was smooth, blank, unreadable.

Slowly he walked over to the wall where three of Annette's works were hanging. Two were simple spring landscapes. The other showed four gaily dressed people sitting on a picnic blanket, an empty bottle of wine lying in the tall grass beside them.

He went to another canvas, which rested still wet, against a chair leg. It was a scene in a spring meadow, painted in soft greens, yellows and browns. A mare and her foal were running with the foal in the lead. One could almost feel the mare's irritation with her frisky foal who, no doubt, would not stand still for even a moment. On a chair nearby sat another canvas. Chinatown at dusk. Shadows lurked darkly in an alley and an arrow of light struck the street from the open doorway of a crib where two men were entering. The balconies of the crib were strung with glowing paper lanterns. It was a dynamic work and it embodied the exotic, secret atmosphere of the district. It beckoned one to enter the scene, to taste of its bizarre delights. Rolf was stunned.

He drew his attention from the Chinatown scene to one of the waterfront, which sat on the easel unfinished. He swept a hand down the right hand side of the canvas. "If it's morning here, Annette," he said as if to himself, "then the light is wrong. You see," he pointed again, "the shadows indicate noon. The light is wrong. Lengthen the shadows, carefully though."

Annette walked up behind him, speechless. "Yes," she whispered. "Of course. That's eluded me for days. Oh, Rolf!"

He turned to face her, placing his hands on her shoulders. His dark eyes imprisoned hers. "These paintings are excellent." He looked almost shocked. "I mean, they are really excellent."

"You . . . you really think . . ." Her stomach fluttered madly.

"Excellent!"

"Oh, Rolf!" Unashamedly, she hugged her arms around her waist and twirled around. Her golden eyes sparkled with delight. "Are you sure? Do you really think they're excellent? Not just passable?"

"Yes. You're ready for a showing. You'll be an instant success, Miss Annette Tofler, ma'am." He laughed with her.

The light in her eyes quickly faded. "Oh, but not a showing, Rolf. No. I couldn't."

Taking her hands in his, Rolf beamed at her. "You definitely are ready. Listen, Annette," his voice was serious now, "I'm no amateur. In fact, my opinion is valued quite highly in some circles."

"But—"

"Look. You're suffering from the shock of success, that's all. Stage fright. Perhaps I'm going a little fast for you, but believe me, you're good. People will love you."

"Oh, Rolf." Annette looked at him imploringly. "I don't know. I really don't." The warm pressure of his hands on hers was reassuring, comforting. "Did you feel this way your first time?"

He quirked a brow teasingly. "Me? Why, Annette,

don't you know how easily I can bluff my way through anything?"

"The gambler?"

"Always the gambler, ma'am."

"Are you gambling, then, that people will like my work?"

"Not about that. Let me talk to Francis Turner at the Golden Gate Gallery and show him some of your work. He'll love it. We'll arrange a showing and I'll be with you every step of the way."

Suddenly Annette pulled her hands away and turned her back to him. "Rolf?"

"Yes?" he coaxed gently.

"If I do succeed, then I'm free, aren't I?"

"Free?"

"Yes. I'm my own person then. Not the wealthy socialite Annette Tofler, or some vapid female who bats her lashes at dinners and feigns the vapors for attention. I'm my own person then, aren't I? I will have earned it then."

Rolf was still for a long moment. "Yes, Annette. I think success will give you your freedom. That's what you've wanted all along, isn't it?"

"Yes," she whispered ardently. "All my life I've been controlled by someone else, never myself."

"Do you fear control?"

Slowly, she turned and met his gaze. "Not now. I feel very different than I did just a few moments ago. It's strange. I feel as if a door which has been closed to me all my life has suddenly opened."

"Perhaps it has." He studied her thoughtfully. The dark auburn curls, held back by Spanish combs, framed the white oval face with its wide, curious hazel eyes, delicate chin and full, sensuous mouth. She was as elusive as a dream, a challenge for any man. It would take a strong man to saddle this filly and ride her out. He wondered whether Annette ever could be tamed or whether he could accept her this way.

"Someday," he reflected aloud, "a man will try to break that spirit of yours, Annette."

Her chin tilted up in surprise. "Do you seek a woman with a broken spirit, Rolf?" she challenged. "Is that what all men want—an Eleanor Fairchild? A woman who can be led around by the bit?" She cast her eyes down. She hadn't meant to mention his mistress's name, but it had slipped out anyway.

Rolf looked at her closely, his gaze unwavering. "Do I detect a note of jealousy in your words?"

"Heavens no!" she countered quickly, blushing crimson.

"It makes little difference." A smile curved his lips. "If you hadn't locked yourself up in this house all spring, you'd no doubt have heard that Eleanor is in Paris—on her honeymoon."

"What!" Annette was stunned.

"Yes. She married a French businessman nearly six weeks ago. An old acquaintance of her husband's." Tossing his head back, he laughed heartily at the expression on her face. "That's right, Annette. And with my blessings, too."

She looked away in sudden confusion and the moment stretched out awkwardly. One thought was uppermost in her mind: Rolf was no longer seeing Eleanor and unless he had a new lover, which Annette rather doubted, he was fair game.

Rolf cleared his throat, breaking into her thoughts. "If I could take several of your paintings with me, I might be able to stop by the gallery this afternoon and show them to Turner. What do you say?"

"It would be wonderful. But what if he doesn't like them?"

"He will."

"You certainly are sure of yourself, aren't you?" She eyed him carefully.

"Yes, why not?" he replied, smiling lazily at her through half-closed eyes. She was so beautiful, even in her paint-spattered smock, that he wanted only to crush her vibrant, slim form against him and kiss those mocking lips. It was difficult at times to keep his wits about him and carry on a conversation with her. Visions of possessing her naked body filled his head. He wanted to plunder her, to own her, body and soul. But Annette was a free spirit and he knew that he would never possess her soul or her mind. He had been forced to admit that to himself as he tossed restlessly in his lonely bed night after night.

"If you wish to take care of this matter," Annette continued primly, "I would be very grateful."

"It's my pleasure, Annette, and not unmixed with conceit on my part, either. If I discover an up-and-coming young artist, it reflects well on me."

"I should have known that you wouldn't do it merely because you like me."

"*Like* you? Why, certainly not, ma'am. That has nothing to do with it." He struggled to keep his tone light and bantering, just as hers was. He wanted to tell her the truth, tell her that he loved her, adored her, that he would do anything for just her smile, her touch. But Annette had to be approached gingerly. Any hint that he wanted her would send her scurrying for cover. She had to be the one to decide, to make the commitment, and he knew it. He had to give her time and treat her with careful flippancy until she was ready.

Annette's tawny eyes turned suddenly serious. Laying a slim white hand on his arm, she searched his face candidly. "How have you been, really, Rolf?"

"Quite well," he lied calmly. "But I must admit that I've been worried about you."

"I'm sorry. I've been very unsettled. And then, too, I've been working so hard. I should have answered your notes, I know, but there didn't seem to be anything to say."

"You could have said hello at least," he reproached gently.

"Yes." Her eyes were downcast, and he could see only her white forehead and the straight, uptilting eyebrows that delineated it. Then she looked up at him. "But I didn't want to lead you on or give you assurances I didn't feel. It seemed easier that way." She gave a nervous little laugh. "You're a very overpowering man, Rolf. I forget my own mind when I'm with you."

"And what does your mind tell you when I'm not with you?"

"That I'm lonely," she admitted.

"For that, my dear, there is only one cure." He studied her upturned face carefully. Then he reached out and drew her to him. She came willingly into his arms. He lowered his head and his mouth found hers. They clung to one another in an exquisite, agonizing kiss until all sensation was nonexistent but the touch of their lips. The moment seemed both infinitely long and incalculably short. Their bodies melted together and became one as if they had always belonged to each other.

Rolf didn't know how long they remained locked against one another, lost in endless passion, but slowly he became aware of another presence in the room.

Eventually that person coughed and cleared his throat. Annette pushed herself away from Rolf, her cheeks aflame. "Oh Jensen!" she breathed. "I . . . we didn't hear you come in."

"Obviously," her brother observed with some amusement.

"Hello Jensen," greeted Rolf easily, still holding on to Annette's arms possessively.

"Yes, well," said Jensen, "Vivian told me you were here and I thought I'd see if you would care to dine with us this evening."

"Thank you, but not tonight. I promised Annette I'd take some of her paintings down to a gallery."

"A showing?" Jensen perked up.

"That's right," Annette intervened, still embarrassed. "Now shouldn't you be going, Rolf? I mean, the gallery may close soon." Her ale-colored eyes begged him to do as she bid.

"Why, yes, ma'am," he drawled casually. He glanced from her red face to Jensen's amused expression. "Perhaps I should be on my way. Until tomorrow?" he finished, getting the last word.

"Tomorrow, then." Annette turned her back to both of them and left the conservatory. As she walked down the hallway, a smile played at the corners of her mouth. With a finger she lightly touched the spot where Rolf's lips had pressed against hers only a few moments before.

Chapter 27

Annette let herself into the Golden Gate Gallery early and very quietly so as not to alert Francis Turner in his office. She had no desire to fend off his insinuating glances just then.

With the drapes closed and the lights off, the large, white room was dim. She almost didn't see the stand with the sign on it: "First showing of works by local artist Annette Tofler. May 17, 1891."

Her heart thrilled at the sight. Her name, at last, and her own show! She burst into a broad smile. This was her big day. Annette prayed that her work would be well received. Rolf had reassured her constantly, but still, there was that nagging doubt that maybe she wasn't any good. The public might not like her.

Annette hadn't been able to stop herself from coming down to the gallery early. The exhibit didn't open until four o'clock and it was only two thirty, but she'd been too nervous to wait any longer. She had been much too excited to eat lunch or to do anything else that wasn't absolutely necessary. Instead she had rushed over to assure herself that the paintings were arranged well and that they looked all right. She needed to convince herself once more that this was really happening and she wanted a chance to appreciate the showing in solitude before the people streamed in to pass judgment on her.

Slowly she moved into the sweeping gallery and stood in the middle of the vast, empty, echoing room. She turned, trying to look at her paintings with an unprejudiced eye. They hung in the dim light, bedecked in ornate, gilt-edged, carved frames, so official looking that she hardly recognized them as her own. But, yes, there was the scene at Devil's Cove, reminiscent of that work of Rolf's, the one she'd criticized thoughtlessly on that long-ago afternoon when they'd first met. Rolf would never be so cruel as to say anything like that about one of her paintings. She'd been such an immature, spoiled girl then. Oh, how she had changed! And she had to admit that much of it was due to Rolf. He'd sustained and encouraged her during the whirlwind of activity preceding the show. Why, she'd never have been able to get through it without him, for she'd had less than a month to prepare for the big day. He'd set up the showing, helped her choose the works to be hung, arranged for the framing. He had even stood over her and made her finish a few more canvases for the show when she'd been ready to give up.

Now, all alone in the dusky gallery, Annette was pleased with the fruits of her labor.

She looked at another painting, the one of Moor in the stable, gleaming and alive. And over there was a sketch of Rolf that succeeded in capturing the bold lines of his face. She turned again and saw her garden on Nob Hill and then the series of paintings of mares and spring foals. Another turn and there was Chinatown, secret and alluring. They were all there, the canvases that had absorbed her completely, the canvases she'd struggled with and cried over. They could have been her children. Each one was different, yet she loved them equally, for all of them were full of effort and memories.

Annette walked past every one with slow, deliberate movements, remembering every brush stroke, every problem overcome, straightening one here, touching one there. Again she prayed that people would like them.

The gallery door opened behind her. She spun around. Lord above, she thought, I hope it isn't Turner with his hot hands. I couldn't bear it.

A shadowy figure approached her. "Annette?"

"Yes, who is it?"

"Bernard."

She ran to him, happy and excited. "Bernard! How on earth did you find me?"

Taking hold of both her hands, he looked at her soberly for a moment. "Of course you would be here, nervously checking on your paintings. Where else should an artist be on the day of her first showing?"

She laughed and kissed Bernard on the cheek. "You've always seen through me, right from the first, haven't you?" she grinned.

"Certainly," he quipped. "But seriously, I wanted to talk to you privately before the crowds arrive."

"Aren't you going to look at my paintings?"

"Of course. But first I want to know how you are. It's been a long time since we've talked."

"Yes, it has. Since, well since . . ."

"Since Chinatown," finished Bernard.

"You're still my friend, aren't you?" she asked, searching his face.

"Always. But there are other things in your life now and in mine." He shook his dark head. "You weren't good for me, Annette. I began to sympathize too much with you rich people. I began to think you were just like me. I forgot."

"Forgot what, Bernard?"

"My convictions. But never mind. Perhaps it did some good. I'm busier now than ever because of my association with you. The commissions are rolling in. And the money is welcome. The cause can use it."

"The cause?"

"Socialism. We're going to make the world into a utopia one day. But never mind all that." He laughed. "I want you to tell me how you feel about all this." He gestured to the paintings hung on the walls. "It's your day at last."

"You always believed in me." She put her hand on his arm. "I'll never forget that, Bernard. And you'll always be a dear, dear friend. As for my show, well, I'm so nervous and excited I can't even tell how I feel. I'm happy. I'm thrilled. I'm scared. I'm afraid I'll cry if I hear any criticism. I feel very fragile today."

"You, fragile? Ha! You're as tough as the steel they build those new skyscrapers with! You were too strong for my blood, Annette," he admitted with good humor. "I almost fell in love with you. I thank my lucky stars I didn't."

Annette pouted a little. "You've insulted me now."

"Don't be silly. You know it's true." He hesitated, looking around the dim room. "And Rolf?"

Annette walked over to one of the paintings and straightened it the tiniest hair.

"Well?" pressed Bernard.

She turned finally and faced him. "I don't know. It's so strange. It isn't simple, Bernard."

"Do you love him?"

"Yes."

"Does he love you?"

"I think so. He's never told me."

"It's none of my business, of course. But I want you to be happy."

"You sound like my brother!" she scolded. "Will all of you please stop worrying. I'll manage." She took his hand and pulled him over to one of her favorites, the dry grass in the Chinese vase. "See? There it is. That one is yours, Bernard. It isn't for sale. I'm giving it to you, all right? Now look at them all. And you'd better tell me how wonderful they are, every single one!"

When at last Jensen and Su Ling arrived with Rolf, Bernard had gone. He had work to do, he said, and he felt more comfortable in his own circle of friends than hobnobbing with the wealthy. Annette had kissed him good-bye with regret and understanding.

Rolf came to her immediately, his dark eyes proud and shining. "You holding up all right?" he wondered. "You left the house so early, I was a little concerned."

As always his appearance moved her. He was so powerful and so masculine, even in his elegantly tailored dark blue suit. His shirt front was starched and gleaming white, the collar standing up crisply around his strong neck, with his cravat perfectly tied. One could almost take him for a dandy.

"I'm as nervous as a filly," she confessed. "Do I look all right?"

He kissed her hand formally. "You are a vision, Miss Tofler, ma'am." He grinned at her. "That's one thing I didn't have to worry about at my first show—my gown!"

She smoothed down the folds of her pale grey, silk crepe dress. It was a simple, flowing gown with austere Grecian lines. It suited her beautifully, accentuating her curves but not in a sensual manner. It was a stately dress befitting a woman who had made a place for herself in the world. She no longer felt the need to push for recognition of her charms with low necklines and sheer lace. Her dark auburn hair was piled high on her head in gleaming coils through which a strand of pearls was intertwined.

"You look like Athena," he said, "the goddess of wisdom."

"I've always been partial to Aphrodite. At least before," Annette teased.

"Ah, but you're learning, my dear." Rolf winked at her with a lazy, knowing expression.

She would have liked to follow up on his remark, but people were trickling into the gallery and Jensen was trying to get her attention. "I'll see *you* later," she informed Rolf.

"You certainly will." He bowed deeply.

The afternoon burst into action. People arrived and then more people. There were reporters from the *Call* and the *Examiner*, friends, acquaintances, artists from the Monkey Block, Jensen's business associates, the blue bloods of the city, the art critics, even a few curious Bohemians. It went on and on, everyone congratulating her, asking her questions, exclaiming over her work. The gallery was like a carnival where everything was happening so fast that Annette hardly had time to think. Her mind stopped working consciously and she simply did what needed to be done.

People introduced themselves to her, babbled and smiled, and she forgot their names and their words a moment later. It was frenzied, exhausting, tense, wonderful.

Annette even had the opportunity, at last, to meet William Keith, who had taken the time to stop by the gallery and observe a young artist's work. She was absolutely in awe of the man, who was a terribly famous and successful painter. When Mr. Hearst brought him over, introduced her to him and left her face to face with the elderly gentleman, she almost couldn't speak. William Keith had a thick head of silver-grey hair and a long beard. Oddly enough, a package of brushes protruded from his coat pocket.

"I see you have been influenced by the Impressionists," he observed.

"Yes, I suppose so. I studied under Fernand Cormon in Paris."

"Good man. I like your style," Mr. Keith offered kindly.

"Oh, thank you. I only hope someday to be able to paint as well as you, Mr. Keith."

"Hard work and a strict schedule, that's what it takes," he said, his Scottish burr still vaguely discernible after all the years in America. "Well, Miss Tofler," he kissed her hand, "I'd best let you attend to business," and he was off, lost in the throng of guests once more.

She found a moment to dash into Turner's office with Su Ling. It was empty, fortunately. "Is my hair falling down?" she asked Su, biting her lower lip and patting the coils of hair at the back of her head.

"Only one little strand. Here, let me fix it," and Su Ling's tiny, deft fingers quickly repaired Annette's coiffure.

"Oh, thank you." Annette took a deep breath and plunged back into the colorful, milling crowd.

Francis Turner finally managed to back her into a corner. His grinning face was red and damp. "I told you long ago, Miss Tofler, to bring me some of your works. Why, we could have had several shows by now." His small eyes glistened. "Perhaps we could talk about it in my office." She could have sworn he licked his lips.

Thankfully, Rolf came along at that moment, however, and swept her away with a polite bow to Turner. He leaned down and whispered in her ear, "You're quite a hit, you know. They want to know where you've been all this time." His dark eyes glinted with amusement. "I told them I've been hiding you out at Devil's Cove."

"You didn't! Oh, Rolf!"

"Do you care what they think?"

"No!" she vowed staunchly. "But that was an awful thing to do."

"You've told me that before, ma'am, but in much more picturesque ways."

"I haven't the time or energy right now, or I would. Now, really, take me to my brother. I need some family support."

"Of course. This way, ma'am." He held out his arm to her, the epitome of respect. She knew without looking, however, that a devilish grin was playing on his chiseled lips.

"Damn you, Rolf Karman!" she whispered. "I'm trying to maintain my dignity."

"Is it trying to slip away?" he whispered back, grinning insolently as he deposited her smoothly at Jensen's side and slipped away into the crowd.

"You're a success!" Jensen beamed. "I'm so proud of you, Annette."

"Am I?" she asked uncertainly.

"Yes, unquestionably. Everyone's here. And I mean everyone."

"Yes, it certainly does seem so." She glanced around. "But do they like my paintings?"

"They love your paintings, little sister!"

"I wish Cecile were here."

"So do I. But we'll write and tell her all about it."

"I'll send her and Luke a painting to hang in their new house. Do you think they'd like that?"

"They'll adore any one of them." He looked around, worried. "Where's my wife?"

"Always the doting husband," laughed Annette. "Come on, we'll find her."

Su Ling was talking to a young lady from Oakland who had come to the showing with her husband and who didn't know anyone there. The Chinese girl's easy manner and natural poise had captured everyone's interest, if not their hearts. She had made the young wife feel comfortable and had even introduced her to one of Jensen's business cronies.

Jensen claimed Su Ling protectively. "You mustn't exert yourself, my love," he reproved. "Do you want to sit down?"

Su Ling smiled at him. "So nice of you to worry, but I'm having fun. You should, too."

Annette left them, smiling to herself, but a small spurt of envy invaded her delight. It was spring and everyone seemed to be paired off except her. Would she go on alone, always, afraid to submerge herself in a relationship? The thought frightened her a little.

She pushed through the crowd, nodding, smiling, responding to questions, ever the gracious lady artist. It was hot and stuffy in the room, big as it was, and Annette suddenly felt the need for some fresh air. She went to a tall open window and drew in deep breaths of the heavy, warm air. Her head ached from the noise and her corset stays were pressing cruelly into her ribs. All at once she wished that everyone would go home. She had received her accolades and now she was tired.

"Tired of the crowd?" drawled a familiar voice at her shoulder.

"A little," she admitted. "They're devouring me."

"We could go," he suggested.

"Perhaps."

He led her through the crowd, moving people aside easily. She was grateful.

"Oh, there you are!" someone cried over the noise of the crowd. "Annette!"

It was Mrs. Manion, one of her family's oldest friends, a well-to-do elderly lady who'd always been sweet to her. Annette had no choice but to talk to the woman.

"I bought the picture of your garden, Annette!" Mrs. Manion gushed. "I'm going to give it to my daughter, Audrey. She's got the perfect place for it in her sitting room! Why, I can hardly believe you're such a success, and me knowing you since you were born!" On and on went Mrs. Manion. She was so full of excitement at knowing a real artist that her chins literally quivered with it. "And George—that's my husband, you know, Mr. Karman—is just so happy for you, too. You remember Uncle George, Annette? Oh, my land, but wouldn't your mother be proud!" The lady leaned down, her heavy lilac scent assailing Annette's nostrils. "We're all so proud, I just can't tell you how much! Little Annette!"

Annette felt the blood leaving her head and her stomach turned over. It must have been because she hadn't eaten all day in the excitement. A surprising wave of nausea seized her and suddenly it seemed as if the crowd, the noise and the smoke would suffocate her.

"Excuse me, Mrs. Manion," Rolf interrupted as politely as he could, "but Annette has to see the gallery owner about something."

Annette looked up at him gratefully. She felt faint and sick. If only she could get some air. Rolf grasped her firmly at the elbow and steered her quickly out into the hall, then into Turner's office. He eased her down into a big leather chair and threw open the window as wide as possible.

She leaned back thankfully into the chair's embrace. Small droplets of perspiration beaded her upper lip and forehead. Weakly, she tried to wipe them away. She closed her eyes, concentrating on the warm, fresh air blowing on her face.

"Now, do you mind telling me what in hell is the matter with you? You turned green in there."

She kept her eyes closed, not daring to meet his gaze. "It was the heat. And I didn't eat today."

"Don't lie to me, Annette."

Her eyes flew open indignantly. "I'm not lying!"

Rolf stood in front of the open window, his arms folded across the front of his impeccably tailored suit. He looked angry and worried at the same time. "You're pregnant, aren't you?"

She closed her eyes tiredly. She should have known she couldn't keep it from him. The man knew her so well. "Yes," she whispered at last.

He was silent.

Annette forced her eyes open and looked at him. His face was expressionless. Annette's heart sank. "I didn't tell you because I didn't want you to feel that you had to . . ." She couldn't finish.

"Marry you?" he asked softly.

"Yes." Shame and embarrassment washed over her and she felt shy with him. "You don't have to."

"Do you think," he rasped, "that I would leave you to face the world alone like this, that I would . . ." He stopped, his throat working convulsively.

"Rolf?" she asked tentatively.

He came to her and took her arms, lifting her so